# The Lily of the Sky

A Historical Fiction by Terrance D. Williamson

*Dedicated to:*
*My eternal sons,*
*My loving daughter,*
*And my patient wife.*

*"I do not believe in using women in combat, because females are too fierce."*

Margaret Mead

# Chapter One:
# Deception

*"Patience is bitter, but its fruit is sweet."*

Aristotle

Lily sat quietly on her bed with her legs dangling happily off the edge as she retrieved the new textbook on the latest aerobatics from her bag. It was a large, heavy book that was more expensive than she would've preferred. She had been fortunate enough to smuggle it past her mother and brother.

Glancing over her shoulder at the closed door, Lily turned on the lamp that was sitting on her small, rickety bedside table.

Yet as she leaned over, she lost grip of the textbook, and it fell with a large thud on the hollow wooden floor.

With tight shoulders and a clenched jaw, Lily stared at the door and listened closely for any sign of movement. She was certain that her mother, or, at the very least, her brother, would've been curious about the disturbance.

*Good luck explaining yourself to Mother,* Lily thought sarcastically as she grabbed the textbook off the floor and brushed off the dust.

"You'll keep this a secret, won't you?" Lily whispered to her stuffed doll that was sitting up against a pillow and staring back at her indifferently.

She knew she was too old to keep a doll, but her father had purchased it for her when she was born, and Lily didn't dare depart from that memory, especially since it had survived in relatively good condition. She only wished that she had been more creative with naming it when she was younger, but she was christened 'dolly', unfortunately, and a name change now would simply be out of the question.

Returning her attention to her textbook, with the dull orange glow from her little lamp reflecting off the sickly green wallpaper that Lily loathed, she ran her hand along the cover with a swelling eagerness and excitement. It featured a cartoon drawing of an airplane in a barrel roll.

She knew it would be better if she waited until evening, or at least until she was alone in their small, two-bedroom apartment, but Lily's passion for consuming every morsel she could about flying was unbearable. It was an addiction, she admitted, but also one that she had successfully, and surprisingly, kept hidden.

Holding the textbook close to her nose, Lily closed her eyes as she inhaled the scent of fresh paper and relished the feeling of a new book. Setting it back on her lap, Lily flipped through the pages, trying to gather a general overview before diving into the heart of the content.

She ran her hand longingly over the pages of fighter planes as her spirit longed to experience their speed and power. She imagined her hands gripping the controls before glancing at the various instruments for altitude, fuel, and speed.

Lily understood that such imaginings were rather odd, given that she was a young woman approaching twenty and should, as her mother so often put it, be pursuing a husband.

"If a man ever makes me feel the way you do, I'll consider it," Lily spoke quietly to the image of the plane in her textbook.

"Who are you talking to?" a voice asked innocently behind Lily.

Startled, Lily slammed the textbook shut and spun around to find her younger brother, Yuri, standing in the doorway, still clutching the door handle.

"Nothing!" Lily replied swiftly as she tried to recover from her alarm but knew that her wide eyes had given her away.

"Nothing?" Yuri smiled wryly, discovering a secret that he could exploit.

"Go away!" Lily griped as she slipped the textbook into her bag beside the bed.

"I asked who you were talking to you, and you said 'nothing.'" Yuri crossed his arms and leaned against the doorpost.

"Why do you care?" Lily stood and crossed her arms as the two siblings entered a familiar standoff.

"I'm a man of opportunity." Yuri shrugged as he walked slowly into their shared room and sat on his bed, which was opposite Lily's.

"Man?" Lily scoffed. "You're twelve years old."

"In some societies, that is considered adulthood." Yuri leaned back on his bed.

"Really?" Emma titled her head as she feigned interest, although her mind dwelled on her textbook. "Such as?"

"I'm not so easily distracted." Yuri recognized her attempt at diversion.

*Damn!* Lily twisted her lips in annoyance.

"What were you reading that is so secretive?" Yuri sat upright as he squinted at his sister. "An indecent novel? A private letter from a suitor you don't want anyone knowing about? Why? What's so embarrassing about him?"

"The content is irrelevant." Lily sighed, knowing that she would have to barter out of Yuri telling on her.

"Irrelevant?" Yuri narrowed his gaze.

"Boring, I should say. At least, to you, it would be. Still, it needs to be kept secret."

"Fortunately for you, my silence is available. For the right price, that is." Yuri bit his lip, and Lily grew annoyed at how much he was savoring having the upper hand.

"What do you want?" Lily rolled her eyes.

"A favor," Yuri replied swiftly, and Lily grew suspicious, wondering if he was previously aware of her contraband.

"What sort of favor?" Lily asked slowly, not sure if she wanted to hear his answer.

"I'm not sure yet." Yuri stood.

"Oh?" Lily frowned.

"I'd like to see how this plays out." Yuri tapped his chin. "Once I know what I want, I'll cash in my favor."

"I can't agree to that." Lily shook her head. "It needs to be balanced. A fair deal."

"That sounds reasonable." Yuri began walking toward the door before he continued, "Or I can just tell Mother now that you—"

"No!" Lily held up a finger as she interrupted him. "This would devastate her, and then she'd kill me."

"Scandalous." Yuri's eyes lit up. "I like how this is evolving."

"I hate being at your mercy." Lily rubbed her eyes.

"Not yet." Yuri shook his head before adding, "But soon you will."

"You're a cruel little man, you know that!" Lily growled at him.

"My dear sister," Yuri spoke patronizingly as he leaned against the doorpost. "I'm going to spend a good deal thinking of something perfect as my favor. Part of the enjoyment will be watching you squirm in the discomfort of knowing that what I choose will be absolutely awful for you."

"Go away!" Lily gestured for him to leave. "And close the door!"

"Lunch is ready, by the way. Mother sent me to get you." Yuri rattled his knuckles on the doorpost before leaving the room.

*What a little weasel!* Lily fumed. *I've been careful for years, and today, of all days, he catches me?! I should've waited until he was asleep like usual.*

"Lily!" her mother barked, and Lily's shoulders seized as she feared that her brother had already informed on her. "Come eat!"

*He better not have said anything!* Lily thought as she stood in front of the mirror and inspected herself quickly.

She was wearing her favorite yellow dress that accentuated her blonde hair, and a blue scarf with white polka dots that brought out the hints of blue in her grey eyes was wrapped around her neck. She had stitched in a white lily flower near her left shoulder that was small and mostly unnoticeable, but she felt it showcased her craftsmanship in embroidery.

"Lily!" her mother shouted again.

"Coming!" Lily replied as she scurried out of the room, walked down the narrow hallway past her mother's small bedroom, and came to the cramped all-purpose area that served as the dining/living/storage room.

There was a large, and usually streaky, window beside the table that, in the spring or summer, was a blessing, but in the winter, permitted an intolerable draft. The view was less than bleak as it faced another apartment block across the street, and the dull grey brick complimented the austere color scheme of whites and dark browns surrounding Lily in her apartment. It almost made her appreciate the tint of green in her room. Almost.

"Vegetable salad," Lily's mother announced dismally as she set the plates down on the table.

About an inch over five feet, or about the same height as Lily, Anna Litvyak was adorned in her usual navy blue dress with a white shawl and a light brown head scarf.

Shuffling her feet while hunched over and worn out from the trials of life, Anna sat down at the table with a huff before retrieving her handkerchief and dabbing the sweat from her forehead.

"Sit! Sit!" Anna waved for Yuri and Lily to take their places at the table.

"Remember, you owe me," Yuri whispered.

"You're fortunate we only live on the first floor." Lily threatened as she nodded to the window.

"What was that?" Anna looked up at her children.

"I merely mentioned that Yuri looks adorable." Lily tussled Yuri's hair as he swatted her hand away in annoyance.

"He looks like a mess." Anna waved for him to come closer to her.

"I can clean myself!" Yuri took his spot at the table.

"Then this will teach you to do so before you come near your mother looking like a street rat." Anna grabbed his arm roughly with her thick, strong hands and pulled her son close to him before generously licking her thumb and wiping away a smudge in the corner of his mouth.

"Stop it!" Yuri complained, but Anna ignored his protest.

"There." Anna released him. "Now you look respectable."

Yuri generously brushed away whatever dampness had been left with his sleeve as he glared menacingly at Lily, who was offering a large smile, enjoying his suffering.

"At least you have one child who takes care of themselves," Lily spoke proudly as she pulled her plate of carrots, cucumbers, tomatoes, and onions that were dressed in smetana closer to her.

"Too good of care, I would argue." Anna stabbed at her plate with her fork like she was angry at the salad, and the dinging and scraping on the porcelain set Lily's teeth on edge. "Vanity is just as perilous."

"I've been blessed with beauty." Lily held her chin high. "Should I not use that to my advantage?"

"Beauty fades." Anna pointed to her face as she stared at her plate gloomily, and Lily understood that her mother was exhausted.

"I think you're absolutely stunning." Lily squeezed her mother's tough, round shoulder.

"Heh." Anna shook her head in dismissal before pointing at Yuri and adding, "I haven't been beautiful since this one was born."

"Me?" Yuri asked in surprise, wondering how he was to blame.

"You took the last of my beauty." Anna glared at him. "I used to attract the sort of attention your sister does. I was bright-eyed, full-breasted, and I could make any man stop in his tracks. Now, my belly juts out further than my bosom."

"Gross." Yuri scrunched up his nose in disgust.

"Kept your father away." Anna chuckled slightly.

"Was that necessary?" Yuri's countenance turned sour as he let his fork fall against his plate.

"That's alright though. After you, I wasn't all that interested in him, if you gather what I'm saying." Anna grew a secretive smile, and Lily understood that her mother loved torturing Yuri.

"Other mothers wouldn't be discussing this with their children." Yuri squeezed his eyes shut in disgust.

"Other mothers give a damn." Anna laughed at her own joke, but then turned toward Lily and added, solemnly, "Land yourself a husband, a nice one, before you look like me."

"Then I could finally have a room to myself." Yuri also encouraged Lily.

"Get a man who won't abandon you," Anna spoke softly as she grew emotional.

The table grew silent as both Yuri and Lily glanced at each other, not entirely sure what to say. They knew their mother was grieving, but she rarely showed any such emotion, and Lily knew they had to tread carefully.

"He didn't abandon you," Lily spoke tenderly.

"No?" Anna glared at her daughter as she asked rhetorically. "I told him to keep his political ideals quiet. I told him what would happen if he kept opening his mouth. He disregarded me, and guess what happened? He was labeled an 'enemy of the people' and shipped off to who knows where. So, yes, because he didn't listen to me and put his own stupid principles above his family, he abandoned us."

The table again returned to silence as Lily recalled the day her father was taken. It was during The Terror, as some were now calling it, almost four years ago to the day. Mr. Litvyak was a Trotskyist, and he was a proud proponent of a version of Leninism which, unfortunately, was opposed by Stalin.

His disappearance was so sudden, so unexpected by Lily, who was still ignorant to most things political at the tender age of fifteen, that she still really hadn't processed his absence. One day, he was singing and smoking by the window, and the next day, he was gone. All his belongings remained in the apartment, and it was almost as if he had vanished into thin air.

Anna, while trying to remain strong, packed away his possessions almost the day after he had been taken. Lily had only caught her crying on a few occasions. Otherwise, Anna refused to permit any emotional outbursts, even from her children.

Now that she was a little older, Lily understood that her mother was simply trying to be brave for them, but she would've preferred to see her mother truly grieve for her husband.

"Is there any salt?" Yuri glanced around the table.

"You know well enough there's no salt." Anna finished her meal before retrieving a cigarette and lighting it. "If you want some, go back to the kitchen."

"It smells in there." Yuri played with his food with his fork. "And there's always some other mother who wants to pinch my cheeks. Why can't we have a kitchen of our own?"

"Communal living is important to our Soviet way of life," Lily chimed in. "We're doing our part for the community, for everyone."

"If you ask me, these policies are because they are cheap," Yuri spoke quietly.

"Shush with that!" Anna pointed an angry finger in his face. "What did I just say about your father?"

Yuri drew silent as he slunk down in his chair and assumed the role of the impatient and unamused adolescent.

"You would be wise to remember what Stalin has done for this country." Anna took a puff from her cigarette as she glanced at the door, and Lily understood her paranoia.

"When is Uncle Boris coming home?" Yuri glanced at his mother.

"Not till tomorrow," Anna replied briskly.

"Tomorrow?" Yuri turned toward her with wide eyes. "I thought he would be back tonight?"

"He sent a telegram that there was an issue. An engine needed repairs or something of that sort." Anna stared at the ceiling.

"I wanted to show him my set." Yuri slunk back down.

"Your set?" Lily frowned. "What set?"

"I bought a train set. Same engine that Papa used to work on," Yuri replied brightly.

"With what money?" Anna glared at him.

"Money that I earned." Yuri grew proud of himself.

"You stole it?!" Lily asked in a hushed voice as she glanced at the apartment door to make sure it was closed.

"Stealing is a disease of capitalism," Yuri replied with a good measure of attitude toward his sister. "So, no, of course I didn't steal it."

"First, you complain about our wonderful living conditions, and then you steal?" Anna was beside herself with concern.

"I didn't steal!" Yuri defended adamantly.

Leaning back in her chair, Anna examined him thoroughly before sighing and waving to dismiss the subject.

"I was thinking," Lily cleared her throat as she asked her mother, "that we could see a play again soon? There's supposed to be a new production that is receiving positive reviews."

"Not another play." Yuri leaned his head back in despair. "They're so long and boring. The only plays you two care about are the romantic ones."

"The theater costs money." Anna raised her eyebrows. "But that does sound nice. Maybe I can scrounge something together."

"Can we turn the radio on?" Yuri whined.

Leaning over, Anna flicked on the little radio, but the static was so terrible that it was impossible to tell if music or an announcement was broadcasting.

"I'll fix that." Yuri began to stand.

"After you eat!" Anna held up her finger to stop him.

"Then can we turn it off? Just listening to static is worse than no music at all." Yuri slouched over his meager portions of vegetables.

"So ungrateful," Anna muttered as she flicked the radio back off.

"I heard a joke today." Yuri perked up.

"Jokes are for the weak-willed," Anna replied as she stamped out her cigarette in the ashtray before retrieving another one.

"I'd like to hear it." Lily shrugged.

"No!" Anna shouted and pounded her thick fist on the table. "I won't permit it."

"Why not?" Yuri frowned, and his rebuttal sent his mother into a state in which Lily had rarely seen her.

Leaning forward on the table with wide, angry eyes, Anna pointed a round finger in her son's face as she spoke slowly and menacingly, "Your attitude is terrible! If you ever speak to me that way again, I'll turn the rest of your life into a joke. A cruel one at that."

"Sorry." Yuri swallowed as he stared at his plate of food.

"Eat!" Anna shouted, and her loud voice reverberated throughout the apartment.

"Yes, ma'am." Yuri obeyed without hesitation and scarfed down the meal.

"All your jokes are anti-Soviet," Anna continued softer than before, and Lily sensed she was feeling guilty for possibly overreacting. "I wouldn't be able to stomach it if you met the same fate as your father."

Yuri didn't reply as he continued eating, but Lily sensed he felt much the same as she had with their father's absence. She imagined, for a younger boy, not to have a father figure was a harsh burden. Then again, it was the sad state of their nation. Many fathers were taken by the civil war, or the Revolution, or the Great War, or The Terror, or any other aspect of the seemingly unending violence perpetuated upon them from forces both internal and external.

"You're a good boy." Anna patted his shoulder roughly, showing the only affection she knew. "But there's no room in this world for good boys. I need you to remain clever and alert. Can you promise me that?"

"Yes, ma'am." Yuri swallowed.

"Good." Anna drew a deep breath. "I need to work this afternoon. There is some sort of inspection at the store that I'm required to be present for. I'll need you to watch him." She pointed at Lily. "I've seen him enough."

"I have drama class this afternoon." Lily shook her head. "I can't watch him."

"Take him with you." Anna shrugged.

"I'm not going with her!" Yuri's sour disposition returned.

"You knew this was the arrangement." Anna rubbed the back of her neck, and Lily felt for her, understanding how exhausted she likely was. "Your grandmother had to leave."

"I don't understand why she left, though." Yuri offered a begging look to his mother for an explanation.

"Your grandmother is Jewish," Anna clarified. "After your father was taken, she thought it best to distance herself from the family. She didn't want any of us rounded up for having association with her."

"But that makes us Jewish also." Yuri frowned in his confusion.

"You're of Jewish descent." Anna puffed her cigarette. "Don't ask me to explain that one because I don't understand how they came up with these rules on who is suitable or not."

"I'm old enough to be at the apartment by myself." Yuri remained defiant. "I don't need Lily to watch me."

"The drama club is for members only," Lily lied as she began to panic. If Yuri was forced to tag along with her, then he would discover her secret and more than likely hold that as another bargaining chip for a future favor.

"Then you'll have to stay home, my little Lily." Anna grabbed the plates and walked over to the small sink.

"I can't stay home!" Lily drummed her fingers on the table. "I have a...um...a presentation."

"The drama club can wait." Anna looked at her daughter with annoyance mixed with understanding. "This life doesn't permit us to do what we want, only what we need, and sometimes not even that."

"It—" Lily was about to protest, but the look from her mother warned that further debate would prove catastrophic.

"Turn the lights off before you leave." Anna grabbed her purse and headed toward the door.

"I only have money for my subway fair. I need some for Yuri if he's coming along." Lily called out.

"Grab what you need from my drawer, but only what you need. I know how much is in there," Anna spoke swiftly as she shut the door behind her.

"I'm not going with you to your stupid drama club!" Yuri crossed his arms tightly.

"You think I enjoy this?" Lily raised her eyebrows. "We don't have a choice."

"You could just leave me. You'll be back before Mother gets home. She wouldn't know the difference."

"Are we talking about the same woman?" Lily scoffed.

"Why is she so mean?" Yuri asked solemnly as he stared out the window at the grim grey sky.

"She's stressed, is all." Lily shrugged.

"She used to be so happy." Yuri bit his lip.

"She likes to pretend she's tough, but sometimes I think she misses Papa more than she lets on." Lily reached across the table and grabbed Yuri's hand.

"Don't touch me!" Yuri pulled back sharply. "Your hands are cold."

"You used to worship the ground I walked on." Lily stood and pushed her chair in.

"But then I grew up." Yuri tilted his head with a flair of immaturity.

Lily smiled slightly before stating, "I'll make you a wager."

"A wager?" Yuri's interest piqued. "On what?"

"By the end of the day, you'll adore me as you once did."

"That is bold." Yuri examined his sister hesitantly. "And if not?"

"I'll owe you another favor."

"Interesting." Yuri tapped his chin.

"You have nothing to lose." Lily stretched out her hand.

"This better be one exciting drama club meeting." Yuri shook her hand in agreement before asking in annoyance, "Why are your hands so cold?"

"Yuri, you idiot." Lily leaned on the table as she spoke with intrigue, "There is no drama club."

# Chapter Two:
# Not A Drama Club

*"As far as we can discern, the sole purpose of human existence is to kindle a light in the darkness of mere being."*

Carl Jung

"Where are we going then?" Yuri asked curiously as they arrived at the subway station.

"You'll see," Lily replied with a note of inflection in her voice that was equivalent to the dangling of a carrot.

"You're a woman of conspiracy, is that it?" Yuri asked as he eyed his sister apprehensively while the two passed through the busy Moscow crowds anxious to either exit or enter the station.

"My dear brother, you have no idea," Lily replied as she paid the fare for the subway.

"Why do you never take the escalator?" Yuri groaned as they walked down the stairs.

"It's faster to walk down," Lily replied with a bounce in her step as she half skipped down the stairs despite some annoyed looks from passersby for her chipper attitude.

A breeze rushed through the station and up the stairs from a passing train, striking Lily in the face and rustling through her hair. The familiar smell of engine oil in the poor circulation of the concrete underground was an offense to some, but to Lily, this smell indicated that freedom was mere minutes away. She could, however, do without the insufferable heat that accompanied the trains and loathed the mixing of temperatures that seemed the staple of subway environments.

While many despised the swarm of people in the busy city of Moscow, Lily held an appreciation for the chaos. She felt alive or part of something greater than herself when she was among the crowds. She loved watching the mothers shepherding their children, the bankers and businessmen with their noses stuck in newspapers, the buskers singing old Russian songs that instilled a patriotic fervor, and, increasingly in the last few years, the soldiers.

They looked marvelous in their smart uniforms. They were tall and bright and ready to defend the motherland should they be called into action.

While most women adored the soldiers in a romantic sense, Lily instead revered them from a position of envy. Not that she blamed girls for throwing themselves at these men, and Lily concurred that they were handsome and alluring, but what she would give to don such a uniform herself.

Not that she was eager to fight or had an odd thirst for violence, but Lily was desperate to belong to something meaningful.

While she had found a mediocre substance of belonging in the secret she was about to reveal to Yuri, there was an appalling lack of appreciation shown to her due to her sex. Still, for the sake of passion, Lily persisted.

"New poster." Yuri nudged Lily as they came to stand beside a pillar while awaiting the next train. "They're pushing recruitment lately. I bet they're worried about Hitler."

Glancing over, Lily noticed a poster showcasing the pride of the Red Army and enticing other young men to join their ranks. Soldiers displaying the red star on their helmets and offering steely looks of determination marched in front of a towering statue of Lenin. Above the statue were formations of fighter planes, and Lily's heart ached with excitement.

But beside this poster was another that caught Lily's attention. It was dedicated to the Soviet Air Force, and it was calling upon all available fighters, asking them to submit their applications to the nearest recruitment office.

*It's silly to even try.* Lily shook her head as she dismissed the thought.

"You don't need to worry about Hitler." Lily examined her brother as he studied the poster. "And don't permit yourself any silly notions of joining once you're old enough, either."

"It would be an honor to fight for my country." Yuri nodded proudly.

"You're as clumsy as a bear. You'd accidentally kill yourself before the enemy ever shot you."

"Then I'd die with honor." Yuri remained smug.

"If you enlisted, I'd be more worried about Mother's reaction than bullets flying at you." Lily raised an eyebrow as their subway car arrived.

Pushing their way through the commuters hastily exiting the car and those anxious to get onboard, Lily and Yuri found a seat across from two young soldiers.

They were reading a report that captivated their attention and appeared rather downcast. Whatever was indicated in the report had clearly caused the soldiers to be a little shaken.

Yet, as soon as Lily sat down, she noticed the gloominess of the soldiers lessening a degree as they tried not to be obvious in their ogling of her.

Aware of her effect on men, Lily smiled a touch in her appreciation of their attention. She had no intention of meeting whatever romantic or erotic expectation she knew they were formulating, but still, Lily took enjoyment of the fact she held a power over these men of war that only a few could wield.

While it was true, in some cases, she agreed that she may lead a few too many men on before breaking their hearts, Lily wasn't convinced any of them deserved her affection.

"She's my mother," Yuri interjected, also taking notice of the soldiers' immediate infatuation with his sister. "She's much older than she looks."

"Yuri!" Lily offered a swift backhand to his leg.

"We also don't know who the father is." Yuri held his gaze low like he was an abandoned puppy.

The soldiers laughed, realizing Yuri's jest.

"I do apologize." Lily held her hands gingerly on her lap as she offered a pleasant smile.

"I have a sister as well," one of the soldiers responded with understanding. "I know what it is like to be protective of those we hold dearest."

At this, Yuri frowned sharply before adding, "I'm not being protective!"

"You might not know it yet, but you are." The soldier smiled at him, and Lily noticed the other soldier was simply staring at her with the sort of fixation she was so accustomed to.

"Are you shipping out?" Lily asked as she leaned forward, enjoying their adoration of her before adding flirtatiously, "Or is that a state secret?"

"We're being sent out west," the soldier who had been staring at her replied quickly, almost too quickly, and Lily found his nervousness, while unattractive, also endearing.

"What's out west?" Yuri asked as he grew intrigued.

"Hitler," the first soldier replied uneasily.

"I thought we had a non-aggression pact with Germany?" Lily rubbed her finger along her chin.

"It's precautionary." The first soldier shrugged.

"I'm less optimistic," the other soldier interjected as he began to reclaim some of his nerves.

"Oh?" Lily tilted her head. "You think there will be war?"

"Would Hitler want a war with the Soviet Union?" Yuri asked as he attempted to sound rather mature, and Lily thought she heard his voice dip a little lower than usual. "Seems ambitious."

"Can I trust you?" the soldier asked as he tilted his head while studying Yuri.

"Of course." Yuri nodded eagerly, and Lily knew he was relishing this experience and likely already planning how he was going to retell the story to his peers.

"I'd wager," the soldier glanced around him before leaning in and whispering, "If Hitler attacked right now, he could personally walk all the way up to Moscow."

"We have millions of men on that front, though." Yuri shrugged.

"Millions of *unprepared* men." The soldier cocked his head to the side. "Have you read *The Art of War*?"

Yuri shook his head.

"'He will win who, prepared himself, waits to take on the enemy unprepared,'" he quoted Sun Tzu.

"We're wide open," the other soldier also leaned in, and Lily caught the stench of vodka on his breath. "We saw how they invaded France just over a year ago. If Hitler employs the same tactics on our western flank, we'll be overrun."

"The French were weak." Yuri turned his nose up. "We're Soviets!"

"Let's hope, young comrade, if it ever comes to war, that such determination will prove true." The first soldier grinned at Yuri. "How old are you, by the way?"

"Much too young to fight." Lily took her turn being protective.

"I would be a good soldier." Yuri nodded proudly.

"I don't doubt it." The first soldier threw his lips upside down. "But what do you think that entails? What is a good soldier?"

"A good fighter." Yuri held his chin high.

"No, young comrade." The first soldier pulled down his uniform a little to reveal a wound on his chest. "A good soldier is someone who knows how to die, and how to die well."

Lily watched with a mark of dissatisfaction as Yuri's countenance shifted from misplaced confidence to excitement. Despite the surprise of the man revealing his scar, Lily had hoped that such a stunt would at least stir Yuri to think twice about his enthusiasm for war.

Lily, at least, understood that the posters, the films, the papers, and the parades all projected a false narrative. She

26

knew that war was hell, or at least, that was how her father had experienced it.

Lily had known her father as being a rather bright, intelligent, and cheerful man. But when he returned home from the Great War, he spent every penny they could afford on vodka, sang his songs with waning enthusiasm, and openly criticized those who had 'destroyed him' on the front lines.

"Can I touch it?" Yuri asked eagerly.

"Go ahead." The soldier nodded.

"No!" Lily held out her hand to stop Yuri, who looked at her with annoyance and disappointment.

"It's good to listen to your sister." The soldier winked at Lily.

"Mother," Yuri corrected with a smile.

"You're funny." The other soldier smirked.

"I know another joke." Yuri's eyes lit up.

"No." Lily shook her head, regretting bringing him along, although she didn't have the choice.

"It's not anything inappropriate!" Yuri pressed his case.

"It's fine." The first soldier waved to dismiss Lily's concerns. "We're part of the Red Army. We're accustomed to off color jesting."

"Alright, so." Yuri held his hands in front of him as he set the stage. "A father comes home to his family after work. His young son runs up to him and excitedly states, 'Papa, I heard that they're raising the price of vodka. Does this mean you'll drink less?' The father replies, 'No, it means you'll eat less.'"

The two soldiers roared with laughter, but Lily could only think of her own father and his obsession with drink, and the humor was lost on her.

"This is our stop." Lily stood and nodded for Yuri to come along.

"Why don't I stay with them?" Yuri asked innocently.

27

"Let's go." Lily waved, growing impatient with his antics.

"I was enjoying myself for once," Yuri moaned as they walked up the stairs, again refusing to take the escalator, and exited the station.

"Where are we?" Yuri frowned when they came to the outskirts of Moscow.

Lily didn't reply as she hailed an approaching vehicle.

"Who is that?" Yuri asked.

"Larisa."

"Larisa?!" Yuri's breath left him.

"Is that a problem?" Lily asked with a smirk, understanding how infatuated he was with her friend.

"You should've told me!" Yuri ran his hand quickly through his hair and straightened out his shirt and suspenders.

"You look nice." Lily examined him briskly.

"Forgive me if that doesn't mean a lot coming from you. I've seen your standards of beauty."

"And I've smelled yours," Lily muttered.

The black car pulled up to the subway station, and Larisa, sitting in the back seat, rolled down the window before excitedly waving from them to enter.

"Let me go first!" Yuri argued quietly with his sister as she reached for the door.

"You just want to squeeze up against her, you little pervert."

"Don't say it so loud!" Yuri continued to whisper harshly.

"She can't hear me!"

"Yes, I can!" Larisa called from inside the vehicle.

"See!" Yuri berated his sister.

"Oh, just get in!" Lily swatted his backside.

"Miss." Yuri removed his hat politely as he sat beside Larisa and Lily squeezed in next to him.

"We're all set," Larisa spoke kindly to the driver as she leaned forward and tapped on the glass with her gloved hand.

Impeccably dressed, as usual, Larisa was wearing a white dress that was cut off just after the knees and was complimented with a white fur hat. It was much too ridiculous an outfit for the spring weather, but far be it from Larisa to spurn a chance to show off yet another new outfit.

She was, as Yuri confirmed with his lingering gaze, a rather pretty young woman who was only three years older than Lily.

Lily was eternally grateful for their friendship as the disparity in their social and economic status was, thankfully, overlooked with their unified passion for flying.

"This is a nice surprise," Larisa spoke warmly as she looked at Yuri. "I wasn't expecting you. Did you come to watch?"

"Watch what?" Yuri glanced at his sister.

"You still haven't told him?" Larisa glanced at Lily in shock.

"Told me what?" Yuri grew annoyed.

"What about your mother? Please tell me that she's aware of your activities. You know that she'll rake me over the coals along with you if she believes I colluded in this conspiracy." Larisa looked worried.

"I..." Lily paused as she shuffled her jaw. "I haven't found the time yet."

"Really?" Larisa tilted her head in disappointment. "You'll have plenty of time when you're locked up inside your room."

"Will you please enlighten me?!" Yuri looked crossly at his sister.

"You'll see soon enough." Lily stared out the window as they took a road out to the country.

"That's pretty." Larisa gestured to the white lily that Lily had sown into her yellow dress.

"It's not too much?" Lily asked as she patted it.

"Delicate and eye-catching." Larisa nodded her encouragement. "Are you hoping to win the attention of any new young gentlemen today?"

"Far from it." Lily huffed.

"Oh, I'm surprised this wasn't the first thing I mentioned, but Lily," Larisa began formally, "Did you hear that Major Raskova will be making a tour of our facility?"

"What?" Lily turned sharply toward her friend, who was grinning from ear to ear with pride at sharing the news. "Major Raskova is coming?!"

"The very one." Larisa beamed with pride.

"Who is Major Raskova?" Yuri glanced at his sister.

"Who is Major Raskova?!" Larisa asked with indignation.

"Is she a ballerina or something?" Yuri shrugged his disinterest.

"A ballerina of the sky, perhaps." Larisa smiled.

"She's the Soviet's first female navigator," Lily explained excitedly. "She's set a handful of long-distance records."

"Oh?" Yuri's interest was piqued before asking warily, "In what capacity is she involved with the Soviet Union?"

"The Soviet Air Force," Larisa replied proudly.

"Really?" Yuri's interest soared. "Are we meeting her today?"

"No, no, no." Larisa shook her head. "Next month, I believe."

"Who told you she was coming?" Lily asked her friend eagerly.

"Mr. Romanov received the telegram yesterday."

"Why would she be coming to see you two?" Yuri remained confused. "What do either of you have to do with flying?"

As if in response to Yuri's question, an engine roared overheard, causing the vehicle to rattle and the windows to shake before a single propeller plane sped above their vehicle at an incredibly low altitude.

"What was that?!" Yuri ducked down.

"Hitler's invasion," Larisa jested, and the driver chuckled.

"That, my dear brother, is why we're here," Lily explained with a grin as the vehicle came to a stop near a hangar that was filled with a few planes and some crew inspecting and preparing them.

Beside the hangar was a small clubhouse with men and women dressed pompously, like Larisa, and they were clapping in the manner afforded to the wealthy. The plane, which had made the previous low pass over their vehicle, was now flying upside down, displaying both the capabilities of the pilot and the vehicle.

"Whoa!" Yuri grew amazed as they stepped out of the car.

"That's nothing special." Lily threw her lips upside down in dismissal of his exhilaration.

"Like you could do that," Yuri scoffed, and Lily glanced at Larissa with a hidden smile.

"So, instead of going to drama club, you delight in an airshow?" Yuri asked as they began walking toward the clubhouse.

"Something like that, I suppose." Lily again offered Larisa a secretive grin.

"There's a lot of them," Larisa spoke with worry to Lily as they approached the club. "We might be here a while."

"Don't worry," Lily whispered back. "It's likely the herd will thin itself out."

"What are you guys talking about?" Yuri grew confused.

"Ah, just on time!" a tall, thick man called excitedly from a group of about eight men who were still watching the plane conduct impressive aerobatics.

The men in question were all rather wealthy, although Lily understood that they took pains to hide their material gains, especially with The Terror still fresh in everyone's mind.

Still, little hints of status snuck out here and there. Gloves that were made from fine leather, jackets that had been freshly pressed and were virtually brand new, and black boots that glimmered after a fresh coat of polish that was undoubtedly applied by someone else.

"Mr. Romanov." Lily held her hands firmly yet politely in front of her as she, Larissa, and Yuri, pulling up the rear, came to a stop about five feet away from the group.

Mr. Romanov, while about half a foot taller than most men and with broad shoulders, seemed to be unaware of his daunting stature. With a slouch and a soft demeanor, Mr. Romanov bent to the will of anyone who contended with him.

While Lily preferred that he showed a greater deal of backbone from time to time, this did work in her favor when she convinced him to allow her to fly solo when she was only sixteen.

"Gentlemen, as I promised, our finest instructor." Mr. Romanov pointed at Lily as his pudgy face beamed with excitement that was mixed with apprehension for their reaction.

As Lily had grown well accustomed to by now, some men considered this a joke, others looked past Lily, wondering if the flying instructor was somewhere behind her, and others, who were sharper, offered Lily an unappreciative scowl.

On the opposite spectrum, however, there were two men among them who seemed more than appreciative to have a beautiful young woman as a flying instructor. While this would be cause for concern to some, Lily was adept at handling herself, and being alone with a man in an airplane, of which she was intimately familiar with, was an advantage some had unfortunately overlooked.

"Who is he talking about?" Yuri also glanced over his shoulder.

"Mr. Romanov, I took you for a serious man." One man scowled. "I didn't pay all this money to be mocked."

"Is he talking about you?" Yuri offered his sister a double take.

"You asked for the best, I give you the best." Mr. Romanov pointed adamantly at Lily, who raised her hand gingerly to signal that his attempt, while noble, was falling flat.

"She's a little girl," another man grumbled. "How are we supposed to learn from her?"

"What about him?" one of the men pointed at a pilot who was climbing out of the very plane that had performed some stunts only moments ago.

"She trained him," Mr. Romanov spoke with a shaky voice as he detested confrontation of any sort.

"Where are your experienced men?" another demanded.

"All of us *experienced* men were trained by her," the pilot, who was passing by and heading toward the clubhouse, interjected before offering a wink to Lily.

"This all some sort of ruse," one of the gentlemen's face flushed crimson with rage. "You're having us on, aren't you, Mr. Romanov?"

"We were given the impression that we would be learning from your best man!" Another griped.

"Gentlemen, if you're too afraid of a little girl, how will you overcome your fear of heights?" Lily asked condescendingly as she held her hands firmly in front of her.

"Afraid?" They scoffed, but Lily understood that she had pinpointed their frustration.

Status counted for everything in the Soviet Union, especially in Moscow. Women had a designated role, and any deviation was treated with harsh deterrents. She understood that these men didn't frown upon her flying or cared that women took part in such activities, thanks to women like Major Raskova and her heroics, but for a woman to teach them, that was out of the question. Women were inferior in their eyes, and to be taught by a woman was an embarrassment few could overcome.

"She actually instructed other pilots?" another man asked quietly.

"Forty-four other pilots, to be exact." Lily reached into her purse and retrieved her worn brown leather gloves. "Whoever passes my test today will be awarded the privilege of being the forty-fifth cadet under my wing, so to speak."

A couple men chuckled slightly at her quip, but the majority remained incensed with what they perceived as both an insult to society at large and to their own person.

"If I'm not mistaken, Mr. Romanov did provide you all with reading material a week in advance of today's lesson?" Lily asked with a commanding voice as she fastened her gloves, taking firm control of the situation.

Lily watched their reactions closely as a couple gazes remained fixated on her confidently while the majority glanced awkwardly at each other, wondering if they were the only ones who had neglected reading the material.

"If you didn't read the material, you are dismissed." Lily pointed toward the clubhouse. "By all means, you're welcome to partake in a drink and watch the demonstration, but you will not be participating today."

"Dismissed?" the men grumbled angrily. "How dare you dismiss us? We paid good money to be here."

"What is the procedure for stalling?" Lily threw her hands behind her back as she took a couple steps toward the men while assuming her instructor role. "It was part of the reading material, so I assume you would know."

Looking at each man in the eye, Lily studied their reaction. She wasn't particularly looking for the right answer, although that would be helpful, but rather, she was inspecting their intuition. She wanted to know how familiar they were with the mechanics of the vehicle, and how well they could adapt in situations that called for a quick response.

When no one gave an answer, she continued, "The plane we will be taking to the sky with today is the Polikarpov Po-2. While wonderfully aerobatic and majestically maneuverable, it has a slower speed, meaning that it can stall on occasion. I ask again, what is the procedure when this occurs?"

"You're supposed to teach us this!" another man pointed at Lily.

"I did. I ordered you to read the material."

"If I'm not mistaken," one of the men who had remained confident began, "the procedure is rather simple. The pilot should point the nose down and roll the wings level, if possible, reattaching the airflow to the wing. This will help the aircraft recover and power can be restored. Of course, this is all dependent on altitude."

"Very good." Lily grinned at him. "Mr.?"

"Mr. Morozov," He replied smoothly and with a touch of class that Lily appreciated.

He was a tall man and strikingly handsome with bright blue eyes and dark black hair. Yet even he, in his upper-class jacket and shining boots, Lily found ill-suited for her. Not that she considered herself of a higher status than all these men, but there was no spark, no ignition of romance. She thought it best to keep such movings of the soul contained until love was truly awakened.

"I paid good money for you to teach me how to fly." A fatter man stepped forward and glared at Lily. "I'm a busy man with much to attend to and many people relying on me. I don't have time to read material that you are going to show me anyway."

"I'm sure Mr. Romanov would be happy to reimburse you. Failure to understand the mechanics of the plane, intimately, can result in catastrophic failure," Lily replied fiercely. "I'm sure you're a wonderful gentleman, but I would prefer not to be scraped off the pavement with you."

"How dare you!" His eyes flew wide with outrage. "No man wants to be instructed by someone who only learned how to fly yesterday."

"I've been flying for three years," Lily replied coldly to this man's fury, refusing to yield to his vile temper.

"That can't be. The club doesn't permit anyone under the age of seventeen."

"Unlike you, sir, I devoured the training material. Every book, every article, every piece or scrap of paper that had any information on flying, I read it. I knew every aspect of that plane, every response to the controls, every reading on the instruments. Because of my robust knowledge, Mr. Romanov was kind enough to bend the rules for me."

"Not to mention writing to me every day, sometimes twice a day," Mr. Romanov muttered.

"I'm leaving!" The fat man barked as his large cheeks jiggled.

"This is ridiculous!" another man agreed, and as he departed, four other men left with him.

"I'll process your refunds." Mr. Romanov slouched, but Lily knew full well that he was accustomed to such prejudice.

"That leaves only two of you." Lily glanced at the men undeterred by her sex, one of whom was Mr. Morozov.

"I'm ready." Mr. Morozov nodded as he offered Lily a seductive gaze.

"Meet us by the hangar." Lily pointed in the direction, and the two men left eagerly.

"I'll take Mr. Morozov in my plane," Lily spoke to Larisa as they devised a plan.

"Why do you get him?" Larisa stomped childishly. "You don't even like him!"

"Which is why he's coming with me." Lily raised her eyebrows in understanding. "You'll be too distracted."

"Doesn't matter." Larisa scratched the back of her neck. "I'll probably fall in love with my guy anyway."

"Please don't fall in love again." Lily groaned.

"I'm so lonely I'd fall in love with the wind if it brushed against me the right way." Larisa glanced at the man who was assigned to her as she judged if there was any merit.

"If anything, you're always entertaining." Lily chuckled. "Let's go."

"What about me?" Yuri asked.

"You can watch from the hangar," Lily spoke over her shoulder as they walked to their charge.

"What?! Why can't you take me up with you?" Yuri protested.

"Mother," Lily replied swiftly. "That's why."

"How did you afford to be a member anyway?" Yuri caught up with them.

"I have my means."

"Means?" Yuri squinted.

"Not those sort of means!" Lily grumbled angrily.

"Gross!" Yuri's nose scrunched up. "That's not what I was implying!"

"Are you ready?" Lily asked Mr. Morozov, who offered a confident nod that was trying to mask his nervousness.

"Miss." An attendant handed Lily her helmet and goggles, and then offered the same to Mr. Morozov.

"If you need to relieve yourself, please do so now," Lily spoke patronizingly to Mr. Morozov. "I do detest when you men soil my airplane."

Mr. Morozov chuckled, but Lily detected his apprehension.

"I'll be over here, I guess." Yuri shook his head in annoyance as he dug his hands into his pockets and leaned against the main hangar door.

Climbing into the cockpit while Mr. Morozov climbed into the seat behind her, Lily offered a wave to Yuri, indicating that everything was alright. She assumed that it was likely odd, at best, to see his sister, whom he had heaped so much prejudice upon, as siblings naturally do, in this precarious position so confidently.

Kicking out the blocks from the wheels and starting the propeller, the assistant waved to Lily that she was clear for takeoff.

With a smile that was impossible to contain, Lily pushed the throttle slowly forward, feeling the roar of the machine coursing throughout her body.

Turning the vehicle toward the runway, Lily beamed with anticipation. Even though she had flown hundreds of times, she still felt the drop in her stomach during takeoff, and she loved it.

"Should I be doing anything?" Mr. Morozov shouted.

"I almost forgot you were there!" Lily shouted back. "No, don't touch anything. This is merely to give you the experience. Oh, did you put your parachute on?"

"Parachute?!" Mr. Morozov asked with panic, and Lily grinned as she listened to him rustling around behind her. "What parachute?"

"Too late!" Lily yelled as she increased speed and the plane hurried along the runway.

"What parachute?!" Mr. Morozov remained in a state of panic.

"It's alright, comrade," Lily called over her shoulder as she pulled the nose of the plane up, and they left the safety of the earth. "You're fortunate that you're with me. Otherwise, you may need one."

"Are you sure you know what you're doing?" he asked impatiently as they continued to climb.

"You're strapped in?" Lily confirmed.

"Yes! Why?"

"No reason." Lily licked her teeth as she tried to suppress her grin.

With a deep breath of gratification, Lily felt the peace that she could only experience in this environment. The wind rushed through her curly blonde hair, gravity pulled on her stomach, and the thrill of flying was not lost on her.

Here, in the air, there was no Soviet Union taking her father away. There was no Nazi Germany threatening invasion. There were no politics, money was absent, her mother's nagging for romance was null, and her father's death was pushed far to the back of her mind.

Still, she wondered what he would think if he saw her now. She imagined he would be proud. She imagined he would be diving into all the reading material with her or scouring the textbooks.

Whatever Lily was involved with, her father took an active part, even if he had no interest. She recalled the days of him sitting on the floor playing dolls with her. If any of his peers had seen him in that state, he would've been ostracized, but for his sweet Lily, as he often called her, he played out the fantasy of shopping for food at the market or feeding the rock that was designated as the dolls' baby.

Then again, if her father hadn't disappeared, Lily wondered if she would've engrossed herself in flying or if she would've settled for a more typical life. Not that she appreciated what happened, but she was glad that she, at least, made some good of the circumstances.

Still, at this moment, all that mattered was Lily and her aircraft. Nothing else was even worth considering or thinking about. Flying was all-consuming and encompassing, and Lily already hated the idea of landing again.

Then, with a large grin, Lily suddenly tipped the plane almost entirely vertical as they aimed for the clouds.

"What are you doing?!" Mr. Morozov grew flustered.

"What's the procedure for stalling?" Lily asked.

"What?"

"The procedure. What is it?"

"It's…uh…it's…"

The plane's engine began to sputter with a put-put-put, and Lily glanced at the instruments to see that their altitude was nearing three thousand feet.

"Are we stalling?!" Mr. Morozov screamed.

"We are, indeed, sir." Lily let go of the controls as the plane, which was once ascending, began spinning and tumbling toward Earth.

"You're going to kill me!"

"What's my first step?"

"Ah! Its! Ah!" Mr. Morozov slammed his fist against the side of the plane in frustration.

"Knowing the material counts for nothing if you can't apply it when necessary," Lily spoke calmly, although she wondered how far she should push her luck. "What's our altitude?"

"Two thousand six hundred feet!" he shouted back.

"What should I do at this altitude to correct my stall?"

"I can barely think with this blasted machine spinning out of control."

"Take your time," Lily spoke calmly as the world spun and spun while they came closer and closer to their awaiting death.

"Turn the nose toward the ground!" Mr. Morozov finally yelled.

"Very good, Mr. Morozov." Lily followed his instructions.

"Bring power back to the engine once you are reconnected to the airflow."

"Excellent." Lily did as instructed, and the engine roared back to life.

"Set me down!" Mr. Morozov ordered, and Lily glanced over her shoulder to find him clutching his chest.

"Are you sure you don't want to try any of the controls?" Lily asked. "You have some in front of you."

"No! I'd like to return."

"If we return, you'll likely never come up in the air with me again," Lily warned.

"That's quite alright with me."

"Very well. Just one barrel roll and then we'll land."

"One what?"

Without offering clarification, Lily began her roll while giggling with delight as Mr. Morozov shouted in terror.

Eventually, they were back on the ground, and Mr. Morozov nearly fell out of the plane in his desperation to return to the safety and surety of solid earth.

"How did your demonstration go?" Lily asked Larisa, who had landed just before them.

"We're not in love." Larisa smirked. "But I think he's a good fit. He handled the situation well and without panic."

"Too bad I can't say the same." Lily glanced at Mr. Morozov as he stood with shaky legs.

"I'm surprised you brought him." Larissa pointed at Yuri, who was still standing with his hands in his pockets near the hangar entrance and staring in their direction.

"I didn't have a choice, really. What is surprising is how long I was able to keep the secret." Lily grinned. "I should go speak with him."

"I'll speak with Mr. Romanov to advise that my demonstration was a success."

Walking slowly over to her brother, who was looking back at her with fresh eyes, Lily didn't say a word as she came to stand beside him.

The two stood silently for a moment, brother and sister side by side, watching the planes take off and practice with their instructors.

"This is amazing," Yuri spoke, and Lily glanced at him with a smile.

Throwing her arm around his shoulder, Lily kissed his head as he tried to pull away.

She had won the wager.

# Chapter Three:
# Barbarossa

*"Any man who has once proclaimed violence as his method is inevitably forced to take the lie as his principle."*

Aleksandr Solzhenitsyn

<u>June 22, 1941</u>

"Please let me come with you!" Yuri urged Lily as the two of them were getting ready for the day.

"Once was enough." Lily shook her head. "Mother will kill me when she finds out what I've been involved with. If she finds out that I brought you along, there's no force in Heaven or Hell that will be able to contain her wrath."

"I'm good at keeping secrets!" Yuri pressed as he sat beside her on the bed.

"I know you are." Lily grabbed a little mirror and began inspecting her appearance.

"So, can I come?" Yuri pleaded with his eyes.

"When you're older." Lily fluffed her hair.

"I'm tired of hearing that." Yuri looked defeated.

"Because all you hear is the privilege that age brings. No one is eager for the responsibilities. I'd rather be tired of hearing a patronizing phrase than be weary from carrying these responsibilities."

"What responsibilities do you have?" Yuri rolled his eyes.

"Excuse me?" Lily frowned. "You, for one."

"Me? How am I your responsibility? It's not like you have to change me or feed me or clothe me."

"If only it were that simple." Lily raised her eyebrows.

"I'm not a burden!" Yuri growled, and Lily knew she had hurt his feelings.

"Responsibility and burden are not synonymous." Lily looked at him with soft eyes before offering a kiss on his head. "At least not in this situation. You're a pleasure, and it's a great privilege of mine that I get to call you my younger brother."

"I could be an asset to you," Yuri pressed. "I'll look after the planes. I'll help with the refueling and the maintenance."

"You can't even maintain your hair." Lily glanced at the mess sitting like a mop on top of his head.

"Teach me." Yuri knew his pleading was in vain, but he continued nonetheless. "I can learn. I want to be involved."

"Soon." Lilly ran her hand along her blue summer dress as she inspected herself in the mirror.

"What does soon mean?" Yuri shrugged.

"I had to beg, daily, for Mr. Romanov to allow me to fly, who, by the way, would be the one deciding if you're permitted to join. I can tell you already that it's a no."

"Maybe I can help inside the club? You know, serving drinks. Anything that can help me get my foot in the door."

"The club members smoke, drink heavily, and discuss things a boy's ears should never hear." Lily pinched his cheek.

"I'm not a boy!" He defended as his voice squeaked.

"Puberty is nature's way of humbling us, isn't it?" Lily asked rhetorically as she applied some lipstick in the mirror.

"You know what I think your problem is?" Yuri crossed his arms as he slumped down onto his bed in frustration.

"At the moment, you."

"You're lucky."

"Lucky?" Lily scoffed and turned to face him. "This is a problem?"

"One day, your luck will run out." Yuri glared at her. "Then, you'll wish you had been kinder to me."

"Well, Yuri, one day you'll grow up, and then you'll realize what you perceive as restraint is actually love and kindness." Lily tilted her head before glancing around the room and asking with confusion, "How am I lucky? I live in a two-bedroom apartment with my mother while sharing a bedroom with my younger brother. Our father

45

was taken, we eat scarcely better than the peasantry, and I've yet to find a man that interests me. It's likely that I will live out the rest of my days in mother's shadow and become a spinster that looks after all her needs."

"I suppose the distinction between a fortunate life and general good chance should be arrived at, but still, it pains me that you don't see how blessed you are."

"By all means, educate me." Lily watched him closely.

"I've yet to meet anyone who thinks ill of you." Yuri examined his sister. "I've yet to hear a bad word about you, or some strange rumor, or a snarky remark. Besides the obvious with the men at the club, but that was more to do with your gender and not your person. You're unique in that jealousy, which plagues many other beautiful women, flees from you. People appreciate you as Lily, and there aren't many others who could claim the same."

"You think I'm beautiful?" Lily grinned.

"Objectively speaking." Yuri shuddered in disgust. "As difficult as it is to say, you need to hear the truth. Providence won't always be on your side."

"Well, that is —"

"Lily! Yuri!" Anna shouted.

"What's wrong?!" Lily jumped to her feet, trailed closely by Yuri, as they exited the room quickly to find out what was so emergent.

Entering the dining room, Lily was surprised to find Anna sitting by the radio and glaring at it angrily.

"What's happened?" Lily knelt in front of her mother and took her hand.

While brandishing a hateful scowl, Anna didn't reply as she stared at the radio with a menace that shocked Lily.

"I repeat, the Germans, under Hitler's directive, have invaded the Motherland," the announcement began, and a cold chill ran down Lily's spine.

Her arms and legs turned to jelly as she listened to the terrifying broadcast. She imagined that this day would inevitably come, but part of her didn't believe she would ever hear such terrifying words.

She recalled the horror stories her father shared of war, but Lily was wise enough to fear the stories he didn't share with her. Lily knew what an invasion of the Soviet Union meant and how destructive this would be for their nation and way of life.

Selfishly, Lily's first thought dwelled on her flying club. She wasn't ignorant enough to believe it would last forever, but she wasn't ready to give up that part of her life just yet. She doubted that the club would continue to operate during an invasion.

"Our initial estimates have indicated that this is the largest land invasion in the history of the world. The German brute seeks to uproot the inhabitants of our land so that they can carry out their barbaric Fascist ideal of repopulating the Soviet Union."

"I don't understand," Yuri spoke quietly, and Lily detected the nervousness in his voice. "Hitler and Stalin had a non-aggression pact. Why would he break it?"

"The pact only gave Hitler all the time he needed to prepare," Anna spoke through gritted teeth, and Lily imagined that if they sent this ferocious woman to the front, the Germans would be in a full retreat.

"Without a declaration of war," the broadcast continued, "German forces fell upon our country, attacking our frontiers in many places. The Red Army and the whole nation will wage a victorious Patriotic War for our beloved country, for honor, for liberty. Our cause is just. The enemy will be beaten. Victory will be ours!"

*Our cause is just,* Lily repeated in her mind as she felt a stirring in her soul as she recalled the poster she had seen in the subway recruiting pilots for the Soviet Air Force.

A moment passed, an infinitesimal break in the passage of time while Lily knelt in front of her mother. Her next actions, she understood, would decide her fate.

She could choose the path of safety, staying with her mother to assist her with Yuri, or finding some sort of work to provide financial support.

Or, the dangerous thought beckoned, she could use her skills for good. She could make a real difference as a fighter pilot against the Nazis.

It was a ridiculous notion, she agreed, and the very thought almost made her burst into laughter. And, still, there was another aspect to this idea that was altogether humorless. She was the best pilot at the club, no one questioned that. Such skills could be employed against the invaders and, if her luck, as Yuri pointed out, held strong, then maybe she could return home after the war.

Looking into her mother's menacing, hate-filled eyes, Lily squeezed her hand before glancing over at her brother with his frightened countenance, wondering what this meant for him. She knew that, like most boys, he wanted to be tough, but when faced with real tribulation, their character was tested.

"I'll be right back," Lily spoke quietly as she stood.

"Where are you going?" Yuri asked with concern.

Lily didn't reply as she burst into her room and rummaged through the drawer of her bedside table as she retrieved a pencil and paper.

"I saw how you looked at the poster in the subway." Yuri closed the door behind him after he trailed Lily into the room.

"You intend to stop me?" Lily began writing furiously.

"Mother might."

Lily glanced up from the bed as she looked intently into her brother's eyes.

"So, I won't tell her." Yuri cleared his throat.

"She might find out when I'm no longer around the apartment." Lily grinned.

"My sweet sister," Yuri began as he sat on the bed beside her and spoke in a patronizing tone. "I'm not going to tell her, because I know that they won't accept your application."

"I have to try." Lily felt downcast. She knew her brother was right. If the way the men at the flying club reacted was any indication of how the Soviet Air Force would respond, then her chances were already destitute.

"Unless..." Yuri stared at the ceiling as he was lost to thought.

"Go on." Lily urged.

"Major Raskova." Yuri glanced at her.

"She *is* a female pilot in the Soviet Air Force." Lily tapped her pencil against her cheek as she considered it. "She would know who I should reach out to."

"I shouldn't be helping you with this." Yuri rubbed the back of his neck.

"Stop!" Lily demanded. If her brother requested, Lily knew she would divert her course.

She was frightened as well and knew that any reason for her not to pen the letter would divert her from her course. Still, something seemed to be guiding her. She couldn't explain it. She wasn't religious or spiritual in any regard, but Lily felt that something greater than herself was calling her.

*Is that you, Papa?* Lily asked inwardly.

There was no response.

*In either case, I'll make you proud. I promise. I know you hated Stalin, but you loved Russia and Mother. I'll defend them both for you, if I can.*

Without further hesitation, Lily wrote the letters. One to the Soviet Air Force recruitment office, and one directly to Major Raskova. She detailed her flying experience, including how she had been an instructor and trained many other men and women.

Glancing over at her brother, who was watching her intently, Lily wondered what he was thinking. Words were difficult to come by in a situation like this, and Lily understood that Yuri was likely terrified.

"I wish I could help." Yuri half-heartedly kicked at an imaginary object on the ground in frustration.

"You shouldn't overlook your importance to mother." Lily squeezed his hand.

"Neither should you," Yuri retorted.

"You're her golden child. We all know that." Lily wrapped her arm around his shoulder.

"That's surprising, considering the way she talks about you." Yuri raised an eyebrow. "When you're not here, you become her every thought."

"She's just worried." Lily shrugged. "Want to mail these with me? We can find out more about the invasion while we're at it."

"Sure!" Yuri's eyes lit up as he glanced at his sister in surprise at the request.

"We'll have to deceive mother." Lily tested.

"I am a man bred for duplicity." Yuri stuck his nose in the air, and Lily chuckled.

She appreciated the levity her brother brought to this terrifying situation. This was the end of the world, especially if the Nazis won. They would eradicate everyone to achieve their goal of replacing the population.

A loathing set into Lily's bones as she thought of such a wicked goal. She thought of her mother and brother and knew that she had to protect them—no matter the cost.

# Chapter Four:
# Broadcast

*"Success is stumbling from failure to failure with no loss of enthusiasm."*

Winston Churchill

September 8, 1941

"Let's open ours together." Larisa beamed with excitement as she sat across from Lily outside a café in Moscow.

"It feels odd being so excited for rejection." Lily played nervously with the letter in her hand.

"You don't know that!" Larisa scowled.

"You know I'm usually optimistic, but this is the fourth letter we've received." Lily let her letter flop down on the table. "The last three were rejections. I doubt they'd change their mind now. I'm not certain I can handle any bad news today."

Not that she could concentrate much as it was. The street outside the café was bustling with citizens anxious to flee deeper into Russia. The Nazis were pushing further into the Soviet Union, and Lily, among many others, knew that if no counteroffensive were launched, the Nazis would continue their unrelenting push and they would be forced to flee.

Cars were piled high with belongings, and people half ran this way and that, organizing their journey or else preparing for the worst. Adding to the confusion, the Red Army seemed to be just as disordered. Soldiers, in a disorganized sprawl, fortified positions that seemed to be useless while others stood around awkwardly as officers shouted conflicting and unclear orders.

"Do we have to sit out here?" Lily rubbed her eyes in frustration. "Can't we sit inside?"

"You're just nervous." Larisa opened her letter, and Lily watched eagerly.

"Go on! You, too! At the same time!" Larisa pointed.

"Alright," Lily grumbled as she also opened her letter and the two girls impatiently read their responses.

"How bad is yours?" Larisa's shoulders slouched.

"'The Soviet Air Force is not so desperate that we need to employ girls,'" Lily read her letter aloud. "Short and to the point."

Neither woman spoke a word as the waiter brought them tea, and Lily noticed how often he glanced at the soldiers and cars. She wondered if he was considering leaving as well or if he, like her, even had the means to leave.

"Anything else?" the waiter asked as he retrieved a pen and pad but kept a nervous eye on the street.

"This is excellent, but thank you," Lily replied, yet the waiter remained staring out at the commotion.

"I'm terribly sorry." He shook himself back to reality. "I didn't catch that."

"Are you alright?" Larisa asked with concern.

"Yes, miss." The waiter forced a smile. "I was simply lost in thought."

"Your name is Ivan, correct?" Larisa squinted.

"Yes, actually." Ivan tilted his head as he returned a curious gaze.

"I'm Larisa. We went to school together. You were a year ahead of me, though, so I don't think you would've noticed me."

"My apologies." Ivan looked a little embarrassed. "The only thing I paid attention to in school was the clock."

"You seem worried." Larisa stirred her tea gently, and Lily grew annoyed at her pursuit of romance, even with the end of the world looming over their heads.

"It's not appropriate for me to burden you with my troubles, miss." Ivan waved to politely dismiss her concerns.

"Please." Larisa held a limp hand to her chest. "I would love to hear what troubles you."

Glancing over his shoulder, Ivan knelt and whispered to Larisa and Lily, "My brother is on the front. I'm worried about him. It's been almost a month since we last received news. He was taken prisoner and sent to some sort of camp, but that's all we know. The Germans are getting closer to Moscow every day, and my mother is crippled. Getting her out of the house is difficult as it is, but if we have to flee, I fear the worst."

"That is troublesome." Larisa drew a deep breath.

"Excuse me!" another patron called to Ivan from a table not far from them. "May we have the bill?"

"Thank you for sharing." Larisa touched Ivan's shoulder gently before he stood and left to attend to his duties.

"Thank you for sharing," Lily mocked.

"Quiet!" Larisa growled. "He's a troubled man who cares for his mother. That's adorable."

"Well, if—"

Lily was interrupted by the sound of glass shattering across the street.

Glancing in that direction, Lily, to her horror, saw a man throwing bricks into the window of a store before grabbing whatever produce and goods he could toss into a bag.

"Looters!" Larisa shook her head with frustration.

"After all this country is going through, he decides it's a suitable time to be greedy!" Lily concurred.

Immediately, the police gave chase and tackled the man to the ground, where they began beating him relentlessly.

"If anyone deserves disappearing, it's men like him." Larisa took an angry sip of her tea.

"This is so infuriating." Lily cracked her knuckles.

"Oh, I despise when you do that." Larisa scrunched up her nose.

"We have talents, advanced skills, that could be used to help turn the tide of this war." Lily ignored Larisa's annoyance as she went through each finger, paying special attention to crack every joint. "Yet we're sitting here having tea simply because of our sex. It's not right. I want to be out there. I want to be helping. I'm not some silly housewife who concerns herself with nothing more than the latest fashion."

At this remark, two women with large hats, who were sitting at the table near Lily, turned toward the girls and offered large scowls.

"Mother keeps insisting that if I want to be involved, I should volunteer for nursing," Larisa continued in a softer voice as she tried to thwart the attention of the ladies.

"If I have to hear of another woman who enters nursing, I'm going to vomit." Lily began to chew her nails.

A huff of annoyance for the impolite conversation came from the two ladies near Lily, who, at this point, found the weight of their opinion null.

"She's frustrated." Larisa leaned over and offered an explanation to the two women.

"Frustrated doesn't even begin to describe what I'm feeling." Lily squeezed her eyes shut as she bit her tongue, preventing herself from offending them any further.

"Your soup, miss," Ivan spoke courteously as he returned to the table with their pea soup.

"This looks delicious. Did you make it yourself?" Larisa asked cheerfully as she stared up at him with her bright blue eyes.

"No, miss, the kitchen prepares the food." Ivan pointed over his shoulder.

"But of course." Larisa grabbed her spoon gingerly.

"I'll return shortly." Ivan offered a slight bow of his head before assisting the table beside them.

"They're being very rude!" one of the ladies whispered her harsh complaint to Ivan.

"Did you seriously ask him if he made the soup?" Lily leaned forward.

"Shush!" Larisa held her finger to her mouth as she pointed to the back of Ivan. "He can hear you!"

"Too bad he didn't make this. It's delicious." Lily grinned. "Are you hoping to find a househusband?"

"You love torturing me." Larisa offered an unappreciative glare at her friend.

"You do make yourself an easy target." Lily took a generous mouthful of the pea soup and accidentally slurped, which again drew the ire of the posh women.

"Sorry." Lily mouthed her apology to them.

"Feels odd, doesn't it." Larisa grew reflective. "To be sitting here, knowing that this will come to an end soon. There's a war on our doorstep, but the theater is still in production, the opera is organizing new events, and café's like this are operating."

"Yeah." Lily didn't know what else to say, and now whatever enjoyment she was experiencing from the pea soup turned bland.

"I'm not sure what I'd do without flying right now."

"About that," Lily paused as she looked at her friend with sorrow. "The club is postponed until further notice."

"What?!" Larisa dropped the spoon into her bowl, and it clinked loudly, again drawing the attention of the other patrons.

"It's too dangerous." Lily raised her eyebrows. "According to Mr. Romanov, that is."

"That man has no backbone." Larisa frowned. "Though I suppose that makes sense. They recruited most of the cadets."

"They did?" Lily glanced at her in surprise.

"They even took Mr. Morozov," Larisa scoffed.

"Mr. Morozov?" Lily jutted her jaw to the side in anger. "The man who joined me once in the plane while not even handling any of the controls himself, and since then, every time he comes to the club, merely drinks and smokes with his friends? They took him over experienced instructors such as ourselves? If he tells anyone where he learned how to fly, that will forever tarnish our reputation."

"He asked me to dinner, by the way." Larisa took a sip of her tea.

"Mr. Romanov?" Lily shot her head back in surprise.

"No, silly." Larisa chuckled but then added with a touch of annoyance, "Mr. Morozov."

"You don't sound pleased." Lily tried to seem attentive, but her mind dwelt on the devastating news of their rejection.

"He asked me after inquiring if you would be interested." Larisa tilted her head. "I'm not all that attracted to the idea of being picked second."

"What am I without flying?" Lily shook her head, mesmerized, as she shifted the subject. "It's been my life for years. I'm consumed by it."

"We started around the same time." Larisa stared at the table. "At the club, that is."

"I never asked why you joined, by the way. Were you always interested in flying?" Lily took a sip of her tea, which was, unfortunately, colder than she would've preferred.

"Same reason you did, I suppose." Larisa continued to stare at the table. "My brother was also taken."

"I see," Lily spoke tenderly. "I didn't know that."

"He was obsessed with planes. I thought I would join in a sort of silent protest or to somehow honor his memory. What about you? Was your father interested in flying?"

"Not that he mentioned." Lily drew a deep breath as she attempted to hide her discomfort with the subject. "He was fixated on trains."

"Why was he taken?" Larisa asked quietly, but Lily noticed the stolen glances from the ladies near them. It was dangerous to discuss such things openly, and especially in public. While The Terror was long over, the effects still lingered, and many were being taken as 'enemies of the people', never to be heard from again.

"We shouldn't talk about this here." Lily shook her head.

"So, why did you start flying then?" Larisa understood her friend's concern.

"Seemed like a suitable escape." Lily tilted her head.

"Why didn't you change your last name?" Larisa returned to the previous subject.

"What do you mean?" Lily watched her closely. She knew exactly what she meant but was merely playing for time to think of an excuse.

"You kept your father's last name." Larisa offered her a knowing look. "Your mother and brother changed their last names, but you kept yours. Why?"

Lily pondered for a moment as she again glanced around her to ensure they were out of earshot before replying, "My mother and brother reacted out of fear. I don't blame them for it, but I refused to follow that path."

"Why?"

"You're rather persistent today." Lily chuckled.

"You and I are cut from the same cloth." Larisa took another sip. "We both had men in our family taken, we both turned to the sky to save us, and now we're both sitting here holding onto the hope that our nation can see our value. I trust you, unreservedly, but I need you to trust me. Who knows, someday you and I may be in the same plane fighting against Nazis, and we'll need to trust each other like we are closer than family. Tell me why you didn't change your name."

"When that day comes, I'll tell you." Lily turned her gaze away.

Larisa leaned back with a sigh as she also stared out at the busy street.

"So, are you going to dinner with Mr. Morozov?" Lily asked after a moment.

"Of course." Larisa nodded firmly as if the answer was obvious.

"You are?" Lily frowned. "There are many other—"

"Shush!" Larisa threw her hand up as she turned her ear.

"Don't shush me!" Lily grew indignant as she swatted at Larisa's hand.

"The radio!" Larisa stood and ran inside the café.

"Radio?" Lily muttered as she slowly stood and followed her friend, half wondering if she had somehow been driven insane.

"Ivan, can you turn the radio up, please?!" Larisa pleaded as she pointed behind a serving bar.

"What is it?" Lily asked with concern, wondering if she would need to rush home to help her mother and brother evacuate.

"Major Raskova," Larisa whispered.

"Really?" Lily also turned her ear.

"I make this announcement with the unconditional blessing of our Great Leader," a woman's voice came through strongly over the radio. "Every available women flier is encouraged to submit an application without delay to our all-female fighter and bomber regiments."

"What did she say?!" Lily latched onto Larisa's arm, who simply stared at the radio with tearful eyes.

"Recruitment will begin shortly," Major Raskova concluded, and Lily didn't believe that a sweeter or stronger voice existed.

"Did you hear that?!" Larisa spun toward Lily, still in shock.

"This is actually happening!" Lily squeezed her friend's arms as she squealed.

"We're that desperate, are we?" a man near them muttered under his breath.

"Major Raskova is a Hero of the Soviet Union!" Larisa barked at him. "By the end of the war, we will also be awarded the prestigious title."

The man scoffed.

"Drink your tea while us women go off to fight!" Larisa growled as she grabbed Lily's hand, and the two stormed out of the café to submit their applications.

# Chapter Five
# Major Raskova

*"The best revenge is not to be like your enemy."*

Marcus Aurelius

"I don't suppose there's anything I can say to stop you," Anna spoke plainly from the doorway as Lily packed a few summer dresses, a couple blouses and skirts, and her flying textbooks into a tiny suitcase.

With the approaching Germans, coupled with Anna's increasing anxiety, the family had moved to a small town outside of Moscow. It was isolated and quiet, but Lily feared that they had not fled far enough and possibly in the wrong direction. Regardless, it was all that they could afford, and the decision to leave the apartment was not easily made.

While the new place was more spacious than their cramped apartment in Moscow, Lily and Yuri were still forced to share a room despite his protests.

"I'm of little use here," Lily replied solemnly as she squeezed her doll into the suitcase.

"My dear girl," Anna chuckled as she grabbed the doll. "You can't take this with you to war."

"Why not?" Lily asked innocently.

"There are already men who look down on your position because of your gender." Anna studied the doll lovingly. "If you bring this with you, it will only provide them with the ammunition to further dismiss your determination."

"I've never been without her." Lily looked at the aged doll fondly.

"I remember when your father gifted it to you." Anna's lips trembled before she broke down and threw the doll angrily onto the bed. "You're just a girl, Lily! What do you know of war?!"

Startled by the outburst, Lily nearly jumped backward before reclaiming her nerves.

Sitting on the bed with her face in her hands, Anna wept, and Lily's heart shattered for her mother. Kneeling in front of her, Lily wrapped her arms around Anna as she sobbed into her shoulder. Resting her head against her mother's, Lily drew a deep breath, inhaling her scent, which plunged her into happier memories.

She recalled the days when her father was still with them, when life seemed pleasant, and Lily yet carried the blind optimism of youth. She recalled the times when she would sit on the floor with her mother as they listened to their father, or Uncle Boris, telling stories. Lily wished she could cut a lock of her mother's hair to take with her. She would only need to sniff it, and at once, she would be back at home and in happier times.

If she was honest, Lily was terrified. War was not something she had ever imagined for herself, nor was it something she would have ever dreamed of enlisting for. Still, for the first time since her father was taken, Lily felt a sense of purpose. She had delved into flying to cope with her father's loss, and now she was able to use that gift to hopefully save her mother and brother.

"I may not know war, but I know flying." Lily squeezed her mother's arm as she broke from her embrace.

"Drama club." Anna sniffled. "I should've known. You should've told me."

"You wouldn't have let me go." Lily looked back at her with understanding.

"Of course not!" Anna growled but then looked at her daughter with softer eyes as she rubbed Lily's cheek. "There's too much of your father in you. Even if I refused, you would've found a way. You're too mischievous."

"Is that a bad thing?" Lily shrugged.

"Evidently." Anna grinned before turning to the suitcase and throwing her hands onto her hips before sighing, "If I had a minute with a needle and some thread."

"They're a little tattered, but I'll be wearing a uniform anyway." Lily shut the suitcase.

"Wait, wait, wait." Anna squinted at something she had spotted in the suitcase. "Open that back up."

"Why?" Lily did as requested.

"You can't take these!" Anna dug out a handful of summer dresses.

"Because?" Lily tilted her head.

"Lily!" Anna shook the dresses in front of her as if the answer was obvious. "You're going to war! War, my girl! You don't take summer dresses into battle!"

"This is for when we're not in uniform." Lily shrugged. "I'm sure there'll be dances and such. Besides, you're always nagging at me to find a husband. These will help."

"My goodness." Anna slapped her hand over her face in despair. "Dances? Do you really have no idea what you're getting into?"

"At least let me take a couple." Lily bartered.

"Absolutely not. Especially considering that winter is approaching, and who knows where you'll be stationed."

"One dress," Lily pressed. "That's all I ask. They mentioned bringing suitable clothing. If I am selected, I won't be returning home."

With a heavy sigh, Anna looked through the summer dresses in her hand before relinquishing with a nod.

"Thank you!" Lily kissed her mother on the cheek. "Besides, I may not even pass the interview."

"They'll love you," Anna spoke with regret. "Everyone loves my Lily. It sounds cruel, but I wish you had some sort of problem with your eyesight or that you would have been born without a limb or something, anything that would keep you from flying."

"I promise I'll come back to you." Lily kissed her mother's hand.

"If only you could keep such promises." Anna patted Lily's face gently. "It's quiet in this new house. You could stay here until the war is over."

"It's too quiet for me."

"Typical. Do you have enough money for the train?"

"I do." Lily double-counted the coins in her purse.

"Write often, please." Anna stared at her feet before shuffling toward the door where Yuri was standing with his arms crossed.

"Don't slouch!" Anna barked at Yuri as she slapped his backside to make him stand upright.

"Hey!" Yuri grumbled as he massaged his wound.

"Have you come to talk me out of it?" Lily watched him closely as she held the suitcase down by his side.

"Are you kidding?" Yuri chuckled. "All my friends are jealous. They wish they had sisters like mine."

"Well, I'm glad my sacrifice has elevated your social status." Lily grinned.

"But..." Yuri paused.

"Yes?"

"I'm worried." Yuri cleared his throat to force the tears away.

"So am I." Lily nodded. She intended to lie, to pretend that she was strong and unbothered by the idea of not only being shot at but also shooting at others.

"I think I'm going to cash in on that favor." Yuri shuffled his jaw as his eyes flooded with tears.

"How so?" Lily swallowed.

"Come back. Please." Yuri drew a shaky breath as he sniffled. "That will fulfill the obligations of my favor."

"I promise." Lily offered her brother a large embrace.

"Yuri! Come help me with the dishes!" Anna called.

"You can't leave me alone with her!" Yuri pleaded. "It goes against human decency!"

Lily chuckled as she patted her brother's shoulder before adding, "Give me a moment alone. I need to get ready."

With a nod, Yuri sauntered out of the room to help his mother.

Closing the door, Lily stood alone in the quiet room as she contemplated if this was truly the correct course of action for her life. She knew how devastated her mother would be if the worst came to pass, but somehow, Lily felt a strange reassurance that nothing terrible was going to happen.

Without further thought, Lily drew a deep breath, donned her perky smile, shook her head to get that bounce in her curls, and opened the door.

With her battered leather suitcase banging against her knees while she walked, Lily arrived at the small train station, which was the route's last stop before Moscow.

The sun was beginning to set as it painted a beautiful array of oranges, purples, and blues against the fall horizon. It was Lily's favorite time of year. She loved the changing leaves, especially from the view of a plane where whole valleys, hills, and forests were decorated in oranges, yellows, and reds.

Waiting with her on the platform were a few other families, mostly women, whom Lily assumed had some pressing matters inside the city. Otherwise, no one dared to venture to Moscow unless it was absolutely necessary.

A whistle bellowed, and Lily glanced in that direction to find an engine puffing down the line toward the station. She felt her heart climbing into her throat as she clung to her suitcase. Her shoulders tightened, her stomach churned, and Lily was forced to take a deep breath to calm her nerves.

To her surprise, as the train came closer to the station, Lily noticed that it was littered with bullet holes and looked as if it had come from the front line. The windows were shattered, some of the doors were barely hanging onto the hinges, while others were missing altogether.

With a piercing squeal, the train came to a halt, and Lily noticed that many of the passengers were huddled together inside and shivering. Without windows or doors, and paired with the cool fall air, Lily agreed that the journey must've been unbearable, especially for the younger ones.

Without delay, the families on the platform near Lily entered the train, and she trailed after them.

Immediately, Lily was hit with the unmistakable stench of body odor. The train car she entered was littered with soldiers, and many were covered in mud or dirt or had serious wounds. Lily concluded that they had recently returned from the front, and the state of so many injured was demoralizing at best.

Glancing around, Lily wasn't sure where to sit. Almost every seat was taken, and the ones that were free lay between groups of men who looked less than enthused.

Covering her nose while trying to be discreet, Lily moved through the train car, hoping to find a suitable and respectable seat.

"Hello," a sweet voice spoke cheerfully.

Looking in the direction of the voice, Lily met the eyes of a younger woman, likely about her age, sitting near a group of men. Her brightness and enthusiasm almost seemed sarcastic, given the bleak circumstances that surrounded them. Either that or this young woman had gone entirely mad.

She was modestly dressed in respect to fashion, and Lily assumed that she hailed from a similar economic background. But her startling brown eyes above a cute nose and a charming smile made her a whirlwind of positivity.

"Hello," Lily replied cautiously as she noticed a large sack at this woman's feet.

"Come, sit." The woman scooched closer to the soldier sitting next to her, who grumbled at the intrusion as she made room for Lily.

"Thank you," Lily spoke warmly as she brushed the glass from the window off her seat before sitting down.

"I'm Nadia." She extended her hand in greeting. "Nadia Popova."

"Lidya Litvyak." Lily shook her hand. "But I go by Lily, or Lilya. Whichever you prefer."

"Lily it is then." Nadia nodded enthusiastically, and Lily found her energy endearing, and possibly inspiring, if not entirely overwhelming.

"You're awfully cheerful." Lily took notice of the fact that not a single man paid her much attention. Not that she was seeking their interest, but she understood that this was a telling sign of how serious the situation was.

"Not in the slightest." Nadia shook her head but still smiled brightly. "I'm excited, but cheerful, no."

"Dare I ask what you're excited about?" Lily placed the suitcase under her feet.

"I'm finally going to kill some Germans." Nadia held her chin high.

"You're heading in the wrong direction," Lily muttered dryly, and a soldier near her chuckled.

"I'm hoping to be selected for one of the regiments under Major Raskova," she explained brightly.

"Major Raskova?" Lily watched her closely.

"You've heard of her?" Nadia perked up, which surprised Lily, who considered this new acquaintance to have already summited the peak of excitability.

"I'm also being interviewed."

"What are the coincidences?!" Nadia latched onto Lily's hand eagerly and yet roughly.

"Rare, I'd imagine." Lily smiled back at Nadia.

"I hope you're familiar with Moscow? I've been worried sick, wondering how I can possibly navigate such a large city. I'm apparently supposed to take the subway, but I've never used one before, and, to be honest, I'm not even sure what a subway is." Nadia ran through every available emotion as she bared herself to Lily.

"I've spent a considerable amount of time in Moscow." Lily nodded. "I can guide you."

"Oh, thank goodness!" Nadia threw a limp hand to her chest in relief. "I'm so glad I met you, Lily."

"And I you." Lily smiled. "So, what have you prepared for the interview?"

"Prepared?" Nadia asked as the color left her face. "Like a presentation?"

Ignoring an opportunity to torture the poor thing, Lily answered honestly, "No, no. I meant, have you mentally prepared?"

"Oh, I see." Nadia chuckled, but Lily noticed that her good spirits were setting some of the soldiers on edge, and they offered glares in their direction.

"I presume," Lily began in a quieter voice, hoping that Nadia would follow suit, "that Major Raskova is seeking serious women. I'm hoping that I can substantially repress any bright temperament and showcase an austere Soviet woman of war."

"That's grim." Nadia's eyebrows bounced. "I like it."

"What is your background in flying, Nadia?"

"It's a touch scandalous," Nadia leaned in and whispered. "But I started flying at the local flying club much younger than was permitted. I'm from Donetsk, in Ukraine, and one day, a pilot landed in a field nearby. As soon as he stepped out of the plane, I was in love. With flying, that is, not him. Well, actually, him too, but more so the idea of him rather than the actual person. I mean, he was nice and all but—"

"And this ignited your love of flying?" Lily interrupted, understanding that Nadia was the sort of woman who required helpful direction from time to time.

"Yes, and at sixteen, I completed my first solo flight. Two years later, I had my pilot's license and became an instructor."

"Doesn't sound too scandalous to me." Lily threw her lips upside down.

"My parents didn't know about it." Nadia giggled. "I didn't tell them, actually, until my application was accepted by Major Raskova."

"Interesting." Lily squinted. "I think you and I are cut from the same cloth, my friend."

"How did you become interested?" Nadia asked Lily.

"Replace your name with mine in the story you just told me, and that's how."

"You're from Ukraine?" Nadia frowned.

"No."

"A pilot landed in a field near you?"

"No, no." Lily shook her head in frustration. "I, too, joined a flying club, completed my first solo very young, and hid the whole endeavor from my mother."

"Is that right?" Nadia threw her hands onto her hips, but in doing so elbowed the soldier sitting next to her, who grunted loudly.

"We're coming up on Moscow." Lily glanced past the broken glass on the window.

"Again, I'm so very thankful you're here. Looks scary."

"We'll be meeting a friend of mine, another flier who is also being interviewed. You'll love her. Her name is Larisa."

"Larisa," Nadia sighed endearingly. "What a beautiful name. Larisa."

"And a beautiful person."

"I love that." Nadia tilted her head. "What a sweet friendship."

*Don't give this girl a plane, just give her a dinner date with Hitler. Her positivity will exorcise his demons, or he'll be driven to insanity. Either outcome would be suitable.*

"There are no lights," Nadia commented on the peculiarity. "Why is the city so dark?"

"The lights are kept off at night so as not to give away our location to enemy bombers," Lily explained.

"Do you think we'll still be able to find our way?" Nadia asked nervously.

"It shouldn't be a problem," Lily replied confidently.

The train came to a stop in the station, and the jolting caused some of the loose glass remaining to fall and shatter onto the floor and seats.

"If they get me up in the air, they won't have to worry about this train being strafed again." Nadia cocked her head arrogantly.

"Somehow I believe you," Lily muttered as she stood and grabbed her suitcase while Nadia threw her bag over her shoulder.

"Where's your friend?" Nadia asked as the two stood on the platform.

"She should be here. She's...ah, there she is!" Lily pointed in the direction of a waving Larisa.

"Rather elegant, this friend of yours." Nadia grew impressed as Larisa was dressed in the latest fashion, as was her custom.

"I don't think she's ever taken the subway either, to be honest," Lily whispered to Nadia.

"She probably knows what it is, though."

"Well, yeah, she has that advantage over you."

"Is it another train, then?" Nadia continued, and Lily knew how desperate she was for answers.

"Exactly."

"So, why isn't it called a train?"

"Because it goes under the ground."

"Oh...so why not call it a subtrain?"

"You'll have to ask the Ministry of Transportation," Lily replied with a measure of annoyance.

"Hello!" Larisa wrapped her arms around Lily in greeting.

"Larisa, this is Nadia. Nadia, this is Larisa."

"Hello." Nadia beamed. "Lily tells me you're being interviewed as well?"

"Yes, and we should probably be leaving." Larisa glanced at the large clock in the station. "We don't want to set a bad impression by being late."

"I love your thinking," Nadia grew excited, and Lily offered Larisa a knowing look as if to say it was safe to play along with her genuine enthusiasm.

With a bounce in their step, the three women left for the subway, which was every bit as enthralling as Nadia had expected. Lily grinned as she watched her new friend take in the sights like a child first experiencing all the wonders of life.

"Were your parents as enthused about your joining our ranks as mine were?" Larisa asked Nadia with a knowing smirk as they took their seats on the crowded underground train.

"I..." Nadia paused, and it was the first time Lily had witnessed her brightness diminish. "I'm not sure where they are."

"I'm sorry." Larisa glanced down at her hands apologetically.

"The Donetsk region was overrun." Nadia swallowed, and Lily noticed that she was having difficulty discussing this. "I haven't heard from my parents since. I have, however, heard of the stories of what the Germans are doing in those regions."

"It's best not to dwell on such things." Lily placed a gentle hand on Nadia's back.

"The Germans are forcing themselves upon every woman they can find." Nadia clenched her jaw. "I heard that young girls, very young girls, as well as the elderly, aren't spared. The Germans are perverting every good and beautiful thing for their demented pleasures. I've heard of others being sent to camps where the stories there aren't any more favorable."

Neither Lily nor Larisa said a word as they felt a righteous fury burning within their hearts. Lily couldn't imagine what she would do if her mother had been subjected to such horrors, and she couldn't understand why Nadia had such a bright spirit despite the tragedies befallen her family.

"Do you have any other family?" Larisa asked after a moment.

Nadia shook her head before adding, "My brother fell in the first month of fighting. He was engaged, but I've yet to hear from his fiancé. I imagine she's devastated."

"I'm sorry, my friend." Lily inched closer to Nadia.

"That's why I'm joining." Nadia sniffled before her voice grew low and brooding as she continued while nearly shaking with rage, "Not to serve my country, or because of any patriotic fervor, but because I want to kill as many Nazis as I possibly can. I'm of little use with a rifle or a pistol, but give me a plane and I'm a weapon unparalleled. If I discover that my mother endured tortures at their hands, I'll turn all of Germany into ash."

Both Lily and Larisa glanced at each other before Lily spoke softly, "I have goosebumps."

"That's my story." Nadia returned to her chipper disposition as her bright smile resurfaced, and Lily knew better than to mess with this woman's demons.

"This is our...um...this is our stop." Larisa pointed as she watched Nadia with understandable concern.

"I love the subway," Nadia spoke quietly, but still with cheer, as they left the train.

Exiting the subway station, Lily and the two other women with her stopped in their tracks when they noticed that the plaza and the surrounding streets were crowded with hundreds, if not thousands, of people.

As it was now late in the evening, many people were lying down, covering themselves in whatever they could so that they could try to sleep. Others warmed themselves around small fires they were permitted to start while they chatted quietly. A musician played near the fountain with an accordion and a little bell attached to his feet.

Some children wailed while others played happily with new friends, families bickered with each other or with temporary neighbors, and laughter could be heard from some corners. This was Lily's first taste of the war.

This, after all, was war. The battles were fought with bullets and machines, but war, as it was when she was just born, was waged against civilians. The innocent people who cared nothing more than to raise a family and live in peace and quiet were those who suffered the most. Lily's heart ached for them, and she prayed that her mother and brother would be spared this destitution, especially if this were to happen to them during the winter.

"Why are they all here?" Nadia asked with concern as the three women watched the scene with a sense of pity.

"Is there somewhere else we can go?" a voice called from behind them, and Lily turned to see an elderly man smoking a cigarette as he sat on the cold pavement. "I'm asking genuinely. If you know of anywhere else to go, please share."

"Where did you come from?" Nadia asked as she knelt beside him, but Lily glanced at the clock as she feared their time was running short.

"A little town near the front." The old man waved in the direction. "We came here in the hopes that we would find shelter."

"We're pilots," Nadia spoke cheerfully as she pointed to herself and then to Lily and Larisa, who both offered polite but cautious nods of greeting. "We're going to fight for you."

With a slow laugh, the man glanced between them as he judged their sincerity.

"We're going to fight for your home," Nadia added proudly.

"I'm glad you're confident." The man chuckled sarcastically.

"Me too." Nadia nodded eagerly before standing and walking past the other two girls.

"Is she alright?" Larisa asked Lily quietly. "Nothing seems to bother her."

"I'm perfectly fine," Nadia called over her shoulder after overhearing them.

"Do you know where you're going?" Lily asked Nadia as she glanced at Larisa with a slight frown.

"Oh, right." Nadia giggled. "I should be following you."

"As it happens, you were going in the right direction." Lily looked around them. "I think."

"You think?" Larisa asked as she studied her friend.

"It's difficult to determine where we are without any lights. It looks so different than in the day or when it's all lit up."

"Excuse me," Larisa hailed a passing patrol as she raised her gloved hand in a delicate manner. "Would you kindly provide directions to Zhukovsky Academy?"

"Two hundred yards, then take a right," the patrol replied quickly, and Lily sensed that he was exhausted.

"Thank you!" Larisa placed a limp hand on her chest flirtatiously.

"Give it a rest." Lily rolled her eyes.

"Have either of you met the major?" Nadia asked as they walked along the street.

"No. Have you?" Lily asked.

"No." Nadia shook her head. "But I remember when she made her long-distance flight. Six thousand kilometers. I spent every available minute sitting beside the radio, hoping to catch the updates."

"Is that the building?" Lily asked, but all she could see were large shadows.

"I can't tell what anything is!" Larisa grew flustered.

"Maybe he can help?" Nadia pointed at a small orange glow that flickered from near a brick building.

"Where?" Larisa looked in that direction, but the light had already been snuffed out.

"Someone was lighting a cigarette." Lily grabbed Nadia and Larisa's hands. "Let's ask them if we're in the right spot."

"You can't just walk up to a stranger in the dark!" Larisa whispered harshly.

"He's probably a soldier." Lily pressed onwards while dragging along her reluctant friends.

"A little late to be out," a voice came from near the direction Lily had spotted the glow, and the embers of a cigarette burned bright before dimming again, revealing the face of a tired and bored soldier.

"We're expected to report to Major Raskova," Larisa announced boldly, shunning whatever previous trepidation she had been feeling.

"Never heard of him." The man took another puff, and with the slight glow from the cigarette, Lily noticed that he had a large scar on his cheek.

Then, out of the corner of her eye, Lily noticed a shape that caught her attention. Glancing in that direction, Lily noticed that it was an anti-aircraft gun, and its long nozzle was pointing threateningly at the dark sky.

Lily knew that if she was about to embark on this arduous and perilous journey, she would likely encounter such weaponry. It felt cold, looking at the mechanism of violence capable of tearing crude holes in aircraft, flesh, and bone. There was an absence of humanity in it as the enemy became a distant object rather than a person.

"Major Raskova is heading the female aviation regiments," Larisa explained with impatience.

"Oh, right, her." The soldier stamped out his cigarette and seemed embarrassed. "Yes, I know Major Raskova. She's a hero."

"And are we in the right place?" Larisa pressed.

"If you're fliers, you're supposed to be excellent navigators," the soldier snickered. "I'd say the all-female regiments are off to a predictable start."

"It's dark, comrade," Larisa spoke with a clenched jaw. "Neither of us have been to this location before. We simply need to know which direction—"

"It's the building behind me." He pointed with his thumb over his shoulder.

Without a word of thanks, the girls walked into the building that, at least, had a few dim lights glowing from some of the offices and classrooms.

A sign on the wall pointed to the end of the hallway where an office with Major Raskova's name was pasted on the door.

"I feel unprepared." Larisa clicked her teeth as she looked at Lily with wide eyes.

"None of that!" Lily held up a stern finger. "She needs to see that we're every bit of a soldier as the next man that comes through here. We need to be tough and give strong answers. We're fighters, we're fliers. We're here to protect our families, and avenge those who've fallen."

"You're right!" Larisa drew a deep breath and shook her arms to rid herself of any nerves, although Lily was worried that her adherence to fashion may inhibit any illusion of ferocity.

Nadia, Lily noticed, needed no convincing. While she remained cheerful, she also carried a burning passion that was written on her narrowed gaze. Lily feared that even if

Major Raskova did not permit her to proceed, that Nadia would find herself behind the controls of a plane anyway.

Standing tall, the women walked proudly with their suitcases, and Nadia's bag, toward the office.

Stopping in front of the closed door, Lily felt her limbs freeze. There was no returning after passing the threshold. The life she had known, flying planes leisurely, and the simplicity of her family life, would be gone forever. The Lily that went beyond this door would never return.

"Knock already," Larisa whispered.

"What about our bags?" Nadia asked quietly. "We can't go in there looking like drifters."

"Good point." Lily bit her lip as she set her tattered suitcase down beside the door, and Nadia slumped her bag onto the floor.

"Go on." Nadia encouraged Larisa, who remained firmly holding onto her spotless suitcase.

"There are a few keepsakes in here that—"

"Oh, give it." Nadia ripped the suitcase out of Larisa's hands and set it on the floor before ordering Lily, "Knock."

"I like you." Lily grinned at Nadia.

Drawing a deep breath, Lily raised her fist to the door and offered a few polite rattles.

No reply.

"Is she in?" Larisa whispered.

"I doubt she heard you. I could barely hear it, and I'm standing right beside you." Nadia stepped up and offered a full-fisted pound against the door. "We're soldiers, remember. Stop being little girls."

"Enter," came the response, and Nadia turned to Larisa with raised eyebrows as her point had been proven.

Opening the door, the three women entered the office, and Lily's attention was stolen by the major. With her hair pulled back sharply, bright blue eyes, and a smart uniform, Major Raskova was the very essence of who Lily aspired to be.

She was in command, confident, and the head of a regiment. Major Raskova had broken barriers that Lily never dreamed of achieving until she saw this woman sitting behind a large desk, poring over applications and looking every bit as competent as Lily had imagined her.

"Ladies." Major Raskova stood, and Lily noticed the Hero of the Soviet Union award pinned to her chest. "Take a seat."

After a few pitiful and unpracticed salutes, the three women sat in the small chairs in front of Major Raskova's desk, eager to begin the interview.

With a quick glance at Larisa, Lily nodded her encouragement to be strong, confident, and, most importantly, to answer any question with unwavering accuracy.

"These are impressive flight logbooks." Major Raskova tapped the applications as she sat again, but Lily noticed that she took particular interest in Larisa's fur hat and soft blue dress.

"Thank you." Larisa nodded.

"But they mean nothing to me." Major Raskova looked each woman in the eye before continuing. "Do you understand what it is I'm asking of you? This is not the flying club offering a luxurious experience. If you are accepted, you will be shot at by the enemy. Do you understand?"

"Not if we shoot at them first," Larisa replied, and Lily couldn't help a grin from forming at her friend's self-assurance.

"Overconfidence will get you killed," Major Raskova replied without sharing in Lily's amusement. "You will be fighting against men, and to do so, you must yourselves fight like men. You may be burned beyond recognition, you may be killed, you may lose a limb, you may break every bone in your body, and you may even be captured by the Germans, and we all know how they treat beautiful young women."

The air left Lily's lungs as Major Raskova detailed these gruesome scenarios. Yet, still, the confidence of youth dissuaded the notion that such terrible things would ever befall her.

"All these things can happen to our enemy, too," Nadia spoke commandingly. "If that's the case, how soon can you get me into a plane?"

"Training is required first," Major Raskova replied as she interlinked her fingers across her chest, and Lily thought she was made a touch nervous by Nadia's enthusiasm for violence.

"When can we start?" Nadia pressed.

"Why do you want to join?" Major Raskova narrowed her gaze as she studied Nadia in particular.

"I want to do my part for my country." Nadia nodded.

"This is personal for you." Major Raskova looked disappointed as she unveiled Nadia's reason.

Nadia didn't reply as she glanced out the corner of her eye at Lily and Larisa.

"I…" Nadia started, but Lily gathered that she couldn't seem to stress the sentiment she wanted to convey.

"You will be flying in squadrons," Major Raskova continued. "You may be the navigator for the pilot. You may even be the engineer maintaining the planes. No matter what, you are not in the air by yourself. This is not you against the Nazis. This is not you against those who hurt you or your family. Pursuing vengeance may put your wing mates at risk. Do you understand?"

"I do, ma'am."

"I'll keep a close eye on you during training." Major Raskova stood and held her hands firmly behind her back.

"Does this mean I'm accepted?" Nadia asked with wide eyes as she and the other two girls also stood.

"You wouldn't be here otherwise." Major Raskova looked at all three girls closely. "I already accepted you. I merely wanted to meet those who would be under my command. The real test will be if you can pass training."

With, again, painfully unrefined salutes, the girls maintained their composure, but Lily assumed they, like her, were dying to scream with excitement.

"We'll have to practice those salutes." Major Raskova clicked her tongue before gesturing toward the door for them to leave. "Report back here tomorrow morning. You'll be given orders for training then and you can become acquainted with your other flying partners."

Quietly, and with restraint, the three women left the office, grabbed their luggage, and headed toward the exit.

Lily's heart was racing with exhilaration, and she didn't know how much longer she could withhold an outburst. She intentionally refused any eye contact with Larisa, or she would otherwise crumble.

Yet as soon as they were outside the building, and with the door firmly shut behind them, all three girls immediately dropped their luggage and embraced each other as they squealed and laughed in delight.

# Chapter Six
# Engels Wings

*"It is difficulties that show what we are."*

Epictetus

"Is this it?" Larisa asked with an expression that Lily believed would be better left hidden.

Lily, Larisa, Nadia, and nearly one thousand other young women, whom Lily noticed were almost entirely in their late teens or early twenties, were being transported by trucks from Moscow to Engels.

"Were you expecting another flying club?" Nadia asked from the seat in front of them as she watched a few Po-2 planes, the ones Lily was accustomed to, performing military maneuvers above them.

"It's a little rudimentary," Larisa explained quietly to Lily.

"A little?" Lily also spoke quietly. "It's the epitome of depression."

"At least some men will be here." Larisa grinned as she fluttered her eyebrows.

"Is that all you can think about?" Lily rolled her eyes.

"It's all I can think about," Nadia chimed in as she stared at the ceiling of the truck with dreamy eyes. "A tall pilot as a husband. Can you imagine?"

"Everyone is tall compared to you," Larisa snickered.

"They must be at least five foot ten. Six feet is preferable." Nadia nodded confidently.

"Did you pack your measuring tape?" Lily grinned.

"I imagine they're lonely." Nadia grew an inappropriate smile as she stared out the window again. "They've probably been here for months without seeing a proper woman."

"There's nothing proper about you," Larisa muttered under her breath as she offered a smirk to Lily.

Driving quickly up to the main gates of the airfield, and much too quickly over a pothole that the passengers bitterly complained about, that the truck eventually came to a stop near about twenty other trucks that were already parked.

Exiting the vehicle, after grabbing her luggage, Lily had a better opportunity to review her surroundings, and she found the military base to be rather intimidating.

A barbed wire fence stretched around the entire perimeter with guard towers placed strategically throughout, anti-aircraft guns pointed menacingly at the sky, and guards who looked serious yet bored protected the main gates or else patrolled around.

The women chatted lively and excitedly as they pooled outside the trucks they had just exited, but Lily and Larisa remained guarded. Lily assumed that her friend, like her, was feeling nervous about her new surroundings. She had felt confident in her skills, but the austerity of this environment hinted at a harsh evaluation.

"Form a line!" an unkind shout echoed from a tall officer, startling most of the women.

After a quick shock, the women fell in a line for the main entrance while Lily, Larisa, and Nadia joined near the rear.

"Have your papers ready!" the officer shouted again.

Kneeling quickly, Lily unlocked her suitcase and grabbed her passport and official letters from Major Raskova.

"Shit!" Nadia panicked as she rummaged through her bag.

"Please tell me you didn't forget!" Larisa panicked on behalf of her new friend.

"I hope not!" Nadia offered a worried look.

"Have your papers ready!" the officer shouted again as he paced down the line that was moving steadily toward the main entrance.

"Shit! Shit! Shit!" Nadia continued to search frantically through her bag.

Lily offered Larisa a quick shake of the head for their friend's antics when she noticed a woman, a few spots ahead of them, holding a photograph of a small girl, about the age of two.

The woman held a serious expression as she studied the photo and seemed to be more concerned with the child than retrieving her papers.

Lily's heart went out to her, and she understood that she had likely sacrificed a great deal to play a part in the salvation of her nation.

"Found it!" Nadia breathed a heavy sigh of relief as she pulled out a crumpled paper that had a stain from some old food in the bottom right-hand corner.

"Papers?" a guard at the main gates asked apathetically, and Lily handed hers to him as he scanned it quickly before nodding for her to proceed.

"I could've handed him a menu and he still would've let me in," Larisa grumbled as she caught up to Lily. "He barely looked at it, or me."

"I hope that gets addressed soon." Lily glanced over her shoulder at the main gate as the last few women came through.

"Keep going!" another officer shouted as he waved them along toward an old school near the hangar.

"Where are the barracks?" Nadia asked as she looked around the airfield.

"Good point." Lily also looked around in confusion.

"Move!" another shout came, and the women hurried along, keeping as close to a line as they could until they came to the school where a lieutenant, along with Major Raskova, were waiting with hands held firmly behind their backs.

"Form five columns of two hundred women!" an officer shouted, and the women quickly, and what Lily perceived as efficiently, organized themselves accordingly.

"Keep silent!" the lieutenant near Major Raskova shouted as he blew a whistle, and, at once, the airfield, apart from the puttering of the planes circling above them, drew deathly silent.

Lily sensed that the other women, like herself, were aware of the gravity and seriousness of the charge they were about to undertake. Glancing again at the woman who had been studying the photograph of the young child, Lily was reminded of her brother and mother. She wondered how they were doing and knew they would be eagerly awaiting a letter from her.

"You are not at your flying clubs!" Major Raskova began with a commanding, strong voice, and a terrible fear was instilled in Lily as she listened to this woman she had sat across from in her office mere days ago. Major Raskova had seemed endearing, almost motherly, when she had met with them, but now Lily saw only the officer who wouldn't tolerate any deviation or defiance.

"Whatever flying experience you thought was relevant, forget it. This is war. You do not know more than your instructors, despite whatever level of proficiency you may have. If you believe you know better, you will either die or kill your wing mates. Is that understood?"

"Yes, ma'am!" the women shouted in a somewhat pathetic attempt at unison, to which the lieutenant smirked arrogantly.

Lily already hated him. Everything about his manner and behavior indicated he didn't, for a second, believe that any of these women were either capable or could certainly best him. She couldn't wait to rise to the challenge and put him in his place.

"Your time as instructors or as patrons of your flying clubs are over. You will learn how to shoot the guns on your plane. You will learn how to drop bombs accurately at targets. You will learn how to kill. You will learn what to do if you are captured. You will learn how to take your own life to prevent capture. You will learn how to fight as men."

Lily felt a tightening in her shoulders as she listened to Major Raskova addressing them, especially with respect to taking their own lives. A detail she considered best left out of any letters she sent back to her mother.

"You will be forced to learn two years' worth of training in six months' time," the major continued. "The preparation will be grueling. You will spend fourteen hours a day flying or being instructed on theory."

"Fourteen hours?" Larisa muttered behind Lily, who shook her head in agreement at the shocking tally.

"At the end of the six months, we will assess who will be assigned to what regiment. The 586th Women's Fighter Regiment, the 587th Women's Bomber Regiment, or the 588th Women's Night Bomber Regiment will be filled according to your capacities. Best of luck." Major Raskova saluted before she promptly turned and headed toward a small office near the school.

"On me!" the lieutenant shouted as he pointed to the line at the end, who were then guided into the school by other soldiers.

"We should try for the fighter regiment," a girl in the line next to Lily whispered to the girl in front of her.

"I'm a skilled pilot, I should be in a fighter plane, not some clunky bomber," the girl concurred.

"Something tells me I'll be one of the bombers," Nadia whispered over her shoulder to Lily. "Somehow that seems suitable."

"As long as I'm not an engineer and stuck on the ground, I'm happy." Larisa nodded.

"I'm surprised there were this many women fliers!" Nadia looked around.

"There are over one hundred and fifty flying clubs in the Soviet Union, and nearly a quarter of the instructors are female," Larisa explained.

*I need to be a fighter,* Lily thought to herself. *I'm the best pilot here. Sounds arrogant, but it's the truth.*

"Move out!" a soldier demanded as he came to their line, and Lily grabbed the suitcase that was resting against her leg as they marched into the school.

Peeking into the different classrooms as they walked along the hallway, Lily noticed that the school had been repurposed as barracks. Rickety bunkbeds had replaced the desks and chairs, but it was evident to Lily that this had been done in quite a haste as some of the old schoolwork had been left up. Even the chalkboard in some of the classrooms still had math equations left unsolved.

The rooms that had been already assigned were filled with lively chatter as the women became acquainted or old friendships were reignited. While the sound of giggling was appreciated, Lily was eager to start the training.

"These are your quarters." The soldier who was guiding them stopped quickly as he pointed to a classroom. "You will find your uniforms laid on the bed. You are not permitted to switch rooms, nor are you permitted to fraternize with any of your male comrades. Training starts at zero six hundred. You're welcome to familiarize yourself with the airbase. Food will be provided in the officer's mess hall."

Entering the room, Lily inhaled a strong scent of mold and musk. This room, clearly, had not been properly cleaned in quite some time. There was also only a small amount of light allowed into the room by the narrow windows, and after Nadia tried the light switch that proved ineffectual, Lily and the others tried to acclimate in the dim light.

"I guess I'll take this bunk." Larisa placed her suitcase on the top bunk.

"Why do you get the top?" Lily asked grumpily.

"There are plenty of top bunks available." Larisa gestured to the room. "We don't have to share."

"Like hell you'd be rid of me that easy." Lily threw her suitcase onto the bottom bunk as Larisa smiled.

"I'm Nadia." Nadia held her hand in greeting to another woman who didn't return the gesture but instead threw her luggage beside the bunk.

"Marina," the woman replied as she retrieved a cigarette and immediately lit it as if a second longer and she would have expired.

"I don't suppose smoking in here is necessary, is it?" Another woman asked nervously.

"Believe me," Marina pointed at her as she kept her gaze low. "You'll be begging me for one soon."

"I'll take one." Nadia shrugged.

"Yeah?" Marina asked hesitantly.

"Why not?" Nadia held out her hand.

"There's no going back." Marina offered a cigarette to Nadia.

"Ever forward." Nadia smiled brightly, and Marina chuckled.

"These are our uniforms?" Larisa scoffed as she held up a large dark green shirt and matching trousers.

"You could fit two of me in there." Lily chuckled. "You're going to look so silly. I'm sure they'll fix their mistake shortly."

"I'm going to look silly?" Larisa narrowed her gaze. "You have the same uniform, love."

"What?!" Lily panicked as she also held up an oversized uniform before noticing a gigantic pair of black boots beside the bunk. "And these are the boots?"

"Something tells me this wasn't a mistake." Nadia inspected her uniform as well.

"They have no faith in us." Marina shook her head as she took a puff. "They expect us to fail."

"I'm sorry, but you have to try it on." Larisa bit her lip as she tried to restrain her smile at Lily.

"I'm not trying it on." Lily threw the uniform onto her bunk.

"You don't have a choice." Marina scoffed. "They're not bringing you another set just so you can look pretty while you're fighting."

"Well, if there's no choice." Larisa grinned as she slipped out of her dress before becoming engulfed in what looked more like a blanket than a uniform.

"Oh my goodness." Lily held her hand over her mouth at the sight of her friend.

"Put the boots on!" Nadia urged, and by now, the whole room was surrounding Larisa and giggling at the spectacle.

"What do you think?" Larisa tried to walk, but the boots were so large and clunky she reminded Lily of when Yuri would put on their father's boots and walk around the apartment.

"I have to try this!" another woman ran to her bunk, and soon the whole room was giggling and laughing at their extraordinarily ridiculous outfits.

"Might as well indulge," Lily muttered as she let the uniform envelope her.

"How are we supposed to fly in these?" Nadia looked down at herself as she laughed liberally.

"Are you sure these aren't parachutes?" Lily asked as she pulled at the sides of her uniform and held them outwards. "I swear they deliberately gave us the largest uniforms they could find."

"This simply won't do." Nadia took a puff of her smoke but coughed loudly, and the whole bunk laughed at her.

"You look like a child with a cigarette in that big uniform," Larisa chuckled.

"Have you seen yourself?" Nadia threw her hands onto her hips as she grew annoyed, but the whole bunk only laughed harder.

Nothing serious could be achieved while one looked like they belonged in the Moscow circus, and while it was humorous, Lily couldn't help but decipher the hidden intent of their superiors' apparent wish for failure.

"I bet this is all that lieutenant's doing," Lily whispered to Larisa. "He seemed rather cruel."

"I wouldn't be surprised." Larisa still played with her uniform as she shook her head in wonder.

"I have some thread and needle." Nadia held up her finger as she returned to her bag.

"Why? We're already in stitches!" Marina interjected dryly, and the room roared with laughter.

"She's right," Lily spoke loudly, using her instructor voice, and the bunk quieted a measure as they listened to her, although a few giggles still escaped here and there. "They want us to fail. Let's prove them wrong. We are soldiers, but we also happen to be women. We don't need to sacrifice our femininity in order to kill the Germans. Besides, what would the Nazis think if they saw us like this?"

"What do you suggest?" Larisa asked.

"We have the day." Lily shrugged. "Let's get to work."

# Chapter Seven
# Fight Like Men

*"Women should do for themselves what men have already done – occasionally what men have not done – thereby establishing themselves as persons, and perhaps encouraging other women toward greater independence of thought and action."*

Amelia Earhart

Loud banging came against the other side of the wall early the next morning.

"Wake up!" a shout came from the hallway, and an officer burst into the room with a baton at the ready. "You've slept long eno—"

The officer stopped himself short when he discovered that the women, every last one, were already dressed in their uniforms and prepared for the day.

The officer's surprise at their readiness made Lily immensely proud of both herself and the group. Heaping satisfaction to her grin was the additional stunned look from the officer as he quickly inspected their uniforms.

Lily assumed that he had expected to find them in the silly state that they had all been yesterday, but after staying up all night sewing and mending, the women stood before him in the best possible outfits they could hem. It was far from perfect, but Lily was proud, at least, that she could provide some figure to her uniform. She had even stuffed her boots with extra bits of cloth or a shirt so that she didn't shuffle awkwardly.

While the women looked as stunning as was permitted them, Lily had added a few extra personal details to her uniform. With a small belt pulled tight around her slender waist and a white lily sown into her cap, she was convinced that she stood out as the brightest among them.

"You're all ready?" The officer played nervously with the baton in his hand.

"I think you'll find, sir," Marina began, "that a group of highly focused women don't require the sort of discipline that men do."

"Enough!" The officer shouted as he tried to reclaim whatever authority he had lost. "Roll out!"

"Rather bold," Nadia whispered to Marina as they marched past the officer and toward the courtyard. "I think he fancies you."

Grinning at Larisa for Nadia's remark, Lily marched with the group into the courtyard where the officer organized them into a square formation while making sure that they had enough room in front of and behind each individual woman for exercises.

"Roll call!" the officer shouted, and Lily noticed that Major Raskova was approaching them from the small office attached to the school.

With a glance of anticipation to Larisa, Lily could hardly wait to hear what the major had to say. Lily was eager to learn all she could from this extraordinary woman.

Without the slightest touch of familiarity or affection, Major Raskova read off the names from a clipboard as each woman responded in kind to confirm they were present.

"Soviet forces have withdrawn from Odessa," Major Raskova began reading from another clipboard after roll call. "The Germans have reached Mozhaysk, which many of you will know is close to Moscow. Most of our Soviet government has evacuated Moscow, although Stalin has elected to remain to provide a degree of calm to the panic."

Lily's heart sank into her stomach as she thought of her mother and brother. They were on the dangerous side of Moscow, and she prayed that they were safe.

A woman in front of Lily shuddered, and Lily noticed that she was straining to withhold the tears. It was the same woman on the truck who had been staring at the picture of the little girl, and Lily's heart broke for her.

"Quiet!" one of the officers barked at the woman, who was now sniffling.

Capturing Major Raskova's attention, she handed the clipboard to the officer before she walked into the midst of the women.

"What's your name?" she asked tenderly, and Lily appreciated her tact.

"Katerina." The woman cleared her throat and stood tall and proud.

"Katerina." Major Raskova nodded. "You have family, I'm guessing?"

Katerina nodded before adding, "My husband was killed in the first month of fighting. My daughter, Margarita, is with her grandparents. They're in the very region you just named."

"How old?" Major Raskova asked gently.

"Two years."

"That must be difficult for you." Major Raskova looked sympathetically at Katerina.

"Forgive my outburst, it won't happen again." Katerina clenched her jaw as she stared straight ahead and resolutely.

"I know." Major Raskova nodded. "Because if it does, you will be sent home."

"Understood," Katerina replied firmly.

"That goes for everyone," Major Raskova began loudly as she returned to the front of the column. "My door will always be open to you. If you need to discuss personal matters, you may see me. If you display a wanton lack of emotional control publicly before your peers or superiors, you will be dismissed. I promise you that nothing you have experienced so far will be able to prepare you for combat. If you can't contain your emotions here, you won't be able to in the sky, either. No man is shown a morsel of sympathy for emotional outbursts, and the same will be applied to you. You will be fighting men, and you must fight like men. This is your first and final warning. Is that understood?"

"Yes, ma'am!" the women replied in unison.

"Good." Major Raskova grabbed the clipboard before continuing, "Remember who we are fighting against. It was just announced this morning, publicly, by the German authorities, that any Jew found outside the ghetto in Poland will be executed. This, ladies, is the barbaric enemy we are fighting against. To victory!"

"To victory!" the women resounded, yet the words stuck in Lily's throat.

Being of Jewish descent herself, Lily found the announcement particularly jarring, if not harrowing.

"As you were." Major Raskova nodded to the officer before she returned in the direction of her office, and Lily didn't believe she could respect another person greater than she respected the major.

Then, while again annoyed at how easily the women fell into line and did as commanded, the officer began ordering exercises as he paced up and down to ensure they were doing them properly and with appropriate enthusiasm.

"I'm not sure I see how this benefits our flying," Larisa muttered to Lily during crunches.

"I'm sure it will help keep us fit in case our plane crashes or something." Lily grunted.

"If my plane crashes —" Larisa wiped the sweat from her forehead — "and I'm in enemy territory, I'm using the gun on myself."

"You can be a touch dark sometimes, you know." Lily frowned at her friend.

"I prefer the term 'realistic'," Larisa replied curtly.

After the exercises, and still unpleased that he was absent of an excuse to berate the women, the officer ordered a march around the perimeter.

Again, Lily found the atmosphere to be rather bleak and hostile. The large anti-aircraft guns were pointed at heaven while the men beside them continually scanned the sky for any sign of enemy aircraft. It reminded Lily that, while they were mostly safe, the enemy could be upon them at any time.

"Is she crying?" Larisa asked as she glanced over her shoulder, and Lily also looked to find that Katerina was trying to stifle her tears.

"Hey," Lily whispered to Katerina as she kept an eye on the officer. "Stay close behind me."

"Thank you," Katerina whimpered as she pressed right against Lily to shield her from the officer.

"Don't let him see you," Larisa also whispered as she tightened the gap.

"I owe you both."

"You don't owe us anything." Lily shook her head. "This is what separates us from the men. They're stronger apart. We're stronger together."

The familiar puttering of planes caught Lily's attention, and she glanced at the sky to find a couple of planes who were in a simulated dogfight. These were not the ordinary Po-2 planes that Lily and the others had been accustomed to, but rather, the sort in her textbooks that she dreamed of commanding. They were fast, sleek, and designed with the latest technology and understanding of aerodynamics.

Months had transpired since Lily had the pleasure of operating an aircraft, and she couldn't wait for the moment when she was back in the air. These drills and regiments were tiresome on their own merit, but to have the carrot of flight dangling in front of Lily made them all the more tedious. To be so close to what she wanted and yet so far drove Lily to near insanity. Besides, the maneuvers they were performing were amateurish, and Lily craved the moment she could display her skill.

Eventually, the march came to a halt at the hangar where the two planes that had been dogfighting were now landing.

With the planes coming to a firm stop about twenty yards away from them, the lieutenant from the previous day exited the cockpit and began walking toward the women.

Some male pilots who were inspecting their aircraft inside the hangar left their duties to stand near the women, and Lily expected a debrief from the lieutenant.

Larisa, however, had difficulty prying her gaze away from the male pilots, and Lily didn't blame her. They were rather dashing in their smart uniforms with brown leather jackets, silk scarves around their necks, goggles on their heads, and their woolen-insulated leather flying caps.

Nudging Larisa with her elbow, Lily nodded for her to pay attention as the lieutenant came to a halt in front of them.

"Mr. Morozov is staring at you," Larisa whispered.

Glancing out her peripheral, Lily didn't dare look in the direction of Mr. Morozov, and was surprised that he was even at this airfield. She despised how hard she had to work to even be considered for a position like this, while he had spent a panicked moment with her in a plane and was promptly selected.

"I'm Lieutenant Dobkin. Are any of you familiar with the plane behind me?" the lieutenant asked condescendingly as he removed his gloves.

He was a taller man with striking blue eyes under thick, black eyebrows. Although Lily assumed that he was likely twice her age, his hair still clung to youth and didn't lose any of its shading or veracity. It was still a thick, dark black that reminded Lily of Yuri.

Still, Lieutenant Dobkin's unmistakable prejudice turned everything that was attractive about him sour. Lily perceived that he loathed his charge and thought it beneath him to instruct women.

Not waiting for anyone else to answer, Lily shot her hand up.

"Go on." The lieutenant rolled his hand impatiently.

"That is the Yak-1," Lily replied proudly. "Capable of reaching a max speed of five hundred and ninety kilometers an hour. Its maneuverability will give the German Messerschmitt a hell of a fight."

"Interesting." Lieutenant Dobkin threw his hands behind his back as he strolled closer to Lily. "Miss?"

"Litvyak," Lily replied strongly, which drew some chuckling from the male pilots.

"She's adorable." One of the men mentioned which drew further laughter, and even Lieutenant Dobkin offered a slight grin.

"You're correct, but all of that counts for nothing unless it is piloted skillfully." The lieutenant raised his chin as he looked down his nose at Lily.

"Permit me in the cockpit, and I'll show you skill."

"Wow!" another man spoke patronizingly, and it took Lily everything within her to restrain herself from walking over to him and offering a large slap across his face. Still, Lily knew the real test would be in the air, and she would outshine all of them. She had to. For her mother, for her brother, Lily knew she had to be the best.

"I appreciate your confidence, even if it is misplaced." Lieutenant Dobkin did not join in the men's enjoyment of Lily's determination as he remained glaring at her. "But until you can prove your worth in the Po-2, you won't be touching the Yak-1."

"I'll prove my worth right now." Lily nodded toward a pair of Po-2's and a collective gasp came from the women as the men ceased their merriment.

"Miss Litvyak," Lieutenant Dobkin began slowly with a large scowl. "I very much doubt you will impress me in any regard. Even the very idea of you women fighting alongside us men has given the Germans great cause for mockery. When a pilot is in the air, he is not flying solo. He has wing mates that he must trust with his very life. I know how a man operates. I know how he thinks. It's instinctive, innate. But you, I have no idea what you're thinking, nor has any man been able to summarize a woman adequately. Don't get me wrong, young lady, I have nothing against your sex as a whole, but we each have our place in society, and certainly in war. The gifts of nature bestowed upon you in beauty and mystery are such that a man like me could never possess, and it wretches at my heart to see you throw it away needlessly, recklessly."

"Wouldn't you agree that my unpredictability, as a woman, would prove an advantage against the enemy?" Lily tested, but she instantly regretted it for the look he returned her.

At once, Lieutenant Dobkin rushed toward her and came within inches of her face as he screamed, "You mistake me for someone who cares about your opinion! We are not here to have a conversation. I give orders, you follow. That's it! Do you understand?!"

Standing her ground, Lily nodded as she swallowed in fear with the stench of his breath lingering in her nostrils. Without flinching or wavering, she stared straight ahead like a good soldier.

"That goes for everyone!" Lieutenant Dobkin retrieved the baton by his side and gripped it tightly. Lily glanced down at it quickly as her heart raced, fearing he would use it against her. "Step out of line, and I won't hesitate to put you back in your place. Because if you can't follow my orders here, when, and if, you make it to the front, you won't survive a day. Is that understood?"

"Yes, sir!" the women responded in unison.

"Little bitch thinks she can talk back to me!" Lieutenant Dobkin shouted as he stormed away, and Lily noticed the stolen glances in her direction from both her female and male comrades.

*I'll make him see my worth.* Lily clenched her jaw.

"Take breakfast in the officer's mess." The officer who had been guiding them instructed, and the group, including the men, quietly and orderly walked back into the school.

Grabbing a tray of food from the officer's mess, which was a bland serving of black bread and some sort of cereal that had lost its structural integrity, devolving into mere mush, Lily sat beside Larisa and Nadia at a table.

The atmosphere was tense, and Lily struggled to hide the burning in her cheeks from her goading such a severe reaction out of Lieutenant Dobkin.

"May I join?" Marina asked rhetorically as she sat beside Nadia before retrieving a cigarette.

"I'll take another, please." Nadia smiled brightly as she held her hand out to Marina, and Lily noticed that she was holding a broach in the shape of a beetle.

"What's that?" Larisa asked, also taking notice.

"A broach from my parents," Nadia replied as she lit her cigarette. "It's my lucky charm. Do you have one?"

"She's my lucky charm." Larisa nodded to Lily.

"You should probably rethink that," Marina muttered as she looked around the room.

"And what's your lucky charm?" Nadia asked Lily with a bright smile, but even she, Lily gathered, was trying to forget the previous interaction with the lieutenant.

"Skill, determination, perseverance," Lily replied quickly.

Marina scoffed as she continued to eat.

"My brother is convinced that luck seems to follow me," Lily continued as she stared at the table.

"He should've been here today." Marina grinned at her own quip.

"Providence plays the long game. She'll outshine us all." Larisa defended her friend.

"We'll see." Marina ran her tongue along her teeth.

"What's your story then, Marina?" Nadia asked enthusiastically.

"Please be careful," Larisa whispered to Lily as she leaned over her plate while Marina avoided Nadia's question.

"The lieutenant is wrong about us," Lily whispered back.

"Don't worry about his opinion." Larisa looked at her friend sympathetically. "Show him how well you can fly. After that, when we're on the front, it's the opinion of the Germans we'll need to worry about. The lieutenant will have become a small fly by then in terms of severity. I know how you try to prove yourself to other men, but maybe let this one slide. I don't know if I could stomach being without you."

"You're a good friend." Lily squeezed Larisa's hand.

"A good friend would find you something better to eat than this." Larisa lifted her spoon out of the bowl as the mushy cereal slopped back in with a splatter.

"Don't complain," Marina spoke with a mouthful as she shoveled the food while holding a cigarette in the other hand. "It's in poor taste."

"There's a joke about taste in there somewhere." Nadia narrowed her gaze as she tried to think of something clever.

"Yes…it's the food," Larisa grumbled.

Lily chuckled slightly, enjoying a measure of levity from her friends when she noticed Katerina was sitting by herself at a table. Lily imagined she was worried sick about her daughter.

"Katerina!" Lily called out to her, but she didn't respond. "Come sit with us."

Still, no response.

"Alright, I'll come sit with you." Lily grabbed her tray and stood.

"Stay where you are!" Katerina barked. "I have enough trouble of my own. I don't need to be associated with you."

The mess drew silent as everyone stared in Lily's direction, and her cheeks again burned crimson as she had inadvertently created another uncomfortable interaction.

"Fair enough," Lily spoke quietly as she sat back at her table.

"Don't let her get to you, sweetheart," a man's voice spoke from behind Lily, and she turned to see Mr. Morozov approaching them.

"How can this day get any worse?" Lily squeezed her eyes shut.

"May I sit?" Mr. Morozov asked.

"No!" Marina barked, and Lily offered a nod of gratitude.

"She trained me, you know." Mr. Morozov pointed at Lily.

"I took you on one test flight where you nearly soiled yourself in terror," Lily began shoveling the slop into her mouth in anger as a couple chuckles escaped from Mr. Morozov's comrades.

"I wouldn't say ter—"

"You kissed the ground when we landed," Lily continued, and the mess laughed at Mr. Morozov's expense.

"I don't understand why you're so hostile toward me?" Mr. Morozov looked offended. "I'm a nice guy. I just want to talk to you."

"No man is interested in talking!" Lily stood as she came face to face with Mr. Morozov, unleashing the pent-up rage from her morning experiences. "You want to know why I'm so hostile toward you? Do you? It's because men like you can coast through life while women like me, like us, need to work twice, three times as hard just to earn a morsel of what is given to you hand over fist. You took one pathetic flight with me and you're immediately granted entry. While I, an experienced instructor, was rejected time and again due to my sex."

"I, um..." Mr. Morozov was at a loss for words, and Lily relished in his stupid appearance.

"I'd like to finish my meal." Lily returned to the table, and Mr. Morozov walked gingerly away.

Suddenly, a woman from another table picked up her tray and sat across from Lily. With a slight smile, the woman leaned forward on her elbows and stared at her.

She had rather refined features with a seemingly permanent inquisitive glare where the right eyebrow was thinner in the corner, making it appear like it was raised. Her jaw was thick yet still feminine, and her shoulders were broad, although she carried herself with grace. Unlike the other women, she didn't seem to need as much hemming with her uniform, yet somehow, this made Lily jealous.

"Hello?" Lily asked warily as the woman continued to stare at her.

"I'm Katya Budanova." She extended her hand, and Lily accepted the gesture. "I like that you speak your mind."

"You do?" Lily tilted her head, not sure if she should be cordial or concerned.

"It's refreshing." Katya grinned.

"I'm glad someone thinks so." Lily raised her eyebrows.

"Listen," Katya paused as she stared at the table. "Like you, and I'm sure every other woman in this room, I've faced men like Lieutenant Dobkin. The only way to humble him is to beat him at his own game."

"And how do you suggest I do that?"

"They'll be taking us up in simulated dogfights soon." Katya grinned. "I'll help you prepare so that you can defeat him."

"Why would you help me?" Lily remained cautious.

"I hate him." Katya shrugged.

"Bit harsh." Nadia's countenance grew sour, and Lily sensed she was worried about where this was heading.

"Are you as good as you say you are?" Katya pressed.

"Better," Larisa interjected.

"Then you're our best hope." Katya nodded eagerly. "The lieutenant needs to see that we're capable. If we can beat him, maybe then he'll respect us."

"Maybe," Lily replied unconvincingly as she stared at the remaining slop in her bowl.

# Chapter Eight
# Dogfight

*"Sometimes from her eyes I did receive fair speechless messages."*

William Shakespeare

<u>February 2, 1942, Engels.</u>

*You may just be right about my luck after all,* Lily wrote in a letter to Yuri. *Today, after three months of training, we're having our first official inspection. To our horror, the order was given that we were to cut our hair. Our gender does not exclude us from military standards, and we must look ready for service during our inspection.*

*As fortune would have it, my hair is short enough as it is. My friends, Nadia, Marina, Katya, and Katerina, all of whom you should meet, were adamant that my curls were too precious to cut. Thankfully, I can disguise it rather well by pulling my hair under my hat. Poor Larisa is still in tears and holding her locks in her hand as if they were family members. Don't worry, she's just as gorgeous as ever, but still not interested in you.*

*The training has been rather intense, and that's putting it lightly. Flying for fourteen hours a day would be a pleasure, but often, that's not the case. They instruct us in classrooms with theory on how to outmaneuver our opponent, or tactics for defense, or how to fire the weapons properly.*

*Mercifully, today we are putting these theories to the test. I'm going to be in a simulated dogfight with my lieutenant. He's a nasty man. You'd appreciate him, I'm sure.*

*Also, do you remember Mr. Morozov? I took him up on a flight when you came with me to the flying club. Anyway, my shunning of him both at the club and here, have proven inopportune. He's my flying instructor, you see, and to say that things have been awkward would be an understatement. Still, it boils my blood that he, of all men, would be instructing me. And, as much as it pains me to write this, he actually knows the new aircraft rather well. I don't imagine admitting this to him would be suitable. He'd take it as an opening to try and flirt. On the other hand, I am thankful that the Yak-1 only has one seat, so he's unable to be with me in the plane.*

*My goodness, Yuri, is there ever a lot of power behind that machine. We practiced for a good while in getting used to the* controls and how fast it can go without taking off. My face is still at the beginning of the runway by the time I reach the end.

Speaking of power, you should see the guns they have on these planes. The trigger is on the control stick, there's a safety switch, don't worry, and it fires all three weapons on the plane at once. The power is unparalleled in anything I've experienced before. We've practiced shooting at targets dragged behind other planes, and it's much more difficult than you'd imagine.

Speaking of which, any misses or mistakes are chastised mercilessly. The officers, and that nasty lieutenant, scream at us until they lose their voices. Even slight mistakes are shown little clemency. Which, to be fair, I understand. In war, mistakes could cost your life, or the life of your wing mate, or even turn the tide of the battle.

One thing I didn't anticipate was how sore my neck would be. In the cockpit, I'm constantly looking around for the other aircraft, or navigation points on the ground. We've been taught how to find our way at night using our instruments and landmarks. Even if there's no moon, or it's overcast, we use a map, a stopwatch, and our instruments. It's easy to get lost or to lose altitude without even realizing it. The little light on the instrument panel leaves much to be desired, but it provides enough illumination to study the maps we keep on our laps.

We'll be organized shortly into our different regiments, and I hope that I'm assigned to the fighter regiment. Being in the bomber or night bomber regiments, I feel, would be a squandering of my talents.

All my love,

Lily

"Lily, let's go!" Larisa rattled her fist against her bunk. "We can't be late for inspection."

"What time is it?" Lily glanced at the clock, worried she had let the moment slip away from her.

"Almost noon. Come! Quickly!" Larisa waved.

"I need help with my hat!" Lily panicked. "You need to make sure my hair is tucked in properly."

"Here!" Larisa grew flustered as Lily secured her hat.

"Can you tell?" Lily asked as Larisa inspected her closely and tucked any flyways or strands under the cap.

"Not in the slightest." Larisa smiled brightly, but Lily thought her friend resembled a little boy with her hair cut so short. "Though I am rife with jealousy."

"You can't even tell you cut anything off," Lily lied.

"The major is able to keep her hair." Larisa twisted her face in annoyance. "I don't see why we couldn't have kept ours."

"She's a major. That station permits some privileges."

"Incentive to seek a promotion, then." Larisa glanced again at the clock.

"Alright, let's go." Lily nodded, and the two girls rushed out of the school quickly to find that the rest of the women, and even the men, were already in their assigned positions.

"Where were you?" Nadia asked quietly from behind Lily as she took her spot.

"Writing a letter," Lily answered quietly as she waited.

"Silence!" Major Raskova shouted from the front of the column.

Standing still, Lily glanced out her peripherals to see if she could spot the general's aircraft. It was quiet at the airfield, and Lily thought this was, by chance, the only time she had not heard the sound of the Po-2s or Yak-1s roaring above their heads.

The bright sun shone down on them on the cold, clear day, and Lily felt her fingers turning numb and wished she had brought her gloves. She prayed that the inspection would happen soon, and she wasn't certain why they were required to keep silent when the general hadn't even arrived.

Then, eventually, the distant roar of an engine could be heard, and everyone's attention was fixed on a military truck rushing into the airfield from the main gates. It was almost ridiculous how fast the truck was driving, and Lily wondered as to the hurry. For some reason, she assumed that the general would be arriving by plane.

Finally, the truck came to a halt near the columns of men and women as a short, pudgy, red-faced man stepped out of the passenger side. Fastening his hat to his head, the general, who looked less than enthused, marched toward the men with a retinue of three soldiers trailing him.

Inspecting each man diligently, and without a word, the general looked more and more indifferent and even displeased. Lily wasn't certain if this was a tactic or if he was genuinely upset with his findings. Whatever the case, Lily tried to contain her grin when the general ripped Mr. Morozov's scarf off his neck before examining it quickly and then throwing it back in the pilot's face.

Her amusement quickly diminished when the general began walking toward them, and she prayed that he wouldn't notice her hair.

Stopping at the end of the column, near Marina, the general drew a deep breath as he surveyed the group with much less attention than he had paid to the men. While Lily was thankful that he wasn't actively seeking any flaw he could use to delegitimize them, she wished that he would take greater scrutiny. She felt that the group looked rather sharp and would pass even the most intense inspection.

Walking down the line, the general offered a brief glance at each woman until, that is, he came to Larisa. Stopping in his tracks, the general threw his hands behind his back as he looked her up and down.

"I know you." He squinted.

"Sir?" Larisa asked loudly as she stared straight ahead.

"You instructed my son at that little flying club just outside of Moscow." He wagged his finger at her as he recalled. "How does this airfield compare? Are the instructors adequate?"

"I'm privileged to learn from the best, sir." Larisa nodded.

"You have a fine crop here, Major," he spoke quickly to Major Raskova.

"Thank you, sir," Major Raskova replied swiftly, but Lily caught the tone of pride in her voice, which made her happy indeed.

"If you ever happen to—" the general stopped, and Lily's heart dove into her stomach. He was staring directly at her.

"You!" He pointed his large finger at her. "Come here."

"Sir?" Lily swallowed as she marched to the head of the column and stared straight ahead.

Then, and before Lily even had a chance to react, he swung his hand at her hat, knocking it onto the ground as her short hair fell to just above her ears.

"What is the meaning of this?!" the general asked angrily as he turned to Major Raskova.

Major Raskova didn't reply as she stared back at the general before glancing at Lily, whose heart was shattering with the thought that she had let down her hero.

*Why the hell did I let them talk me into not cutting it?!* Lily wondering. *So stupid! They're going to send me back home now! All because of my damned vanity!*

"Why don't they all look like her?" the general continued angrily.

"Sir?" Major Raskova asked with confusion.

"They all look like little boys!" The general pointed to the other women. "The Fascist snakes will think we're pitting them against juveniles! They'll be convinced we've run out of men to fight. Let them grow their hair out."

"Yes, sir." Major Raskova nodded as she drew a hidden smile.

"Pick up your hat," the general demanded, and Lily obeyed immediately.

"Fall back in line," he ordered, and she did so with enthusiasm.

"I'm told that there is going to be some simulated combat maneuvers?" the general asked impatiently.

"We can commence now, general, if you believe that is suitable?" Major Raskova waved for Lieutenant Dobkin to join them.

"I wouldn't have asked if I didn't think it was suitable." The general huffed, and Lily understood there was little that pleased him.

"Sir?" Lieutenant Dobkin arrived with a prompt salute.

"We may begin." Major Raskova gestured to his plane.

"Excellent." Lieutenant Dobkin threw his hands behind his back. "With your permission, General?"

"Get on with it!" the general barked.

"Ladies." Lieutenant Dobkin stood tall and commanding. "Today, we put your training and theory to the test. We will be taking to the sky in the Po-2s for some one-on-one combat training. I will take off. When the flair is launched, one of you will join me in the air at four thousand feet. Don't worry, I will find you. Your objective is to best me, but I doubt any of you will."

*This is it.* Lily drew a deep breath. *This is where I prove my worth.*

"At ease," the general announced, and the women relaxed as they all walked briskly and excitedly toward the hangar.

"Best of luck," Lieutenant Dobkin spoke condescendingly as he climbed into his plane and was shortly in the air.

"Larisa." Major Raskova waved for her to enter a plane. "Humble him a little for me, will you?"

"Yes, ma'am." Larisa nodded, but Lily noticed that her hands were shaking a touch.

*You've got this,* Lily wished to tell her friend. She wanted to best the lieutenant herself, but Lily would be just as happy if any woman reduced his pride.

"They're making wagers." Nadia poked Lily's side as she pointed at the general who was now visiting with the men.

"Good." Lily grew an arrogant grin. "Make note of the man who makes a wager on me."

"Keep a keen eye on the lieutenant," Katya spoke from behind Lily as the women were now huddling together.

"Where is he?" Marina asked before muttering, "I need a smoke. My nerves are shot."

"I can't see him." Nadia scanned the sky.

The green flair fired, and Larisa began her approach. Lily felt as if time had slowed down as she watched Larisa's plane crawling to the edge of the runway before eventually becoming airborne.

"He's likely taking cover in the clouds." Lily pointed to some large white clouds.

"Smart." Nadia nodded.

"Then how would he see us approaching?" Marina asked grumpily.

"Maybe he can see the flare?" Katya shrugged.

"She must be at four thousand feet now." Nadia covered her eyes from the sun.

"I believe you're right." Lily nodded.

Suddenly, and before Lily could even detect where he had come from, Lieutenant Dobkin's plane was hot on Larisa's tail.

"Come on, Larisa," Lily muttered as her friend performed admirable maneuvers, but nothing would shake the lieutenant.

"Damn!" Marina sighed when it was evident Larisa had failed and began returning to the airbase as some of the men groaned in their lost wagers while others cheered at their winnings.

The plane came to a halt, and Larisa, who Lily noticed was both embarrassed and enraged, stepped down from the plane.

"It's not fair that he performs maneuvers he didn't teach us in class." Larisa removed her goggles and tossed them at Marina, who had been designated as the next target.

"Poor thing." Nadia shook her head nervously as she watched Marina. "She's a wreck."

Again, the green flair was launched, and Lily paid special attention to the sky, desperate to catch a glimpse of where the lieutenant was coming from.

"How does he do it?" Katya asked with annoyance as, again, the lieutenant seemed to appear out of nowhere and was right behind Marina.

"She had no chance." Nadia threw her hands onto her hips. "He's going to disgrace the very idea of women flyers."

"Litvyak." Major Raskova gestured for her to take a plane when Marina returned.

"Do us proud." Katya patted Lily's shoulder as she walked boldly toward the plane.

"Don't let us down," Major Raskova spoke firmly as she handed the hat and goggles to Lily. "Whatever you do, don't let us down."

With a nod, Lily climbed into the cockpit. Fastening her gloves, checking her instruments and controls, and securing her hat, Lily gripped the throttle eagerly. She had been waiting for this moment since they arrived back in October. This was the moment where she could finally prove her worth, and not just hers, but all those with her.

The flair fired, and Lily felt her stomach drop. It was her time. Pressing on the throttle, Lily built up speed until she almost reached the end of the runway, where she pulled up sharply. She watched the sky closely, inspecting each and every cloud, wondering if the lieutenant was indeed taking cover behind them.

*He's nowhere,* Lily thought as she looked at her altimeter, which read four thousand feet.

Glancing over her shoulder to her left, the sky was clear. He wasn't on her right, in front of her, or above.

"Where are you?" Lily asked aloud when a thought suddenly struck her.

Glancing over her right shoulder, Lily shielded her eyes as she looked directly into the sun. Sure enough, a black dot was heading straight toward her.

*Genius!* Lily grumbled. Her opponent had used the cover of the sun to blind his target. Although she had spotted him, it was too late. He was closing in on her, and quickly, and Lily recognized that she was about to face the same defeat as the other two women before her.

But then, a thought crossed Lily's mind. A passing thought that transformed into instinct.

"Five, four, three," Lily began counting as she wrapped her hands tight around the controls.

He was nearly within range, and Lily knew she had to execute this with perfect calculation. Any mistake and she would suffer a humiliating defeat, or worse yet, she could crash her plane right into his.

"Two, one!" Lily pulled back sharply on the stick while pressing against the right rudder pedal.

In a swift and perfectly executed barrel roll, Lily's plane was now upside down, and her eyes locked with the lieutenant's as he glared up at her with shock and menace. She would've smiled had she the opportunity, but Lieutenant Dobkin, despite being outwitted, was not about to go down easy.

Bringing her plane back level, Lily was now tight on his tail. Employing every trick within his retinue, he tried to shake Lily, but her instincts were sharp, her reactions swift. No matter what he tried, Lily was right behind him.

She imagined he was a German, the very man responsible for destroying her way of life, for putting her mother and brother in jeopardy. Squeezing on the controls, she fired pretend rounds at the lieutenant's plane, bringing him down in a blaze of fire.

Snapping her back to reality was the lieutenant's signal that he was surrendering.

Her shoulders relaxed, and Lily felt a lump in her throat as she grew emotional. She had proved herself worthy. And not just for herself — but for all the women down on the airstrip watching her.

As Lily descended, she caught the waves and cheers from her comrades. Even the men were clapping their approval.

With a large, gratified smile, Lily climbed out of the plane and was surrounded by her friends, who clung to her tightly. This was a victory of small measure, but Lily sensed this meant more for her gender than she could realize.

"Nadia," Major Raskova spoke dryly, and Lily noticed she was not sharing in their cheer. "You're next."

"Here." Lily handed Nadia the goggles and hat. "You've got this."

"I don't think I can pull off the same stunt, especially now that he's expecting it, but him being rattled may help me." Nadia strapped her hat on and climbed into the plane.

"You cost the men a fortune." Major Raskova stood beside Lily, who still couldn't contain her smile.

Looking at Major Raskova, Lily was distracted by a large wad of bills in her hand.

"I never gamble." The major shook her head before adding quietly, "Unless I'm sure of the outcome."

"Thank you." Lily grinned at her.

"You were lucky today." The major looked her in the eyes. "You may not always be so fortunate."

"My younger brother cautioned me the same." Lily returned her attention to the sky.

# Chapter Nine
# Selections

*"Knowing your own darkness is the best method for dealing with the darkness of other people."*

Carl Jung

<u>May 17, 1942</u>

*Dearest Yuri,*

*We're nearing the end of our six-month training. I find out today which regiment I'll be stationed with, and I hope it's with the fighters! I think I will wallow in disappointment if I'm assigned to a bomber regiment.*

*I know that's not what's important, really, but I can't help feeling like I would make the best contribution with the fighters. Still, perspective on what matters most is pressing on me. Two of our best navigators perished in an accident back in March. I've tried to digest the tragedy, but every time I climb into my plane, I'm reminded how dangerous it is.*

*Don't repeat any of this to Mother, I know she'd worry incessantly, but Nadia, if you remember me telling you about her, was leading a formation in a blizzard. Two of the fighters were separated due to the storm. We later discovered their bodies among the wreckage of their planes. Poor Nadia, despite this not being her fault, has yet to forgive herself. She hides it well behind her chipper attitude, but every once in a while, I catch her staring off into the distance, which is rather unusual for her.*

*It's tragic that they perished in training and weren't able to be effective against the enemy. Still, their memory lingers, and we will carry their spirits into the fight. Many of the women here are worried sick about their families under occupied territory. Katerina stares at the picture of her daughter all day long. I imagine that would be devastating as a mother.*

*In lighter news, some of the girls' hair has grown back, but others have actually enjoyed their hair being shorter and are adopting the style. Their hair is out of the way, and, besides, it's nearly impossible to maintain a style under a flying hat. Luck has been my constant ally in that regard, with the wonderful benefit of my curls. As soon as my cap is pulled off, they pop back into place as if they were freshly curled.*

*Also, please make sure to remind Mother that when she sends letters to me, she can't address me by name. You never*

*know who may be intercepting the correspondence. Please
remind her to write to Pilot Litvyak, or L. Litvyak.*

*All my love,*

*Lily*

Lily folded the letter and placed it in an envelope on
the makeshift table beside her cot.

Glancing at the clock to determine how much time was
left on her brief recess, Lily lay down and stared at a
picture of her mother and brother. She wondered what
they were up to and how they were getting along. She
imagined the fights they were having without her there to
provide some calm to the situation. She hoped that Yuri
was at least enjoying his own room.

"Hey," Larisa spoke quietly as she sat on the edge of
Lily's bed.

"It's going to be fine," Lily consoled her friend, already
perceiving her worries.

"What if I'm not selected for the fighter regiment?"
Larisa rubbed the back of her tense neck.

"Then you'll go to one of the bomber regiments."

"I'm a skilled pilot," Larisa grumbled. "They should be
using me where I can be the most impactful."

"You're also an excellent navigator." Lily raised her
eyebrows as she tucked the photo of her family back into
her breast pocket. "Don't discount how important that is."

"Would you be happy as a navigator?" Larisa asked
knowingly.

"Goodness, no." Lily shook her head quickly.

"But I should be?" Larisa tilted her head.

"I'm trying to help you see the positive side."

"There is no positive side." Larisa huffed and lay
beside Lily.

"There's barely room with me on here!" Lily barked.
"Get your elbows out of my side!"

"So fussy." Larisa smirked.

"I'm realistic." Lily frowned. "I believe you once referred to yourself with that term."

Larisa chuckled quietly as she stared at the bunk above their head before uttering sadly, "This may be the last few times we're together."

Lily glanced out of her peripheral vision at her friend as she thought of the photo of her mother and brother.

"The Germans are launching a counteroffensive." Larisa drew a deep breath. "It's nice to know that our Red Army was able to recapture some land, but I doubt the Nazis will give way so easily."

Lily remained silent as she thought of how close they were to being sent to war. She had been excited for as long as she could remember about fighting for her country, but now, with that possibility being only days away, Lily felt a sense of dread.

"Do you think —"

"Let's talk about something nicer." Lily turned onto her side as she smiled at her friend. "Something to lift our spirits a bit?"

"Like what?" Larisa shrugged.

"You and Mr. Morozov?" Lily grinned and fluttered her eyes at her friend.

"Please!" Larisa rolled her eyes. "All he talks about is you!"

"Really?"

"Every time you jump into a plane, he watches you the whole time."

"He doesn't." Lily frowned.

"They all do." Larisa tilted her head. "All the men, that is."

"Do they think I'm going to crash?" Lily scoffed.

"They have never seen anyone push the plane the way you have." Larisa lifted an eyebrow as she began inspecting her fingers. "I used to be so clean."

"You used to smell nicer, too." Lily bit her lip as Larisa's mouth fell open in shock.

"Blame the soap." Larisa's head slumped back onto the pillow. "Though I suppose that's part of being a soldier now."

"Put you on the front and the Nazis will run away from your smell." Lily giggled.

"You're so cruel!" Larisa swung at Lily, but she rolled out of the way and landed with a thud on the floor.

"Are you alright?" Larisa grew concerned as she leaned over the cot.

"I'm fine." Lily laughed.

"They'd never forgive me for injuring the best of us." Larisa breathed a sigh of relief.

"The regiments have been posted!" a shout came from the hallway as a woman ran down the corridor, shouting into each room.

Immediately, Lily and Larisa bounded toward the door, rushed out into the hallway, and sped along to the front of the school, where a crowd of other girls were huddling around a message board.

"Yes!" Katya squeezed her hands into fists as she grew excited with her designation.

"Where am I?" Larisa asked rhetorically as they attempted to get to the head of the group to see the list of names.

"As if there was any doubt where you were going." Nadia smiled at Lily.

"I'm a fighter?" Lily asked, unsure if she should allow herself to believe the news she so desperately wanted to hear.

"Yeah, look." Nadia pointed to the list of fighters and then ran her finger down to Lily's name.

"I'm a fighter!" Lily squealed and then wrapped her arms around Nadia, who laughed heartily.

"Where am I?" Larisa asked as she eagerly searched the list.

"Night bomber," Marina spoke dryly as she pointed.

Lily watched as the air left Larisa's lungs and her countenance morphed into despair while her shoulders dropped.

"You're with me!" Nadia beamed.

Larisa didn't reply, staring at the board as if she were reading a list of deceased relatives.

"Word spread quickly, I see," Major Raskova spoke with a smirk from behind the group of women who, at once, stood at attention.

"Major Raskova," Larisa addressed her officially. "I would like to formally object to my designation. I taught thirty other men how to fly before I came here. You know how I have excelled during training. I can be of greater service to our cause if I—"

"Request denied!" Major Raskova boomed, and the excitement in the air immediately deflated as all eyes turned to her. "This is not some game. Our people are dying by the thousands, and who knows if we'll survive another winter. Instead of being grateful that you're part of this great endeavor, you whine to me because you're not getting exactly what you want. Childish! Never bring it up again!"

With that, Major Raskova stormed away, and Larisa, looking sheepishly about the room, turned and walked back to her quarters with her head bowed low.

"I hope that doesn't stifle the atmosphere of the dance this evening." Nadia chewed on her cheek.

"Dance?!" Lily's eyes flew wide as she grew excited. "What dance?!"

"We received permission from Major Raskova to host a dance, seeing as it is our last night here," Marina chimed in.

"You're excited about a dance?" Lily raised an incredulous eyebrow at Marina.

"There'll be vodka." Marina grinned in her reply.

"I see." Lily smiled back.

"And the boys are joining!" Nadia squealed in her seemingly impossible-to-dampen spirits.

"Does our little Nadia have her eye on a certain boy?" Lily tilted her head.

"Little? I'm nearly a foot over you!" Nadia stood tall as she compared their heights.

"A foot?" Lily laughed. "Don't flatter yourself. You still need to sit on a cushion to see out of the cockpit."

"I hope that Mr. Morozov fellow is attending." Nadia stared off into the distance. "That is, if you don't mind me trying my luck with him."

"It's not luck you need," Lily replied quickly.

"Then what?" Nadia shrugged.

"A strong stomach." Lily grinned at her own quip as Marina chuckled loudly.

"Oh, you're terrible!" Nadia swatted Lily's arm. "He's a perfectly reasonable gentleman!"

"And he's all yours."

"Quickly! The men will be here any moment!" Nadia panicked as she organized their room later that evening. "Help me push the beds against the wall to make space for a dance floor."

"I'm not sure I'm in the mood to stay up late this evening," Katerina complained as she grudgingly helped Nadia. "Why couldn't we have done this in the men's quarters?"

"Are you kidding?" Katya scoffed. "Have you smelled their quarters? Stinks like tobacco and body odor. No offense, Marina."

Marina offered a daggered glare as she puffed her cigarette by the window, which often had the opposite effect when the wind blew the stench into the room.

"None taken," Marina finally responded. "I personally enjoy the smell of body odor. I like a man with the aroma nature intended."

"Nature also provided water for them to wash in," Katya mumbled. "Goodness knows I could do with a good washing. My hair hasn't been this unkempt since we were forced to cut it."

"We're all aware of the washing you need," Marina muttered.

"I'm bathed daily in your affections, what else do I need?" Katya asked sarcastically, and Lily chuckled.

Lily and Katya had grown closer over the last six months, and Lily was excited that she would be Katya's wing mate. Although her heart did shatter for Larisa, as Lily understood how devastated she would be if she had been assigned to the night bomber regiment. At least in the fighter regiment, they had proper planes. The night bombers were forced to use the Po-2s, and they were little more than sitting targets at such low speeds.

"Hey." Lily sat beside a dejected Larisa.

"Hey," Larisa replied feebly.

"I'll miss you." Lily took her friend's hand in hers.

"Really?" Larisa looked at Lily with concern.

"What do you mean, really?" Lily offered her friend an annoyed look. "Of course I'll miss you."

"That's good to hear." Larisa drew a deep breath. "I'm not sure I can survive without you."

"Survive? You'll thrive without me. I'm the one holding you back."

"How?" Larisa glanced at her friend, baiting her for compliments.

"You're the second-best pilot here. You might even be better than me." Lily raised her eyebrows.

"It's rude to exaggerate." Larisa frowned.

"It's true!" Lily pressed. "You're definitely a better navigator."

"That is, actually, true." Larisa bounced her head from side to side as she contemplated.

"With me out of the way, they'll see your full potential. You never know, maybe you'll join us someday. Keep petitioning and making requisition."

"Thank you," Larisa sighed as she stared at her friend in the eyes.

"Come on!" Nadia came over to the cot they were sitting on and waved for them to stand. "They'll be here any minute. We need to make it look presentable."

"The men aren't coming to inspect our aptitude for décor." Larisa stood with a groan.

"Which is a shame." Lily threw her hands onto her hips as she looked about the room. "It really is nice in here."

A sense of nostalgia dawned on Lily as she took in the sights for one last evening. The nice curtains draped across the windows, the little sewing corner for mending uniforms or adding designs that they snuck here and there, Marina's smoking corner that Nadia frequented with her newfound enjoyment of the habit, and the bunks that had been personalized with photos and hidden etchings into the wood frames.

"Look what we found!" a shout erupted from the doorway, and Lily glanced over to see Mr. Morozov, along with the other men, pouring into the room with an accordion, banjo, small drums, and even a piano that they wheeled into the room.

"Yay!" Nadia clapped excitedly. "Who plays what instrument?"

"We were hoping some of you knew." Mr. Morozov looked timidly at the banjo in his hand.

"Knew what?" Nadia asked innocently.

"How to play, obviously!" Marina griped as she tossed her cigarette out the window before waltzing over to Mr. Morozov, grabbing the banjo out of his hand, and stating, "I might be able to do something with this."

"You play?" Nadia's exhilaration grew, and Lily found it difficult to believe that there were levels of Nadia's excitement that were previously undiscovered.

"Supply me with vodka, and I'll play as long as you want me to." Marina dragged a stool back to her corner.

"It's been years, but I might be able to follow along with you." A man shrugged as he sat near Marina with the accordion.

"And I can play the piano." Katya nodded at another woman to help her push it over to the corner.

Lily watched as the room delved into a buzz of excitement, and soon, the bottles of vodka were popping open and pouring liberally as the band began playing to the tune of what Lily could only describe as a cat screeching.

Yet the merriment was lost on one soul, and Lily watched with a heavy heart as Katerina excused herself from the room. Lily understood Katerina was beside herself with worry, and this revelry was not appropriate for her nerves.

"A drink, my lily," Mr. Morozov spoke confidently as he handed Lily a glass.

"I will take your offer of a drink if you never call me your lily again." She tilted her head and raised her eyebrows in warning.

"Agreed." Mr. Morozov cleared his throat. "Felt strange saying it, anyway. What should we toast to?"

"To hopefully never seeing each other again." Lily raised her glass, but Mr. Morozov's shoulders slouched.

"Sorry, that was harsher than I intended." Lily looked sheepishly at him. "How about to war?"

"To war!" Mr. Morozov raised his glass, and the room erupted in a cheer.

"Celebrating war?" Lieutenant Dobkin grumbled as he and Major Raskova entered the room.

"Celebrating our fight against Fascist snakes!" Nadia corrected as she raised her glass.

"Now *that* I can drink to!" Lieutenant Dobkin grabbed a glass, and the room erupted into another cheer as he poured and then drank.

"May I have this dance?" Mr. Morozov set down his glass and held his hand out charmingly to Lily.

"No." Lily shook her head quickly.

"Just one dance. That's all I ask."

"You, Mr. Morozov, are gifted with persistence." Lily took a sip as the alcohol burned her throat.

"You won't talk to me, and now you won't even dance with me?" Mr. Morozov continued to hold his hand out to Lily.

"Because you don't care for either. All you want is what every man wants."

"If you can't face a man on the dance floor, how will you expect to face them in the air?" Mr. Morozov grinned cheekily.

"You remembered what I said back at the flying club?" Lily squinted as she tried to measure his sincerity.

"I remember every word you utter, no matter how cutting." Mr. Morozov looked intently into Lily's eyes, but still, she felt nothing for him.

"One dance." Lily gestured for him to take the lead, and they entered the chaotic dance floor with couples dancing awkwardly and yet enjoyably with each other.

"May I have a word?" Major Raskova approached Larisa, who was still sitting on the cot, and Lily strained to listen in.

"Yes, ma'am." Larisa stood at attention.

"I spoke harshly to you earlier, and I apologize," Major Raskova began, and Lily leaned closer as she danced with Mr. Morozov so she could hear this startling conversation. "The new regiment is going to need skilled navigators, and few are better than you. It may not be the position you desired, but I need women like you as navigators."

"I understand." Larisa nodded adamantly, and Lily smiled as she saw the look of pride smeared across Larisa's face.

The fact that the great Major Raskova mentioned that she needed Larisa was, Lily assumed, more than merely a ploy.

"Thank you." Major Raskova smiled at Larisa. "Now, grab one of the shy boys and dance with him."

"Yes, ma'am!" Larisa giggled as she ran over to a boy leaning against the wall, grabbed his hand, and yanked him onto the dance floor.

The song ended, and the room erupted into supportive clapping. The music was terrible, Lily admitted, but there was something moving about it. The piano and accordion were out of tune, the drummer was off-beat and the vocalist was pitchy, but it was somehow memorable.

Lily assumed that she wasn't alone in recognizing that this may be their last night of peace. There was no telling what war would bring, and Major Raskova's warnings, from when she had interviewed them, of maiming and dismemberment, rang through Lily's mind.

"May I have the next dance?" Lieutenant Dobkin approached Lily with his hands firmly behind his back and sucking in his cheeks.

"Uh, yes, uh, sir. Yes, sir," Lily stumbled over her words, shocked by his interest.

"Thank you, Lily." Mr. Morozov offered a quick bow of the head as he departed.

With an oddly serious expression, despite the jovial music, and softer hands than Lily would've imagined, Lieutenant Dobkin danced with her around the room.

"I'm a veteran of the Spanish Civil War," he finally spoke.

Lily didn't reply as she wasn't entirely certain what his point was, and, in the back of her mind, she suspected he was about to unleash a rather unflattering argument.

"I have never seen women in war before," he continued as they danced closely. "It's unnatural."

Still, Lily wasn't entirely sure what his purpose of dancing with her was. She was more than aware of his poor opinion of her, and Lily found his proximity unnerving.

"That being said," he cleared his throat. "I have also never flown with anyone as talented as you."

"Thank you, sir." Lily beamed with pride.

"Nor have I flown with anyone as lucky as you are."

"Oh?" Lily frowned.

"I can't count how many times you should've crashed, or the wind suddenly turned in your favor, or your last-minute maneuver snuck you out of terrible danger."

Lily threw her lips upside down as she also recalled how fortune had gifted her with many chances.

"I'd hate to be there when your luck ends," he warned. "You're the best pilot I've ever had the privilege of training, and it would crush me to hear of your falling in battle. Please ensure that you rely not only on your luck but also on everything I've instructed you."

"I will." Lily nodded as the music ceased and a round of applause erupted.

With a polite bow of his head, the lieutenant left Lily, grabbed a bottle of vodka, and exited the room.

Sitting back near her bunk, Lily grinned as she watched the revelry in the room. The music continued, and Lily thought that the little thrown-together band was starting to find their rhythm, the dancing grew less constrained, and the vodka continued to pour.

"Will you wait for me?" Mr. Morozov asked as he sat beside Lily.

"Wait?" Lily asked, half paying attention. "Wait for what?"

"To marry me?"

Lily coughed liberally, surprised by the unexpected proposal, and then covered her mouth as she tried to regain her composure and limit whatever insult she had levied upon the poor Mr. Morozov.

"Promises in war shouldn't be made so lightly." Lily turned her gaze away, hoping to spur any further conversation.

"At least write to me and to no other man." Mr. Morozov got down on his knee.

"You're drunk." Lily gestured for him to get up as she made sure no one else had seen him.

"I'm drunk with love," he professed, and Lily rolled her eyes.

"Let's get the fighting over with first, darling, and then maybe we can discuss love, yeah?" Lily patted his shoulder patronizingly.

"Alright, ladies." Major Raskova clapped to gain their attention. "It's late, and you fly out in the morning. Gentlemen, if you would kindly vacate back to your quarters."

Awkward and youthful groans of separated love gushed around the room as the women and men, who were smitten with each other, were forced to part ways, and with the understanding that some of them would never see each other again.

With a slight sulk, Mr. Morozov left Lily's side, but not before offering a pleading look, which she was more than happy to ignore.

"I had too much to drink." Larisa moaned as she leaned on the side of the bed.

"Which means I'll be taking the top bunk tonight." Lily stood and climbed up to the top.

"What? Why?" Larisa grumbled, but then suddenly rushed toward the garbage where she vomited loudly.

"That's why," Lily muttered.

"Good thing we cut our hair, hey?" Nadia laughed. "Nobody needs to hold it back when we've outdone ourselves."

"Shut up!" Larisa barked and the ladies laughed liberally as another girl or two ran to a garbage bin near them.

"It may not be a good look for us at our new regiments tomorrow. Showing up drunk and overtired." Nadia chuckled to herself as she climbed into her cot. "Hard to sleep when someone is vomiting beside you."

"I doubt any of us were going to sleep anyway." Lily stared at the ceiling.

"You're nervous about tomorrow?" Marina asked as she smoked in her corner.

"Nervous?" Lily asked rhetorically as she shook her head while a smile grew on her face. "I can't wait!"

# Chapter Ten
# War

*"Sound trumpets! Let our bloody colours wave!*
*And either victory, or else a grave."*

William Shakespeare

"Write often." Larisa squeezed Lily tight as they embraced in the hangar.

"I will! I promise!" Lily held her friend close.

They had been wing mates for many years, and flying almost felt empty without Larisa. Still, Lily was glad that her friend had made it through the training program and that her dream of fighting was about to be actualized.

"I got you something." Larisa sniffled as she broke her embrace and handed a brown paper bag to Lily. "I didn't have time to wrap it in anything prettier."

"You shouldn't have!" Lily took the bag but then added, "I didn't get you anything!"

"Just open it." Larisa tapped Lily's arm excitedly.

Obliging Larisa, Lily pulled out a tin mug that wasn't necessarily worn in, but not all that new, either.

"It's nice," Lily tried to sound pleasant, but she wasn't sure what she was missing.

"Turn it around, you goof!" Larisa chuckled.

"Oh! It has my name on it!" Lily smiled as she looked at her name printed in beautiful, gilded lettering.

"Do you like it?" Larisa pressed.

"It's my instant favorite!" Lily offered Larisa another hug.

"It's time," Katya tapped on Lily's shoulder, and she turned to watch as the rest of the women were climbing into their Yaks.

"You'll do well." Larisa held back tears as she nodded proudly at her friend.

With a trembling lip, Lily nodded back at her friend before climbing into her Yak. Words clung to Lily's throat as she offered one last glance at her friend. She prayed that they would meet again, but she wasn't ignorant to the fact that they were going off to war, and a war that was not swinging in their favor.

The green flare shot into the sky, and Lily, positioning her plane, was shortly in the air with her squadron. They were the last to leave the airfield, and passing by the hangar, the squadron offered a salute with the wave of their wings.

They had been ordered to test their weapons before leaving, and Lily squeezed off a round at a target, feeling the mighty firepower rattling through her arms.

"Just breathe," Lily spoke quietly to herself as she felt her hands sweating in her gloves.

Their destination was Saratov, a city right across the river from where they had spent six months training, and Lily was certain their baptism by fire was about to begin immediately.

A sense of pride swelled within Lily as she glanced to her right and then to her left at the formations blackening the sky. She was among the fiercest of women, and some of the most skilled pilots she ever had the privilege of flying with.

She glanced down at the Volga River on this clear spring morning and watched the mesmerizing display of the golden sun shimmering off the waves, reflecting the light back into the sky.

"We're here," Katya announced over the radio.

Without further explanation, each fighter did exactly as they had been trained to do over the course of the six months. One by one, a fighter peeled off from the formation and landed, with Lily pulling up the rear.

Climbing out of her plane, Lily joined the rest of the women and came to stand close to Katya as they took in the sights of their new home.

The stench of smoke and oil lingered in the air, and Lily understood that these were from not-so-distant battles. Glancing at the horizon, Lily knew that the danger was just beyond, and the Nazis and Soviets were engaged in brutal fighting even at that very moment.

"Roll call!" an angry shout erupted from a soldier near them, and Lily and the others fell immediately into formation and stood tall and proud, eager to make a good impression on their new commander.

As the soldier read aloud each name, Lily heard the clipping of boots approaching them. Walking swiftly, but with a limp, to the front of the column, a woman came to a hurried, regimented stop before looking at each of them closely as if she was searching for flaws.

"I'm Major Kazarinova," she began loudly and with a booming voice. "Let me make one thing clear: training is over. You will no longer be shooting at practice targets, but at real planes who will be shooting back at you. This is war. Just this morning, we learned of the successful Nazi counteroffensive. Hundreds of thousands of our soldiers have been taken prisoner, including hundreds of tanks."

The major paused as she again studied each of their faces, and Lily thought she seemed rather impressive. She had a strong jaw with small eyes that seemed ever inquisitive. She carried herself with authority but didn't carry the aura of command Major Raskova came by so naturally.

"You will be flying by day and by night. Your duty is to destroy any approaching bombers, or otherwise force them to abandon their pursuit. Saratov is your city now. These are your mothers and fathers, sisters and brothers. Protect them as if you were protecting your own blood. Understood?"

"Yes, ma'am!" The women shouted in unison.

"The city is divided into four quadrants. During the night, only four fighters will be dispatched at once in order to eliminate the chance of collision. Each fighter will be responsible for their quadrant. Eight of you will be placed on standby during the nights. You are expected to be prepared to take to your plane within a moment's notice."

"Yes, ma'am!" the women again responded.

"The enemy bombers generally attack under the cover of night. In the event that they attack during the day, you will be called upon. Many other missions, including attacking enemy troop formations, or reconnaissance, may be required of you."

Turning to the soldier who had completed the roll call, the major grabbed the clipboard from him before announcing, "These are the women who will be assigned to tonight's standby. Lily, Katya, Olga, Galina, Galia, Valeria, and Valentina."

Lily's heart skipped a beat at her name, and she knew that her resolve would be tested this very night.

"Get some rest today. It will be the last you will have." The major looked at them indifferently, and Lily missed Major Raskova's underlying motherly nurturing. "You will be taken to your quarters."

"On me!" the soldier called, and the women fell in line after him as he led them toward a row of underground bunkers.

"At least we're together this evening," Katya whispered to Lily, who glanced over her shoulder with a nod.

*Thankfully, I didn't drink nearly as much as the other ladies did last night.* Lily thought as she glanced at a few who were struggling to hide their fatigue.

Entering the underground bunker, Lily was at least pleased to find that the cots were an upgrade from the ones at Engels. Not that they were luxurious by any stretch of the imagination, but Lily was happy to not have her feet dangling off the edge. She was a petite woman, too, and she knew that if she had struggled, others of a normal height had exponentially suffered.

"Get acquainted with your quarters," the guard called loudly as the women continued to file inside. "You may collect your rations from the office."

*Rations?* Lily frowned. She wasn't expecting to be fed much, but to have small, carefully cut-out portions was not what she had in mind either.

"Let's take this one." Katya grabbed Lily's arm gently as they walked to a bunk near the furnace in the middle of the bunker.

"Quick thinking," Lily whispered as she glanced over her shoulder at some of the other ladies who were ignorantly happy to have the bunks near the door. "Winter will be unkind to them."

Throwing her little rucksack onto the bottom bunk, Lily watched as a woman, Valeria, beside them began pinning newspaper clippings to the wall.

She had joined their training regiment later than most women, about two months ago, and Lily wasn't afforded the chance to become more than acquaintances with her. She did, however, find it unusual that the rest of them had to endure six months while she only had to take two months of training.

"What are those?" Lily asked Valeria.

"Newspaper clippings," she replied briskly.

"We can see that." Katya glanced at Lily with annoyance as she stood beside her. "What are they of?"

"They're my inspiration." Valeria stood back and threw her hands onto her hips as she studied the clippings. "These are the aces and pilots that have been making life hell for the Nazis."

"That is inspiring." Lily threw her eyebrows up.

"Someday, my name will be printed in a paper like this." Valeria turned to them while offering a confident raising of the chin, not in arrogance, but rather, determination.

"I sure hope so." Katya rested her head on the stiff cushion on the top bunk.

"All those men are dead," Olga interjected solemnly, and Lily turned to see that she had been listening to them.

Lily glanced again at the papers attached to the wall as the gravity of their charge began to sink in. Still, a part of her was convinced, maybe the foolishness of youth, that such things wouldn't happen to her. She was still persuaded that she would make it out of this war unscathed. She had to. It would be impossible for her to leave her mother. She understood that fate would crush poor Anna.

"Don't worry, as your squadron leader, it's my duty to make sure you come home alive," Olga added. She was another woman that Lily had not had the opportunity to become familiar with, but she appreciated her leadership qualities.

"Get some rest." Olga nodded to their bunks. "We're on duty tonight."

Lily didn't need much encouragement to lay in her bunk. The cot, however, was firm, and Lily struggled to find a position that was comfortable.

Retrieving her tin mug from her rucksack, Lily stared at the letters written across it, and her heart ached for simpler days. How she missed the ease of the flying club, and she hated that the invasion had turned her greatest passion into an instrument of death.

Still, she was determined that if she was going to be a device of war, then she would unleash all her fury upon the Nazis.

Her mind wandered to her bother and mother, and she wished with all her heart that she could be back at their two-bedroom apartment, sitting at the small table while her mother smoked and Yuri complained. What she would do for her mother's vegetable salad, which now seemed like a delicacy compared to the mush she had eaten for the last six months.

The clock struck two in the morning, and Lily yawned as she and the other women sat around a table in the crew room. In the center of the table was a radio, a few lit candles, and a telephone.

Olga, the squadron leader, held her hand flat on the table near the phone, desperate to not miss any reports. She was anxious, Lily assumed, to make a good impression. Either that or she was simply terrified.

"We could play some cards." Katya pointed to a deck sitting idly on the table.

"Sure," Lily replied quickly, but no one moved to pick them up.

"It's pretty late." Valeria glanced at the clock. "I think even the Devil is resting."

"I'd rather face him than Nazis." Katya offered a trying attempt at humor, and a light, tense chuckle reverberated around the room as each woman, while nervous, tried to hide their own anxiety.

Lily wanted to prove to them that she was capable, strong, and fierce. But her leg bounced rapidly as she kept glancing at the phone, waiting for that dreaded call.

She wasn't sure why she was so nervous. She had waited for this moment since the invasion of her homeland, but somehow, now that it was actually upon her, Lily could scarcely think straight. Her stomach was tight, her shoulders tense, and she had nearly chewed her nail off.

"Did you see the reports coming out of Ukraine?" Katya asked after a moment.

The clock ticked patiently and loudly as no one answered.

Lily shook her head after a moment before rubbing her jaw, which she was unconsciously clenching tight.

"My family is there," Valentina spoke quietly and without emotion. "A letter was smuggled out. They're killing people at random. Stealing, looting, murdering, and raping. Even girls as young as eight years old aren't spared. Barbaric people. They killed the entire Jewish population in Kyiv. Seventy thousand people were gunned down. Their bodies were thrown in the ravine."

A hate arose within Lily. A burning, boiling hatred for these monsters who had invaded their land. She couldn't imagine how she would respond if anything similar happened to her mother, and Lily seethed inwardly with sweltering resentment.

The room returned to silence as the clock seemed to grow increasingly louder. It ticked, ticked, ticked, reminding Lily that at any second, they could be called into action.

"Are we the first?" Olga asked quietly.

"First what?" Lily asked while barely paying attention.

"Have there been other women who have shot down enemy planes?" Olga clarified.

"None." Katya shook her head.

"Who will be the first to get that honor, then?" Olga asked as she glanced at the women waiting by the telephone.

"No moon tonight," Katya spoke quietly when no one answered Olga.

"We'll be entirely dependent on our instruments." Lily nodded.

"I'm glad they trained us well. I swear, sometimes I think I'm upside down when all you can see is black." Valeria chuckled nervously, but no one joined in the forced amusement.

"I wish the radio worked two ways." Katya drew a deep breath as she shivered. "I'm glad the tower can contact us, but it would be helpful if we can contact them back."

"That is frustrating." Lily blew warm air into her hands.

The phone rang.

Everyone froze.

Olga glanced quickly around the room with wide eyes before grabbing the receiver and repeating into her mouthpiece, "Twenty plus enemy. Six thousand feet. Heading zero nine zero. Twenty miles from Saratov."

Slamming down the phone, Olga stood and threw on her cap as the others with her promptly followed suit.

"This is it!" Katya spoke with excitement mixed with unease as they ran toward their planes.

"Good luck!" Olga called as she climbed onto the wing of her plane and entered the cockpit, but not before adding, "Stick to your quadrant! You'll be alright. To victory!"

Retrieving the picture of her mother and brother, Lily set it on her lap beside the map, which was now spread across her knees. Her fingers shook as she ran them along the map, reminding herself of her quadrant.

She had practiced navigating at night for nearly six months, but now that they were about to employ these techniques in battle, all her knowledge seemed to evaporate into thin air.

She couldn't think, she couldn't feel. All Lily could do was obey her instinct to move the throttle forward and apply power to her aircraft.

Olga was first in line, and she followed along the hooded flairs on the runway until she was in the air and lost to the black of night, heading directly to her quadrant.

Lily was next, and as she turned the plane to the runway, she was certain that she was going to vomit. Air control mumbled something into her radio, but Lily couldn't react. Her arms were frozen, and she simply sat in the plane staring into the dark void that seemed so menacing and full of danger.

"You're clear for departure," the call came again.

With a quick wave, Lily tried to appear commanding, but she was certain she had revealed her nervousness.

With a deep breath, Lily moved the throttle forward, giving some power to the aircraft, and she picked up speed quickly until that blessed moment when, as her stomach dropped, she was in the air.

The instant she left the ground, all her nerves departed. She couldn't explain how, or why, but in the air, even though she was headed toward combat, Lily was at ease.

Flying was to Lily as breathing. It was in her nature, her blood, and she turned her plane toward her quadrant, using the light from her instruments to illuminate the map, her stopwatch, and her altitude to determine where she was.

Little fires were blazing around the city from destroyed tanks or other machinery. The smoke rose to the sky as the bodies continued to burn, and even from such a distance, Lily needed to look away.

Glancing at her altitude, Lily noticed that she had reached seven thousand feet. Yet, even though the instruments were reading that she was right side up, Lily's instincts were telling her that she was upside down. The fires below her seemed to be burning in the sky instead. It was unnerving, but Lily knew to trust her instruments that she was in the right spot and at the right heading.

*Where are they?* Lily glanced out the window. *They should be about a thousand feet below me.*

Nothing.

At least, that is, nothing that Lily could see.

A burst of bullets and tracers erupted in the sky from another quadrant.

*That must be Valeria.* Lily glanced at her map to double-check the quadrant. *Should I move to help her?*

Suddenly, a shadow passed underneath Lily's plane.

Glancing in the direction, Lily peered into the dark night sky, but she couldn't detect any movement.

Until, that is, Lily caught the light from a cockpit just below her plane.

*Found you!* Lily grinned with anticipation.

She was in the perfect position. The enemy was entirely unaware of her presence, and the routine ground into her during training had mimicked this exact scenario. This was her chance to fully prove her worth.

Lowering her speed slightly, Lily made sure that the distance between her and the enemy bomber would be adequate.

Then, dipping her nose down, Lily dove on an angle toward the back of the enemy plane.

"Don't shoot too early," Lily reminded herself as she took the safety off and prepared to fire.

"Now!" she shouted to herself and squeezed the trigger.

Her plane rattled under the firepower as the sky was lit with sparks from the bullets, cannon, and tracers. Her cockpit grew bright with the flashes that were blinding her from her bearings.

The enemy took evasive maneuvers, but Lily, despite being nearly blinded by her own weapons, pursued until, at the last moment, she pulled up and away, nearly striking the back of the enemy plane.

Glancing down at her enemy with a smile of anticipation, Lily's countenance morphed into despair when she realized that every single bullet had missed the mark. She was certain that she had struck the bomber, but it returned to its original path as if Lily was a minor hiccup.

The bomber was nearly over the city, and Lily knew that if she failed to stop their approach, it would drop its payload, killing civilians or destroying military targets.

Pushing her aircraft to its fullest extent, Lily climbed back into the atmosphere, again attaining seven thousand feet. She knew the trajectory of the bomber, and despite being essentially blind, Lily employed her trust in the instruments.

Scanning the sky again, Lily feared that she had lost the enemy to the black of night, or that they had indeed changed their trajectory.

Looking at her stopwatch and glancing down at her map, Lily calculated where they might be. Firing off a quick burst, the tracers illuminated the back wing of the bomber. She had narrowly missed.

Firing off more rounds as she dove down at the enemy, Lily had to again pull up just before ramming into the back of the bomber.

This time, Lily was certain not to lose them, and she kept the vague, shadowy figures in her sights as she spun the plane around to make another pass.

Regardless, the bombers broke off their formation, and Lily watched as they dropped their bombs into an empty field.

"Yes!" Lily shouted to herself as she pumped the air with her fist.

Tears streamed down her face as Lily allowed herself to purge the pent-up emotions. She cried liberally as she guided her plane back to seven thousand feet.

While she wished that she had at least been the first woman ever to shoot down an enemy plane, Lily was contented that she had not failed in her mission to drive the enemy away. She looked down at the lightless city and wondered how many people she had just saved.

*I hope you're proud,* Lily spoke inwardly to her father, and then blew a kiss to the picture of her mother and brother. Even though they were miles away from this danger, Lily knew she was playing a part in protecting them, and that meant everything to her.

Suddenly, an explosion in the sky erupted over another sector. Glancing down at her map, Lily tried to determine who it was, and she prayed that it was the enemy and not a comrade.

"Valeria," Lily spoke aloud once she realized who it was.

Glancing at her fuel gauge, Lily recognized that it was time to land, which she was more than eager to do. She was desperate for news on Valeria, and Lily feared the worst.

With the dull glow of hooded flares on the runway, Lily landed safely and jumped out of the plane to find that nearly the entire airfield crew, including all the men and Major Kazarinova, were huddling around something in a corner.

They were chatting lively and hugging each other, and Lily's heart shattered. She didn't know if she could stomach the death of a comrade on the first night.

Pushing her way to the center of the circle, Lily was surprised to find Valeria sitting on a chair with a bright smile.

"Thank goodness!" Lily ran over to her and embraced her.

Lily found her reaction odd, given that she and Valeria were barely acquaintances. Still, they were fighting for a common goal against a common enemy. Any loss of life was detrimental to morale.

"I have to say, I'm a little offended," Valeria laughed as she spoke. "Everyone saw the explosion and assumed that I was dead."

"Wait!" Lily stood back as she held up her finger. "Do you know what this means?"

"She's the first woman in history to shoot down an enemy plane." Major Kazarinova nodded her approval.

A cheer erupted from everyone surrounding her, and many leaned forward to pat Valeria on the back.

"But the enemy won't stop," Major Kazarinova said, returning to a serious demeanor. "Let's remain vigilant. Next group, get to your fighters."

# Chapter Eleven
# Hell

*"I hate war as only a soldier who has lived it can, only as one who has seen its brutality, its stupidity."*

General Dwight D. Eisenhower

<u>August 23, 1942</u>

*My dearest and sweetest Lily,* Nadia began in her letter. Lily smiled at the charming opening.

She was sitting in the cockpit of her plane early in the morning, waiting to be called into action at any moment, and decided to take the opportunity to catch up on some correspondence.

*This is a long letter, but please be patient. It is worth the read. I promise you!*

*You may have heard of the night bomber's recent success, but we started off rather poorly, and, as much as it pains me to admit this, embarrassingly.*

*On our first, yes, the first, trip to our new base, we were attacked! We had been enjoying our leisurely trip, watching the beautiful blankets of snow passing below us, the bright orange sun against a light blue sky, and Marina's pleasant chatter over the plane's intercom.*

*Me and Marina are on the same plane, you see. I'm the navigator, and she's the pilot. We argued about who should be the pilot, but, oh dear, I'm rambling and you're not here to stop me.*

*As I was saying, we were leisurely heading toward our new base when, out of nowhere, two fighter planes were spotted above us and from the rear.*

*It pains me, Lily, pains me to say this, but we scattered. In an instant, our formation was broken up.*

*Marina piloted us skillfully, bringing us very low to the ground, scaring some horses in a field nearby while doing so, when the enemy planes passed overhead without firing off a single shot.*

*We were stunned! We couldn't understand why the enemy had ignored us. If they had shot at us, we would've become one with the snowbanks in an instant.*

*We arrived at our new base and immediately reported the enemy activity when we were agonizingly advised that the* 'enemy' planes were, in fact, our escorts who had decided to play a little trick on us.

Needless to say, the men with lesser opinions of women, which is essentially all of them, considered their prejudice justified.

You should've seen how much that upset Larisa. I've never seen a woman more impassioned with proving herself. Well, besides you, that is.

Still, we proved them wrong! Very wrong!

You've likely already heard, but the Germans have begun to refer to us as the 'night witches.' They've even invented stories that we perform magic, or take special chemicals to make us see better at night.

The superior, more expensive bombers are piloted by the men, while we're left to use the Po-2s as bombers. The little planes can barely make it off the ground with the bombs strapped to their wings. It takes Marina all her strength to pull back on the lever to get us airborne. It's moments like that I'm glad I lost the argument about becoming the pilot. I don't think I could muster the strength. She's not supposed to smoke while we fly, but she still does. I shouldn't have written that. They monitor all correspondence. I shouldn't have written that, either.

Still, what our superiors intended for ill, we turned around for good. As you're aware, our little planes have a max speed of one hundred kilometers an hour. This, as it happens, is the stalling speed of the swift German fighters. Catching us has become a nightmare for them.

I don't think I shall ever tire of the exhilaration of our bombing runs. At night, in complete darkness, we climb to a certain altitude, and then cut the power. We glide down to our target silently before releasing the payload.

It's tough trusting in your instruments. There were a good number of times I was certain we were about to crash into the ground, but the instruments said otherwise.

Apparently, the whooshing of our planes as we glide by has given the Germans the impression that we're on brooms, thus the prestigious title of 'night witches'.

But, my sweet and adorable Lily, there is little in this life that matches the feeling of hitting a target. When the bomb drops and lands squarely on its mark, spreading fire and destruction to the enemy, I feel like I'm fighting for my family. I keep the broach they gave me close by, and I imagine they're with me in that cramped navigator's seat.

Regardless of our efforts, few men here respect us. Our accommodation is an old cow shed while the men are secured in underground bunkers. We got rid of the smell of the previous inhabitants as best as we could, but Larisa still claims she can detect traces of cow feces. I'm convinced she's the source of the smell. In either case, the men have taken to calling our little shed the 'Inn of the Flying Cow.' Humorous, I'll admit, but hurtful, nonetheless. We're gaining their respect slowly, but at least we have the respect of the enemy. We've become such a nuisance that they're awarding medals to anyone who can shoot us down.

Sadly, they are occasionally successful. I'll never become accustomed to the feeling of losing a friend. I thought I would be numb by now, but it still feels fresh, like opening an old wound. We lost another two girls last night. Luba and Vera. They were behind me and Marina on our sortie, and after we dropped our bomb, the Germans threw on the searchlights. They opened fire with their anti-aircraft guns, and the shrapnel tore through their plane. Some locals found them the next morning, but it was too late. They had bled to death from their wounds. I can't imagine that would be a good way to go.

The Fascists, being the barbarians that they are, stripped the bodies of everything useful and left them lying in the field. If not for the locals, I think they would still be there. The villagers cleaned the bodies and washed them before offering a proper burial. They knew that they were heroes.

I do feel a touch bad, though. I used to get snarky with Luba. She was so strict about our bunks being tidy. Marina would *make a remark under her breath, which I would then take great pleasure in repeating so Luba heard. It was petty, and I hate that we resented her for simply trying to do her job.*

*It provides perspective. Death, that is. There are so many silly things I've attached myself to in this life, and then I realize how trivial they are. I seem to never fully learn that lesson, but I hope to before this war is over.*

*Oh! Marina was promoted! She's a lieutenant now! Poor thing was beside herself with doubt about her leadership capabilities. We all knew she could do it. The problem is, we're all very close, and while we have a hierarchy and rank, socially, these titles fall away. We've made a pact that, while the men are around, we address the women in position over us with their proper title. We can't let the men in on our secret of simply getting along and achieving a unified goal. The world would delve into chaos if men became aware of our gifts.*

*As always, you have my love.*

*Nadia.*

"What a sweet woman," Lily spoke to herself before muttering, "And somehow just as exhausting in her letters as she is in person. I miss her."

Rubbing her eyes and yawning, Lily kicked her feet out the side of the cockpit as she drew a deep breath. She knew that at any moment she would be called into action, but she found the waiting in between combat tiresome. It forced her to think about her mother and brother, and Lily could scarcely bring herself to contemplate their fate.

Part of her was certain that the worst had come to pass for them. Every day, letters for other women or men at the airfield arrived, breaking the horrible news that their families had perished or been captured by the Germans, and Lily's heart skipped a beat each time she received a letter.

*Dearest Mother,*

Lily began in a letter.

*I'm writing to you from the cockpit of my plane. I'm awaiting to be called into action at any moment. The Yak-1* planes are incredible, and don't worry, they're much warmer than the Po-2s. The canopy in the Yak-1 retains a lot of warmth. Still, I could use some better gloves, and maybe a scarf or two if you could send them. Also, I need a book for writing. I would like to jot down my experiences here.

I have yet to shoot down an enemy plane, which is frustrating. I've been in a handful of skirmishes, but most of my combat has been during the night, and it's incredibly difficult to see anything, let alone the enemy.

If you could kindly send a picture of father, that would be appreciated. I don't really know how to describe it, but sometimes I feel that while I'm flying, I'm closer to him.

The reports out of Stalingrad are rather abysmal. Apparently, there's no food, and some have turned to eating clay. A mother reported that she was filtering the clumps of clay, throwing away the stuff covered in blood, and giving it to her children. There's nothing else for them to eat. Those poor souls.

"I told you she was here!" a shout came from in the hangar, and Lily glanced to see Katya and the rest of the squadron rushing toward their planes.

"What's the target?" Lily asked as she set her letter aside and sat upright while strapping on her helmet.

"Cover for our troops!" Katya shouted back as she hastily climbed into her plane. "A panzer column has reached the north of Stalingrad."

Lily's heart climbed into her throat as she fastened her gloves, put on her goggles, checked over her instruments, and blew a kiss at the photo of her mother and brother.

The signal was raised, and Lily pressed forward on the throttle as she taxied to the runway. As soon as her plane had left the hangar, Lily noticed smoke rising from the other side of the Volga River. The enemy attack had already begun.

As soon as the squadron was in the air, Lily noticed that they were not alone. To their right, she spotted a squadron of bombers, and Lily wondered if some of her friends were among them.

"We're going to strafe the enemy ground formations," Olga called into her headset. "We need to be low, about two or three hundred feet. We'll go in pairs. Katya and Lily, you two will take the first pass."

Lily tried to calm herself as she and Katya drew their planes closer together, but her heart was racing, her mouth suddenly turned dry, and her hands and face began to tingle. It was one thing to fly at night when the enemy couldn't spot her, but to be so exposed in the day was unnerving.

Then, distracting Lily was the unexpected singing of a patriotic Soviet song. At first, Lily thought she had intercepted a radio transmission, but when she glanced over at Katya, she realized the source. Katya, using the full range of her voice, was singing loudly and proudly without reservation.

"It looks like the river is on fire," Katya ceased singing as she spoke over the headset, and Lily glanced down at the approaching shore.

"It is on fire. Must be from an oil spill," Lily replied. "The whole city is burning, too."

"There are boats not far from the fire. Looks like they're being loaded with civilians."

"I'm glad they're getting out." Lily felt a measure of relief for their suffering, but it was short-lived when she noticed an array of black dots in the sky.

"I see them, too," Katya spoke, and Lily glanced over to see she was looking in the same direction.

"Should we intercept?" Lily asked.

"Negative," Olga interjected. "Our orders are to attack the enemy ground formations."

"Those are bombers," Katya replied. "They're heading straight toward the transports."

"If the ground troops take Stalingrad, then everything will be lost," Olga explained.

"We should protect the civilians," Lily pressed.

"We have our orders. The bombers are going to attack military targets before they strike at civilians."

*What targets? The whole city is ablaze*, Lily thought, but in the back of her mind, she was worried about the people below. She was nearly one thousand yards from the shore, and she could see that the transports were being loaded with civilians carrying whatever goods they could while also holding their children.

"Let's proceed," Katya continued. "Lowering altitude."

"Confirmed." Lily followed suit as she and Katya descended to about three hundred feet.

"Are those fish?" Katya asked with disgust, and Lily looked down at the river to see thousands of floating scaly bodies with wide eyes staring back up at her.

"The oil probably killed them."

Suddenly, bullets pinged and ricocheted off Lily's plane.

"Who is shooting at us?!" Lily shouted.

"It's our own men!" Katya yelled back. "Tip your wings so they can see the red star."

Swiftly, Lily turned her plane, displaying the bright red star to their comrades down below, and the firing stopped shortly.

"They're trying to protect the transports. They're likely terrified."

"Let's go to two hundred feet." Lily glanced at her altitude. "We're too high."

"Two hundred feet." Katya nodded in her agreement, and they both descended again.

Staying dangerously close to the ground, the two women scanned the horizon for enemy troop formations.

"There, one o'clock!" Lily pointed toward a battalion that was rushing into the city.

The Nazis were entering a heavily destroyed part of Stalingrad, where Lily noticed there were hundreds of civilians fleeing toward the river.

At once, the Soviets opened fire on the Germans, who sought cover among the rubble. Without regard for the sanctity of life, the Nazis began firing back indiscriminately, killing, maiming, and wounding the civilians who were merely trying to flee.

A rotting, painful pit formed in Lily's stomach as she couldn't understand the inhumanity she was witnessing. Lily's heart was wrenched out of her chest as she watched a mother curl up in the middle of the road and cover her baby. The mother had nowhere to go, nowhere to turn, and Lily pushed the throttle to hurry to her rescue.

"I see them!" Katya confirmed, and, without another word, the two acted as one as they pointed the noses of their planes almost straight up into the air.

They ascended quickly, and Lily glanced down at the German troops, glad that they paid little attention to them in the chaos.

Explosions rocketed the little pocket of the city, bullets fired back and forth, bursts of pinks and reds could be seen as grenades or mines turned men into dust, and blood was splattered against the walls of freshly destroyed houses.

Then, at one thousand feet, Lily and Katya leveled out before beginning their descent.

Lily's heart raced as the earth drew closer and closer with each passing second. Taking off the safety, Lily steadied her finger over the trigger.

Lily had never taken a life before, and even though these were enemy troops rushing into the city, they were people. These were brothers, fathers, sons, uncles, and friends.

"Good!" Lily spoke aloud when she noticed the mother and baby were still alive and crawling along the road to escape the danger.

But whatever inhibition Lily felt toward killing the Germans vanished when she watched an advancing Nazi soldier deliberately rush over to the mother, where he put his gun to her head and pulled the trigger.

"No!" Lily screamed as the soldier then pointed his weapon at the child before offering it the same fate.

With a rage unlike anything Lily had felt before, she unleashed a spray of cannon and machine gun fire.

Dirt flew into the air from her and Katya's unleashing of their weaponry, obscuring Lily's view.

"Pull up!" Katya shouted, and Lily pulled back on the throttle.

"Did we hit any of them?" Lily asked as she looked down at the ground.

"I don't think so, but we gave them a proper scare."

"Let's make another pass!"

"Two fighters at a time, remember?" Katya shook her head. "The others are making their pass as we speak. There are other formations ahead. Let's attack them."

"Agreed." Lily nodded.

Yet as they flew over the city in pursuit of other pockets of Germans invading the city, Lily's heart took another blow.

Hundreds of bodies were scattered about, lying in the dirt or among the rubble. No one was able to approach and bury them. She assumed they had been killed by previous bombing runs or by the enemy entering the city. Whatever the case, a hatred arose in Lily's heart for the Nazis for this indiscriminate and cold-blooded murder.

"Two o'clock." Katya pointed at a group of about thirty to forty Nazis entering the industrial section of the city.

Again, the two immediately pointed the noses of their planes in the air and began their ascent.

This time, however, Lily noticed that the Germans didn't meet any resistance and they would likely fire upon the two women.

Regardless, Lily was eager to avenge the innocents cut down so cruelly and mercilessly.

They began their approach again, and, as Lily expected, the enemy began firing at their planes.

A bullet cracked Lily's windshield on the right side, another embedded itself in her left wing. She could scarcely see past the little explosions of light from bullets hitting against the metal of her plane, she could barely hear Katya in her headset begging her to disengage, and she could hardly contain her rage as she opened fire.

Pulling up just in time, Lily glanced behind her in dismay to find that she hadn't killed anyone. They had all hid among the rubble or inside destroyed homes. Still, Lily was pleased she had been somewhat effective in delaying them a measure as she watched Soviet reinforcements rushing to meet the Nazis.

"Check your fuel." Katya reminded, and Lily glanced over at her to see that black smoke was bellowing out of Katya's engine.

"Don't worry about that! You've taken a hit!" Lily pointed.

"Really?" Katya replied sarcastically.

"I have just enough to make it back to base." Lily checked her fuel.

"Let's head back and refuel. I'll see if they can fix my plane so I can make another sortie with you."

"The bombers!" Lily pointed as they turned back toward their base. "They're heading toward the transports."

"We can't interfere!" Katya shouted.

"Damn the orders!" Lily screamed.

"They're too close now. If we hit them from above, we run the risk of missing and hitting the civilians."

"We can't just watch!"

"We don't have enough fuel as it is!"

"We can land in the field or something!"

"There's too many of them. What's the point of us throwing away our own lives? We're more useful alive than dead. We can come back and hit them again, or we can die here trying in vain."

Lily's lips trembled as she watched, in horror, as Nazis bombers unleashed their payload on the civilian transports. The Soviet soldiers, in a desperate act of heroism, used their own bodies in an attempt to shield those they were protecting.

But it was of little use as bomb upon bomb was dropped on the transports. Soon, the river that had been filled with dead fish and black oil was now swollen with the remains of the dead innocent.

Legs, feet, hands, and heads bobbed beside the bodies of those whose only care in the world was to live in peace and quiet.

Removing her mask, Lily screamed into her cockpit as she wept openly. It was too much for her to bear. She couldn't handle the depravity, the immorality. She couldn't stomach the thought of all those poor people dying needlessly. She didn't understand the rationale of the Nazis murdering the children trying to flee or mothers protecting their babies. It was heartless, callous.

"Lily," Katya called, and Lily glanced over at her as they sped away from the city. "We did what we could. It's not your fault. We'll make the Nazis pay. I promise."

# Chapter Twelve
# The Regiment of Men

*"The best way to keep a prisoner from escaping is to make sure he never knows he is in prison."*

Fyodor Dostoevsky

<u>September 5, 1942, near Stalingrad.</u>

It was late in the night when Lily and Katya approached the runway of their new airbase. For their particular skill in piloting and combat, they had been assigned to the men's 73 Guards Fighter Aviation Regiment.

The assignment was an extraordinary privilege, and Lily was confident that she could play an integral role in this new regiment. Although she didn't relish the idea of being away from the friendships she had formed with the other women, she was eternally thankful that Katya, at least, had also been assigned with her.

The airfield had been hastily made and well camouflaged. If not for the coordinates provided earlier that day through a coded message, Lily would've never found the base.

The runway had been built in two days, and Lily was advised that they were using concrete slabs that were laid down in a honeycomb style. So, when a portion of the runway was damaged, it could easily be taken away for repairs or replaced. It was a tribute to the ingenuity of those of a collective mind, mostly women, who were passionate about defending their country.

Landing and parking the plane in the designated area in a row of about twenty other planes, Lily climbed onto the wing when a mechanic, eager to begin the inspections, bent down under the plane.

Slowly, Lily sat on the wing before leaping onto the ground. Without the availability of a suitcase, or any room in the plane for most of her belongings, Lily found the best solution was to wear most of her clothes. With three pairs of socks, her summer dress underneath overalls, a light jacket underneath a sheepskin jacket, and two pairs of gloves, Lily felt almost as silly as she had when they first tried on their uniforms during their initial training.

"She's in good condition," Lily spoke to the mechanic, who had his back to her.

"I'll be the judge of that," a high, sweet voice replied, causing Lily to narrow her gaze.

Trying to be discreet, Lily leaned over to get a glimpse of the mechanic who was now checking the wheels. The mechanic was wearing thick overalls, large gloves, and a cap, but Lily was convinced she had heard a feminine voice.

The mechanic, growing aware of Lily's gaze, turned suddenly toward her.

"Oh, you're a woman!" Lily spoke aloud and was entirely grateful that it was dark enough to hide the blushing in her cheeks.

"I'm glad you can still tell," she replied sarcastically.

"Sorry." Lily swallowed as she watched Katya's plane being taxied. "I'm—" she cleared her throat "—I'm from the women's fighter regiment. 586th Regiment, to be specific. I've been assigned to the men's regiment."

"And women can't be engineers?" the mechanic asked with annoyance when she stood and wiped the oil off her hands with a cloth that was so dirty, Lily wondered what the purpose of it was.

"That's not what I meant." Lily felt her shoulders tightening and thought she preferred to be shot at by the enemy than to endure this encounter any longer.

"Then what did you mean?" she crossed her arms and stared at Lily unreservedly.

"Well..." Lily paused as she thought. "I—"

"What's this, by the way?" the mechanic tapped the side of the plane where a large number three was painted in white.

"It's my signature." Lily tried to sound confident but felt that she had merely proved herself as inadequate.

"Signature?" the mechanic scoffed. "So the enemy can find you easier?"

"No, it's—"

"I'm torturing you for sport." The mechanic grinned before extending her still-oily hand in greeting. "I'm Sergeant Pasportnikova. But you can call me Ina."

"Ina." Lily shook her hand with relief but regretted it for the remnants that were now stuck to her skin.

"There aren't many of us women engineers." Ina leaned against the plane as Katya approached them. "I don't blame you for the confusion."

"Katya, this is Ina. Ina, this is Katya." Lily introduced them.

"Nice to meet you." Katya nodded formally. "I'm excited to be part of this regiment and to fly as soon as possible."

Ina offered a slow and mocking chuckle as she grinned at both Katya and Lily before stating, "Good luck with that. The last two women didn't last a day. I imagine you'll be back with your previous regiments shortly."

"I don't understand." Lily frowned as she glanced at Katya for the confusion. "We were sent here to fight."

"And Colonel Baranov will send you back." Ina shrugged coldly.

"Surely he's seen our logbooks." Lily threw her hands onto her hips.

"We must be able to speak with him." Katya shared in Lily's offense. "I'm positive we can sort out anything that he—"

"He won't give you the time." Ina shook her head. "Regardless, why don't you follow me to meet your new team. Then I'll show you where we women sleep. It will be nice to have another female around."

"Another? You've been here by yourself?" Lily asked with surprise. "For how long?"

"You don't remember me, do you?" Ina squinted at Lily.

"Remember you from where?" Lily glanced at Katya, who seemed to be just as lost.

"Typical fighters. You think you're better than the rest of us?" Ina crossed her arms as she grew incensed.

"I don't think that's fair." Lily again glanced at Katya, wondering how to escape from this discomfort.

"Lily, I was with you during training." Ina tilted her head in annoyance.

"Oh…" Lily clicked her tongue, wondering if she was merely torturing her for sport again or if she was being genuine. Regardless, she had no memory of her at all.

"We ran in different circles." Ina grinned as she dismissed Lily's worry. "Only reason I knew who you were is because I checked the logs before you arrived. You were popular during training. I wasn't."

"Popular?" Lily scoffed. "I don't remember being well-liked, especially not by the instructors."

"Because you were too good." Ina raised her eyebrows before adding, "Lieutenant Dobkin finally saw the worth of a woman in the end. I think."

Neither Katya nor Lily replied, and Lily assumed her wing mate was just as desperate to rest her eyes as she was.

"So, why is the number three your signature?" Ina continued.

"If you recall when I bested Lieutenant Dobkin, I was third in the air that day." Lily rubbed the back of her neck, feeling foolish. "I took it as part of being lucky. The plane is my Troika."

"Hopefully, your luck continues." Ina nodded for them to follow her. "Actually, if you are lucky, the colonel will send you away from here. Many take off from that runway but few return. Luck would steer you elsewhere."

The women left the strip beside the hangar and began walking to the entrance of an underground bunker that was barely visible in the dark. If not for a couple lanterns hanging beside the steel-reinforced door, Lily would've never spotted it.

"May I ask how you ended up a mechanic if you were in training with us?" Katya asked as they walked while staring at their feet to make sure they didn't trip over anything in the dark.

"I was beside myself with resentment when I was designated as an engineer," Ina replied quickly. "I'm a good fighter. I probably even rival you, Lily. But I understand the Yak-1 like few people, even the men, truly do. My work is important, even if it isn't glamorous."

"Have you tried to become a fighter here?" Katya asked.

"No!" Ina laughed loudly. "That would never happen. Besides, I'm actually quite enjoying what I do. I'm good at it, and I get to embarrass a few of my male comrades in the meantime."

"I'm glad it's you looking after my plane, then." Lily glanced at Katya, but it was difficult to determine her facial expressions in the dark.

"A word of warning - they don't like when women take part in the planning," Ina spoke over her shoulder just before they reached the door. "I tried to offer my strategic input once, and let's just say that it went disappointingly for everyone."

Ina held the door open for Katya and Lily as they walked into the bunker only to find that it was nearly as poorly lit as outside. A couple of shaded bulbs hung from the ceiling, and a group of about ten men were sitting at a table directly under one of the lights.

A map was spread out on the table with different colored pins that Lily assumed were marking objectives or targets, cups and mugs littered the floor, the room smelled of both stale and fresh cigarette smoke, mud had been dragged in from the boots that the men cared little to clean, and Lily loved it.

"Close the door!" a man who was huddled up on the floor in the corner of the room shouted.

He was rocking back and forth and chewing his nails angrily. Lily recalled her father behaving in a similar manner after a nightmare, and in an instant, she was transported back to their apartment in Moscow, watching her father curled up like a little boy and weeping. She recalled the look in his eyes as if he were viewing something terrifying in the distance.

Snapping back to the present, Lily stepped gingerly around another man who had pushed a few chairs together and was fast asleep.

"Take a seat," a man at the table spoke to Lily and Katya without so much as looking in their direction as he stood and walked over to the large potbellied stove in the middle of the room. It was clear to Lily that neither he, nor anyone else, had realized that they were women.

He was a handsome man, Lily thought. At least enough to catch her attention. His hair was thick and wavy, and Lily found herself a touch jealous of how natural it appeared. His eyes were fierce, and yet, they seemed to hide a mischievousness, as if he knew a secret about Lily that she herself wasn't aware of.

"Did you see a parachute?" the man asked as he chucked another log into the stove.

"No, sir," another from the table replied with his head down.

"The intelligence stated five planes," another man interjected as he leaned back and crossed his arms.

"How many did you count?" the man at the stove asked, still unaware of the presence of the women in the bunker, and Lily, surprised by her own behavior, allowed her eyes to linger on his backside for a little longer than was likely appropriate.

"I didn't take an official count, but there must've been thirty."

"The Luftwaffe have complete air superiority." The man at the stove threw his hands into his pockets in dismay. "The counterattack by our comrades on the panzer divisions was catastrophic. The report states that thirty of our tanks were lost, and that was mostly due to the Luftwaffe."

"We need more fighters. Every German we down is replaced with five more."

Listening intently to the men, Lily and Katya walked over to the stove, where they began to warm themselves. Still, the man hadn't noticed them, but Lily understood that he was preoccupied.

"Hopefully this provides our enemy with, at the very least, a false sense of security." The man rubbed the back of his neck.

"How so?" another pilot asked.

"We're going to be changing our tactics," the man replied, and Lily caught the tone of despair in his voice.

Warming up a little in the underground bunker, Lily began removing her jacket. Then, grabbing a chair, Lily sat by the stove and began removing her sheepskin boots and the two pairs of woolen socks overtop her regular socks. Finally, she removed her helmet and goggles and stood again beside the stove.

"Tomorrow we'll have a chance at—" the man stopped abruptly as he locked eyes with Lily, who was staring back at him with as much confidence as she was able to muster.

Even without a mirror to inspect herself, Lily was confident that she appeared striking. The hemmed uniform, she was convinced, accentuated her gifts of nature, and the pistol by her waist seemed to magnify her slender physique.

Curious at the man's sudden ceasing, the rest of the men in the room turned toward him when they, too, spotted Lily, then Katya, and then Ina.

It was an odd encounter, Lily thought, but she had grown more than accustomed to such reactions by male comrades. She wished that such outcomes would be a thing of the past, but the fact remained that their society was largely predicated on defined gender roles.

"I'm Lieutenant Litvyak." Lily extended her hand in greeting with a serious expression. "I'm your new pilot."

The man simply stared back at her with wide eyes, and the silence in the room only seemed to swell before he pointed at her and mentioned, "You have oil on your forehead."

"I do?" Lily touched her forehead quickly, but she didn't feel anything.

"Lieutenant." The man turned to Ina. "Can you show our new pilots to their quarters?"

"Yes, sir." Ina nodded.

Glancing down at the layers of clothes that Lily had recently removed, she knew that it wouldn't be appropriate to argue with her superior the night of the arrival.

Without further thought, the man returned to the table as he began speaking in a hushed tone. The rest of the men leaned in, and Lily understood that her presence had, again, caused a rather exclusive reaction from them.

"Do I have oil on my forehead?" Lily asked Katya quietly as she leaned toward her friend.

"I don't see anything," Katya whispered.

With an unkind glare, Lily looked back at the man who was now smirking at her, and she realized the game he was playing. It was clever, but unkind. He had played upon her vanity, thus reinforcing his bias toward her sex while also making her feel foolish.

"Colonel Baranov would like to see you two in the morning," the man spoke up from the table at Lily and Katya. "Be ready at first light. He'll meet you in the hangar."

*That's a good sign, at least. Right?* Lily wondered as she gathered her jacket, goggles, hat, and socks before following Katya and Ina out of the bunker.

"I'm surprised you didn't speak your mind," Katya muttered to Lily.

Lily didn't reply as they walked back across the field. She didn't know what to say, really. She imagined she was merely tired and prayed that was the only reason for her reservedness. The man was rather handsome, but never had anyone caused Lily to become speechless.

*You're just tired,* Lily thought as she shook it off.

"Where are our quarters?" Katya asked as she shivered.

"Just there." Ina pointed to a smaller bunker, which was guarded by a sentry.

"You have your own personal guard?" Katya asked in surprise.

"He's there to protect us in case the Germans arrive, but, really, it's to discourage the men who may be missing the 'comfort' of a woman."

The distinct popping of gunfire echoed in the distance, and all three women looked in the direction. In the dark of the night, they could see the tracers from bullets firing back and forth.

"I'll have to get used to sleeping through that noise." Katya tried to sound chipper, but Lily sensed she was nervous.

"It's not noise. That's the sound of our people dying," Ina replied somberly. "That's the sound of innocent men,

169

women, and children being gunned down like they're merely rodents for extermination."

Lily and Katya glanced at each other in the darkness, and she sensed that sleep would evade them permanently. Each crack of gunfire set Lily into a rage. She hated hearing the shots, knowing, as Ina put it, that the Nazis were showing no discrimination for who they gunned down. She remembered the mother and her baby who had been shot so callously by the soldier in Stalingrad, but she shook her head to rid her mind of such terrible images.

"Evening," Ina spoke politely to the sentry, who offered a lingering gaze back that he struggled to keep hidden before he examined Lily and Katya's papers closely.

Entering the bunker, which was of a simpler design, Lily and Katya once again began removing the layers as they inspected their new quarters.

Quickly constructed with concrete, the bunker was quiet but warm. There were two rooms and a main area that had a plain cot. Still, Lily found the space much to her liking. She had shared a schoolroom with more women than she cared to spend that much time with in close quarters, and to have an inkling of privacy restored was welcome indeed.

"It's not much." Ina shivered as she began throwing wood into the stove. "But the stove does well in keeping it warm. I've taken the room on the left for my own. You two can decide your sleeping arrangements."

"So, you and the sentry?" Katya asked, and Lily was glad she had also picked up on the subtleties.

"What?" Ina glanced up sharply as she sat on a chair near the stove and began pulling off her boots. "What sentry?"

"Oh, come on!" Katya chuckled as she grabbed a chair and sat close to Ina, who, Lily noticed, was less than comfortable with the proximity.

"You're alone in this little bunker all by yourself while a handsome young man stands guard?" Lily also grabbed a chair and sat on the other side of Ina with a large grin.

"I'm barely here!" Ina grumbled as she stood and rushed her boots over to the entryway.

"And you've never taken pity on the poor man left to the cold all by himself?" Katya pressed, and Lily sensed she was desperate for a captivating diversion.

Ina glanced between the two girls as she shuffled her jaw while removing her jacket before stating, "I've let him stand in the entryway on particularly cold nights."

"Was that for his warmth or yours?" Lily chuckled, and Katya joined in the amusement.

"It's late." Ina tried to restrain her smile.

"Better call him inside, then," Katya giggled.

"I'll stand guard instead." Lily snorted.

"We're due early in the morning," Ina continued, undeterred by the mockery.

"Maybe you're due in nine months?" Katya asked as she grinned at Lily.

"Don't make me enjoy watching the colonel dismiss you tomorrow." Ina offered a warning look.

"Sorry, I tend to get carried away." Katya offered an apologetic look but still couldn't restrain her amusement at Ina's expense.

Ina paused for a moment as she stared at the floor before muttering, "So can he."

Both Katya and Lily's mouths dropped open at the admission, and they turned to each other in excitement for the juicy gossip.

"Goodnight!" Ina shouted as she walked toward her room.

"What was it like?!" Katya chased after Ina.

"Katya! Leave her!" Lily yelled, but it was too late, her friend was already hounding at the heels of the poor mechanic.

"Get out of my room!" Ina yelled as Katya forced entry.

Lily chuckled to herself as she sat alone in the main area, half catching the muffled whispers from Ina and Katya.

It was then that Lily noticed this was the first time she had been alone since, well, she couldn't remember when. She had been alone in her plane many times, but being alone here, in the dim bunker with the only light coming from the stove in the center of the room and a dull orange bulb overhead, felt suffocating.

The image of the Nazi soldier executing the mother and baby in Stalingrad flashed before Lily's eyes. But then the memory morphed into something entirely more personal, and the face of the woman on the ground took on that of her mother's while the infant became Yuri.

"Stop that!" Lily grumbled at herself, annoyed at how cruelly the vision had sprung upon her.

Jumping up from the chair, Lily sped over to Ina's room to join in the gossip of forbidden love, and hopefully distract herself from such awful images.

# Chapter Thirteen
# Clipped Wings

*"Whoever battles monsters should see to it that in the process he does not become a monster himself. And when you look long into the abyss, the abyss also looks into you."*

Friedrich Nietzsche

Tired yet eager, Lily stood with Katya near their planes as they waited for the colonel and the rest of the pilots early in the morning. Ina, Lily noticed, had awoken before either of them and was already prepping the planes when they arrived at the hangar.

Black smoke rose on the horizon, and little pops and booms from gunfire and explosions echoed in the distance. It was harrowing to be so close to so much death and destruction and yet be so helpless against it. Lily prayed that she would never get used to such a sight.

"What time is it?" Lily asked with a yawn as she leaned against the wing of her plane with the bright white three painted on the side.

"Early," Katya replied dryly as she stared at the concrete at her feet. "Too early. But, yet again, it is the women who are the punctual ones while we wait for the men."

"Here's one man, at least." Lily nodded to a pilot who was approaching a hard-at-work Ina.

The man, Lily noticed, seemed to be more interested in the mechanic, but not from any amorous pursuit. Even from a distance, she deciphered his untrusting gaze.

After a minute or two, Ina also noticed his unkind stare and began to question him. Lily wished that she was close enough to hear the conversation, but she supposed it wasn't necessary, given the body language of the male pilot.

"Does she need our help?" Katya asked.

"I don't know." Lily shook her head. "She doesn't seem too upset."

With a quick shake of his head, the pilot stormed angrily out of the hangar, and Ina, in a startling fit of rage, spit on the ground behind him before walking over to Lily and Katya.

"What was that about?" Lily asked with concern.

"He's refusing to use the plane I worked on!" Ina patted Lily's plane.

"He was going to fly my plane?" Lily squinted in confusion. "Why wouldn't I be flying it?"

"He's going to collect the head mechanic to make him double-check my work." Ina ignored Lily's question as she offered another generous spit in the direction of the pilot.

"Really?" Katya shot her head back before asking nervously, "Do you have a poor track record?"

"My record is perfect." Ina raised a stern finger in defense.

"Then what's the issue?" Lily asked but felt as if she already knew the answer.

"I think we all know what the issue is." Ina offered them a discerning look.

"Is the colonel usually late?" Katya glanced at the clock on the hangar wall. "The man in the bunker last night mentioned that the colonel wanted to meet with us at first light."

"They were discussing strategy." Ina drew a deep breath, and Lily noticed she was rather distraught by the pilot's rejection of her work.

"Why would they discuss tactics without us? Wouldn't it be best if we also knew?" Katya frowned.

Suddenly, a door near the hangar opened, and a shorter, older man with a scruffy, well-worn uniform approached them with a limp.

"Who is that?" Katya asked.

"He's the head mechanic. Very nice man." Ina explained as she awaited his approach.

"Ina, my girl," the man began as he removed his hat to scratch his head, which Lily noticed was struggling to hold onto the hair that remained. "Listen, we have a problem."

"He won't use the plane I inspected?" Ina asked rhetorically.

"He's insisting that I inspect the plane as well. I told him that I usually get you to double-check my work, but he wasn't convinced." The man looked embarrassed to be passing along the information.

"I understand." Ina nodded, but Lily sensed she was hurt.

"You're the best mechanic and engineer we have." The man let his hands slap against his thighs in frustration. "I don't know what else to say."

"Thank you, sir." Ina nodded.

"At ease, or whatever." The man rolled his hand nonchalantly as he glanced quickly at Lily and Katya, almost as if he didn't realize there were two other women standing beside Ina, and she had somehow multiplied.

"I'll see what I can do." The man limped toward Lily's plane.

"The men are coming." Katya nodded, and Lily looked in the direction of the bunker, where she noticed a man of rank, likely the colonel, with his arm around another pilot who was laughing loudly.

The man laughing, Lily recognized, was the same man who was in the bunker the previous night holding the debriefing. He appeared rather familiar with the colonel, who was a tall, slender man that she assumed was approaching his mid-forties.

"They seem to be in good spirits," Lily muttered before she and Katya stood at attention, wanting to impress the colonel.

Without a word or even a glance of acknowledgement, the colonel strode past the ladies while he continued to laugh. The man from the bunker, however, offered Lily a patronizing wink, which she did not appreciate. It wasn't an attempt at seduction, at least she hoped not, despite the fact that he was strikingly handsome, but it carried an unbearably demeaning implication that these two women were far from his equals.

"Did he not see us?" Katya asked Lily quietly as the men began jumping into the planes. The man from the bunker jumped into Lily's number three.

"Excuse me!" Lily rushed over to him. "That's my plane!"

"I appreciate you ferrying it here for me." The man looked about the console before tossing out the stitched white lily, and her mouth fell open in shock at his disregard.

"I'm not a ferry pilot!" Lily growled.

"You're cute." The man grinned at her, and there was a certain swagger in his grin that inexplicably disarmed Lily.

Caught off guard by her own bewildering inaction, Lily simply crossed her arms and stared up at him, dumbfounded.

"I'm Captain Alexei Solomatin." He nodded at her before securing his parachute and double-checking the instruments.

Lily was beside herself with indignation that he didn't even conceive of asking what her name was. Again, she found his demeaning opinion of her less than ideal, and the handsomeness he embodied lessened each time he opened his mouth.

Before Lily or Katya could make requisition, the airfield was drowned in activity. Planes began taking off the runway one after the other, and Lily watched with a terrible sinking feeling in her gut as her number three left the ground and was airborne in the squadron.

"It couldn't have been a mistake," Lily spoke softly as the sound of the planes drew distant when they headed toward Stalingrad.

"He asked us to meet him here this morning." Katya nodded as she recalled. "The colonel intentionally ignored us."

"What should we do?" Lily felt a hopelessness sinking into her spirit.

"I, for one, am not going down easy." Katya turned to Lily with a strong gaze of determination. "I didn't come here just to be sent away. Ina?"

"Yes?" Ina asked almost with surprise at Katya's fierceness.

"Show us how to be useful." Katya threw her hands onto her hips.

"Um, yeah, alright." Ina drew a deep breath. "The planes will be back in thirty minutes. They will need to be refueled and rearmed. There are already others to complete that task, but they're swamped, and it would be a benefit to everyone if you prepared the ammunition."

"Where is it?" Katya demanded as she looked around the hangar but spotted an area before Ina could answer and asked rhetorically, "It's over there?"

"Use the trolleys," Ina called after them. "Otherwise, you'll put your back out. Then you won't ever fly here."

"Come, Lily!" Katya shouted angrily, and Lily hurried after her comrade.

"I think we should request a formal meeting," Lily mentioned as she caught up to Katya.

"How many aircraft took off? Do you remember?" Katya asked angrily.

"Eight."

"We can fit, let's see, two per trolly." Katya rubbed her chin as she calculated, and Lily was impressed with how determined she was to take control of the situation.

"I still think we should discuss this civilly with the colonel." Lily grunted as she lifted the heavy ammo casing onto the trolley.

"I think we're past being civil."

"He has a lot to think about." Lily glanced in the direction of Stalingrad as the black smoke still rose steadily toward the sky.

"I suppose," Katya muttered.

"He's from an older generation, too. Lieutenant Dobkin came around in due time. I'm sure if the colonel can see how well we fly, then he'll be more than eager to employ our skills." Lily looked at the large ammo casings on the trolley.

"Maybe." Katya continued in her pessimism.

In quiet determination, the two ladies soon had the trolleys loaded with ammunition and began wheeling them back to the designated area for the planes when Lily spotted a formation flying in their direction.

"I see them." Katya also took note. "How many do you count? I only see seven."

"Better not be my plane that was lost!" Lily grumbled but instantly felt guilty as she realized she cared more about the plane than the life of the pilot who likely had perished.

Still, Lily's nerves were on edge as she watched the planes land one by one until, finally, her number three was safely down, and Alexei climbed out. She hated how he made her feel. Her firm resolve turned wobbly and her confidence retreated. Their last two interactions had caused her to stumble onto her back foot, and Lily was certain that would be the last of such nonsense.

Quickly, Lily and Katya wheeled the trolleys to the engineers and mechanics, who outfitted the planes and refueled them.

"Come." Katya tapped Lily's shoulder as she pointed to where the pilots were gathering around a table inside the hangar.

Approaching the men, Lily and Katya came within a few feet of them, where Lily noticed they were studying a map.

"Where did he go down?" the colonel asked as he circled his finger on an area near the north of Stalingrad.

"About here." Alexei pointed. "No parachute."

"Damn!" the colonel pounded his fist on the table, and Lily understood that the loss of the pilot bothered him greatly.

"These tactics aren't working," another pilot interjected.

"We've only just begun implementing them." The colonel leaned over the map with a dejected countenance.

Lily was eager to learn what new tactics they were employing but knew now was not the time to interrupt.

"It's throwing the enemy off." Alexei shrugged. "They're used to us going after certain targets and forming defensive circles. They don't know how to counter our current methods. They were lucky. That's all."

"Hmm," Colonel Baranov sighed. "In either case, we'll need a pilot to replace our fallen comrade."

"What about her." Alexei crossed his arms as he examined Lily with a peculiar smile.

"This is not the time for joking." The colonel glared at Alexei. "Take someone from the night shift."

"They'll be exhausted." Alexei shook his head.

"We're good pilots, sir," Lily raised her voice, taking advantage of the situation.

"Good pilots die." The colonel stared at her, paying particular attention to the flower in her cap. "I need fighters. I need men. The Germans are only two miles from the center of Stalingrad. If some strange bout of luck doesn't come our way, we will lose the city before the winter."

"I've been known as lucky, sir," Lily continued.

The colonel took a few steps towards her as he glared at her with unrelenting malice before beginning as he nearly shook. "I've lost more men in the last few weeks than the entire war. I've lost friends, good pilots, and some men who were here for such a short time I didn't even get the chance to learn their names!"

"Have you reviewed our flight records, sir?" Katya asked as she stood tall and proud.

"Of course I have!" Colonel Baranov shouted as he came closer to her before continuing his monologue, "They're impressive, without doubt, but I don't need impressive fliers. I need fighters! I need men of war! The women regiments did an excellent job protecting railways or bombing strategic targets, but this is Stalingrad. There is no equal to this hell. We are free hunters here; do you know what that means?"

Neither Lily nor Katya replied. They were aware that his question was rhetorical.

"We are an elite guard that fights in pairs. We are free to hunt down any target we perceive as vulnerable, and I cannot risk pairing one of my men with an irrational woman who will panic at the first sign of danger!" Colonel Baranov's face beamed red with anger, and Lily knew he was releasing the pent-up rage the war had built within him. "I will not have girls flying with me. There will be no more discussion about it. I'll have you transferred out of here in two days."

With that, the colonel returned to the map and drew up further plans with the other pilots. Yet Lily couldn't help but notice Alexei's lingering gaze that was accompanied by a cocky grin.

"Maybe you should be paying attention," Lily whispered to him.

"Why? Are you worried about me?"

"I'm worried about my plane." Lily ignored his gaze as much as possible while attempting to focus on the colonel's plans.

With the scheme firmly drawn up, Colonel Baranov ordered another sortie in five minutes. The pilots quickly grabbed some water or a slice of black bread, but Lily and Katya refused. Lily assumed Katya was feeling the same sentiment as her. They were underserving of any sustenance after having done so little and were also determined to show the colonel their resolve. The silent protest was, of course, useless as the colonel paid them absolutely no attention whatsoever.

"Seargent," Alexei called to Ina.

"Captain?" Ina saluted him.

"I hear you were scaring my pilots?" he asked with a slight smirk.

"I..." Ina was lost for words.

"He was wrong to treat you in that manner." Alexei nodded. "Fortunately for me, I get to fly the plane you took such diligent care over. Still, it is annoying to find little trinkets like flowers and hair curlers in the cockpit."

*Hair curlers? I didn't leave any curlers in there!* Lily frowned but then caught the look on his face and realized he was joking.

"Help me with this, will you?" Alexei handed his parachute to Lily and turned his back to her.

"Not sure I want someone piloting my plane who can't even strap themselves into a parachute," Lily grumbled as she assisted him.

Placing the parachute on his back, Lily walked around to his front and fastened the clips into place. Yet Lily's proximity to him seemed to stir the very feelings she was hoping to ignore. She felt the warmth radiating from his body, and she looked up into his eyes to see him staring down at her with longing.

Patting his shoulder roughly, Lily backed away from him quickly, wishing to dismiss any inkling of romance. She was here to fight, and falling in love with a pilot was foolish. Even if he was a competent fighter, time and chance were cruel. No one was invulnerable.

"Maybe I'll put a word in for you." Alexei examined Lily quickly as he double-checked the parachute.

"Why would you do that?" Lily held her chin high, but feared her attempt at trying to dissuade any attention from him was falling flat.

"I would hate to see you leave." Alexei patted Lily's plane as he studied the vehicle like he was studying a work of art.

"You barely know me, sir." Lily cleared her throat.

"I was talking to your plane." Alexei winked at Lily before climbing into the cockpit. "And I feel like I know her intimately."

"She is special." Lily agreed as she examined her plane with worry.

"I almost threw this out, by the way." Alexei tossed her the tin mug with her name written on it. "I thought it was junk until I saw your name. Don't worry about your plane. You've taken excellent care of her, although I could do without the strands of blonde curls I keep finding here and there."

"Keep them." Lily grinned before adding, "Maybe some of my good fortune will pass onto you."

"You really want to fly with us, don't you?" Alexei narrowed his gaze. "This isn't some game you're playing at?"

"No, sir." Lily shook her head as she stood tall and confident. "There's a reason I'm here."

"Hopefully it's a good reason." Alexei strapped on his hat as Ina pulled away the blocks on his wheels.

With a nod, Alexei applied power and the plane roared to life as he taxied to the runway and was soon airborne with the rest of the squadron. Again, Lily's heart ached with anxiety as she watched her plane in someone else's hands. Her knuckles turned pale white as she squeezed her hands into fists watching her number three speed off into battle.

"Maybe some of my good fortune will pass onto you," Katya mocked lightly, and Lily offered her a slap on the arm.

"That's not fair!" Lily grumbled as she played with the mug in her hands.

"It was a rather odd thing to say about your hair." Ina threw her lips upside down in agreement.

"You need to focus." Katya encouraged. "We need to be charming the colonel, not the captain."

"Did you see how friendly the two men were?" Lily defended. "I think I may be onto something."

"You are — the captain." Katya raised an eyebrow, and Ina giggled.

"Should we tell everyone about your sentry?" Lily tilted her head as she threatened Ina, who immediately ceased her amusement.

"Come, let's get the next round of ammunition ready." Katya nodded for Lily to follow her.

"If we do that, the colonel will expect us to fill that role. If charming him didn't work, then maybe being a pain in his ass will." Lily crossed her arms defiantly.

"Mail!" a shout came from further inside the hangar.

"Oh! Mail!" Lily's indignation retreated swiftly as she spun on her heels, and pursued swiftly by Katya and Ina, came over to the cart that was full of packages and letters.

"Please let there be something for me!" Katya sifted through the letters eagerly, and Ina followed suit.

"L. Litvyak!" Lily snatched a package off the cart. *She finally wrote it correctly!*

Sitting down on the ground, in the middle of the hangar, Lily ripped open her package, desperate for any of the items she had requested or for news of how her family was.

"What did you get?" Ina asked as she sat beside Lily and began opening her letter.

"Soap!" Lily held it to her nose, took in a deep sniff, and was instantly transported back to her mother's side. "Looks like there are also a couple scarfs, some socks, sweets, a can of beans, and a picture of — "

"A picture of what?" Katya asked, curious as to Lily's hesitancy.

Lily cleared her throat before replying, "My father."

"Larisa told me what happened to him." Katya glanced over her shoulder sympathetically. "My cousin was also taken."

"He spoke his mind." Lily tucked the photo into her breast pocket. "He was killed for it. Might be my fate as well if I speak like that again to the colonel."

"What did you get, Ina?" Katya asked.

"A letter from home." Ina looked concerned as she held the unopened envelope.

"Are you expecting bad news?" Lily asked tenderly.

"Every time." Ina drew a deep breath. "They've been under Nazi occupation since near the beginning of the war."

"Want me to read it for you?" Katya asked.

"You would do that for me?" Ina examined Katya with peculiarity.

"I know what it is to wait for news from home. I'll read it and let you know if it's good or bad." Katya held her hand out.

Ina stared at Katya's extended hand for a moment before eventually agreeing and handing over the letter.

"Let me down kindly if it's poor news." Ina sat a little closer to Lily, much closer than she appreciated. Still, Lily understood that her mechanic friend needed to be close, and she trembled slightly as she stared nervously at the ground while playing with her fingers.

Even Lily was growing nervous for the response as Katya gingerly opened the letter and began reading. Glancing at the photo of her father, Lily remembered the letter her mother received when he was taken. It was brief and riddled with ridiculous lies. Everyone knew the truth of why he had been taken, even the men who handed the letter to her mother knew the truth, but the fabrication of the infallible Soviet state could not be broken.

Lily found it strange that she would fight so strongly and passionately for the same government that had ripped apart their family. Though, she supposed that she wasn't fighting for the state, but rather, for her mother and brother. They were her only thought, and Lily stared at the letter in Katya's hand, wondering when it would be her turn to receive sad news.

"Everyone is fine." Katya folded up the letter, but the look on her face was not one of relief, and Lily watched Ina's countenance shift from liberation before diving back into worry.

"Then why do you look so downcast?" Ina pressed with wide eyes.

"Your mother is unwell." Katya handed the letter back to Ina. "They expect it's a madness brought on by stress and malnutrition."

"She's always been eccentric," Ina explained. "When I was younger, I thought it was merely amusing, but as I grew older I started to realize that she wasn't quite like the other mothers. Which was quite alright with me, but when she worries, she seems to grow stranger and stranger."

Katya and Lily remained quiet for a moment as they watched their new friend with sympathy.

"I've heard the Americans don't know what they're fighting for." Ina drew a deep breath. "The Nazis aren't invading their country like they are ours. They're not raping their women, killing thousands of their citizens, or stealing their land or food. They don't know why they're fighting, but we do." Ina waved the letter in the air.

"They're coming back!" Katya pointed, and Lily glanced up to find the planes returning.

Again, with her heart in her stomach, Lily watched the planes, hoping that her number three had survived.

One by one, the planes landed, and Lily breathed a sigh of relief when she saw her bright white three being taxied into place and Alexei climbing out unharmed.

The other planes, Lily noticed, didn't fare so well. Many had bullet holes in the fuselage or cracked windshields. Black stains were smeared across Colonel Baranov's plane as he climbed out of the cockpit with oil staining his hands.

"They knew we were coming," Colonel Baranov spoke with frustration dominating his voice as he tried to clean the oil off his hands.

"I promised I'd keep her safe," Alexei spoke softly to Lily as he walked past her, but not before offering the slightest of pinches on her elbow.

"Hey!" Lily frowned.

"Oh, by the way." Alexei stopped in his tracks. "I'll talk to the colonel this evening. Keep helping with the ammo and refueling. It shows that you're after the greater good and not just your own vain glory."

With a nod of appreciation, Lily and Katya returned to help with refueling the planes. It was arduous work, and Lily, despite considering herself strong for her size, struggled under the weight of the hoses. One hose was fine enough, but after attaching and detaching plane after plane it wore the muscles down.

The rest of the day proceeded in much the same fashion, with the colonel and his fighters taking to the sky on sortie after sortie until, when it was late in the evening, he retired to the bunker with the other men.

Many of the planes had returned peppered with bullet holes or gashes caused by shrapnel, but Lily's little three remained mostly unscathed. She attributed this to her luck, and refused to accept it was due to the captain's skill in piloting.

Lily, however, was not satisfied with leaving her fate to either the colonel or the captain's hands and wouldn't accept any other answer than being able to fight with them tomorrow. She knew Alexei would speak with him, but Lily wasn't convinced he wasn't properly concerned with her cause.

Storming into the bunker, Lily peered into the darkness to find the colonel sitting behind his desk in the corner of the room where Alexei and he were clinking glasses of vodka. They were laughing liberally and loudly, despite the fact that other pilots were eager for some sleep.

"Here she comes," the colonel muttered to Alexei, his cheer evaporating when he noticed Lily approaching.

"I would like to discuss my time here, sir." Lily spoke as she cleared her throat.

"I told you my decision." The colonel leaned back in his chair before lighting a cigarette. "What else could you possibly want?"

"I came here to fight," Lily spoke courageously, knowing that the answer was almost assuredly a no.

"And I'm sending you to fight somewhere else."

"We wouldn't have been sent here if senior command didn't believe it appropriate," Lily pressed. "We're good fliers. We were sent here to fulfill a purpose."

"My answer is final." The colonel shook his head before squinting at her and asking, "What the hell is in your cap?"

"It's a flower, sir," Lily replied boldly and unashamedly.

"Do you see any other man in here with such frivolous accessories?" The colonel scoffed. "If any of my pilots displayed that behavior, they'd be dismissed immediately. Don't you understand the difference between us? I barely have enough planes for the men as it is. I'm not giving up one so that you can fulfill whatever reckless dreams you might have."

"And I'm not leaving until you allow me to fight." Lily grabbed a chair and dragged it over to the desk, where she promptly sat and crossed her arms. "If I may be so bold, you're not being fair to Katya and me. I was born on Aviation Day. Flying is in my blood, it's part of me."

"So keep that vision alive." The colonel looked at Lily with sympathy. "Don't you understand? It disturbs me greatly when I lose a pilot. Losing two girls like you would be unbearable. No, Lieutenant Litvyak, you would not survive this war. Please recognize that my refusal is compassion."

"With respect, sir, why do they get to fight?" Lily pointed to the men in the bunker with her. "Why are they afforded that privilege?"

"They aren't women," the colonel replied briskly.

"And their sex gives them privileges that I can never achieve?" Lily grew incensed.

"Naturally." The colonel furrowed his brow. "And watch your tone with a commanding officer."

"I want that privilege, sir," Lily continued tactfully.

"Why do you call it a privilege?" the colonel scoffed before a sudden rage overtook him, and he shouted, "Don't you understand?! Men are expendable! We're supposed to die! We protect you! We protect your innocence, your beauty, your near divinity. And in thanks you want to throw that away for a chance to see what men experience? We're the scum of the earth. Look at us! Look at you! You don't belong here."

Taking the colonel's words to heart, Lily looked around the bunker at the tired men sleeping, others drinking or smoking as they played cards or rested their heads while staring blankly at the ceiling, and others writing letters to their loved ones.

But then a thought dropped into Lily's mind. A courageous yet foolish notion. She didn't know where it had come from other than, again, her good luck, but Lily pressed the portrait of her father against her chest, wondering if he was playing some part in this.

"I know I have the body of a weak and feeble woman," Lily began after a moment, "But I have the heart and stomach of a king."

"Hmm." The colonel squinted at Lily, and in the twinkling of his eyes, she could see that he was already viewing her in a different light. She had consented to his chauvinistic viewpoint of her sex's physical inferiority while also appealing to the transcendental spirit that lived and breathed in every man and woman's chest.

"That's Elizabeth I," a pilot in the bunker spoke after a second.

"Correct," Lily replied while still gazing at the colonel.

"Sir," Alexei, who had watched the interaction silently while slowly sipping on his vodka, interjected. "I believe we should give them a chance."

The colonel shot Alexei a surprised glance before looking back at Lily, almost wondering if she had also heard the captain correctly.

"They came here to fly. They went through all the training. They're pilots who have experienced combat. Let's give them a shot." Alexei shrugged.

Colonel Baranov clenched his jaw as he stared at the captain, and Lily understood, in that moment, that there was little he refused Alexei.

"She can fly with you." He pointed at Alexei without so much as looking in Lily's direction.

Lily nearly burst into tears as she felt the relief spreading through her shoulders. Regardless of how she felt, Lily remained disciplined and showed as little emotion as possible.

190

"She's your responsibility." The colonel looked sternly at the captain.

"And Katya?" Lily pressed.

"You're persistent." The colonel offered Lily an unappreciated glare.

"She should also be given a chance." Alexei shrugged.

"She can fly with me, then." The colonel closed his eyes as he clenched his jaw tighter. "Tomorrow morning. The other girl will fly with me. Then this one will fly with you."

*This one?* Lily grew annoyed at the designation and the fact he wouldn't dare look her in the eyes, but she had a chance to prove herself, yet again.

"Get out of here." The colonel nodded for both of them to leave. "I have much to prepare."

"Sir!" Lily saluted, but the colonel did not return the gesture.

"Let's go tell your friend the good news." Alexei touched her elbow gingerly, and Lily felt a strange sensation run through her body.

Explaining it away as nerves, Lily focused her attention on what she needed for tomorrow's flight. Her heart raced in her chest, and Lily didn't believe she would sleep a moment tonight.

"Do you suppose she'll be excited?" Alexei asked as he opened the bunker door for her.

"Why are you helping me?" Lily asked as she ignored his question. She wasn't sure if she wanted to know the answer and assumed he was possibly assisting her with another goal in mind.

"The pilot who refused to fly in your plane, he died today," Alexei spoke quickly as they left the bunker and headed toward the hangar.

Lily glanced up at him in surprise as she waited for him to continue.

"He took the plane I was supposed to fly in." He looked down at her with his piercing eyes, and Lily glanced away. "I've survived this long by learning through other's mistakes. Tomorrow, you'll have the chance to prove whether he made the mistake — or I did."

# Chapter Fourteen
# What Nazis?

*"If a man knows not which port he sails, no wind is favorable."*

Seneca

As she had predicted, Lily had not slept a wink the previous night. She was so excited that all she could envision was climbing into the plane. Yet she regretted it now, as the early morning hours rolled around, and she stood as a shell of herself in the hangar, waiting for the call to action.

Katya was already on a sortie with the colonel, and Lily was jealous that she wasn't the first in the air with the free hunters. Or maybe it wasn't jealousy but rather eagerness. Lily couldn't decide as her mind was spinning with excitement, nervousness, and anxiety to get into her number three.

With a pitifully weak cup of coffee in her personalized tin mug from Larisa, Lily stood in the hangar as she watched Ina prepare her plane. The mechanic was paying special attention to the aircraft, ensuring that it was in the best possible condition. She had wiped the windshield clean, made sure the instruments were reading accurately, double-checked every aspect of the engine, and ensured the ammunition was stocked.

Lily was thankful for her new friend and understood that her and Katya's performance today would be a step forward for women. Flying in the Soviet Air Force with the female regiments was one thing, but flying with the men as free hunters was another entirely. This would, essentially, place women as equals among men, and the significance of this morning was not lost on Lily.

"Do you want mine?" a voice asked from behind her, and Lily turned to see Alexei approaching her with a piece of black bread in his hand.

"I'm not hungry." Lily shook her head.

"Probably for the best. It was moldy." Alexei tossed the bread onto the ground.

"You were going to give me moldy bread?" Lily raised her eyebrow in disapproval.

"You could pick around the moldy bits." Alexei shrugged as he took a sip of his coffee.

"Very generous of you," Lily muttered.

"Are you nervous?" Alexei asked as he took another sip.

"Are you?" Lily watched him drinking the coffee now with large gulps.

"Always." Alexei studied his now empty cup before adding in a hushed tone, "Don't tell the others. If they know I'm nervous, it'll destroy whatever resolve they're clinging to."

Lily didn't reply as she watched him closely. She couldn't quite gauge his character. He seemed interested in her yet didn't make a pathetic appeal like Mr. Morozov had done at the dance.

Yet he also seemed familiar, as if Lily had known him her whole life. There was a sparkle in his eye that seemed confident and even happy despite the fact that hell was all around them.

"You're staring," he spoke after a moment.

"I was looking at the plane." Lily turned away but noticed that he was smirking slightly.

"Don't worry about today. Stay tight on me when we're up there, and you'll be fine. You don't need to demonstrate any heroics. Just stay on me. Can you do that?" Alexei studied her closely.

"I'll stay so close you'll think our planes are one," Lily replied boldly but felt foolish for answering so arrogantly. She was merely overcompensating for her nerves.

"We'll see now, won't we." Alexei went to take another sip of his coffee when he remembered that it was empty.

"They're coming back." Lily pointed to a couple of black dots heading in their direction.

"They must've taken damage." Alexei glanced at his watch. "They shouldn't be back for another few minutes."

"They're flying pretty low." Lily squinted.

"Yeah." Alexei also took note of the oddity.

"Those aren't ours!" Lily panicked.

"You're right!" Alexei latched onto her arm before shouting back into the hangar, "Take cover!"

Within mere seconds, the air raid siren was blaring, and the anti-aircraft guns were unloading their weaponry upon the approaching enemy.

The sound was deafening, and Lily could scarcely hear a word of what Alexei was shouting. She could, at least, understand that he was pointing to the trenches near the hangar where Lily spotted Ina taking cover.

Without hesitation, Lily and Alexei ran toward the trenches. The hangar, and the planes nearby, were undoubtedly the target of the enemy, and being anywhere near them was too dangerous. There was no time to get into an aircraft of their own to counterattack.

A burst of machine gun and cannon fire pelted the earth about ten yards from their feet as they ran, covering Lily and Alexei in a mound of dirt. Latching onto Lily's arm, Alexei guided her toward the trenches, where she came crashing against Ina.

"What do we do?!" Lily asked Alexei more so out of anger than fear. She was beyond livid that her chance at fighting the enemy was potentially cut short by this attack. She hated the injustice of it. She hated being pinned down and unable to properly fight back. It felt so inhumane and dishonorable.

The Nazi planes roared overhead as they passed by at daringly low altitude, trying to avoid the fire from the anti-aircraft guns, and Lily noticed that they were turning to make another pass.

"Get me in my plane!" Lily shouted as she stood.

Suddenly, the anti-aircraft guns stopped, and Lily looked at Ina in confusion, hoping that she had some sort of explanation.

"Look!" Ina pointed to the sky, and everyone in the trench looked up to see that another two planes were approaching.

"Those are ours!" Alexei laughed in relief. "That's the colonel! That must be your friend with him!"

"Katya!" Lily shouted in her excitement as the planes roared overhead before engaging the enemy fighters.

Seemingly caught by surprise, the Nazi planes noticed their enemy when it was too late. They broke formation, but the colonel and Katya stayed hot on the heels of one plane.

A burst of cannon and machine gun fire erupted from both planes, and the enemy was soon nothing more than a ball of fire plummeting to the earth amidst cheers from those being saved on the ground.

The other enemy plane was still within striking distance despite a frantic attempt to escape the danger, and the colonel and Katya were soon firing upon him as well. With a billow of smoke, the Nazi plane lost altitude quickly before crashing some distance away.

Leaving the safety of the trenches, Lily, Alexei, and Ina ran onto the runway as they waved their scarves or handkerchiefs excitedly and in salute for their thanks.

The colonel and Katya flew over the airfield, tipping their wings in salute to those on the ground in recognition of their swift victory.

"If that doesn't impress him, I'm not sure I know what will," Alexei spoke to Lily over the cheers of the crowd.

If their own Soviet fighters had not returned in time, the Nazi planes could've done irreversible damage. No one was ignorant of this fact, and the cheers continued unimpeded as Katya and the colonel taxied their planes to a final stop.

An ecstatic crowd rushed to the planes and surrounded their heroes. Lily forced her way through the crows as she embraced her friend.

"That was amazing!" Lily squealed as she held her friend close.

"That's one way of putting it." Katya broke off from her embrace as she removed her flying hat, where her sweaty short hair fell across her forehead. Her eyes were wide, and she seemed to be trembling slightly.

"You seem dazed," Lily asked with concern as she held her hands on Katya's arms.

"Just a little shaken is all." Katya nodded as she looked around at the still-excited gathering.

"How'd she do?" Alexei asked the colonel as he stepped down from his plane.

"Alright," he replied briskly as he walked toward a table with a map spread out.

"I don't think I've ever seen him so emotional," Alexei added as he came to stand beside Lily and Katya.

"From what I could see, her form was perfect." Lily threw her arm around Katya's shoulder. "She stuck to the colonel without any deviation."

"It's time to test your skills." Alexei offered her a curious glance, as if he was trying to determine if he wanted her to even succeed. "Get to your plane, and remember to stay close to me. Whatever you do, stay close."

"You'll do well." Katya swallowed and patted Lily's arm as she repeated, "You'll do well."

With a deep breath, and as the crowd began to disperse and resume the terrible business of war, Lily climbed into her number three.

Again, and almost every time she had flown into combat, sitting on the runway was intolerable. Her heart raced, her stomach churned, her hands sweat inside her gloves, and Lily had to continually remind herself to breathe properly.

Giving the signal to Ina, who took away the blocks under the wheels of Lily's plane, she was taxied to near

Alexei. With a signal from his right hand, Alexei indicated that it was time to take off, and Lily matched his speed as they approached the end of the short runway.

"You're doing better than I expected," Alexei spoke into her headphones as they became airborne, and Lily heard a chuckle.

"We've barely begun," Lily replied.

"Check your weapons." Alexei fired off a quick burst, as did Lily, to make sure everything was operational.

"All clear." Lily again reminded herself to breathe.

"Keep an eye out for the enemy." Alexei returned to a serious demeanor, and Lily checked out her peripherals as best she could while maintaining a dangerous proximity to the captain's plane.

She did, however, take note of the other two free hunters that were flying near them. She hoped that they would pay special attention to their surroundings so that she could keep as close to Alexei as possible.

The smoke from Stalingrad grew closer and closer, and Lily found the city to be nearly unrecognizable from when she had first seen the Nazis invading. Almost every building was demolished, fires were raging in different quadrants or around the city, and Lily understood that life in the city would be as close to Hell as she could imagine.

Suddenly, Alexei turned to his right, and Lily, with swift reflexes, followed him closely, again nearly running into him.

Alexei's moves were so sudden and unexpected that Lily was certain he was trying to lose her. He dove down sharply and began to roll as if in a corkscrew before pulling up sharply.

Lily felt that she was almost losing consciousness as she pushed her plane to the brink and her body to the limits of human capabilities. For the briefest of moments, she thought that she saw gunfire from the other pair of

Yaks that were with them, but her attention was still on Alexei. She didn't dare lose him. This was her chance to prove she wasn't only a fighter but that she deserved to be treated equally.

Lily's arms grew weary as she pulled against the throttle, making sure that she matched his speed and almost anticipated his moves.

After what felt like an hour, Alexei finally broke off this routine and glanced over at Lily with a nod. His oxygen mask was covering his face, but Lily was certain she could see him smiling.

"Let's head back," Alexei spoke, and Lily thought she could hear him panting.

The short journey back to the airbase was quiet. No other planes, not even Soviet, seemed to be around. Lily was once again reminded of her love for flying as she watched the late morning sunrise painting the sky in a beautiful array of oranges and pinks. She looked down at the beautiful countryside and the lovely winding lakes and rivers.

Still, she wondered if she had passed Alexei's test. She had kept close to him, as he stated, but there was no combat. Katya had been tried in the crucible of air battle, but Lily remained unproven. At least, that is, with this regiment.

Arriving back at the base, and with her plane taxied to her place near the hangar, Lily couldn't keep a grin away as Katya and Ina came running over to hear about her experience.

"So?" Katya asked with wide eyes.

"I did exactly as he commanded," Lily replied with excitement as Ina helped her take her parachute off. "He told me to stick to him like glue, and I did exactly that. He couldn't have lost me had he parachuted out."

"Do you think this means we can stay?" Katya asked eagerly. "We both did so well today!"

"I'm not sure what other test they need?" Lily shrugged as Alexei and the other two pilots approached her.

"I think that strategy worked," one of the pilots threw his hands onto his hips, and Lily noticed that his face was red from exertion.

"Attacking them from both angles was smart." Alexei concurred.

"What did you think?" the other pilot asked Lily, who hadn't been paying as much attention to the conversation as she should have.

"About?" Lily asked with wide eyes, wondering what she had missed.

"About our strategy." The pilot chuckled. "How did you think that tactic faired against the Germans?"

"What Germans?" Lily shrugged, and the pilots, including Alexei, burst into a laugh.

"Do you have such contempt for the Fascists that you didn't even realize when one was attacking you?" The pilot laughed liberally, and Lily smiled a touch, playing along with his jesting but still feeling lost.

*Did I really not notice?* Lily wondered. *I was so focused on Alexei. How could I not have seen enemy fighters? Though, I suppose I do recall some gunfire.*

"You're quite something." The pilot smiled at her before extending his hand in greeting, "I'm Boris, by the way."

"Boris." Lily shook his hand. "I'm Lily."

"I'm well aware of who you are." He offered her a cocky grin, and Lily glanced away, hoping to stamp out any idea of affection before it took flight, so to speak.

"Go get some food." Alexei waved for Boris to leave them alone.

"I'm alright." Boris continued to stare at Lily.

"I need to speak with the lieutenant alone." Alexei continued to shoo him.

"She's good, you know." Boris tilted his head as he remained in place.

"Come over here, then." Alexei threw his arm around Lily's shoulder as he led her a few paces away from the other pilots and the prying eyes of Ina and Katya.

"I stuck close to you." Lily swallowed, hoping the conversation was going to be positive.

"He's right, you know. You're good." Alexei glanced back in the direction of Boris. "I've never had a pilot stick to me like that before. Don't tell him I said this, since he's clearly smitten with you, but Boris spun out when I first took him up."

"He probably saw a pretty girl in the air," Lily muttered.

"Or a squirrel," Alexei added with a grin. "Anyway, I'll talk to the colonel. I'll let him know you're ready."

"Thank you," Lily sighed.

"Get some rest." Alexei patted her shoulder before walking toward the command bunker. "We'll leave in twenty minutes for another sortie."

"Yes, sir." Lily nodded as she watched him walk away.

Again, Lily wasn't sure if her emotions were merely being mixed with what she was experiencing, but in her heart, for the first time in her life, Lily felt what she thought might be something akin to love.

"He's smitten with you." Katya crossed her arms as she came to stand beside Lily.

"You think?" Lily asked as she continued to watch the captain.

"He's still staring at you." Katya nodded in the direction of Boris, and Lily gathered she was talking about him and not Alexei.

"He's no bother." Lily paid him no attention. "I'm used to men like him."

"Good thing they have our living quarters separated then, hey?"

"Indeed. I'd hate to have to hurt him." Lily smiled.

"He's walking this way now," Katya muttered under her breath.

"Should I tell him you're interested?" Lily tested Katya.

"I'd rather kiss a German."

"I don't mean to be too forward," Boris spoke as he arrived beside Lily, who braced for a strange proposal of the likes of Mr. Morozov. "But I was watching you with Alexei. I've never seen anyone with as quick of reflexes as you. Don't tell anyone, but I spun out my first time with Alexei."

"Is that right?" Lily glanced up at him with feigned surprise, but her attention was stolen by the colonel, who was now leaving the command bunker with Alexei and approaching them swiftly.

"This is it." Katya pressed against Lily as they waited with bated breath for the colonel's official reply.

"Litvyak! Do you have any other boots?!" the colonel called from a distance.

"Sir?" Lily shouted back, not sure if she had heard him correctly.

"Your boots!" He pointed with annoyance as he came closer. "Are those the only ones you have?"

"Yes, sir." Lily nodded.

"You, too?" the colonel asked Katya as he was now within speaking distance.

"Yes, sir," Katya replied quickly.

"I'll order some new ones for you." The colonel scratched the stubble on his chin before ordering Katya, "Get to your plane. We're due for another sortie. Let's go kill some more Germans."

"Sir." Katya saluted as the colonel continued to his plane.

Without a word, Lily and Katya grinned brightly at each other. They had won. They had fought for a chance to be seen as equals, and they had earned that right through merit.

"Thank you." Katya squeezed Lily's shoulder when the colonel's attention was diverted.

"For what?" Lily shrugged.

"For making sure I also got a chance. You could've been selfish, but you made sure I also had an opportunity. I'll never forget that."

With that, Katya ran toward her plane, and Lily watched with amusement, her friend full of life and vigor. Lily knew that they were going to make a difference at this regiment. She understood their contribution was too small to affect the overall war, but still, the fact that they were playing a part was enough for Lily.

"Boris! Go eat!" Alexei barked as he returned to Lily with another cup of coffee and another slice of black bread.

"Maybe we could chat later?" Boris looked at Lily eagerly.

"She's not interested." Alexei swatted at Boris' backside, and he scurried away.

"I'm capable of handling him." Lily glanced up at Alexei.

"I don't doubt it. Anyway, when we get back in the air, there are couple of things you should know," Alexei spoke with a mouthful of black bread, and Lily noticed that he was picking out pieces that weren't moldy. "Now that I'm aware of your capabilities, I'll explain our tactics. We free hunters use a strategy of attack and cover. The German planes are faster and have a better rate of climb, but our planes are more maneuverable. When one of us attacks, the other drops back to provide protection. Understood?"

"Yes, sir." Lily nodded.

"Good. Now, when we attack the bombers, specifically the Heinkel 111, they have defensive machine guns on the rear. Try and get behind them, just below their tail, where they have a blind spot for their guns and reduce your speed to match theirs. Unleash hell upon them, and you'll be heaping kills upon kills."

"I'm aware of the blind spot." Lily shuffled her jaw, anxious to get back to the sky.

"I should've known." Alexei smiled at her warmly, but then his face turned sour as he scrunched up his nose in disgust.

"You ate some mold?" Lily asked rhetorically.

"I ate some mold." Alexei looked at the remaining bread in his hand before offering some to Lily.

"Again, thank you, but I'm alright." Lily held up her hand to politely decline.

"You should eat soon." Alexei tossed the bread onto the ground. "It's going to be a long day."

"I will." Lily glanced back at her plane to see that Ina was nearly finished.

"How can someone so small like you handle such a large and powerful aircraft?" Alexei shook his head in bewilderment.

"Men have been asking me that all my life," Lily replied swiftly.

"And? How do you answer these men?"

"You'll have to get to know me better, captain, if you're going to unravel my secrets." Lily grinned at him. "In either case, words count for nothing when action is a suitable answer."

"Then action it is." Alexei patted her arm as he indicated that it was their turn to take to the sky again.

With energy, and an untamable smile, Lily climbed into her plane after giving Ina a happy wink.

"Be safe!" Ina called as she pulled out the blocks from Lily's plane.

"Tell that to the Germans!" Lily called back but knew that Ina couldn't hear her with her windshield closed.

The green flair was fired, and Lily and Alexei were back in the sky, en route to Stalingrad. Lily's nerves were much steadier now, and she was able to scan the sky more diligently than before.

Still, the sight of the burning city never ceased to cause Lily's heart to ache. All she could envision was her mother and brother in that burning Hell. Glancing at the photograph of Anna and Yuri on the console, and then at the photograph of her father, Lily was imbued with passion and resilience.

"Bombers. Three o'clock." Lily spotted a formation heading toward the city.

"Ignore them."

"Ignore them?" Lily frowned. "Shouldn't we try to break up their attack?"

"Negative. We should attack the bombers after they've dropped their bombs. Strike when they feel safest, en route home."

"But they're attacking civilians!"

"The Germans have no shortage in their supply of bombs, but we can limit their bombers. If we attack now, the bomber will drop its payload and then return for restocking. We will take the momentary loss so that we can destroy the bomber forever."

"I don't like it." Lily shook her head as she watched the bombers passing by underneath them without being disturbed.

"They're not alone, either." Alexei pointed, and Lily glanced in the direction to find a squadron of eight fighters protecting the bombers from a higher elevation, hoping to ambush any Soviet fighters that dared to attack.

"Good catch."

"Let's circle the city. We'll find some for you to kill."

Agreeing, although finding it strange that she, a little blonde girl from a quaint flying club outside of Moscow, was now actively seeking men to kill, Lily followed Alexei while staying close to him.

To be honest, Lily wasn't sure that she could kill another person. It had been easier to attack the bombers during the night and under the cover of darkness where the act was veiled. Even with the soldiers killing civilians in Stalingrad, she had no issue unleashing her weaponry on them. But now, on this sunny Fall day, illusion would be stripped bare, and she would have to face the harrowing reality of taking another life.

After about ten minutes of flying at a high altitude, Lily spotted a single bomber being escorted by a couple fighters. They were returning from a bombing run, and the fighters were flying at a much higher altitude than the bomber.

"I see them," Alexei spoke into her headset after she pointed. She wasn't sure why she didn't simply mention it to him, but in her nervousness, she almost felt as if the enemy could hear her.

"What's the plan of attack?" Lily asked.

"Follow me. We'll use the clouds for cover until there's a clear opening. I don't think the fighters have noticed us yet."

Following closely behind Alexei as he dove down so as to be behind the bombers in their blind spot, Lily approached the bombers, who, she realized, were still unaware of them.

"Where are the fighters?" Lily asked as she looked around but couldn't see them anywhere.

"Stay on the target," Alexei replied calmly.

Switching off her safety, Lily drew a deep breath as she continued to approach the bomber. She lowered her speed to match the bombers, lined her sights up with the underbelly of the enemy, and, while holding her breath, squeezed the trigger.

Her plane rattled with the loud crackle of machine gun and cannon fire, ripping holes in the bottom of the enemy plane. It felt like ages, but Lily knew it was likely only a handful of seconds. Still, she continued firing as the Heinkel's engines were set ablaze with fire and smoke before it began to descend quickly.

Pulling up moments before colliding with the back of the bomber, Lily noticed the other Heinkels were breaking off their formation.

"Did you see that?!" Lily asked excitedly as she looked down to watch the bomber continuing its rapid decline toward the earth.

It felt uncomfortable, knowing that these men were plummeting to their deaths with the expectation of a rather gruesome end. Still, she reminded herself that these were the same men who were more than content to drop bombs on innocent civilians in the hopes of eradicating every ethnicity they deemed inferior.

"Captain?" Lily asked again when she realized that he hadn't responded.

Glancing around, she couldn't see him anywhere. She looked at the enemy bombers, wondering if he had broken off to attack one of them, but Lily was certain he would've remained in formation with her.

"Lily! Break right!" Alexei called into her headset.

Without waiting for further explanation, Lily engaged her swift instincts and did as commanded.

Despite her best efforts, a burst of cracks and banging clattered against her hull and windshield. The enemy was right behind her and in perfect positioning. His bullets had found their mark, but Lily's trusty troika had taken the pounding bravely.

"I can't lose him!" Lily yelled as she took evasive maneuvers.

She was trying every trick she had used in her training or at her flying club, but the German pilot was just as swift in his reactions as she was.

Suddenly, a burst of fire, followed by an explosion, filled Lily's rearview mirror, and she nearly yelled with excitement when she watched Alexei's plane surge out of the ball of flame from the enemy he had just killed.

"The tactic works," Alexei spoke into her headset calmly, but Lily detected hints of worry in his voice which made her happy. "Attack and cover. Let's move on to the next bomber."

"Sir." Lily nodded as she followed suit, and they approached the other Heinkel that had broken away from the formation.

"I'll let you take the attack again. I'll provide cover."

Lily needed no further motivation as she approached the bomber in the same fashion. She remained behind it and approached from the bottom so that the gunners couldn't target her.

Once she was in position, she released the full arsenal of her weaponry, tearing holes into the underside until, again, she pulled up at the very last moment.

With smoke billowing from the engines, the Heinkel began spinning toward the ground. Lily and Alexei circled above until, finally, the plane landed with an explosion.

Glancing over at her wing mate in the air, Lily caught his gaze while they were locked in this heavenly dance. He seemed proud, but even from a distance, Lily detected that he was tired. It was a measure of pride to take down the enemy, but Lily wondered if he felt as uncomfortable as she did with the taking of a life. She wondered if that feeling would ever pass, and if she would eventually grow numb to this. A part of her hoped not. She wished to retain her humanity. Otherwise, she wondered what she was fighting for.

"We should refuel." Alexei gave the signal, and they returned in the direction of their airfield.

"Thank you, by the way," Lily spoke to Alexei as she glanced down at the picture of her father, wondering if he had played some part in protecting her.

"Just return the favor sometime." Alexei chuckled. "Let's do a victory roll to let them know we killed some Germans."

"I shouldn't." Lily looked at the bullet holes near her cockpit. "I don't know where else I was hit."

"You scared?" Alexei challenged.

"I'm not scared of anything," Lily replied confidently, but she glanced again at the damage, praying it would hold together.

*How would that appear?* Lily scoffed to herself. *First woman with a kill on this regiment, and during my victory roll I, crash my plane?*

Regardless of her trepidation, Lily and Alexei performed their victory roll over the airfield to waves from scarves and handkerchiefs on the ground.

Eventually, their planes landed safely, and they were taxied to their positions, where Ina swiftly threw the blocks under the tires and a concerned Katya ran over to Lily's plane.

"Are you hurt?" Katya asked as she inspected Lily closely, looking her up and down and checking her jacket and parachute for any damage.

"I'm fine!" Lily laughed.

"You ran into trouble?" Ina asked as she inspected the underside of the plane.

"We were the trouble." Lily glanced over at Alexei as he approached them with his hat in his hands.

He looked profoundly handsome, even with his sweaty hair swept over his forehead. They made a great team, and Lily was beginning to wonder if the chemistry they had in the air could be transferred to other areas of their relationship.

"She's going to be an ace in no time!" Alexei shouted excitedly as he wrapped his arm around her shoulder. Lily had to strain against blushing as others were now surrounding them, including the colonel.

"How many?" Boris asked.

"Two bombers and a fighter." Alexei nodded at Lily before adding, "She took out both bombers."

"She did?" Colonel Baranov pointed at her in surprise as he clarified.

"We used the tactic of attack and cover. Worked beautifully." Alexei almost laughed with delight.

"Two bombers and a fighter. That's about eleven men." Boris counted on his fingers.

"It's not even eight in the morning." Ina glanced at her watch. "You killed eleven Germans already?"

"And we're hungry for more." Alexei patted Lily's plane. "We'll make another sortie in an hour."

"I'll need more than an hour to prepare the plane." Ina shook her head. "I need to make sure nothing hidden was damaged."

"Fair enough." Alexei waved.

"What's your symbol?" Boris asked as he drew close to Lily, and she wondered if he was entirely oblivious to her and Alexei's budding relationship.

"Symbol?" Lily shook her head in confusion.

"What are you going to paint on your plane?" Boris shrugged as if the answer was obvious. "You know, for your kills."

"Ah, right." Lily glanced at her plane as she thought. "Well, bring me some paint."

# Chapter Fifteen
# Gladiator

*"Life is very short and anxious for those who forget the past, neglect the present, and fear the future."*

Seneca

December 25, 1942

Lily sat at the table in the main area of their little bunker, sewing repairs into her jacket. A piece of shrapnel from an anti-aircraft gun had ripped it, nearly missing her shoulder and again reminding Lily of her incredible aptitude for luck.

Ina and Katya were also sitting with her in the bunker as they wrote letters home or took a moment of quiet reflection to read while listening to the radio.

Swan Lake was playing, and Lily relished in the soft strings, imagining the refined movements of the ballerina.

Suddenly, the music on the radio dimmed, and Lily turned to pay attention as this usually indicated an announcement was incoming.

"Yesterday, Soviet tanks broke through the German defenses and have taken the Tatsinskaya Airfield," the broadcast began.

"That's good news!" Kayta threw her lips upside down in surprise.

"The Soviet 62nd Army has retaken the Red October factory in Stalingrad," the announcer continued.

"More good news." Ina looked brightly at Katya.

"The following is an address by Pope Pius XII for the Christmas address."

"Odd that they would allow a religious broadcast." Katya frowned. "Especially for a Western Christmas."

The voice of the Pope began over the radio, but Lily couldn't detect what language he was speaking and looked at the other girls in confusion before asking, "Can you understand him?"

A moment later, a translator began speaking over the Pope's words, and Lily and the girls giggled at her impatience.

"Humanity owes this vow to those hundreds of thousands who, without any fault on their part, sometimes only because of their nationality or race, have been marked down for death or gradual extinction."

"He sounds sad." Katya stared at the radio.

"What's he talking about?" Lily squinted.

"Probably how the Nazis are treating the Jews, or how they're treating the Poles, or how they're treating just about anyone they have deemed as inferior or subhuman," Ina explained.

"Why doesn't he say that then?" Lily pressed.

"He needs to stay neutral." Ina shrugged.

"Why do they celebrate Christmas early?" Katya asked with a frown.

"They follow the Gregorian calendar. The orthodox follow the Julian calendar," Ina continued dryly.

"How do you know so much about this?" Lily looked at Ina suspiciously.

"I enjoy the subject." Ina leaned back and crossed her arms. "I find it a shame that our Soviet policy banned Christmas as a religious holiday. We never treated it in that manner. I miss decorating the tree or gathering by the warm fire with my family while my father read stories."

A knock came to the door of the bunker, and Ina and Katya both glanced at Lily.

"What?" Lily shrugged.

"Everyone knows who it is." Katya rolled her eyes.

The knock came again as Alexei called through the steel door, "It's cold out here!"

"Lucky guess." Lily offered glares at the ladies as she walked over to the bunker door and opened it to find a shivering Alexei with a package in his hand.

"What's this?" Lily asked as he handed it to her.

"Some correspondence for you and the others," he explained as he rubbed his arms to try and warm himself.

"Invite him in already!" Ina called. "You're letting the cold air in."

"I'm not prepared to receive company," Lily called back over her shoulder but took notice of the sentry posted outside the bunker, who looked more than annoyed at Ina's remark about the cold.

"Tonight, then?" Alexei asked eagerly. "I would like to see you."

"Perhaps." Lily tried to look indifferent, encouraging Alexei to continue the chase.

"What does that mean?" Alexei shook his head in confusion.

"It means you've yet to prove your worth. Also, it depends on how I'm feeling this evening." Lily closed the door and returned to the table as she tried to ignore the grins from Ina and Katya and set the package in the center.

"So, you and—"

"I don't want to talk about it." Lily feigned indifference but found it impossible to contain her own grin.

"Too bad." Ina inched her chair closer to Lily, as did Katya.

"Spill." Katya rattled her fingers against the table. "We want every detail."

"There's not a lot to say, really." Lily returned to sewing. "We've shared hidden looks, he gives me a great big hug after a successful sortie, but there's been no profession of love, no commitment or devotion."

"The whole airfield is aware of your romance." Katya leaned in.

"We've seen you holding hands, by the way." Ina also leaned in.

"You have?!" Lily looked at her in surprise before backpedaling and stating, "That would be strange indeed seeing, as we have never engaged in anything even remotely improper."

"And he's never snuck in here late at night either." Katya grinned, and Lily's face went pale.

"Your secret is safe with us." Ina laughed.

"We were so careful!" Lily's eyes grew wider and wider as she grasped the potential consequences. "If you know, then the colonel must know as well!"

"Please. He's a man." Ina raised an eyebrow.

"We haven't…you know…been intimate in that way." Lily cleared her throat. "It's sometimes just nice to be close to someone."

"Well, I, for one, am jealous." Katya leaned back and crossed her arms. "I'm stuck mailing letters off to some man who probably has given his heart away to another woman."

"He's giving something away, that's for sure." Ina snickered, and Katya reached across the table to slap her arm, but Ina withdrew quickly.

"Speaking of correspondence." Lily pointed at the parcels on the table.

Without further encouragement, Ina grabbed the parcels and began dispersing them to Lily and Katya.

"Nadia?" Lily picked up a letter from her old friend and opened it quickly.

"Please read aloud, if you can." Katya watched Lily unfolding the letter. "I would like to hear how she is."

"Let's see." Lily skimmed past the usual greetings. "Oh no."

"What is it?" Ina paused as she watched Lily.

"Valeria fell in battle." Lily grew emotional as she stared at the table in disbelief.

"How?" Ina asked as she cleared her throat.

"During a crash landing." Lily continued to read. "Nadia states that an investigation is being launched. Valeria had been without sleep for nearly two days when Major Kazarinova ordered her to perform another sortie.

They believe her eyes hadn't adjusted to the dark yet when she crashed."

"She was the first female to shoot down an enemy in combat." Ina also stared at the table.

The room drew quiet as they reflected on the tragedy. While Lily was still of the mind that such a fate would not be hers, she was becoming more and more aware of how fleeting her time as a pilot would likely be.

"What else does Nadia say?" Ina asked, and Lily sensed she was hopeful for some good news.

"Oh, looks like she's in love?" Lily tilted her head as she read.

"Who is it this time?" Katya snickered.

"She says that she was forced to make an emergency landing behind enemy lines. There was a man there who was badly wounded. His face was covered in bandages, but she says that she spotted him reading her favorite novel. She fell in love with him, and she knew it was genuine since she couldn't see what he looked like."

"That is romantic." Katya grinned with jealousy.

"Does she know what he looks like now?" Ina asked.

"Ina!" Katya scowled.

"What?" Ina shrugged. "It's relevant."

"They've decided not to promise each other anything, though," Lily read, but she was immediately reminded of her and Alexei as she continued, "She states that nothing is guaranteed. They don't want to promise a love that may never be realized."

Again, the room drew silent as they took to heart Nadia's statement in light of Valeria's death.

"I need a good wash," Lily stated after running her hand through her hair. "Alexei won't want to be anywhere near me if he sees how greasy I am."

"I don't think he's after your hair, Lily." Ina smirked.

"In any case, I don't think I can wait for the bath train to return." Lily stood and walked over to her bunk, where she grabbed a neatly folded towel.

"Are you going to dip in the river?" Katya asked sarcastically, but when Lily didn't reply and began walking toward the door with her towel and a bar of soap, Katya pressed, "Lily? The river is frozen. You know that, right?"

"Just going to wash my hair. I'll be right back." Lily threw on a jacket before rushing out the door.

"I have to see this." Ina chuckled as she followed closely after Lily.

"Good. I could use the help." Lily smiled at her friend who was now locking her arm in hers as they walked across the field toward the hangar.

Arm in arm, the two girls walked into the hangar and then approached Lily's plane, which was still warm from the last sortie she had undertaken.

"I need a bucket." Lily tapped her chin in thought as she looked around the hangar.

"For?" Ina squinted.

"The water, of course."

"Of course." Ina continued to squint before retrieving a bucket from a shelf.

"I could also use some cold water," Lily continued as she grew increasingly aware of the stares from some of the men in the hangar, including Colonel Baranov.

"Alright," Ina spoke slowly.

Wrapping the towel over her neck, Lily grabbed the tray of water from the radiator, poured it into the bucket, and mixed it with some cold water, and leaned down to wet her hair.

A couple of the men began to chuckle, but when they realized that she was serious, the entire hangar ceased what they were doing. No one was talking, the hammering or prying of metal from the engineers stopped, and Lily wondered why this was so astounding to them.

"Let me help you." Ina grabbed the bucket. "Lean forward."

Lily did as requested and let Ina pour the water over her hair while she used the soap to lather and wash away the grease.

Wrapping the towel around her head after she had finished, Lily stood and noticed that all the men were still staring at her in a state of shock. Then, slowly, the men began to look over at the colonel. Lily assumed that they were expecting him to offer her a harsh rebuke, and by the look he was offering her, she wondered if she had made a grave error.

"Huh." The colonel expressed his slight amusement before returning his attention to the map, and at once, the hangar returned to their activities as if the whole event had never happened.

Taking Ina's arm, Lily walked out of the hangar with her hair up in the towel.

"The power you have over those men, Lily," Ina spoke with reverence as they returned to the hangar.

"It's fun, isn't it." Lily giggled.

Returning to the bunker, Lily found Katya reading a letter near the table where she offered them a double take before asking in disbelief, "You didn't?!"

"Could you put my hair in curlers?" Lily ignored Katya as she asked Ina.

"I have some paper ones. They're not that great." Ina looked disappointed.

"Anything will do, really." Lily sat in the chair at the table as she dried her hair.

"These should work," Ina replied after she had rummaged through some drawers.

"I'm due for another sortie soon." Katya yawned as she leaned her elbows on the table.

"How many have you claimed now?" Lily asked as Ina began putting the curlers in her hair.

"Three and two shared," Katya replied plainly as if she were listing something trivial.

"I think we've made quite the impression here." Lily nodded. "And to think the colonel was going to transfer us away."

A knock came to the door.

"He's back again?" Katya frowned.

When no one moved to answer, Lily grumbled, "I can't answer looking like this."

"If it's true love, he'll appreciate you even with curlers in." Katya raised an eyebrow.

The knock came again.

"Answer!" Lily demanded of the girls as she pointed at the door.

"You're afraid of what he'll think? You can face Nazis, but you can't face Alexei?"

"You know how much I hate being manipulated," Lily grumbled as she stood up from the table and marched over to the door where she boldly swung it open.

Yet instead of the captain she was expecting to find, stood a civilian with a pen and notepad in hand.

"Yes?" Lily panicked as she retrieved her blue scarf and threw it over her head before tying it under her chin, entirely embarrassed to be seen in this state.

"I'm looking for Lily Litvyak," the man began.

"It's Lieutenant Litvyak," she corrected him sternly.

"Lieutenant." He held up his pen in recognition of the correction. "And that would be you, then?"

"Yes," she replied briskly as she began to form panicking thoughts. "Is everything alright? Is this about my mother or brother?"

"I'm not here about them, Lieutenant. I'm here for you," he explained as he shivered. "May I come in?"

"What is it you want with me?" Lily asked grumpily.

"I would like to interview you. Have you not seen the papers? You're in every one of them. There are reports that you have shot down six enemy planes by yourself."

"I'm in the papers?" Lily crossed her arms.

"Yes, actually." He held up a finger as he set his briefcase down and retrieved a newspaper that he handed to Lily. "I've been writing about you."

"You have?" Lily raised an eyebrow as she looked at the paper, which had a column on the side reading *The White Rose of Stalingrad.*

"Rose?" Lily tilted her head.

"The English papers mistranslated what I had written. I called you Madonna Lily, but they translated it to White Rose. I thought it sounded better, anyway. More feminine."

"And more feminine is good?" Lily frowned as she read through the brief column.

"I would say so. I'm still surprised that such a beautiful young thing like you is a menace to the enemy." He examined her in a manner that no woman would appreciate as he continued, "Is it true you've shot down six planes yourself? And that for each plane you shoot down, you paint a white rose on your plane?"

Lily bit her lip from cursing him out for his patronizing tone, and without hesitation, stood back and slammed the door shut in his face.

"Lily!" Katya tilted her head in disappointment. "He didn't deserve that."

"I don't like being written about." Lily tossed the paper onto the table. "He's barely said anything about me that isn't about my looks."

"You can change that narrative, you know." Nadia urged. "Go invite him in before he gets too far. He's going to write about you anyway. He might as well have the facts."

"I'd rather not have the attention." Lily crossed her arms as she sat.

"Well, why don't I give him the facts, then." Katya stood and threw on her jacket.

"What?" Lily frowned. "Why?"

"I'll go with you." Nadia also stood.

"You really don't have to. I'm—"

"You don't understand, Lily," Katya began as she secured her hat. "How that man writes about you in the paper is going to determine, without exaggeration, how the rest of the world sees us as women combatants. I'm going to make sure that they know that we're not silly girls playing at a man's game. They're going to see us as the Fascists do: a serious threat."

A cold chill ran down Lily's spine as Katya and Nadia were soon out the door and running after the reporter. Lily felt a twinge of guilt as she understood this went well beyond merely an article on her. Still, Lily despised that sort of attention.

Sitting alone in the quiet bunker with the dim light glowing above her, Lily began to feel uncomfortable with the silence. Leaning over, Lily turned the volume up on the radio, but she could still feel her thoughts rising in contention with her peace. Turning the volume as high as it could go, Lily leaned back in her chair as she listened to the blaring and passionate tenor singing an aria.

Closing her eyes with her face raised to heaven, Lily began taking out her curlers, enjoying the immersion in the loud music that was drowning out her thoughts. She couldn't think of the images of Stalingrad, or the idea of all the men she had killed, or her mother or brother, or even Alexei. In this blaring tune, all she could feel were the curlers in her hair, the cold draft from the slit under the door, and the heaviness of her eyes.

Still, like a tide slowly rising, a thought began to climb to the surface. She began to think of her recent combat missions, and how she and Alexei, as excellent a team as they were, had killed so many men. She had yet to grow numb to that feeling, but each time she set an enemy plane ablaze, she knew that the pilot was experiencing an agonizing death by burning alive until the plane crashed with the earth. She knew that at any given sortie, that could be her or Alexei's fate.

The phone rang.

Lily was startled and turned down the radio.

The phone rang again.

"Yes?" Lily answered it quickly.

"There's a plane circling the airfield," Boris spoke into the receiver.

"A plane?" Lily frowned before adding sarcastically. "How unusual. At an airfield you say?"

"An enemy aircraft, Lily," Boris replied with a slight groan.

"And you need me to go shoot him down for you?" Lily asked with a smirk. "Why haven't the anti-aircraft guns taken him down?"

"He's too high for them. We believe he's offering a challenge."

"A challenge?" Lily's interest was piqued. "To single combat?"

"Yes, and I thought I would—"

"I accept," Lily spoke boldly.

"That's great and all, but—"

"Tell Ina to have my plane ready. She's chasing after some reporter at the moment. I imagine this would make a great story. If—"

"Alexei has already been given permission by the colonel," Boris spoke quickly.

Lily's heart fell into her stomach.

"I thought you would want to know," Boris continued softly.

"I see." Lily swallowed. "Thank you."

With that, Lily hung up the phone before rushing to grab her coat and running out the door.

Looking up into the sky on the clear winter day, Lily spotted the unmistakable shape of the Messerschmitt circling above the airfield.

"What the hell is wrong with him?!" Lily asked aloud as she ran toward the hangar.

She knew that she couldn't stop Alexei from pursuing the challenge, and Lily prayed that this wasn't the day when his pride got him killed.

Lily ran across the field, shielding her face from the bitter bite of the cold air, and her stomach lurched when she heard the start of an engine.

*He better wait for me to at least wish him luck!* Lily grumbled to herself, but as she ran, she watched as his plane took off down the runway and was shortly in the air.

*This is not the day I say goodbye to you,* Lily watched his plane ascend quickly into the sky. *You idiot! He has the advantage of height over you. Why would you risk this?!*

Entering the hangar, Lily noticed that nearly the entire airbase had gathered to watch this spectacle.

"What is he thinking?" Lily asked as she came to stand near Boris.

"The Germans think little of our skill. The captain wants to prove our worth," the colonel interjected.

"He'll be alright." Boris placed his hand on her shoulder, but Lily rolled away after offering him a cruel glare.

*Men are so stupid! Does he think I'll run into his arms if Alexei dies?* Lily fumed inwardly as she moved into a better position to view the fight. Her shoulders were tight, her jaw was clenched, her brow was furrowed, and Lily felt as if she might pass out at any moment.

"Lily!" Katya called out as she arrived by her side. "We just heard the news."

"I can't watch!" Lily turned away as the German unleashed his weaponry on Alexei, who was able to dodge and avoid the fire masterfully.

"He's going to be fine!" Ina also arrived by Lily's side.

"Don't worry, Lily," Katya spoke softly, but Lily caught the trepidation in her voice.

Such maneuvers and feats were dangerous even when gunfire wasn't part of the equation, and Lily, with her eyes squeezed shut, prayed that he would be swift and accurate and not rely on his ego.

An explosion echoed throughout the sky, and Lily's first thought was the worst possible outcome. She was pleased, at least, that his death was quick and he didn't burn alive in the cockpit as he hurdled to the earth.

Then, suddenly, a cheer erupted from everyone inside the hangar, but Lily still didn't allow herself to believe everything was alright.

"He's alive?" Lily looked intently into Katya's eyes.

"I told you not to worry." Katya placed her hands on Lily's shoulders before pulling her in close for an embrace.

"Good!" Lily pulled away as she frowned sharply. "I'll be in the bunker."

"You don't want to wait for him to land?" Ina asked with confusion.

"I never want to see that man again!" Lily half-shouted as she stormed back across the field.

*The absolute nerve of that useless captain!* Lily seethed with rage. *How dare he put me through that! I would never do that to him! Clearly, he means more to me than I do to him!*

"Papers," the sentry demanded as Lily approached the bunker.

"It's me!" Lily barked. "The White Rose of Stalingrad! Haven't you heard?"

"It's my job." The sentry held up his hand to refuse her entry.

"What Ina sees in you is beyond me." Lily growled at him but then relaxed her shoulders a measure before handing him her documents and stating, "Sorry. That was uncalled for."

The sentry didn't reply as he took an extra minute looking over her documents, and Lily knew he was lingering to keep her in the cold.

"I apologized," Lily snatched the documents back out of his hand before opening the door and adding over her shoulder, "I've been punished enough today with lessons in humility."

The sentry chuckled as Lily closed the door behind her, and she stormed over to the table where she sat and crossed her arms, refusing to take off her jacket, gloves, or boots.

The clock ticked patiently as Lily bounced her leg, running over every possible argument, stockpiling her arsenal of cutting quips and remarks, and preparing for Alexei's visit.

"Careful," the sentry spoke to someone outside. "She's riled up."

"Riled up?!" Lily spoke aloud as she pursed her lips together angrily.

"That's not tough to do these days," the reply came, and Lily recognized the voice of Alexei, and she nearly wished that he had, indeed, met his end by the enemy plane. At least then, his passing would be merciful.

The knock came to the door.

Lily remained with her arms crossed, refusing to budge, and instead turned the radio on and blasted the volume.

The knock came again.

"Lily!" Alexei called. "I know you're in there. Can we have a moment to speak?"

"I'm alone. It would be improper," Lily called back.

"Never stopped you before," the sentry replied.

At this, Lily stomped over to the door and flung it open, where she pointed a gloved finger at the sentry and, with gritted teeth, stated, "Stay out of this!"

"So, have I earned the right to see you?" Alexei looked at her with bright, eager eyes.

"You think that's what impresses me?" Lily pointed to the sky. "You nearly gave me a heart attack!"

"You were worried about me?" Alexei offered her a cocky smile.

"I'm worried about what is going to happen to you if you keep looking at me like that!" Lily frowned sharply at him.

"Listen, Lily, I knew that I had him." Alexei shrugged.

"You didn't know that!" Lily shouted. "You guessed! You put all your confidence in chance and in your own skills."

"I'm a good pilot," Alexei grew defensive.

"The best I've seen," Lily countered. "But no one is free from time and chance."

Alexei drew a deep breath as he studied her, and Lily noticed that Katya and Ina were approaching the bunker as well.

"I'm sorry," Alexei spoke slowly.

"Thank you." Lily avoided eye contact as she played with the handle on the door.

"I have a responsibility to the men under my charge," Alexei continued. "I would never have been able to live with myself had I sent another man in my place."

"You're a good man, Alexei." Lily looked at him with soft eyes. She knew she was being selfish with her opinion of how the events played out. She had never felt this way for a man before, and Lily didn't know what she would do if the worst came to pass.

"May I come in?" Alexei asked tenderly as he took a step closer to her.

"Did he see your papers?" Lily asked sarcastically as she glanced at the sentry, who offered her a frown of his own.

"He's just annoyed because you're the reason he and the mechanic don't have their usual alone time." Alexei nudged the sentry with his elbow.

"I have no knowledge of what you're insinuating," the sentry replied quickly, but Lily noticed that he couldn't keep his eyes off the approaching Ina.

"Come in already. You're letting in the cold." Lily nodded as she backed away and let him inside the bunker.

"Thank you." Alexei removed his hat and jacket, and Lily did the same.

She smiled at him as she allowed a dangerous fabrication to form. She imagined the two of them were in their bedroom after a long, rewarding day. They had a house in Moscow near her mother that wasn't too big but comfortable enough for when their children came along. She could already hear Anna demanding grandkids for her to spoil, and Lily knew she would dote on them in such a manner that she refused to her and Yuri.

It was a dangerous reflection because Lily knew that such things were beyond the realm of attainable. If she focused too much on that invention, she would lose sight of the goal. She would react poorly, again, like she had only moments ago when Alexei took on the perilous challenge.

Grabbing a couple chairs, Alexei dragged them over in front of the stove, where he sat with an exhausted huff. Lily soon joined him, and the two sat in the stillness and quiet while warming themselves by the potbellied stove.

Katya and Ina burst into the bunker shortly, in such a manner that Lily was certain they were hoping to catch a glimpse of something scandalous but were instead disappointed to find the captain and lieutenant behaving with propriety.

"Let's give them a minute," Katya whispered as she and Ina shuffled by them and into Ina's room.

Again, in the silence, Lily sat beside Alexei before turning the radio back on. The soft strings played beautifully as she leaned back in her chair and let her hands fall to her sides.

After a few minutes, Lily felt Alexei's rugged hand take hold of hers, and she could scarcely contain her smile.

Words didn't need to be conveyed between them, and further affection than the simple act of hand-holding wasn't required. Even the modest, common act of interlinking fingers sent shockwaves against the unrelenting waves of trauma and despair.

Lily, in this moment, was at peace.

# Chapter Sixteen
# The Georgian

*The tall one wouldn't bend; the short one wouldn't stretch and the kiss was lost.*

Georgian Proverb

<u>January 30, 1943</u>

Lily smacked her gloves together as she stood near her plane to try to warm her hands. Ina was busy working on the engine, and seeing what she had to endure, Lily was thankful she had not been assigned as a mechanic.

It was nearly forty degrees below Celsius, and Lily didn't believe that such a cold was possible. It had, of course, been cold in Moscow, but out here, with the bitter lashing of the wind against the skin, Lily thought there were times she would lose consciousness.

"Would you like any assistance?" Lily asked Ina as she shivered.

"No." Ina licked her finger before placing it on a screw, using her spit as an adhesive so she could get the screw into the small opening.

"Anything the matter with her?" Lily asked about her plane worriedly.

Ina shook her head quickly.

"We're due for another sortie shortly," Lily pressed. She didn't want to be rude in asking Ina for an exact time, especially when she was working so diligently in these extreme conditions, but Lily was anxious to return to combat.

"I know!" Ina barked. "Go get some food while you wait. I can't work with you staring over my shoulder."

*What food?* Lily grumbled to herself as she left Ina alone and headed toward the field kitchen, where she spotted Alexei and the colonel talking together in a lively manner.

"The Fascist dogs have all but surrendered," the colonel began excitedly as he held a cup of warm water to thaw his fingers.

"They're persistent, though." Alexei tilted his head in wonder. "You have to admire their determination."

"I'm not sure if it is determination," Lily interjected as she came to stand beside Alexei, close enough that their arms rubbed up against each other.

Any further display of affection would be, of course, inappropriate, especially in front of the colonel, but Lily took whatever measures she could to be close to Alexei.

Colonel Baranov ran his tongue along his teeth as he took notice of Lily's proximity to Alexei but then glanced away as if he hadn't seen anything peculiar. Lily, for one, was thankful for Alexei's close relationship with the colonel, otherwise both she and Alexei would likely have faced unkind reprimands, at best.

"If not determination, then what?" Alexei asked her.

"Is stupidity too rude of a word?" Lily chuckled.

"We should be careful not to underestimate the enemy," the colonel was quick to chastise.

"Yes, sir." Lily nodded. She was, of course, merely jesting, but she understood his point.

"Lily!" an excited voice called behind her, and Lily turned to find that Boris was approaching her quickly with a newspaper.

"Boris," Lily spoke with indifference as she turned away from him.

"Need me to send him away?" Alexei leaned over and whispered.

"I'm capable of handling him by myself," Lily replied quickly.

"I sure hope not." Alexei smirked as he winked and walked away with the colonel as they continued talking about the positive news from Stalingrad.

"They put another picture of you in the paper," Boris spoke excitedly as he handed her the newspaper, which showed her climbing into her airplane.

"Not as bad as I expected." Lily threw her lips upside down in surprise.

"You're two kills away from ten." Boris tapped the article eagerly. "How about that?"

"I'd say be careful when you're in the air with me, my friend." Lily smiled at him. "You don't want to end up as one of those two remaining."

"Even from the air, you're beautiful." Boris smiled brightly at her, and Lily rolled her eyes.

"That wasn't my best line," Boris continued, undeterred by Lily's obvious dissatisfaction.

"I never did ask where you were from," Lily began as she turned and walked back toward the planes, hoping to shift the conversation.

"Georgia," Boris replied proudly. "Same region as Stalin, actually."

"You should lead with that next time you're trying to seduce me." Lily smirked.

"You mistake me." Boris stopped in his tracks, and Lily, curious, turned toward him.

"You have my attention." Lily rolled her hand for him to proceed.

"I'm not trying to seduce you." Boris stared at the concrete at his feet.

"No?" Lily tilted her head.

"Look," Boris took a small step toward her before continuing softly, "If we weren't in such perilous circumstances, I would keep my mouth shut. As it is, I think you should be aware of my feelings for you."

"I don't think anyone is left in the dark in that regard." Lily raised her eyebrow.

"My affection is a mask, Lily."

"A mask?"

"I don't want to turn you into some sort of score or a notch in my list of accomplishments to tick off." Boris shook his head as he looked intently into her eyes. "I want to serve you. I want to be the man who is exactly who you need me to be. If that means being a comrade in arms and nothing more, then that's what I'll be. If that means standing at a distance while I watch you and the captain experience a love I'll never know, then I'll be content in my isolation, knowing that you are happy."

"Well, I'm glad you're happy." Lily smiled briskly as she tried to brush away the discomfort. She was used to men making pleas of affection before, but the way Boris was looking at her was genuine love. Not even Alexei looked at her in that manner, and Lily was actually quite pleased that he didn't.

"Maybe happy is the wrong word." Boris clicked his tongue as he thought.

"We're due for another sortie." Lily nodded for them to continue walking toward the planes. "We should prepare."

"Do you think you'll add another rose to your plane?" Boris asked as he shoved his hands into his coat pockets.

"I'm running out of room." Lily pointed at the white roses decorating the side of the fuselage. "I would rather have the war over with."

"Did you eat?" Ina asked as she cupped her hands over her mouth before blowing warm breath into them.

"I was distracted." Lily shook her head.

"You have to eat!" Ina barked loudly at Lily. "If you're malnourished, you make mistakes. Mistakes that I have to correct, by the way."

"I'll make note of that next time." Lily nodded as she studied her friend, who was beside herself with frustration.

"If there will be a next time," Ina muttered before continuing angrily, "You have to be careful. I'm careful, but they're not writing about me in the papers. Nobody cares about the thankless jobs on the ground. You wouldn't have any of those kills if it weren't for me making sure your Troika was in perfect condition. Every thirty minutes, I'm fixing up someone's stupid plane. No rest, no food, no time, and no damn thanks for what I do."

Lily didn't reply as she glanced at Boris who, she noticed, seemed ready to defend Lily as he scowled at Ina.

"Thank you, Ina." Lily patted her friend on the arm.

"Too late for that." Ina brushed Lily away before storming off to the next plane that needed inspection, or refueling, or more ammunition.

"Poor thing," Lily mumbled as she climbed onto the wing of her plane.

"No need to pose. There's no cameras around," Boris called as he walked toward his plane as well.

"Thank goodness for that, at least." Lily secured her hat and goggles and looked around the cockpit.

She stared at the picture of her father, imagining what he would say if he could see her now. She was already an ace pilot, an achievement she would've never envisioned for her life. Back at the flying club, she thought that someday she would undertake exploits like Major Raskova had, but now as she glanced out the windshield at the white roses, she almost didn't recognize her past self.

Ina returned to Lily's plane, and, still without losing any of her irritability, smacked the side of the fuselage roughly after removing the blocks under the tires.

With a signal of gratitude, that Ina entirely ignored, Lily taxied her plane to near Alexei's, and the couple took to the air, followed shortly by Boris and another pilot.

"The Luftwaffe are trying to halt our advance, if they can," Alexei spoke into the headset. "They're trying to bomb our ground troops. Let's drive the German Air Force into the ground once and for all."

The squadron of four free hunters passed over the war-torn city of Stalingrad, and Lily's heart ached when she spotted the hundreds, if not thousands, of bodies that were either decaying or recently deceased. It was so inhumane that scores upon scores of innocents had not only died but were now left to rot.

The only uplifting sight were the hundreds of Soviet tanks heading toward German lines, and the dozens of men following behind each engine. This was the beginning of the end; Lily could feel it. She would finally, once this war was settled, be able to fly for pleasure and not as an instrument of death. She wondered what would become of her and Alexei. She imagined a man of his caliber would not be content with a routine family life, and wondered if they would even have a relationship outside of war.

Crack!

Lily flinched as a bullet struck her windshield. It left a mark but nothing more serious, and Lily looked around for the source.

"Lily! Break right!" Boris shouted. "Captain! Break left! I'll cover your six."

Without hesitation, Lily did as commanded as bullets narrowly missed her engine, and she glanced in the rearview mirror to find that a German was tight on her heels.

Flashes of light reflected in the mirror as the enemy unleashed his weaponry on her, and Lily engaged in evasive maneuvers.

"Break left!" Boris commanded, and Lily obeyed quickly.

Glancing again in the rearview mirror, Lily watched as the enemy plane was struck by Boris' shots, and it quickly descended to the earth in black smoke.

"Thank you, my Georgian friend," Lily sighed her relief.

"He came out of nowhere," Boris replied with suspicion. "Why was he alone?"

"He wasn't alone," Alexei interjected. "Five o'clock. One thousand feet."

Glancing in the direction, Lily spotted a bomber that was being escorted by two fighters.

"He was going to lead us away from them." Lily nodded. "Brave sacrifice."

"I'd hate to assume you're starting to admire the Fascists?" Boris laughed while Alexei and even Lily joined in the amusement.

"Boris, you two attack the bomber. Lily and I will provide cover."

"Lily should attack. She needs more kills," Boris replied as if they were discussing a trivial hunting trip, and not men's lives.

"She'll get her kills when the fighters break off to attack you."

"Ah, yes, send poor Boris as bait." He chuckled.

"You're very good at it. I almost want to attack you," Alexei laughed.

"Cover us." Boris and his wing mate increased speed as Lily and Alexei stayed back in preparation to counter.

Drawing a deep breath, Lily steadied her nerves to attack the enemy fighters. She wondered if there would ever come a time when going into battle would feel normal. She wondered how Alexei appeared so casual every sortie.

But then something caught Lily's eye. About a thousand feet above them, in the cloud cover, were a couple black dots.

"Boris! Abandon target! It's a trap!" Lily screamed.

It was too late. The enemy was already descending upon Boris and his wing mate.

Without a word, Lily and Alexei simultaneously sprung into action to come to Boris' rescue.

The ambushing Messerschmitt's, with the advantage of height and angle, fired upon Boris, striking his engine and starting a fire.

The sound of his screaming was horrendous as Boris was burned by the flames, and Lily wrenched off her headset as she watched his plane on fire.

"I'm...still...on target!" Boris spoke in between screams. "The fire...is...burning my...leg."

"Eject!" Alexei shouted. "Get out of there!"

"It's jammed!" Boris shouted back. "Lily, I—"

All he could do was scream, and Lily assumed the pain was unimaginable.

Still, with a determination and grit that few could summon, Boris rammed his plane into the back of the bomber, and the two aircraft were engulfed in a terrible explosion that sent shockwaves through the sky.

Oddly enough, the first thought that passed through Lily's mind was guilt. She recalled how she had reacted to Boris' advances and thought she could've been kinder to him.

But this guilt was short-lived as a rage began to overtake her. She was incensed at the cowardly ambush, and Lily began to pursue one of the fighters despite pleas from Alexei to remain level-headed.

The enemy, however, had clearly become overconfident in their attack on Boris, and was not expecting Lily's counter. Within mere moments, while in perfect positioning, Lily turned the Nazi plane into a ball of fire.

It was her ninth kill, and Lily was hungry for more.

Another bomber, unprotected, was only a few hundred yards ahead of them, and Lily noticed that the other enemy fighters had broken off formation, severely demoralized by the loss of their bomber and a fighter.

"I'm behind you," Alexei spoke into the headset, and Lily placed it back over her head.

"I'll take out the gunner and then destroy the bomber," Lily replied.

"I'll cover for you."

Approaching the enemy bomber from the rear, Lily was about to release a short burst of fire when the enemy gunner fired back at her.

Immediately, black smoke billowed out of her engine, and within mere seconds, the plane lost all power. The engine was now entirely dead.

It was strange how quiet it was in the air without the sound of the familiar humming of the engine, and despite the fact that the enemy was firing upon her, Lily almost found the moment peaceful.

Still, Lily knew she had to act, and she glided her plane back in the direction of their airfield.

"Can you make it?" Alexei asked, and Lily heard the fear in his voice.

Lily shook her head as she looked at her instruments, map, and watch before replying, "No."

"You'll be fine. We'll find you somewhere to land," Alexei tried to sound calm, but Lily could hear how afraid he was.

Lily's arms shook as she drifted over the earth that was approaching swiftly. She pulled back on the lever with all her strength, but the dead weight of the machine was too much for her.

It was then that Lily became aware of a pain in her leg. Glancing down, she noticed that she was bleeding, and bleeding a lot. Something was stuck in her leg. She couldn't tell if it was from the enemy, or from her own plane, but it was metal. Regardless of where it came from, the pain was growing unbearable.

"There's a field," Alexei spoke softly as he flew as slowly as possible. "You can land there. I'll send someone to pick you up."

Lily didn't reply. She knew that if she did, he would hear the pain in her voice. Instead, she pulled off the headset and oxygen mask and prepared for impact. The field, while somewhat flat, was less than ideal. The snowbanks and drifts would not make for a smooth landing, and Lily knew that this was going to be painful.

*Stay awake, stay awake, stay awake,* Lily forced her eyes wide open. She had lost a lot of blood, and it was almost impossible to remain conscious.

The wheels made contact with the field, and the plane jolted and bounced before hitting a rut and spinning around violently before coming to an abrupt stop.

With heavy breathing, Lily pushed open the canopy and watched Alexei circling above. She assumed that he had sent a message back to base, which was a few miles away.

Glancing down at her leg, Lily felt the blood pooling in her boot. She could smell the strong scent of iron and wondered if that was from blood or from the plane.

Summing every ounce of her strength, climbed out of the plane and fell onto the wing, where she screamed in agony at the pressure on her wound.

Squeezing her eyes shut as she tried to press through the pain, Lily's only thought was on Alexei circling above her, and she wondered how he would cope with her passing. She had been so concerned with Alexei dying in action and being left alone that she never considered the alternative; she might be the first to die.

Static came over Lily's headset, which was still in the plane. She knew Alexei was trying to tell her something, but she couldn't make out what he was saying.

Growing aware of the sound of a truck engine, Lily opened her eyes to find that a vehicle was approaching her and swiftly. She couldn't tell if they were friend or foe, but in either case it didn't matter as Lily's vision faded to black.

# Chapter Seventeen
# Convalesce

*He will win who knows when to fight and when not to fight.*

Sun Tzu

"Welcome back," a familiar voice spoke tenderly.

Lily tried to pry her eyes open, but despite her honest attempts, they remained shut. She felt as if weights were tying them down.

"Lily," the voice spoke again.

Then Lily heard a groan of someone in pain, and peeking out from under a heavy eyelid, she spotted a soldier on a cot near her. He was shaking and gritting his teeth as a nurse tended to the bandage on his chest.

A scream erupted beside her, and Lily turned sharply to find another soldier with an open wound in his arm and blood pouring onto the floor. Again, a nurse was beside him and applied pressure to stop the bleeding.

"Hey," the familiar voice spoke to her again, and Lily looked to the foot of her cot to see Alexei smiling at her sympathetically.

Lily didn't know what to say. Her mind was lost in a fog. She tried to sit upright, but a sharp pain in her left arm stopped her. Glancing at her arm, she noticed that it was bandaged and there was a red stain from blood. She then also noticed that she was hooked up to an IV that held a clear fluid.

"You should've told me how injured you were." Alexei scooched up the cot to sit closer to her. "I saw you waving and thought you were fine. I went on another sortie after the colonel had picked you up, only to be told later by your friend Katya that you were in the field hospital."

"Why is my arm bandaged?" Lily squinted as she looked again at her arm.

"I can answer that," a doctor arrived near her cot with his hands in his pockets. He was wearing a white coat over his army uniform, and Lily thought that he looked exhausted.

"You were the surgeon?" Alexei asked eagerly as he stood.

"I was." The doctor nodded.

"Thank you for your diligent care." Alexei extended his hand in thankfulness, but the doctor ignored the gesture and instead retrieved a metal fragment from his pocket that he then handed to Lily.

"What's this?" Lily asked as she inspected the small, frayed metal piece.

"What remains of the bullet that was stuck in your arm," the doctor replied plainly.

"I don't remember being hit in the arm." Lily squinted.

"I imagine the pain in your leg distracted you." The doctor tilted his head as he thought. "Maybe you should keep that as a reminder to stay out of trouble."

"I will." Lily squeezed the bullet tight in her hands.

"I've ordered a period of convalescence," the doctor continued dryly.

"What?" Lily frowned. "No, no, no. I can't leave."

"You can't fly, either." The doctor pointed to her leg. "You'll need crutches for a while. If you don't rest properly, you'll never fly again."

With that, the doctor left, and Lily closed her eyes in frustration.

"This is a good thing, Lily." Alexei patted her unwounded leg.

"Nothing good will come from me being away from you." Lily scowled at him. "Why do you want me gone so badly?"

"I don't want you gone!" Alexei laughed. "It'll break my heart to be without you."

"What's her name?" Lily pressed. "You've found someone else already, haven't you?"

"Lily." Alexei raised his eyebrows, unimpressed. "Her name is Lily. She's a stubborn little woman who needs to know when to take a moment."

"If you were in my position, what would you do?" Lily continued in her irritability.

"I pose the same question to you. If I had been shot down and the doctor ordered convalescence, would you have me disregard these orders?"

"I would never discourage you from flying." Lily raised her chin high and proudly.

"You know you would urge me to listen." Alexei grinned at her before reaching under the cot and grabbing something that was wrapped in a brown cloth.

"What's this?" Lily asked with intrigue, but then held up a finger as she tilted her head, "I'd hate to assume this is to distract me?"

"You'll have to open it and see." Alexei placed it on her lap.

A shooting pain ran up Lily's leg, and she winced as she tried to readjust her position on the uncomfortable cot.

"I wish I had known how serious your injury was," Alexei spoke with regret.

"Why?" Lily shrugged. "What would you have done differently?"

Alexei didn't reply as he looked intently into her eyes, and Lily thought he was wanting to tell her something that he didn't know how to articulate.

Glancing down at the cloth on her lap, Lily unwrapped it to find a knife. It was crudely made — but not without some craftsmanship. The wooden handle was an attempt at intricacy with elegant designs, but the inexperience was evident. Under the knife was a photograph of both her and Alexei on the wing of her plane.

"It's nice." Lily offered a faint smile as she held up the knife, not entirely understanding the sentiment.

"I made," Alexei explained.

"Oh, how sweet." Lily beamed but winced again in pain at the sudden surge in her leg. She didn't quite care for the knife, but she adored that he had labored on something for her. That was love.

"I'll let you rest," Alexei spoke after looking at his watch.

"How can I leave you?" Lily's lips trembled. "I'll be worried about you day and night."

"Have you ever met a Nazi who is a better pilot than myself?" Alexei offered her a cocky look.

"I'd be surprised if there were any as arrogant as you," Lily grumbled as she frowned and added, "Your overconfidence will get you killed."

"On the contrary." Alexei stood. "My overconfidence will keep me alive."

"I'll be back as soon as I'm able." Lily looked at him as she felt a crushing weight upon her heart.

She hated leaving Alexei's side, hated not being a part of the war effort, and hated that the next weeks would be an exposition in idleness.

"Oh, I almost forgot." Alexei dug into his pocket and retrieved some letters. "These came from your friends. Looks like they were written some time ago, but you know how the mail is lately."

"Thank you," Lily replied plainly as she took the letters from him.

"It'll be alright." Alexei offered her a large grin before turning away and heading toward the tent exit.

Lily watched him eagerly, praying and hoping that he would turn around and look at her one last time. If he did, she knew that he truly loved her. It was an unwritten rule that expressing such sentiments was forbidden. With the unpredictability of war, promises of love were seen as counterintuitive at best, and as omens of disaster at worst.

Lily's heart fluttered when Alexei suddenly turned at the exit of the tent, looked directly at her, and, with the characteristic cocky smile, exited.

"He loves me," Lily spoke to herself as she rested her head against the crude pillow on her cot.

Within minutes, another soldier, with his arms around two comrades, came hobbling into the tent while screaming in pain. Blood was spraying from a wound, and Lily noticed that his foot was dangling from his leg. The only thing keeping it attached was some loose piece of skin.

The nurses, and the surgeon who had talked to Lily, ran to his side as they quickly prepared a cot for him.

Lily placed a hand to her forehead to test her temperature, and she felt that she was quite warm. Still, with the situation of the poor man and his foot, Lily thought it best not to disturb the nurses. Lily opened one of the letters.

*Dearest and sweetest Lily*, Nadia began.

"Here we go," Lily spoke to herself as she smiled, anticipating an engaging letter that would run for pages.

*It's been difficult as part of the Soviet counteroffensive. We've lost so many girls, and the new recruits don't have the proper experience. We lost eight girls in a single night. I was leading a night raid as a navigator for Marina, and as soon as we dropped our bombs, the searchlights came on. It was a trap. The Nazis had become so enraged at us 'night witches' that they designed a fake target in the hopes we would attack it.*

*The light from the search beams was blinding and terrifying, considering our slow speeds in those Po-2s. We were sitting ducks, as the English say, and within minutes, four of our aircraft were shot down. It was awful to witness. Some of the aircraft would burn as they spiraled toward the earth, and to know the fate of those poor girls trapped inside was something I don't think I shall soon forget.*

*Speaking of the fate of our comrades, there's something I need to tell you. It's the reason I wrote to you in the first place, but I can't seem to bring myself to pen the words. It's too painful.*

*Major Raskova is dead.*

Lily's eyes bulged out of her head as she read that phrase over and over, wondering if her mind was playing tricks on her.

"How can that be?" Lily asked aloud.

A man beside her groaned as he turned to his side and began to weep. Lily's heart broke for him as she looked at the bandage on his back that scarcely covered the burn wound.

*Major Raskova is dead.* Lily read the words again.

*I didn't believe she was human, to be honest. A few nights before her accident, we found her asleep at her desk, pencil still in hand. She had given everything for us girls.*

*She was in a blizzard, and we can only assume that was flying lower than she should've been. She crashed into the side of a hill. Her body was flung from the wreckage, where we assume she died instantly. We will honor her legacy forever.*

*I wish I had better news for you. My letters usually are more chipper than this, but...oh, Marina wants me to remind you of something, but she wants to make it seem like it was my idea to tell you and not hers. Too late. She's mad at me now.*

*Anyway, we celebrated Marina's five-hundredth mission! Can you believe that? She flies almost as much as she smokes. Terrible habit she got me into. I wish I never had taken that cigarette when she offered it to me. I smell like a man now. It's horrible.*

*Speaking of men, at the airfield we're at now — I can't even remember the name of it, we have had to switch so many times — we're staying in a bunker that the men had used. The smell, Lily, the smell! We cleaned it out in due time and made it proper.*

*Oh, Marina wants me to tell you about the thing we made for her five-hundredth mission. She's mad at me again. We would've made a cake for her, but with the current situation with food and all, I'm sure you're in the same boots as we are, we used a watermelon instead. We carved out a little bomber and wrote five hundred on it. She cut it up like a cake and handed it out to everyone. We invited the men to join us, making sure they wiped their boots before coming in, and we had a sing-along. It was a wonderful night.*

*Odd how you can tell the difference between the pilots. The bombers seem to walk with a certain gait, and they're more calculated and methodical, while the fighters walk with a touch of swagger and seem cocky.*

*Marina wants me to tell you some last bit of good news before I let you return to killing Nazis. I'm not sure why she didn't just write a letter to you herself. She's walking away. She's lighting another cigarette even though she has one in her mouth already.*

*Anyway, we have been designated as the 46th Guards Night Bomber Aviation Regiment! After all that we have been put through by men who didn't believe we would be any success, we have been made an elite guard. There is no higher honor. I only wish Major Raskova was here to see it.*

*I've been seeing you in the papers and heard reports on the radio. We're all proud of you more than you can imagine. I also see there is a certain man with you in some of the pictures. I want all the gossip. Tell me every detail!*

*Look forward to your reply.*

*Nadia*

With a tearful smile, Lily held the letter close to her chest as she felt her hands trembling. Her fever was increasing, and she knew she needed rest.

# Chapter Eighteen
# Reunion

*Blessed are they that mourn: for they shall be comforted.*

St. Matthew 5:4

The subway train came to a halt near Lily's exit, and, grabbing her cane, Lily stood to leave. The crowds paid her little attention as they crammed toward the doors. Some were eager to leave, while others were pressing to enter. No one cared for Lily's injury, or the fact she was a wounded soldier.

Still, Lily didn't blame them for their disregard. She understood that very few had made it this far into the war without losing someone. The suffering was almost endless, and the dire state of Moscow was proof of that. Many of the people she passed by had the unmistakable mark of hunger.

Hobbling on her crutch, Lily took the escalator to exit the station, where she found hundreds of people, including many other soldiers, begging on the street.

A man without legs sat on a board near a fountain in the middle of the square. A wooden sign rested in front of him explaining that he was hungry and a soldier. He looked dejected and broken, and Lily wondered as to the quality of the man he had been before his injury. In her mind, Lily saw Alexei as this man. Someone who had been tall and self-confident, but now was crestfallen.

Walking over to near the fountain, Lily spotted a dried iris flower that was limped over in the snow. There was a beauty in it, Lily thought, and bending down, she grabbed it before tucking it into her cap. Then, without a smile or an encouraging word, as Lily knew neither would do the wounded man any good, she placed a coin in his cup.

Without looking up at her, the man mumbled a thank you, and Lily wished there was more she could do for him.

"What are you doing?!" a voice boomed near Lily, and, turning, she spotted an officer approaching her swiftly.

"Helping out a comrade." Lily looked back at him with wide eyes, wondering how she had erred.

"Who did you steal that uniform from?!" the officer berated as his eyes bulged with indignation.

"Steal?" Lily shot her head back in surprise.

"And not only that, you disgrace the uniform by adorning your cap with a flower? You want to play the role of soldier while men are given their lives for you to play dress up?" the officer grabbed her roughly by the arm.

"She's not playing," the wounded man spoke quietly.

"What did you say?!" the officer demanded.

"That's Lieutenant Litvyak."

"Who the hell is that?!" The officer threw his hands onto his hips.

"The pilot." The wounded man looked up at them. "The White Rose of Stalingrad."

"The—" the officer's face turned a shade of white as he struggled to swallow. "Can you corroborate this?"

"There are plenty of pictures of me in the paper, sir." Lily scratched the back of her neck bashfully.

"I'm sorry." The officer again struggled to swallow. "What...um...what brings you to Moscow?"

"The Nazis, actually." Lily tapped her leg. "But I'll be returning to the front shortly."

"Hey!" the officer shouted toward some other guards nearby and waved at them to come near them. "This is Lieutenant Litvyak. Offer her an armed escort to wherever she chooses."

"Sir." The two men saluted her.

"That's kind." Lily nodded.

"I also have tickets to Swan Lake tomorrow evening." The officer reached into his jacket and retrieved them, and then he handed them to her.

"That's really not—" Lily tried to disregard the gesture, but the officer shoved them into her hand.

"Take your mother. I'm sure she would love that."

"She would." Lily raised her eyebrows. "Thank you."

"Anything else I can do?" the officer rubbed his hands together nervously.

"Give him some money." Lily nodded to the wounded soldier.

"Of course." The officer reached into his pocket again and tossed some cash to the man.

"And some food," Lily pressed.

"Right." The officer searched through his pockets before finding a bar of chocolate and handing it to the man.

"I'll have the escort take me to my destination now." Lily nodded for the two men to assist her.

Offering a brief salute to the wounded soldier, who paid her no attention, Lily set off for her old home with the escort.

Yet the further she traversed through Moscow, the more Lily became aware of the desperate situation. Long lines of people were outside most of the stores, and Lily noticed that cardboard cutouts of what might be in stock were set in the windows.

Although Lily loathed the food at the front, she wouldn't trade having to wait in line for hours at a time with the hope that some food might be left over.

With the danger passing from Moscow, Anna and Yuri had moved back into their two-bedroom apartment, and Lily, for one, was excited to be back in her childhood home.

After about twenty minutes of painful and slow walking with her injury, Lily finally arrived at the apartment and dismissed the escort with a nod of thanks.

Lily stood outside the apartment complex, and even from outside on the street, she could smell the undeniable scent of onion soup being cooked in the communal kitchen.

Awkwardly, with her crutch, Lily began walking up the stairs. The old wood creaked under her weight, and, even being as light as she was, Lily half expected the stairs to collapse onto themselves.

As she walked up the stairs, Lily could hear some shuffling of feet behind her, followed by the creaking of stairs. Whoever it was, they were walking quickly up the stairs, but Lily's progress was slow, and she felt clumsy trying to not hold up whoever was behind her.

Glancing over her shoulder, Lily spotted a young man with a beard and a cap. His head was down, and she couldn't see his face, but he seemed to be politely waiting for her to make her slow progress. He was carrying a brown sack over his shoulder, and Lily detected scents of garlic and onion.

"It might be best if you go around me," Lily spoke over her shoulder as she paused on the steps.

"I'd rather watch you struggle," a deep voice replied.

Lily shot her head back in surprise at the rude reply, but noticing that there were only a few more steps, decided to continue. She was glad Alexei had given her the knife, and she patted her hip where it was strapped, ensuring it would be easy to withdraw.

"Who are you here to see?" the young man asked.

"Family," Lily replied quickly, still not over his insolence.

"Should I warn them?"

"Warn them?" Lily had heard enough, and spinning around, she locked eyes with a smiling Yuri.

"Yuri?!" Lily tossed her crutch aside and threw her arms open as she fell into him, nearly knocking him over in the process as he laughed loudly and held her close.

"How are you?" Yuri asked while still chuckling.

"Who cares?" Lily broke off her embrace. "How are you? When did your voice grow so deep? You're as tall as me even when I'm a step above you! When did that happen?"

"It's called maturing. You should try it." Yuri smirked.

"Nah, you're still just a boy." Lily knocked off his hat as she rustled her fingers through his hair. "But that beard? Did you start growing it the day I left?"

"I could ask you the same thing." Yuri chuckled.

"Maturing?" Lily raised her eyebrow as she grinned.

"Come on. I'll help you up the stairs." Yuri grabbed her crutch and held it in the hand that was already clutching the brown sack, and with his other arm, he assisted her to the top. "My goodness, Lily, what have they been feeding you?"

"Moldy bread and chocolate," Lily replied briskly, surprised by her younger brother's strength.

"I think you've lost weight, if that's possible," Yuri grunted.

"Does mother know I'm coming?" Lily asked with worry.

"She didn't mention anything to me." Yuri shook his head as they walked toward their apartment. "Did you write to tell her?"

"I wanted it to be a surprise."

"Then how would she know?" Yuri scoffed.

"Maybe my commander wrote to her?" Lily shrugged before adding with annoyance, "You can let go of me now. Give me back my crutch."

"Yes, ma'am." Yuri offered a sarcastic salute as he opened the door for Lily.

Walking into the apartment, Lily was almost surprised to find that nothing had changed. The small table squished into the corner near the window brought back a flood of memories, and Lily almost felt as if she had never left.

"Where is Mother?" Lily asked.

"Cooking, I think." Yuri sat at the table and set down the brown sack. "I was bringing her some more produce."

"How is she?" Lily asked as she rested the crutch against the table.

"She's happy to be back here." Yuri leaned back and crossed his arms, and Lily grinned at him.

"What?" Yuri frowned.

"You're such a little man now."

"No man appreciates the word 'little' when you're describing them." Yuri rolled his eyes. "I'm taller than you are anyway."

"That's not saying much." Lily continued to grin. "I need a cushion to see out of the windshield of my plane."

"How is it? The war, that is? Exciting?" Yuri asked while trying to mask his eagerness.

"Exciting is one way of putting it." Lily stared at the table as she thought of Boris, Major Raskova, and all the others who had lost their lives, in sometimes horrific ways.

"Oh, come on!" Yuri abandoned his reserve and leaned forward. "Tell me everything!"

"My God!" a deep voice boomed, and Lily turned to see her mother standing in the doorway with wide, tear-filled eyes, holding a bowl of vegetables.

"She's not a ghost, Mother." Yuri grinned at Lily.

At once, Anna dropped the bowl, and it clanged loudly on the ground as it tossed its contents onto the floor. With a speed Lily had never seen before, Anna rushed over and embraced Lily tightly before she even had the opportunity to stand.

"My little Lily." Anna wept as she pressed her daughter's head against her breast. "My sweet little Lily."

"I missed you." Lily squeezed her eyes shut as she indulged in the warm embrace.

"They hurt you?!" Anna broke away when she noticed the crutches.

"A little accident. That's all." Lily waved to dismiss the severity of the injury.

"You tell me the name of the man who hurt you!" Anna's face beamed red with rage as she grabbed the crutch, and Lily was thankful she didn't know the name of the enemy; otherwise, she entirely believed that Anna would exact a bitter revenge.

"It was a training accident," Lily lied. "I was assisting one of the recruits. Nothing more."

"I don't believe you." Anna sat with a huff beside her daughter before ordering Yuri angrily, as if it was his fault, "Pick up those vegetables!"

"You dropped them?" Yuri threw his hands out in defense.

"Yuri!" Anna clapped angrily. "Do as I say!"

"Yes, ma'am," Yuri groaned as he stood and walked over to pick up the vegetables.

"Wash them in the sink first." Anna pointed before suddenly returning to a pleasant demeanor as she smiled at Lily and added, "We can't be giving your hero dirty vegetables, now can we?"

"Hero?" Lily frowned as she watched Yuri.

"I'm not certain I would say hero," Yuri mumbled.

"Please." Anna chuckled. "You should see his room. Every possible newspaper clipping, every single mention of you in written word, every photograph ever taken, are up on his wall."

"Mother!" Yuri groaned, and Lily laughed.

"I told you that you'd worship me again as you used to." Lily gloated.

"This visit may be changing my opinion," Yuri muttered under his breath before glancing at his sister with a smirk.

"It's good to have you home." Anna reached out and squeezed Lily's hand, but her rough motion disturbed the bullet wound in her arm and she winced.

"What's wrong?" Anna grew suspicious as she looked over Lily.

"Nothing." Lily shook her head quickly.

"You're lying." Anna narrowed her gaze. "Show me your arm."

"It's nothing! It's—"

"Show me your arm!" Anna yelled, and Lily knew there was no alternative.

With a heavy sigh, Lily rolled up her sleeve and revealed the wound on her arm.

"What have they done?!" Anna's eyes bulged out of her head.

"She was shot down," Yuri explained as he brought the washed vegetables in the bowl to the table.

"Shot down?!" Anna threw a hand to her chest.

"How did you know?" Lily frowned at Yuri.

"It was in the paper." Yuri shrugged.

"You knew?!" Anna offered a rough backhanded slap to Yuri's head.

"Hey!" Yuri rubbed his wound. "I was going to tell you."

"When?!" Anna demanded.

"It doesn't matter." Lily placed her hand softly on the table before continuing, "I'm here now. Let's enjoy the moment."

"Enjoy the moment she says," Anna huffed as she retrieved a cigarette and lit it. "At least you're home now before anything worse could happen to you."

"Well..." Lily cleared her throat and braced for her mother's reaction.

"Well, what?" Yuri pressed.

"I'm only on convalescence." Lily swallowed.

"You're an idiot!" Anna glared at her daughter. "The war is almost won. You want to go back and put your life in further danger?"

"The war is far from over," Lily spoke softly as she tilted her head.

"I think another one is about to break out." Yuri gestured to the two of them.

"I didn't ask your opinion!" Anna barked.

"I'm a good pilot." Lily tapped her mother's hand gently. "They need me."

"And what about me?" Anna threw her hands out. "Are you not considering what your mother needs?"

"The whole reason I'm doing this is for you." Lily looked at her mother tenderly.

"Bullshit!" Anna took a puff of her cigarette as she looked harshly at her daughter. "You're doing this for your own vanity."

Lily didn't reply as she waited for her mother to continue. Part of her knew that her mother was telling the truth, but for the last few years, it was the only life she had known.

"Regardless of my motivation," Lily continued, trying to be as tactful as possible. "I'm doing a great thing for my country. You should be proud of that."

"I was proud. I am proud!" Anna yelled, but then she softened a measure before continuing, "It's not easy, you know. Watching the other mothers receive letters about their sons, wondering when it will be my time."

"There won't be a letter for you, Mother," Lily urged, although she herself knew that it was foolish to try and convince her otherwise.

"There almost was a letter." Anna pointed at Lily's crutch. "That's close enough for me."

The room drew silent as the family sat around the table in their impasse. Oddly enough, Lily rather enjoyed the tension. It was a staple of their home life, and Lily wouldn't have it any other way.

"I have tickets for Swan Lake tomorrow night. Would you like to go?" Lily asked her mother.

"Sure." Anna nodded before standing and walking with her head down toward her bedroom where she slammed the door behind her.

"Give it a moment." Yuri glanced at his sister.

"She's trying to guilt me into staying." Lily looked in the direction of her mother's bedroom.

"Is it working?" Yuri asked with a grin.

"If I wasn't in love, maybe." Lily smiled bashfully.

"Love?" Yuri titled his head. "That's the captain in the photos with you?"

"That would be him." Lily scratched the back of her neck.

"And here I thought your only love was for planes. How does it feel to have your heart split into two?"

"Right now?" Lily huffed. "I might know a little of what Mother is feeling. I'm worried sick about him. We usually fly together."

"They let you put flowers in your cap?" Yuri asked as he pointed to her hat.

"When you're as good as I am, they do." Lily fluttered her eyelids.

"I see the recent crash hasn't humbled you." Yuri raised his eyebrows.

"Helps to be confident when you're fighting." Lily nodded, but the sound of Boris screaming as he burned alive rang in Lily's ear, and she turned away suddenly.

"I'll go check on her." Yuri nodded to their mother's bedroom. "I'll give you a moment to yourself as well."

"I'm happy to be back." Lily smiled at him. "But let Mother know that I must return. As soon as I'm well, I have to go back."

"You think that will help?" Yuri scoffed as she knocked gently on his mother's door before opening it and entering.

Alone at the table in their apartment, Lily felt an odd sensation. She felt as if Yuri would come back out of the room as the little boy she had left behind, and they would be off to the flying club for the first time.

Staring out the window as it began to snow, Lily's mind revolved around Alexei. She couldn't stomach thinking of what she would do if the worst came to pass. She knew that she needed to heal quickly so she could return to his side and protect him.

"Be careful," Lily whispered out the window. "Please be careful."

# Chapter Nineteen
# Larisa

*"The woman who can create her own job is the woman who will win fame and fortune."*

Amelia Earheart

"Did you have to bring that?" Larisa asked Lily as she played with the knife Alexei had given her.

"Sorry." Lily returned it to her hip.

"How did your mother handle the news?" Larisa stirred milk into her coffee while the two of them sat in a café in Moscow.

"Handle? She's still handling it." Lily raised an eyebrow. "And poorly. Not that I blame her. What about yours?"

Larisa shrugged, and Lily knew not to press further.

"Good timing on both of us being in Moscow." Larisa took a sip from her cup. "This is the exact café where we heard the radio broadcast from Major Raskova."

"That's why I picked it." Lily smiled, but her countenance soured when she recalled the major. "I should've told her how much she meant to me."

"I think she understood." Larisa set her cup down gently. Even in a uniform and with lines drawn across her face from the constant use of goggles and the weariness of night combat, Larisa was still as posh as ever, which made Lily glad.

"I'm glad you haven't changed." Lily studied her friend with sad eyes. "I feel like the little girl in me that went off to war hasn't come back yet."

"Who says I haven't changed?" Larisa asked with a frown, and Lily felt as if she had offended her. "Some scars don't require a crutch."

Lily drew a deep breath before mentioning, "It was wrong of me to assume."

"My hair has changed." Larisa shifted the subject to a lighter topic as she shook her head back and forth while her curly hair danced. "Still hasn't grown back to its proper length, but this will do for now."

"If it's any consolation, you look stunning in whatever hair length." Lily raised her cup.

"To stunning women of war." Larisa clanked her cup with Lily's. "So, what's this I hear of romance?"

"Do you read the papers?"

"Of course."

"Then there's nothing else to say. It's as simple as the reporters make it appear."

"Come now, Lily." Larisa remained unconvinced. "Nothing is as simple as it seems."

"I'd rather hear about your achievements on that front." Lily leaned forward with anticipation. "I was informed that you fell in love with a young mechanic."

"Ilya." Larisa stared off into the distance with dreamy eyes. "He's a sergeant. He worked on my plane often, and we would talk in between sorties."

"That's adorable." Lily grinned.

Glancing over her shoulder before drawing closer to Lily, Larisa whispered, "Can we gossip?"

"Please!" Lily's eyes grew bright.

"We've done a lot of naughty things." Larisa raised her eyebrows.

"Oh?" Lily waited for Larisa to continue.

"Oh, dear, no, not like that." Larisa threw a limp hand to her chest. "My sweet Lily, I'm a proper lady."

"Propriety over passion. Is that really how you want to spin this?" Lily asked with a skeptical smirk.

"I took him up in my plane when I shouldn't have." Larisa braced for Lily's response.

"Oh?" Lily squinted, wondering where the scandal was hiding.

"Let me start at the beginning." Larisa grew excited as she shifted in her seat, and Lily steadied herself for a lengthy recounting.

"I was being billeted at a house in a small town. I was part of a special group that, well, that's not what's important right now. Anyway, by pure chance, my Ilya was also stationed in this town, and we both had an evening free. I was excited, but I didn't really have anything to wear. The mother at the house I was staying at kindly washed my uniform for me, but it was still wet when evening came. I had a blouse and skirt, but they were dirty and unacceptable. The daughter at this house took on the wonderful task of cleaning and ironing my clothes."

"Alright." Lily nodded, still searching for anything worthy of gossip.

"This poor girl, about twelve, was so eager to help that she offered to iron my skirt and blouse. I happily agreed and began washing up. To my horror, this sweet girl had accidentally spilled all the kerosene from a nearby lamp and drenched, and I mean drenched, my clothes."

"Oh dear!" Lily covered her mouth with her hands as she was now entirely invested in this story. "What did you do? Were you upset with her?"

"If she wasn't so angry with herself, I think I would've been cross. The devastation was written across her face, and I couldn't bring myself to be rude to her. She attempted to mask the smell by drenching, again, yes, drenching, my clothes in cologne."

"She only made the problem worse." Lily clicked her tongue.

"Right? But I had to still go on a date." Larisa smiled at the recollection. "There was some traveling entertainment in the area, so my Ilya took me with him. The gentleman didn't say a word, but if I couldn't handle my own smell, I don't know how he managed to hide his reaction. That is, until he was walking me back to the house and he asked me what perfume I was wearing. I lied and told him it was some French perfume. He told me that he was certain he knew the name, and that he had barrels of it back at the airfield or he could get it from some of the tractors we passed by on the road."

"Cheeky. Did you invite him in?" Lily pressed.

"I would've if I wasn't being hosted by a sweet family." Larisa bit her lip as she added, "But we had other opportunities."

"Such as?"

"Well, my plane was being worked on by Ilya for some repairs. We decided to take it for a bit of a spin. The sneaky little devil brought some champagne with him, and after a few glasses, he convinced me to let him fly."

"Sounds dangerous." Lily frowned.

"Yes, and I count myself fortunate to still be here." Larisa twisted her face into worry. "There was a point during our little journey when I realized that neither of us was controlling the plane. We nearly crashed straight into a hill. What a precedent that would've set."

"How is everyone else doing?" Lily asked as she changed the subject when she grew aware of some peering eyes from others within the café. The same sort of women from when Lily and Larisa were first in the café were still there, as plump and as pompous as ever, suckling off the sacrifice of girls like Lily and Larisa.

"They're well." Larisa nodded as she stared at the table.

"But?" Lily asked as she sensed her friend was withholding something.

"Sometimes I wonder if the way we reacted to how the men treated us was wrong."

"What do you mean?" Lily frowned.

"I think we pushed ourselves too hard. We had to prove ourselves, and sometimes we went beyond even what the men were capable of."

"How so?" Lily shrugged.

"Do you remember a woman named Galina?" Larisa tilted her head.

"Vaguely." Lily squinted.

"She trained with us at Engels. She really pushed herself." Larisa took another sip. "The airfield was overrun by some German tanks, and we had to flee. Galina and another comrade remained to destroy some of the planes so that they wouldn't fall into enemy hands. Unfortunately, they were surrounded. Galina survived by escaping with another mechanic into some nearby bushes. Fortunately, she was discovered by some locals, and they provided Galina and the other girl with some clothing to disguise themselves."

"Did they make it back to our lines?" Lily asked, anxious to know how the story unfolded.

"Barely." Larisa raised her eyebrows. "She refused to tell us what happened, but I was able to get my hands on the official interrogation."

"Interrogation?" Lily shot her head back in surprise. "I don't understand."

"The Germans knew that the girls had escaped, so they pursued them. A Nazi motorcycle patrol caught up with Galina and the other girl and suspected them of being the girls in question. Galina shot both the Germans dead and was able to make it back to our lines."

"That must've been awful." Lily ground her teeth as she imagined what it would be like to kill at such close range. From a distance, in a plane, it was one thing, but to see the fear in the enemy's eyes when the trigger is pulled, and to smell the iron and blood was something Lily was not eager to experience.

"On top of this, when they returned to our lines, the authorities believed they were spies."

"What?" Lily scoffed.

"They interrogated Galina for days. Her story never deviated. They sentenced her to death."

The air left Lily's lungs as she watched Larisa, desperate for a cheerful resolution.

"Did she fight the charges?" Lily leaned in.

"She wanted to prove her loyalty." Larisa shook her head. "If it wasn't for someone higher up who reviewed the case, she would be hanging from a noose or shot."

"That's terrible." Lily drew a breath of relief that was mixed with terror. She wanted to question the justification for such extreme measures, but Lily knew that even whispering about it would be considered treasonous. In these perilous times, when even murmurs of sedition or disloyalty were punished severely, Lily remained quiet.

"She pushed herself too hard and was willing to end her own life just to prove that she was worthy."

Lily stared into the glass of her cold cup of tea as she absorbed the harrowing tale.

"Do you think we can return to our life?" Lily looked intently into her friend's eyes. "After all we've seen and done, do you think we can simply leave that behind and return to a normal life?"

Larisa paused before replying, "No, but I think that's alright."

"How so?" Lily asked as she felt the tears flooding her eyes. She wanted to believe that normality could be hers again. That she could return to being an instructor at the flying club, that she and Alexei could find a cute home together where she could host dinners for her family, and that her sacrifice would have meant something.

"I don't believe that things are meant to happen." Larisa swallowed as she shifted in her chair. "I'm not convinced the war was supposed to be or that all these men, women, and children were supposed to perish. But I am convinced that, despite these horrors, we can be better for it. I can't unsee the women being burned alive by Nazi flamethrowers in Stalingrad, I can't unhear the screams of the other girls as they crashed to the earth in their planes, and I can't forgive myself for the lives I've taken, even if justified."

"But?" Lily tilted her head.

"But I won't let that break me." Larisa's lips trembled as she stared back at her friend. "I know what it's like to watch loved ones destroy themselves from mental anguish. I'm going to be better. I'm going to live my life with this thorn in my side, and because of it, I won't be able to take anything for granted. The time I have with you, the time I have with Ilya, or any of my other friends, is precious. Truly. I know that tomorrow, when I return to action, I could die. Or you, for that matter. The threat is real, and I'll carry that with me for the rest of my life, granting me the perspective that is lost on so many others."

"That's beautiful." Lily took Larisa's hand in hers, and the two smiled at each other.

"Remember that waiter that worked here?" Larisa frowned when she suddenly recalled him.

"Are you already replacing Ilya?" Lily grinned.

"No, no." Larisa shook her head. "Just wondering what happened to him, is all. I can't even remember his name, but there are many forgotten romances. A girl we flew with would write letters to a man she loved at an airfield not far from ours. We broke protocol by flying by his airfield at the end of the day, where she would throw a tin of letters to the poor man waiting eagerly for them below."

"A tin?"

"A whole tin." Larisa rolled her eyes. "I sometimes think I'm pathetic, but a tin of letters each day? That's a little much."

"All love letters?" Lily chuckled.

"Every last marking on the page." Larisa grinned, but her cheer faded as she remarked, "Then, one day after dropping off the letters, we returned to base to discover that the man she loved had been killed. Somewhere in that airfield is a tin of unopened love letters, waiting to be read by his ghost."

The table drew silent as Lily reflected on the tragedy and foolishness of loving someone in such a dangerous and unpredictable capacity as a fighter pilot. She only prayed that the distance and absence hadn't hardened Alexei's heart toward her.

"Do...do you ever feel that the worst is yet to come?" Larisa chewed on her lip nervously.

"In what way?" Lily tilted her head.

"Stalingrad was brutal, the battles we've fought have been hard and draining, but something tells me that we haven't seen anything yet." Larisa drew a deep breath. "I'm worried, Lily. I'm very worried."

"We'll be fine." Lily nodded unconvincingly.

"I hope you're right."

"Well, I should be off." Lily glanced at the time.

"Where are you meeting your mother?" Larisa asked as she placed some coins on the table, and Lily did likewise.

"Bolshoi Theatre," Lily replied briskly, anticipating Larisa's reaction.

"The Bolshoi?" Larisa threw a limp hand to her chest as she feigned swooning.

"Yes, yes." Lily grumbled.

"Swan Lake?" Larisa squinted.

"Of course you know what play is being performed." Lily shook her head, mesmerized.

"Please tell me that you're seeing Galina Ulanova?!"

"Possibly." Lily shrugged. "I don't care for these things too much, but my mother, of all people, eats up every moment. She's a salt of the earth sort of woman, but when there is a play she wants to see, her transfiguration is as legendary as that of Christ on the mountain."

"I, for one, am rife with jealousy." Larisa offered her friend a little glare that was chased by an apologetic smile as she placed her arm around her shoulder.

"I miss you." Lily squeezed her friend tightly.

"We'll meet again." Larisa offered a quick kiss on Lily's cheek before departing.

*I sure hope so,* Lily thought as she watched Larisa, who walked with her gaze low, out into the street.

# Chapter Twenty
# Swan Lake

*"Being born in a duck yard does not matter, if only you are hatched from a swan's eggs."*

Hans Christian Anderson

"Is that what you're wearing?!" Anna asked crossly when Lily arrived near the Bolshoi Theatre to her awaiting mother and Yuri, who were both dressed dashingly and almost looked nothing like their former selves.

"I only have tickets for you and I." Lily began to panic as she addressed her mother. "I thought I made that abundantly clear."

"You didn't get a ticket for your younger brother?!" Yuri looked hurt.

"Nobody told me that you were coming!"

"He's being an idiot." Anna reached up and smacked the back of Yuri's head, stripping away the fabrication of elegance. "He has a separate ticket."

"You idiot!" Lily also smacked Yuri's head.

"At least I dressed for the occasion." Yuri defended.

"I'm in proper military attire." Lily inspected her outfit. "What's wrong with this?"

"You stand out like a priest in a brothel." Anna glanced around to see if anyone was paying them any attention.

"Must you be so crude?" Yuri groaned.

"Your father liked it." Anna grinned as she tortured her son.

"Lieutenant." An officer walking by Lily offered her a salute, and Lily returned the gesture as she watched Anna's countenance shift from shame into the prospect of opportunity.

"Do you know who that was?" Anna whispered after the officer had walked away.

"No idea." Lily cleared her throat.

"He's very important, but I can't for the life of me remember his name." Anna clicked her tongue as she tried to recall.

"In either case, shall we proceed inside?" Yuri put his arm gently on his mother's back. "The play will be starting soon. I don't want to miss the overture."

With a nod of agreement, Anna led the way and the family walked toward the prestigious building. Lily was saddened that it had been struck by a German bomb, but was happy to see that repairs were already underway as scaffolding was set about to correct the damaged portion.

Despite the damage, the theatre had lost none of its allure. With imposing bright white columns that guarded three large doors, the Bolshoi Theatre was a marvel of sophistication that was not lost on Lily.

She recalled the days when her father would bring her to a play or a ballet, and, in her innocence, life seemed so magical and beautiful. She recalled how her father would often mention how fortunate they were that it still existed. The revolutionaries had destroyed anything that resembled the bourgeoisie, but for some reason they had ignored the theatre. It was actually at this theatre, he would often tell her, that the Soviet Union was announced.

*I miss you,* Lily spoke to her father as the doors opened, and they walked inside where a familiar feeling struck her.

Glancing at the ceiling, Lily felt as if she had returned to her childhood, experiencing true splendor for the first time. For the last two years, she had stared at nothing but smoke-filled skies, the bland walls of underground bunkers, and the horrors of war.

Now, she was staring up at a beautifully bright chandelier that was encircled by a lively painting of dancers, actors, and troubadours.

Her gaze fell to the balconies that surrounded the theatre, which were gilded in bright white with intricate designs. The wealthiest and most prominent among them sat in these balconies, but Lily couldn't get past the irony.

These were the revolutionaries who had condemned the hoarding of private wealth, and yet they had merely replaced the degenerative aristocracy with tyrannical and immoral men.

Taking her seat beside her brother and Mother, and carefully laying her crutch across her chest with the butt end on the floor, Lily felt a building of anticipation within her. She only wished that Alexei could be there with her, experiencing this thrill that hardly compared to that of fighter combat.

Squeezing her eyes shut, Lily imagined Alexei surprising them with an unexpected visit and taking the empty seat beside her. She drew a deep breath as she tried to recall his scent and fantasized about leaning her head on his shoulder.

The conductor's stick tapped the podium, breaking Lily's trance as the lights dimmed and the energy in the room quieted to nothing but the occasional yet somehow compulsory cough.

The curtains drew back, and Lily sat upright to see over the head of the man sitting in front of her as she spotted the character of Princess Odette dancing in her solitary walk by the lake.

Lily had seen this ballet more than a handful of times, and while she didn't consider herself as feminine as others, like Larisa, she was entirely drawn into this tale.

The war, and even her fears about Alexei, retreated to the back of her mind as she watched the dreadful Von Rothbart casting a spell on Odette, turning her into a swan.

Lily's emotions of betrayal and injustice rose and fell with the continuation of the play as she allowed herself to be lost to this story of true love unshackling the genuine. She nearly shouted out to Siegfried that the Black Swan Odile was not the woman he loved, but felt the crushing in her spirit as he succumbed to her seduction.

Then, with tears staining her cheeks, she inwardly begged Odette to forgive Siegfried, which, of course, she knew she would, but Lily's heart was shattered when she understood that his mistake had been fatal, and she would be left as a swan forever.

Love, however, had the final triumph as Siegfried and Odette's devotion to each other breaks Von Rothbart's curse, and their spirits are reunited in eternity.

The final curtain closed as the orchestra beautifully played out the performers. The theatre erupted into applause and cheering, and Lily was certain she had seen the best performance of this ballet that had ever existed.

Lily felt as if she was watching herself on stage. Odette had captured everything she was feeling, and not just from a romantic perspective. She saw her father in Odette, and even her mother and brother. They had been transformed by this brutal war into helpless creatures, and the love they should've had was neglected.

The lights gradually came back on, and Lily wiped the tears from her eyes as she followed the crowd walking at a leisurely pace and speaking quietly with one another about the performance.

Exiting the theatre while remaining quiet, Lily and her family began toward the subway station. It was late in the evening, but the city, now that the threat of bombing was essentially over, was brightly lit. It was refreshing for Lily to see, and she felt that she had played some part in this illumination.

"What did you think?" Yuri asked his mother quietly as he took her arm in his.

"Good," Anna replied quickly, and Lily glanced at her to see that her mother was staring at the pavement as they walked. She seemed to be contemplating something, and Lily feared that a difficult conversation awaited her back at the apartment.

Entering the subway train, Lily and her family sat quietly as the car filled and dispelled its passengers. Lily stared out the window as she tapped her finger nervously against her chin. Her mind dwelt on Alexei, and she wondered if he was alright.

She hated this idleness. The ballet had been a masterful distraction, but now that it was over, the feelings she had been wanting to ignore came rushing back tenfold. All she could think about was getting back into her plane and being instrumental to the war effort. She was useful there, impactful, and here, in Moscow, she felt that she was nothing but a burden to be nursed back to health.

Arriving back at the apartment, Anna walked briskly over to her room, where she shut the door behind her.

"I suppose I should speak with her," Yuri sighed.

"Give her a moment." Lily hobbled over to the table and sat while resting her leg on another chair.

"I think I may lie down for a moment." Yuri rubbed his eyes.

"Did you enjoy the ballet?" Lily asked as she stared out the window.

"Meh." Yuri shrugged. "It's a good story, but the performance was a little off."

"What?!" Lily shot him a daggered look. "How dare you?"

"She's overrated." Yuri shrugged.

"Go lie down!" Lily shooed him with her hands. "You've clearly come down with an illness."

Chuckling softly, Yuri left Lily alone.

Yet the moment he left, Lily wished that he had remained. She hated the loneliness. It was quiet, disturbingly so. The only sound was the clock ticking patiently, reminding her that time was going to drag on for the next few weeks.

In the stillness she was forced to confront the demons that were awaiting her, biding their time until the opportune moment.

As Lily sat in the silence, she began to peel away the layers, trying to understand the root cause of her trauma. The truth of the matter was that she hadn't properly dealt with her father's passing. There was no body, and there was no funeral. He was simply gone, and their family had to find a way to survive without him.

Lily had heard reports of how brutal the Gulag system was, and she didn't know if he had survived for days, weeks, months, or even years. It was possible, she supposed, that he was still alive. Surviving in those horrid conditions must've been brutal, and Lily felt the unbearable urge to climb back into her plane and take to the sky.

With a lump in her throat, Lily began to understand her nature. Adrenaline was her answer to dealing with difficult feelings or situations. When she was in her plane, such thoughts didn't exist, especially in combat. All that existed was her survival or her killing of the enemy.

Larisa's words from earlier reverberated through her mind, and Lily wondered if the worst truly was yet to come. She prayed that the days of combat were behind her, but Lily knew that the counteroffensive, which was beginning without her, was going to be fought brutally by both sides.

Anna's door opened a crack, and Lily glanced over to see her mother peeking out.

"Are you hungry?" Anna asked as she came to stand near the kitchen table.

"Not really," Lily replied plainly as she returned to staring out the window.

"You should eat." Anna walked over to the pantry and began rummaging through some canned goods.

"I'll eat when I'm hungry."

"You should be hungry." Anna set down a can of beans and pork on the table before throwing a spoon beside the can.

"I'm alright. Really, I am." Lily pushed the can away.

"Eat!" Anna barked as she sat at the table across from Lily and pushed the can back toward her.

"I'm not hungry." Lily frowned. "Why are you trying to force me to eat?"

"Because I'm still your mother!" Anna yelled, and Lily watched her closely. "At least, I think I am."

"What does that mean?" Lily crossed her arms.

"Are you still my sweet Lily?" Anna asked with tears in her eyes. "Where was the bouncy girl with bright eyes eager to explore and lie to me about flying? Where is that girl who used to chase her brother around the apartment? Where is that girl who tried to take her doll to war? Where is that girl who, after we went to the theatre, wouldn't shut up about what she liked or hated? Where are you?"

Lily's eyes flooded with tears as she looked back at her mother but didn't know how to respond and simply stared out the window.

"They sent you back to me because you were injured, but I need to keep you because the scars have gone much deeper than the skin." Anna sniffled.

"I can't stay," Lily spoke softly.

"I'm your mother!" Anna screamed, and she shook as she withheld the tears. "You do as I say."

"It's not that simple." Lily huffed.

"Why not?!"

"Because I'm part of the Soviet Air Force. I go where they tell me." Lily threw her hands out in frustration.

"Like that has ever stopped you before. I remember your letter on how you convinced the colonel to accept you into the free hunters. You can persuade him otherwise." Anna shrugged as if the answer was obvious.

Lily shook her head before adding, "They need me."

"They need fighters! You're a little girl!"

"I've been told that by everyone who doubted me!" Lily spun toward her mother but winced at the pain in her leg. "And now look where I am! Look how much I've accomplished! Because of me, women aren't seen as a joke anymore."

"I don't care about any of that!" Anna looked intently into her daughter's eyes. "I can't lose you. Do you understand?"

"I understand how you're feeling," Lily sighed.

"No, you don't." Anna shook her head. "Otherwise, you'd be staying here with me."

"I have to go back." Lily closed her eyes.

"Why?!" Anna screamed again. "Why can't you stay with me?!"

"Because I'm in love!" Lily's lips trembled as she opened her eyes and looked at her mother, who was entirely shocked by the response.

After a loud swallow, Anna retrieved a cigarette from her purse and lit it as she took a quick puff before a deep inhale.

"What's his name?" Anna asked after a moment, and Lily thought she seemed uncomfortable with the discussion.

"Alexei," Lily felt the words grow heavy on her tongue. "Captain Alexei Solomatin."

"Is he good to you?" Anna took another puff.

"Very." Lily nodded.

"Why do you love him?" Anna asked dryly, and Lily found the question odd.

"Why?" Lily frowned. "That's like asking why someone is hungry or why they need sleep. He's my sustenance, the spiritual food I didn't know that I needed. I was wandering in a desert before I met him, and since then, I've been in a lush garden."

"You're bearing fruit, are you?" Anna asked with a cheeky grin.

"He's been a perfect gentleman." Lily's cheeks burned red with embarrassment. "If I became pregnant now, it would crush me. I fear I'd resent the child that took me away from flying."

"Sometimes children bring along other benefits you didn't expect." Anna looked softly at Lily. "To see the world again, rather, to see what the world could be through their eyes, is magical."

Lily didn't reply as she stared at the table, taking to heart her mother's answer.

"On the other hand, you could be stuck with a little brat like Yuri," Anna spoke over her shoulder.

"How did you know I was there?" Yuri asked with surprise as he left his hiding spot in the hallway.

"You need a bath," Anna explained. "You're starting to smell like your father after long shifts at the railway."

"Like a man, you mean?" Yuri asked as he sat at the table with them.

"If agreeing to your aspiration for masculinity will get you to clean yourself, then, yes, you smell like a filthy old man." Anna rolled her eyes.

"Good." Yuri smiled brightly, and Lily chuckled at him.

"I missed that smile." Anna looked at her daughter.

"Maybe Yuri should come to the front with me and amuse me." Lily leaned over and pinched his cheek that was now covered with thick facial hair.

"Can I?"

"No!" Anna boomed.

"It's not fair." Yuri leaned back as he pouted.

"To whom?" Anna frowned at him. "It's fair to me! I'm not giving up both of my children."

"You're not giving up anyone." Lily looked crossly at her mother. "I'm an excellent pilot. I'll be back. You'll see."

"You're not invincible." Anna lit another cigarette after stamping out the old one in an ashtray.

"I'm well aware, which is why I take excellent precautions." Lily held her chin high.

"What I would give for you to stay." Anna drew a deep breath before asking, "Are you hungry now?"

"I'm fine." Lily laughed.

"I could eat." Yuri reached for the can of beans, but Anna lurched forward and struck his hand.

"Those aren't for you!" Anna pointed her chubby finger at him.

"She's not going to eat them!"

"She might!" Anna growled.

Lily smiled brightly as she watched her mother and brother enter a familiar spat over some petty squabble. In her heart, Lily wished to come back, but something told her this would be the last time the three of them would be together.

Yet, instead of finding this premonition miserable, Lily took pleasure in the moment. She smiled and laughed at Yuri's pleading and her mother's intolerance of his antics. This moment, for Lily, was perfect, because she knew it was fleeting.

# Chapter Twenty-One
# Tragedy

*"A woman who is not afraid to be herself is a force to be reckoned with."*

Mata Hari

## February 20, 1943, Rostov-on-Don Airfield

Lily glanced out the window of the transport vehicle as she arrived near the airfield. A couple of Yaks were landing, and Lily wondered if Alexei was among them. She had written a few letters to him but had failed to receive a response. She understood the military mail was less than ideal for punctual delivery, and Lily hoped this was the only reason for the absence of his reply.

The truck came to a halt, and Lily felt her heart lurch in her chest. Still, Lily didn't quite understand her feelings toward Alexei. He was the first man where she had felt something more than disgust or annoyance, and Lily was convinced he was the only one for her.

With a slight limp, Lily exited the vehicle with a small rucksack slung over her shoulder that contained some extra food from home and another summer dress now that spring was approaching.

Walking across the airfield, Lily spotted a group of fighter pilots near the hangar. They were gathered around a blackboard that had names written near different assignments.

Then, out of the corner of her eye, Lily spotted Alexei walking toward this group as well. He hadn't spotted her, and Lily slowed her pace as she watched him.

He seemed sad, dejected, and he stared at his feet as he walked which was entirely uncharacteristic. Lily wondered if his feelings for her had changed, and what could possibly have caused him to feel so low.

"Lily!" Katya shouted from the group of pilots, and Lily watched as Alexei's eyes brightened while he began to look around until, finally, his gaze met hers.

With a shy smile, Lily stood nearly a hundred yards away from Alexei, who was now in a full-blown sprint, racing against Katya and Ina to be the first to embrace her.

"Lily!" Alexei laughed as he picked her up and squeezed her closely before setting her back down, where she was nearly bulldozed by Katya and Ina.

Lily laughed, appreciating the adoration, but her countenance shifted into despair when she noticed that Alexei was once again appearing gloomy as he stood back with his hands in his pockets.

Without another word, Alexei winked at Lily before he continued his miserable stroll toward the hangar.

"How are you?" Katya asked with a bright smile as she broke away from Lily.

"I'm good." Lily nodded, but her attention remained firmly on Alexei.

"Bad news there, I'm afraid." Ina took notice of Lily's worry.

"He doesn't love me anymore?" Lily felt a lump in her throat.

"What? No! Of course, he does! You should've seen how terribly upset he was without you here!" Katya encouraged. "It was pathetic, really. You turned a confident man into a whimpering pup."

"Then why is he so cold-shouldered toward me?" Lily shrugged.

"Colonel Baranov…" Ina played nervously with her fingers. "He's…"

"He's what? Jealous of Alexei?" Lily grew annoyed. "Where is he, anyway?"

"He's dead," Katya blurted, and Lily felt the air escape her lungs.

"How?" Lily asked softly, feeling terribly selfish for assuming Alexei's feelings revolved only around her.

"They were outnumbered yesterday morning," Ina explained. "The colonel's plane exploded on impact with the ground."

"That's terrible." Lily didn't know what else to say. The news was entirely unexpected. The colonel seemed somehow invulnerable in her mind. His strategy and tactics were vital to their success, and she didn't know how they would overcome without his guidance.

"Your captain lover has taken it particularly hard." Katya turned to watch Alexei, who was now with the rest of the group near the blackboard.

"They were very close," Lily sighed.

"We should get back." Ina threw her arm around Lily. "Otherwise, they'll assign us to patrolling or something tedious."

"How have you two been?" Lily asked as they walked but found the rough terrain difficult on her legs.

"It's been quiet without you." Katya chuckled.

"Quiet?" Lily shot her head back in surprise. "I'm the quietest out of the three of us."

"You have a large presence," Ina interjected.

"Large presence?" Lily patted her belly. "How? I haven't eaten properly in years."

"You know what we mean." Katya laughed.

"I'm glad my absence was a reprieve for you," Lily grumbled.

"Reprieve?" Ina scoffed. "Who said that?"

"We hate when it's quiet." Katya agreed with a smile.

"Never realized what an impact I had." Lily remained unamused.

"You have the body of a weak and feeble woman," Katya began.

"But the heart and stomach of a king," Ina finished the quote.

Lily couldn't help a grin from forming as they walked into the hangar and came near the blackboard where another officer was writing names with the chalk. Alexei was standing on the opposite side of the group, where Lily noticed that he was avoiding her. She kept glancing his way, but his attention was stuck to the blackboard. Yet Lily wondered if he was absorbing anything as his eyes looked glassy, and she knew that his mind dwelt on his friend.

Inspecting the blackboard, Lily noticed that her name had already been written in preparation for her return, but her heart sank when she noticed that Colonel Baranov was still on the board. It had been partially wiped out, but the clear imprint of his name remained, and Lily found this a shattering image.

"Thanks for joining us, ladies," the officer spoke sarcastically.

"That's Colonel Martinuk," Ina explained. "He is taking over for Baranov."

"And you need no introduction." The colonel turned swiftly toward Lily. He was a taller man, about the same height as Alexei, and he had a thick mustache under thin glasses that barely hung off his nose.

"Sir." Lily saluted. "Lieutenant Litvyak reporting for duty."

"No." Colonel Martinuk shook his head.

"Sir?" Lily grew confused.

"I'm not sure how to say this," the colonel paused as he looked seriously at her, and Lily found the tension in the room rather unwelcoming, "but you've been promoted!"

A cheer erupted around the room, followed by energetic clapping, and Lily glanced bashfully at Katya and Ina before looking at Alexei, who was staring at the ground by his feet.

"Flight Commander Litvyak." The colonel saluted her. "Welcome back."

"Congratulations!" Ina squeezed her friend's arm.

"Yes, enough of that! Back to business." The colonel returned to the chalkboard as he underlined the word *observation balloon*. "The Germans are obliterating our counteroffensive with extremely precise artillery strikes.

The observation balloon is our highest priority. Do we have any volunteers?"

The room drew silent, and the previous excitement at Lily's promotion evaporated. Even Lily, though usually daring, didn't dare volunteer for such a risky undertaking.

"This is not a request I make lightly." The colonel threw his hands behind his back. "As your silence is screaming that you know the risks, the observation balloon is guarded heavily by fighters, anti-aircraft weapons, machine guns on the balloon, and small arms fire."

"If I may," Katya spoke commandingly, although with a hint of timidity. "We cannot attack it."

"*Cannot* does not exist in my vocabulary." The colonel shook his head.

"He cannot say cannot?" Ina whispered to Lily with a smirk.

"The balloon is at such a low altitude, that if we attack from above, the German fighters will have the advantage of height and speed," Katya continued. "If we attack from below, we will be slaughtered by their anti-aircraft guns. If we attack at the same level as the balloon, their machine guns will tear us to shreds."

The room drew silent as everyone understood that Katya was correct in her analysis. This was a suicide mission. Few among them, if any, Lily considered cowards, but to throw away their lives against impossible odds was not something anyone was willing to do.

"I can do it," Lily spoke after a moment, and all eyes, even Alexei's, turned toward her.

"How?" the colonel squinted at her.

"I have an idea." Lily clicked her tongue.

"Which is?" the colonel pressed.

"With all due respect, sir, if I tell you, I doubt you would permit it," Lily replied boldly.

"What do you calculate as your chance of success?" the colonel asked.

Lily thought for a moment as she made sure that her plan was sound.

"She only returned from convalescence a few minutes ago," Alexei interjected. "I don't think it would be wise if—"

"Fleet Commander Litvyak?" the colonel ignored Alexei as he interrupted him. "What do you calculate as your chance of success?"

"Ninety percent accuracy."

"Done." The colonel wrote Lily's name on the chalkboard under the observation balloon.

"With the greatest of respect," Alexei continued his protest. "She hasn't even told you her plan."

"If she succeeds, then I don't care." The colonel continued to write with his back to Alexei. "And I'm not your friend, captain. You will address me by the proper title next time you speak out of turn. Is that understood?"

"Yes, colonel." Alexei nodded slowly, and Lily's heart broke for him.

"The weather won't permit an attack today, but the forecast for tomorrow is favorable." The colonel drew a deep breath. "Which means that you will have a chance, Flight Commander Litvyak, to review your calculations."

"Sir." Lily saluted, and the pilots each went their separate ways to take a day of reprieve from combat.

All that is, except Alexei. He simply stayed in place, staring at the floor.

"Go talk to him." Ina nudged Lily.

"I think he wants his space." Lily shook her head.

"Then he's being silly." Katya nearly shoved Lily in the direction of Alexei, and Lily glared at her angrily as she pointed to her legs, indicating that she wasn't fully healed.

With a deep breath, Lily plunged into the depths of Alexei's personal space and stood close to him as he took her hand in his.

"I missed you," Alexei spoke tenderly, and Lily's knees nearly melted as she squeezed back on his hand.

Again, her reaction to him seemed almost involuntary. She used to mock women who reacted so pathetically to a man, but with the captain, she had become the woman she loathed. And she loved it.

"I missed you, too." Lily grinned bashfully.

"I'll assist you to your bunker." Alexei nodded in the direction before he grabbed Lily's rucksack and slung it over his shoulder.

"I was worried about you," Lily spoke quietly as they walked across the airfield.

"I was fine." Alexei let go of Lily's hand as he glanced over his shoulder, and Lily understood he was nervous for the new colonel to witness their romance. Baranov had permitted them privileges not afforded to many, and Lily gathered that Colonel Martinuk wouldn't be so lenient.

"I'm sorry about your friend." Lily peeked up at him warily, wondering how he would react.

Alexei didn't reply as he glanced back at her with an appreciative nod.

"You two were—"

"I should've been there." Alexei gritted his teeth. "If I was with him, I could've kept him alive."

"They were outnumbered." Lily looked at him sympathetically. "There was nothing anyone could've done for him. And if you had been up there, then you would've likely been lost too."

"I've faced worse odds and survived." Alexei clenched his jaw. "I should've been there."

"You're being too hard on yourself." Lily patted his arm.

"I'm not being hard enough." Alexei huffed. "I told him I was ready for another sortie, but he refused. He commanded me to rest. I should've been there."

"There are many should haves in this world." Lily looked at him sympathetically. "I should have a normal life, my father should still be here, many of the girls I trained with should still be alive. You can't blame yourself for what the enemy is doing. If anyone is at fault, it's the Fascist pigs who are trying to eradicate everyone they deem undesirable."

"What do you suggest, then?" Alexei asked solemnly. "If there are so many things that should've happened or shouldn't have happened, how do we cope with this? How do you deal with such injustice?"

Lily paused for a moment before she replied, "We find joy in the fact we were privileged to have known such admirable people. The colonel was a good friend, and that is something you can cherish."

"I don't mean to be rude, but I think I need to be alone for a moment." Alexei handed the rucksack back to Lily as they were now close to the bunker.

"Are you sure?" Lily asked with worry.

"Entirely." Alexei's voice cracked before he turned away sharply from Lily and walked with his hands in his pockets and his shoulders slouched.

# Chapter Twenty-Two
# Balloons and Animals

*"You act like mortals in all that you fear, and like immortals in all that you desire."*

Seneca

Lily glanced at her watch early the next morning to see that it was nearing five thirty.

With a stretch and a yawn, Lily sat upright in her cot. It was quiet in the bunker, and Lily gathered that the other girls were either sleeping or at the hangar.

Fumbling around in the darkness, Lily found the matches and lit a little oil lamp.

With another stretch to crack her back, Lily began to gather her clothes. Her legs ached as she put on the trousers of her uniform, and Lily wondered if her wound would ever truly heal. It felt so permanent that Lily was nervous to hope that she would walk normally again.

Then, gathering her jacket, Lily paused when she heard what she thought was someone walking in the snow outside the bunker. She paused to listen, but the noise suddenly stopped.

Believing she had merely imagined it, Lily continued to get ready when she heard the crunching of snow again.

Hovering her hand over the pistol that was now strapped to her side, every possible scenario began to run through Lily's mind. She imagined it was Nazi commandos on a special mission, and they had infiltrated the airfield.

Stories of their brutality with other women flashed through her mind, and Lily was intent not to be taken alive.

Unholstering her pistol, Lily held it down by her side, still not convinced that whoever, or whatever, was outside the door was malicious. She found it strange that the sentry wouldn't have said anything. Then again, she imagined he was likely asleep.

"Who's there?!" Lily called out loudly.

No response.

"I'm armed!" Lily called even louder.

"Who are you talking to?" Ina poked her head out of her room and squinted at Lily.

"Someone is outside," Lily whispered as she held a finger to her lips. "Grab your weapon."

"Who is outside?" Ina's eyes flew as wide as her grogginess would allow.

"I don't know!" Lily shook her head. "They won't respond."

"Katya!" Ina rushed into her room and shook her awake.

"What is it?" Katya mumbled in her sleepy daze.

"The Nazis are outside."

"What?!" Katya shot upright. "What do you mean?"

"I don't know if they're Nazis," Lily whispered over her shoulder as she kept an eye on the door.

"Who is out there?" Katya asked as she grabbed her pistol.

"I don't know!" Lily grew flustered.

"Did you ask?" Katya came to stand beside Lily.

"Of course I asked!" Lily grumbled.

"What do we do?" Ina panicked.

"We wait." Lily swallowed. "Hopefully they pass by."

"We lost that chance when you started shouting at them!" Ina frowned at Lily.

"Then we kill as many as we can before turning our pistols on ourselves." Lily nodded firmly, strengthening her resolve.

"I don't have my pistol." Ina shook her head.

"Where is it?" Lily asked angrily.

"I don't know!" Ina slapped her hands against her thighs as she looked around. "I lost it when I first came here. I've been too afraid to make requisition for a new one."

"Stand in front of me, then." Katya nodded. "I'll shoot you first before I kill myself."

"Why can't Lily shoot me?" Ina shrugged.

"What difference does it make?" Katya asked with annoyance.

"Lily's a better shot."

"It's true." Lily nodded.

"No, she's not!" Katya growled.

The crunch in the snow came again, and both Katya and Lily raised their pistols and pointed them at the door.

Each second that passed felt like an eternity to Lily as she waited for a barbaric Nazi soldier to burst inside and unleash the worst possible tortures on them.

Another crunch came that was followed by a whimper and some sniffing.

With a heavy sigh, Katya threw her pistol in her holster and turned to Lily with exasperation before asking, "How many Nazis do you know that sniff like a dog?"

"I…" Lily cleared her throat. "In my defense, I don't know many Nazis."

"I told you we shouldn't have fed him." Ina marched over to the door and opened it quickly, where Lily was pleasantly surprised to find a black terrier pup shivering in the cold.

"Come here, Antony," Katya knelt and spoke in a mushy tone as the puppy, or Antony, rushed inside happily and into Katya's outstretched arms. "Are you a big bad Nazi?"

"Antony?" Lily asked as she holstered her pistol.

"He came by the day you left." Katya ran her hand through the puppy's long black hair. "We were going to name him Lily in honor of you, but then found out he was a boy."

"Lucky me," Lily mumbled.

"I told her not to feed him, and now here we are, sharing what little food we have with a dog," Ina grumbled as she threw wood into the stove and started a fire.

"I couldn't have turned him away!" Katya held her hands over Antony's ears. "Poor thing would've starved to death."

"How did it make its way here?" Lily frowned.

"No idea." Katya smiled down at the dog.

"He is cute." Lily grinned as well.

"Don't encourage her." Ina frowned at them as she warmed her hands by the stove.

"I don't need much encouraging." Katya squeezed Antony close to her chest as he panted happily. "Do you want some food?"

Antony's ears perked up as he stared at her mouth.

"Food?" Katya asked excitedly.

Antony barked.

"Come on!" Katya stood and ran toward her room.

"We're sure he's not a Nazi?" Lily asked, standing near the stove for some warmth.

"I checked his papers. They were legitimate." Ina nodded with a grin. "I don't like having him around, but if Katya is happy, and it's her food she's sharing and not mine, why should I care?"

Lily didn't reply as she continued to warm her hands with the understanding that she was about to be cold, and for a considerable amount of time.

"What's your strategy then?" Ina asked, reading Lily's thoughts. "What couldn't you tell the colonel?"

"I'm going to attack the balloon from behind their lines," Lily replied bluntly, and Ina shot her a surprised look.

"Tell me you're not serious." Ina studied Lily intently. "That can't be your solution!"

"They'll never expect it." Lily shook her head.

"Expecting is half the danger." Ina remained concerned. "The moment they realize you're in their territory, with all your white roses painted on your plane, they'll be after you with half the Luftwaffe."

"The balloon will be down before they even realize what's happening." Lily stared into the blazing fire in the stove.

Holding her hand close to the flames, Lily reminded herself what dying in such a horrible manner would be like. She remembered the screams from Boris as he burned alive in his cockpit before ramming his plane into the bomber. Even if she survived such an ordeal, she had seen other pilots dealing with the permanent scars on their faces and bodies.

A knock came to the door.

"Another Nazi?" Ina asked Lily sarcastically.

"Don't mock." Lily grinned at her friend. "By all accounts, it could very well be."

Walking over to the door, Lily noticed that Ina was, to an extent, concerned. Hovering her hand over her pistol, Lily called, "Who's there?"

"It's me! Alexei!" he called.

"I think we need to be alone," Lily replied, still a touch bitter from his rejection of her yesterday.

"Very funny," Alexei mocked.

"It wasn't a joke," Lily replied as she began to walk back toward the stove.

"It's cold out here!" Alexei pleaded. "Lily!"

"You didn't write once to me, you know!" Lily shouted back.

"I wrote four times!" Alexei replied. "You know how the mail is! You never wrote to me, either!"

"I wrote three times to you!" Lily called back with a frown.

"Lily! Let's talk about this face to face instead of through this stupid door."

"Just open it," Ina urged her friend.

"Fine. But we really can't take in any more strays." Lily grumbled before opening the door for Alexei.

"Thank you!" Alexei shivered as he moved quickly over to the stove.

"You have Ina to thank. She's the one who wanted you in here." Lily sat near the stove but opposite Alexei.

"I'll give you some privacy." Ina grabbed Antony and quickly exited to the back room, leaving Lily and Alexei to sit in the uncomfortable silence.

"You're attacking the observation balloon today," Alexei spoke after a moment, and Lily sensed that he was worried.

"What of it?" Lily avoided eye contact.

"What's your strategy?" Alexei shrugged.

"To destroy it," Lily replied quickly. In all honesty, Lily wasn't entirely sure why she was being so distant with Alexei. Yes, he had essentially avoided her yesterday when she had expected a warm and loving welcome, but he had lost his friend as well. She supposed that she should extend him grace, but her emotions were getting the better of her.

"I know that's the plan." Alexei rolled his eyes, and with his gaze momentarily away from her, Lily took a moment to inspect him.

He was clean-shaven, his hair had been combed, his eyes were clear and vibrant, and he appeared, for all accounts and purposes, as if nothing had happened yesterday.

"How are you going to attack the balloon?" Alexei pressed.

"What does it matter?" Lily shrugged. "If I bring it down, why do you care?"

"Lily," Alexei tilted his head.

A whimper came from the back room, and, despite Ina's demands, Antony came bounding out to be near the warmth of the stove.

"Come here, you sweet boy," Alexei spoke warmly to the puppy as he scooped him into his lap, and Antony excitedly tried to kiss his chin.

*You're more excited to see him than me*, Lily thought bitterly, but instead said, "Maybe it's the two of you that need some privacy."

"So, how are you going to attack the balloon?" Alexei asked, ignoring Lily's question.

"I have an idea."

"Which is?" Alexei pressed as he petted Antony.

"She's attacking from behind enemy lines," Katya called from the room.

"Katya!" Lily barked.

"That's your plan?!" Alexei frowned severely at her. "That's suicide."

"I've mapped it out." Lily waved to dismiss his concerns. "It's doable."

"And to think you once accused me of arrogance," Alexei scoffed. "Are you trying to prove something? You just came back from convalescence."

"Prove?" Lily threw her lips upside down. "No, I know I can achieve it."

"You're going to kill yourself!" Alexei raised his voice, and Antony glanced up at him as his tail stopped wagging.

"Glad you're concerned."

"What the hell is this attitude?" Alexei threw his hands out in frustration.

"I waited weeks to see you!" Lily pointed at him as tears flooded her eyes.

"You think I enjoyed being without you?"

"He was miserable!" Ina called from the room.

"So much for privacy!" Lily shouted back.

"I'm sorry I wasn't a Romeo to your Juliet when you returned, but my closest friend had just died."

"And your solution to dealing with it was to ignore me?" Lily tapped her chest. "I'm not trying to be selfish, but if the tables were reversed, I'd be running into your arms for comfort."

"It's not easy for me to share emotions." Alexei grew animated.

"You're doing fine now," Lily muttered.

"I needed to be alone. That's how I handle things," Alexei spoke a touch calmer.

"We deal with them together!" Lily stood in her anger as she began gathering her stuff for the sortie.

"Together?" Alexei also stood while holding Antony. "I'll walk with you back to the hangar."

"I think I need to be alone for the walk." Lily offered a sarcastic smirk.

"I didn't mean to offend you." Alexei appeared somewhat hurt, and Lily knew it would be best if she abandoned her pursuit.

"Well, you can think about what you meant and we can discuss it when I return." Lily reached for the door, but Alexei stepped in front of her.

"Your plan is suicide." Alexei offered her an earnest gaze. "Please, I don't know what I'd do without you."

"You'd be fine. There are plenty of petite annoying blondes around."

"You're different." Alexei shook his head as he looked at her longingly.

"She's extra annoying," Ina chimed in, and Katya giggled.

Lily rolled her eyes.

"You're unlike any other girl I've met before or will ever meet again," Alexei continued. "You have my heart and my soul. Lily, I love you."

Lily's mouth dropped open, and Katya and Ina gasped at the forbidden admission. It was an unwritten rule that statements of love were unlucky, given the precariousness of being a combat fighter.

"You what?" Lily swallowed as her eyes welled. She so desperately wanted to hear him say it again.

"I love you." Alexei smiled charmingly at her. "You don't have to say it back. You may not even feel the same way I do, but with your stupid plan, I would be beside myself in agony if I didn't permit expressing myself in that regard."

"You really didn't get my letter, did you?" Lily asked quietly.

Alexei shook his head.

"Then, for the record, I told you that I loved you first." Lily grinned bashfully.

"Kiss him!" Katya demanded, and Lily glanced over her shoulder to see that her friends had abandoned the pretense of privacy and were now standing near the stove.

"Put the dog down first." Lily pointed at Antony. "He's not part of this fantasy."

Alexei chuckled as he let Antony jump down and run over to Katya. Then, removing his gloves, Alexei placed his ice-cold hands on both of Lily's cheeks before he leaned in and planted his lips on hers.

Lily tried to articulate how she was feeling in this moment, but it was so beyond anything else she had ever experienced that she decided to simply immerse herself in the experience.

"I'm going to cry." Katya fanned her face, and Lily glanced over to see her halfway to becoming a blubbery mess.

"You're in my way." Lily patted Alexei's chest.

"You're still going through with this?" Alexei asked with hopelessness, knowing there was little that would persuade her otherwise.

"Yep." Lily nodded. "I could benefit from an escort to the hangar, though."

"I'm due for a sortie as it is." Alexei peeked at his watch.

"Do you think we're allowed to keep him?" Lily glanced at Antony in Katya's arms.

"I won't tell anyone." Alexei tapped his nose.

"Thank you, sir." Katya grinned before kissing Antony all over his fuzzy head.

"Let's give them some privacy." Lily opened the door and she and Alexei half-ran across the open field toward the hangar, desperate to escape the bitter cold.

Arriving at the hangar, Lily marched quickly over to her plane, where she retrieved a map and spread it out over the wing.

"We'll talk more tonight?" Alexei asked as he walked past Lily.

"Tonight." Lily nodded without looking up at him.

She couldn't permit that 'final' or 'one last' look. If she did, she feared that either he or she would never return. This was business as usual. They would commence their sorties and then return to spend an evening together. She was determined that this was not her nor his final flight.

Drawing a deep breath, Lily cleared her mind as she charted her course. She looked at the map carefully, running her finger along the river, over bridges and hills, behind the enemy lines, across railroads, and then back to where the observation balloon was located.

"It'll work." Lily convinced herself as she entered her cockpit, where she placed the map on her knee.

With the blocks removed from the tires, Lily taxied out to the runway, where she spotted Colonel Martinuk standing with his hands firmly behind his back and looking at her with a determined gaze. He seemed nervous, and Lily knew that if she had told him her strategy, he would've forbidden such a dangerous attempt.

With a quick salute to him, Lily applied power to the engine. She grinned with anticipation as she approached the runway until, after more than three weeks, she was finally in the air again.

Her shoulders relaxed, her jaw unclenched, and her furrowed brow eased. She was home. This was where she was meant to be.

Glancing down at her map, Lily lowered her altitude significantly, to nearly one hundred and fifty feet, but kept her speed at about three hundred kilometers an hour. It was dangerous, reckless, but Lily knew she needed to keep low and unspotted and to traverse the terrain quickly. She also knew that she would have to employ all her concentration. Even the slightest miscalculation could pancake her against the side of a hill.

It was early enough in the morning where the black shape of her plane wouldn't be too noticeable, but light enough where she could use the advantage of the sun at her rear when she needed to escape.

Speeding across the terrain, Lily glanced down at the map before starting her stopwatch. The balloon should be about a minute away, and she used all her training to ensure she tracked it accurately.

Bang! Crack!

Bullets pinged off Lily's fuselage, and she looked down at the ground to see some German soldiers firing up at her. Swerving out of the danger, Lily spotted the balloon but noticed that it was being winched back to earth. It was now or never for her attack.

With the advantage of surprise, Lily ascended quickly, firing off rounds of machine gun and cannon fire. She had been trained to fire short bursts in order to track where the rounds landed, but with such a large target, this wasn't necessary, and Lily unleashed her entire arsenal.

Within moments, the balloon was engulfed in flames, and Lily drove her plane up and through the midst of the ball of fire before descending again behind a line of trees, escaping the small arms fire and avoiding the anti-aircraft guns altogether.

It was quick, precise, and within mere seconds, her target had been destroyed. Her gamble had paid off, and not a single enemy aircraft was on her tail. Such a methodical strike was textbook, and Lily screamed in exhilaration.

Flying swiftly back to her base, Lily inverted her aircraft and flew upside down across the runway, signaling to the airfield that she had been successful. She watched with a laugh as the mechanics and pilots on the ground began waving their hats or handkerchiefs in excitement.

Lily was back.

# Chapter Twenty-Three
## Captain

*"Let each thing you would do, say, or intend, be like that of a dying person."*

Marcus Aurelius

## May 21, 1943

"How wonderful it is that winter is over!" Katya giggled as she rolled around on the grass.

"Those flowers you're crushing don't seem so happy about it." Lily smirked.

"They've finally found the sun, and now you're suppressing their beauty." Ina joined in the jest with a laugh.

"You never let me have my fun!" Katya ripped some of the flowers out of the earth and threw them at Lily and Ina.

"Hey!" Lily laughed.

"Speaking of suppressed beauty." Katya paused as she pointed at something behind them, and Lily turned to find Alexei approaching them with a basket.

"Nothing about him is suppressed." Ina raised an eyebrow.

"Excuse me." Lily slapped Ina's arm.

"What?" Ina shrugged. "I know a man when I see one, and that is a man."

"He's my man." Lily tapped her chest.

"Where's the ring?" Ina grabbed Lily's hand and inspected it.

"He'd be foolish to propose now." Katya sat near Lily and Ina as Alexei strolled toward them.

"She wouldn't say no." Ina shook her head as she spoke to Katya.

"Of course she would," Katya countered.

"I can speak for myself." Lily held up a hand to stop them.

"Well, what are you going to say?" Ina pressed.

"He's not going to propose." Lily rolled her eyes.

"But what if he does?" Katya leaned in.

"I..." Lily tried to withhold a grin but couldn't keep it from forming.

"Oh!" Ina giggled.

"It would be stupid to agree to marriage now!" Katya threw her hands onto her hips. "It's unwise to test fate."

"Still, he's a Hero of the Soviet Union now." Ina raised her eyebrows at Lily. "How did you feel when you watched them pin that medal to his chest?"

"Like I wanted to rip that uniform off him," Lily replied bashfully for the immodesty as she played tantalizingly with the knife he had made for her.

"You're too much!" Ina laughed.

"I would hope that a proposal would be in a more romantic setting." Katya looked around them. "If that is what he's planning."

"He's probably just bringing sweets." Lily waved to dismiss their concerns.

"I love when he brings sweets!" Ina jumped to her feet and raced toward Alexei.

"Hey!" Lily bounded after her after. "They're my sweets!"

"You have the sweetness of love!" Ina called over her shoulder.

Laughing, Lily chased after Ina when she was surprised to find Katya passing by both of them, despite having been the last to commence the race.

"Is there an air raid?" Alexei looked back at the airfield with concern at the girls' sudden urgency.

"Just a basket raid!" Katya panted as she peeked into the basket and, before Alexei knew what was happening, swiftly reached in and stole a bar of chocolate before returning in the direction where they had been sitting.

"That's not for you!" Alexei called after her, but it was of no use.

"Thank you!" Ina giggled as she stole a handful of crackers.

"What the hell is happening?" Alexei looked dumbfounded.

"They're being cruel and taking advantage of your affection for me." Lily looked back at the two women now basking in the grass as they relished in their pirating.

"Affection for you?" Alexei scoffed, and Lily offered him a confused look before he continued, "I'm just here for your cooking."

"Well, when the war is over you, can take your comedy on tour." Lily looked away, unamused.

"Speaking of which," Alexei began with a touch of nervousness.

"Yes?" Lily asked as she swallowed, wondering if, in fact, he was about to propose.

"What, um, what did you envision?" Alexei cleared his throat. "After the war, that is."

"I haven't really thought about it, to be honest." Lily shrugged.

"Oh." Alexei looked disappointed.

"I meant with respect to a career," Lily explained. "There are other fabricated aspects I certainly have entertained."

"Yeah?" Alexei's countenance brightened.

"I would like to hear your thoughts, though." Lily watched him closely.

"Well." Alexei cleared his throat as he began walking toward the girls, and Lily took his free hand in hers as she walked with him. "I suppose it's not too surprising to admit I would enjoy having a wife and maybe some children."

"How many?" Lily asked as she tried to withhold a timid grin.

"Just one wife." Alexei looked at her with confusion.

"Children." Lily frowned at him. "I meant children."

"Ah, right." Alexei swallowed nervously. "That depends on how many my wife would like to have."

"Very modern of you." Lily looked at him with surprise.

"So…" Alexei struggled to breathe properly. "How many would you like to have?"

"Before I answer that question, you'd have to propose. Properly." Lily smiled at him.

"In due time." Alexei ran his tongue along his teeth, and Lily didn't recall a time when she had seen him so nervous. "But it's best not to make such promises too early with, you know."

"So, what did you envision for work after the war?" Lily asked as she shifted the subject, although she relished the fact that she could expect a proposal shortly.

"I think I can do about almost anything with this." Alexei patted the golden star pinned to his chest.

"It's looks dashing on you." Lily studied him with open desire.

"But I haven't quite thought what I would like to do with my life." Alexei stared at the grass as they came closer to the girls. "You enjoyed living in Moscow?"

"It's amazing!" Lily squeezed his hand in excitement. "There's plays, ballets, shops, restaurants, cafés, and usually something entertaining."

"Making plans, are we?" Katya asked loudly when she overheard Lily and Alexei.

"Listen." Alexei stopped in his tracks as he glanced at his watch. "I have to train one of the newer recruits. I thought I would come see you first, though. Do you think that maybe we could spend some time together this evening?"

"I'll check my schedule." Lily feigned being in high demand. She knew how much it bothered Alexei for him not to receive a straight answer and how much pleasure she gained from teasing him.

"I'd like to think that even without the war, you and I would've found each other." Alexei looked lovingly as he handed her the basket.

"We're destined to be, is that it?" Lily beamed as she looked into the basket to see that it was empty.

"You have oil on your forehead." Alexei pointed before winking at her and walking back toward the airfield.

Lily watched him for a moment, enjoying the view from the back of him. Making sure he was out of earshot, she turned to the girls and, in a panic, asked, "Do I have oil on my forehead?"

"Every time." Ina rolled her eyes. "You fall for that every time."

"So, you were talking about where you would live?" Katya asked with amusement. "That must mean that you will be making things official soon, no?"

"I think he wants to wait until after the war." Lily sat on the grass beside Katya where she snatched the chocolate out of her hands.

"Hey!" Katya tried to wrestle it back.

"It's mine!" Lily defended. "You're like a little Nazi right now."

"Excuse me?!" Katya's mouth dropped open in shock at such a horrific designation, even if it was made in jest.

"You take what's mine, then when I take it back, you get all upset," Lily explained with a smirk.

"I'm taking the rest of it, just to punish you for calling me a Nazi!" Katya lurched forward and the two were involved in a fervent wrestling match.

"Stop it!" Ina laughed at the girls. "You're being ridiculous. What would Colonel Martinuk think if he saw you two in such a state? Your flying permissions would be grounded for a week."

"She does have a point." Lily looked at Katya as she held the chocolate behind her back.

"Then you had better give it over. That would stop the fighting."

"Me?" Lily scoffed. "It's my chocolate."

"But I want it." Katya resumed her valiant struggle against Lily.

The two girls giggled as Lily shoved the rest of the bar into her mouth, puffing out her cheeks and smearing her lips with the sweet.

"That's not fair!" Katya huffed before she dug her fingers at Lily's mouth, trying to pry out whatever chocolate she could.

Lily tried to speak, but her mouth was so full it was nothing more than a gagged plea.

"Open up!" Katya demanded.

"Is that Alexei?" Ina asked, and Lily thought her tone sounded serious.

"Where?" Lily asked with her mouth full as she looked up at the sky to find two planes involved in a mock battle.

"He's too close." Katya also took note.

"He's—" Lily spit out the rest of the chocolate, and Katya complained at the waste. "He's trying to make the training seem as realistic as possible."

"I get that, but what good will it do if it kills him?" Ina glanced at Lily before adding, "Wipe your mouth."

"Is this an oil on your forehead thing?" Lily chuckled.

"No." Katya looked at Lily and offered her a foul look.

"He's not aware of how low he is." Ina stood as she grew concerned.

Lily didn't reply as she wiped her mouth and watched as Alexei's plane made a tight turn, staying hot on the trainee's tail. And, just as Ina had mentioned, they were losing altitude, and quickly. Lily had been in such situations before and knew that if Alexei wasn't paying attention to the instruments, it would be nearly impossible to see how low to the ground he was.

"Break off!" Lily begged the trainee, who, for what it was worth, was quite a skilled pilot.

"Alexei is pushing him to the brink." Katya held her breath.

Finally, and at the last moment, the trainee pulled out of the twist, and Lily assumed he was unable to handle the pressure. If this had been an actual fight, the trainee would've been in a terrible position, and Alexei would've been in a prime spot to take him down.

Yet, as Ina had mentioned, they were too low to the ground, and Alexei, who clearly wasn't paying attention to his instruments, turned out of the spin but too sharply.

Realizing his error, Alexei tried to correct the plane and turned it to the side, but he was so low that the wing of the plane clipped the ground.

Lily watched, in what seemed a suspended period of time, as his plane slammed straight into the ground, crushing the cockpit.

Both Ina and Katya turned to Lily with tears in their eyes. Lily knew it would be impossible to survive such a collision, and the girls watched her with grave concern.

The siren from an ambulance blared as the medical truck raced across the field toward the plane, and Lily watched the blinking lights in a sort of daze.

"Don't look." Katya stood in front of Lily.

Lily couldn't explain why, but she felt nothing. She didn't feel angry, scared, sad, or surprised. Nothing. She couldn't think of anything either. She was simply void.

"I'll go check," Ina spoke softly as she sniffled.

"I'm coming, too," Lily said but found that her tongue was dry, and her voice seemed to be coming from somewhere else.

"You shouldn't see this." Ina shook her head.

"I have to." Lily nodded as she looked at her friend with wide eyes.

"Come, then." Ina took Lily by the hand, and the three women raced across the field toward the wreckage.

"No explosion or fire," Katya spoke with a measure of optimism, but Lily knew that no hope existed.

The trek across the airfield toward the wreckage seemed to have taken a lifetime for Lily, where every step was heavy, and her feet dragged behind her. Yet, in the same breath, time passed by Lily in an instant, and she was already near Alexei's plane. Lily couldn't grasp what was happening with her perception of time, but she wasn't afforded the capacity to contemplate it either.

It was then when they had arrived about twenty yards away from the wreckage that the emotions surged upon Lily. The medics began to remove Alexei's body, and to Lily's horror, he was now but a fraction of his normal size. The engine of the plane had pushed through the cockpit, squashing and compressing Alexei's body into an unnatural state.

Turning away sharply, Lily burst into tears as she buried her face into Ina's shoulder. It was too much to bear, and Lily would've traded any physical pain in the world to rid herself of the strain on her heart.

With embarrassing sobs, Lily fell to her knees as she was embraced by Ina and Katya, who wept along with her. They knew what a horror it would be to endure such a sudden fate with their own romances, and they clung closely to her.

The airfield became a buzz of activity as nearly every pilot who was aware of the captain's incredible exploits was in shock that he would meet such an unfortunate fate.

"Would you like to pay your respects?" a medic asked Lily gently.

"I can't stand to see him like that." Lily shook her head as she continued to weep.

"We covered his body. His head hasn't been harmed," the medic spoke tenderly, which Lily appreciated.

Taking the medic's comforting words to heart, Lily confirmed that he was telling the truth as she turned to see Alexei's body covered in his parachute with his head untouched.

Ina and Katya helped Lily to her feet as she walked over to his body, where she knelt. His face was just as the medic had stated. There was no damage. He looked to be at peace, and Lily wondered if his last thoughts dwelled on her or if he had been afraid.

In either case, she removed the knife he had carved for her, and, laying across his body, she planted a kiss on his forehead as the tears fell from her eyes and coated his skin. She hated how cold he felt. The skin around his lips and eyes was already tight and pale.

His death was so sudden and violent that Lily was almost convinced that what she was seeing wasn't real. It couldn't be. This wasn't the man who had, mere moments ago, talked to Lily about the future. This wasn't the man, the only man, that Lily had ever loved. This wasn't the captain who had been responsible for allowing her the opportunity to fly with this regiment. This was just his body, and Lily knew his soul was nearby. She prayed it was at peace, and that someday she would be rejoined to him.

"I'll meet you in eternity," Lily whispered as her mind recalled the story of the lovers in Swan Lake.

Then, without another word, and refusing a further tear, Lily stood and turned her back to Alexei. With a hateful, menacing gaze and gritted teeth, Lily was determined to make every single Nazi pay for this grievous loss. Even if their occupation had indirectly caused Alexei's death, that was enough motivation for Lily.

Storming back to her bunker, Lily's mind spun with how she would make the Nazis suffer. She felt the same urge of distraction she had experienced with the passing of her father, but this was different. Now, she had an enemy that she could fight and win against, and an obsession festered in her soul like a weed. Lily understood that, if she were wise, she would pluck it up by the roots, but a part of her wanted the hatred to swell and to grow. She would feed off it until every last Nazi was dead.

# Chapter Twenty-Four
# Kursk

*"One death is a tragedy; one million is a statistic."*

Joseph Stalin

## July 18, 1943, Battle of Kursk

"Six thousand feet!" Katya called into her headset.

"I see them!" Lily replied, and, in unison, the two planes dove toward their target, a group of bombers heading toward Soviet tank and infantry divisions.

Nearly two months had passed since Alexei's passing, and Lily had thrown herself into combat in a manner unprecedented. No other fighter pilot had completed as many sorties and missions as she had since Alexei's death. Fighting was her obsession, and every minute she was not in the air was a minute she was forced to think about Alexei.

The battlefield below, and in the air, was one that Lily found difficult to digest. Well over a million men on the ground fought bitterly over the city while thousands of tanks launched missiles at each other. In the air, in an area of only twelve by thirty miles, nearly three hundred planes locked themselves into vicious dogfights.

Bullets and cannon fire zipped past Lily's windshield or else grazed her fuselage and wings. In such tight quarters, collision with friendly or even enemy planes was common, and Lily employed all her concentration to ensure she kept both an eye on the enemy and her comrades.

Bright flashes of oranges and yellows, followed by thick billows of black smoke came from the earth below as tanks exploded. The sight of the men rushing out of the tanks while burning alive was horrific, and Lily's first thought was of Boris.

A Soviet fighter rushed by Lily's plane, ascending quickly toward the heavens, and was followed swiftly by a German. Lily wanted to assist her comrade, but she knew that if she disengaged from the bombers, hundreds of men and dozens of tanks on the ground could be obliterated.

An explosion erupted about a dozen feet above Lily, and she glanced up to find that a Soviet fighter had been destroyed and was plummeting to the earth. With a horrid screech of twisting metal, the plane passed right by Lily, and the fires were burning so fiercely that she could feel them even from inside her cockpit.

"Lily!" Katya screamed, and Lily glanced over to see bullets striking her comrade's plane.

"Stay on the bombers," Lily spoke calmly as she immediately reduced her speed. "I'll cover you."

Utilizing the tactics that she had perfected with Alexei, Lily dropped to cover Katya, and the enemy fighter was shortly in her sights. Spraying bursts of machine gun and cannon fire, Lily struck the wing of the German fighter, and they immediately pulled away.

An explosion erupted from the bomber. Katya's attack had struck in exactly the right spot, and the enemy plane spun toward the earth.

Pulling up, Lily and Katya swerved around to attack the remaining bombers in the formation.

"They're losing their tactical edge," Lily spoke into her headset. "Sending bombers out in such heavy fighting makes no sense."

"On your six!" Katya shouted, and Lily broke quickly to the right as bullets and cannon fire nearly struck her plane.

With swift maneuvers, Lily tried to disengage the enemy, but he was tight on her heels. Bullets whizzed above Lily's cockpit and then below as she swerved and veered in every direction she could manage.

Spotting Katya's aircraft as she moved into position, Lily turned sharply toward her comrade's direction. It was a dangerous game of patience where Lily would have to convince her enemy that he had perfect positioning.

"Ready?" Katya asked.

"Now!" Lily spun her aircraft as she executed a barrel roll, leaving the enemy exposed to an oncoming Katya.

Returning her plane level, Lily glanced up to see that Katya had destroyed the enemy aircraft.

At once, a song of triumph erupted in the headset, and Lily shook her head as she grinned at her friend's antics.

"How many is that for you now? Eight?" Lily asked.

"Eight?!" Katya replied with annoyance. "Eight?"

"I'm not keeping track." Lily laughed.

"Nine!" Katya nearly shouted.

"Sorry! Nine!" Lily giggled.

Another explosion near Lily's plane erupted, shaking her out of her good spirits and reminding her of the precariousness of their situation. It was jolting, apart from watching a plane plunging to the earth, that she had become so complacent. She was in one of the largest air battles of the war, and she had, for a moment, almost treated it as if she was on a leisurely flight.

"I've got another on me," Katya called before Lily had a chance to rejoin their formation. "Can you take care of them?"

"On it!" Lily increased acceleration before adding, "But then we should return to refuel."

"I'm hit!" Katya screamed.

"Where?!" Lily panicked as she searched for her friend when she spotted her comrade's aircraft that was billowing black smoke from the engine.

"Are you hurt?" Lily asked.

"No! But I've lost power," Katya replied as the plane began to descend rapidly.

"I'll try and scout ahead for somewhere for you to land," Lily called back as she sped ahead of Katya and searched for a suitable area.

Lily's heart sank as she looked everywhere but couldn't see a single location that wasn't peppered with craters from explosions due to artillery, bombers, or tanks.

Miles and miles of land was scattered with the destroyed husks of tanks, and Lily felt a lump in her throat as she knew it was near hopeless for Katya to make even a moderately safe landing.

"Lily?" Katya asked, and Lily could hear the terror in her voice.

"Keep going." Lily swallowed. She didn't know what else to say. She didn't know how to tell her friend that it was hopeless.

Katya had been her wing mate with this regiment since the beginning. They had slept in the same cramped bunker, eaten the same unpleasant food, and shared in the same horrors for a year. Katya was there when Alexei had passed, and she had been a great source of consolation for her.

"Lily?" Katya called again.

"I…" The words stuck in her throat.

"It's ok." Katya's voice shook as her plane continued to descend, and Lily flew as close beside her as she could.

Locking eyes with her friend, Lily's lips trembled as she saluted.

Without returning the gesture, Katya began singing her favorite tune. She sang loud and proud, despite the quivering of her voice.

Lily watched for as long as she could as Katya's plane descended and aimed for a strip of land that was clearer than the rest.

But the inevitable came to pass as Katya, although initially touching her wheels on a flat surface, didn't have the capacity to break in sufficient time, and her plane nosedived into a crater.

In an instant, her song was silenced, and Lily burst into tears. She didn't know if she could handle losing anyone else, especially someone as close to her as Katya.

Wiping her eyes clean, Lily headed back to base. Her fuel was running dangerously low, but she concluded that she should reach the airfield just in time.

*You should be returning with me,* Lily spoke in her heart to Katya when the airfield came into view. *It's not right that I'm returning alone.*

Landing safely, Lily climbed quickly out of the plane as Ina rushed toward her with wide, fearful eyes when she noticed that Katya's plane was absent.

Without a word, Lily shook her head, and Ina covered her mouth with her hands to stifle the tears.

"Stop that!" Lily demanded with a spiteful gaze. "I need you to get to work. You can cry later!"

"Give her a moment," a fellow mechanic spoke tenderly. "She was close to her."

"And I wasn't?!" Lily shouted. "If she can't work on my plane, then you can! I need it refueled and resupplied."

With a nod and a pat on Ina's shoulder, the mechanic set to work on Lily's plane.

Lily stormed off to the field kitchen, where she grabbed a handful of black bread and some beans. She scarfed down the meal quickly when she noticed that Colonel Martinuk was approaching her.

Quietly, the colonel stood beside Lily as she ate like a ravaged beast, not caring to pick off the mold or that the beans were a disgusting, lukewarm temperature or mushy consistency. She needed sustenance, and that was all that mattered. She needed to replenish her energy so that she could return to avenge Katya's death.

"No parachute?" the colonel finally asked with a sigh.

Lily shook her head without looking at him.

"I'll need you to make a report."

"After," Lily replied quickly.

"You may have lost your friend, but I'm still your commanding officer," the colonel spoke with a measure of tact that Lily knew she didn't deserve.

"After," Lily replied again, but sternly, as she glared at him.

After stuffing another slice of bread into her mouth, Lily returned to her plane to find that Ina was still weeping, and the mechanic was working diligently.

"When will my plane be ready?!" Lily demanded angrily, without a shred of empathy for Ina.

"There's some considerable damage," the mechanic replied. "It will take some time."

"I asked when?" Lily continued angrily.

"Maybe a day." The mechanic shrugged.

"Then get me into another plane." Lily clapped. "Hurry!"

"All these planes on the ground need maintenance." The mechanic wiped his hands on his overalls. "They could fall apart before you even reach the battle."

"Listen to me!" Lily stood close to him. "Get me back in the air! Now!"

"Litvyak!" a shout came from about a dozen yards behind them, and Lily turned to see Colonel Martinuk approaching swiftly. "Back away!"

"I need to be back in the air!" Lily pointed in the direction of Kursk, continuing to show no reserve with the colonel despite his rank.

"Unless you grow wings, you're staying here!" The colonel pointed at the ground as he stood close to Lily.

"Get him to fix my plane! Quickly!" Lily clapped her hands to signify the urgency.

"Why? So I can lose you, too?" The colonel asked rhetorically, and Ina began to weep harder.

"They need me," Lily pressed as she tried to calm herself a little, realizing her reaction was souring the colonel's attitude toward her.

"And I need you. Take the sergeant and gather some supplies from the local villages." The colonel nodded at Ina.

"A supply run?" Lily's reserve again retreated to her rising rage. "I'm the best pilot here. You want me and the other woman at this airfield to go gather food?"

"Want?" the colonel scoffed. "No, I don't want anything. I tell you what I need, and you get it. Right now, that is supplies."

"I refuse." Lily stood tall and proud.

"Refuse?" the colonel raised an eyebrow as he stared down at her. "It's not up for debate. It's a direct order. If you don't want to lose your flying privileges forever, I suggest you obey."

Lily took shallow, frenzied breaths as her eye twitched while she stared back at the colonel, understanding that his threat was not made idly.

"Now!" the colonel demanded.

"Sir," Lily spoke through gritted teeth.

"Don't think that your insolence will go unpunished!" the colonel barked as he pointed a finger in her face before storming off.

"Come." Lily grabbed Ina roughly by the shoulder and stood her to her feet.

"Which truck is ready?" Lily asked grumpily as they walked toward the trucks. "Or does that shithead need to inspect it first."

"They're all ready," Ina spoke quietly as she sniffled.

"Stop that!" Lily growled as they climbed into a truck, and she grabbed a map off the dashboard.

"Do you know where to go?" Ina asked coldly.

"One of these villages," Lily replied quickly as she looked at the map of places recently liberated from the Nazis.

"I doubt they'll have much food." Ina wiped her nose with her sleeve. "The Nazis half-starved them."

Lily didn't reply as she looked closely at the map, trying to determine the best course to take. Satisfied that she had found a suitable village, Lily looked around the vehicle, trying to figure out the controls.

"What's wrong?" Ina asked with red eyes.

"How to you reverse?" Lily asked coldly.

"You don't know how to drive?" Ina tilted her head.

"It can't be much different from a plane."

"Switch." Ina gestured with her hand as she exited the passenger's side and walked around to the driver's side.

"You'd think they'd be similar," Lily grumbled as she slumped into the passenger side.

She hated not being in control of a vehicle, and her leg bounced as she chewed her nails while Ina started the truck.

"What direction?" Ina asked, avoiding eye contact.

"North, and then east." Lily pointed as she took the map and studied it.

Yet Lily could barely pay attention to the map as she was so beside herself with rage. All she could think about was getting back into her plane. With a battle raging, her regiment needed her, and she was desperate to avenge Katya.

The short trip was filled with an awkward silence that was only interrupted by Ina's stifled outbursts that Lily couldn't handle. She knew she was dealing with the situation in the worst possible way, but Lily couldn't permit a single thought about Kayta, Alexei, Major Raskova, or any of the other admirable people who had been lost to this war.

"How did she—"

"I'm not talking about it!" Lily half-shouted.

"She's my friend too!" Ina shouted back.

"Was," Lily corrected, but she instantly regretted making the distinction.

"You've been..." Ina paused as she showed restraint.

"What?" Lily pressed angrily. "I've been what?"

"You haven't taken a moment since Alexei—"

"The town is up ahead," Lily interrupted.

"I know what you're feeling. I under—"

"You don't know!" Lily turned away.

Pulling up to a village with about thirty houses and a couple stores, Ina stopped the truck near a home on the outskirts. Lily noticed that some of the villagers were running quickly into their houses while a few, who seemed to recognize that the truck was Soviet, remained watching reservedly.

Stepping out of the vehicle, Lily paid special attention to a few men who seemed surprised to see women not only in uniform but also driving a truck.

"You're the White Rose of Stalingrad!" a younger boy who was modestly dressed, although the clothes were stained and hadn't been washed in quite some time, pointed at her in excitement.

Yet Lily, given her lack of appreciation for attention, retreated further into herself and didn't even bother offering the boy an acknowledging or appreciative look.

"We need food," Lily ordered when they came to a group of two elderly men and a woman who were sitting outside a house and leisurely smoking.

While their skin was wrinkled and leathery, Lily assumed they were younger than they appeared. She imagined living under Nazi rule for so long had severely aged them. There was a sadness in them that Lily felt she could relate to.

"Lily," Ina whispered her discontent with the tactless approach.

"She asked nicer than the Germans," one of the elderly men chuckled sarcastically.

"The Nazis took everything we had," the other man interjected.

"And before that, the Soviets had already taken everything," The woman huffed as she crossed her skinny arms.

"Now the Soviets are back," the first man dug his hands into the pockets of his tattered grey pants.

"Where is your patriotism?" Lily asked, even though she understood there was little, if anything, they had to offer.

"You're young," the woman replied briskly before studying them and adding, "Come with me. I might have something."

"Alina!" one of the elderly men called as he studied the woman with deep concern. "You can't!"

"I can't?" Alina scoffed. "You're sitting on your ass hoping bread will fall from Heaven. Shouldn't you be making ready for harvest?"

"It's too wet at the moment." The man shook his head. "Besides, my back, I—"

"My back, my back," Alina rolled her eyes before she waved at the girls to follow her.

Glancing at Ina, who offered her an indecisive look, Lily shrugged, indicating there was little they had to lose.

Still, Lily double-checked that the pistol by her hip was holstered. She wasn't certain of their loyalties, and Lily thought it best to take precautions.

"In here." Alina opened the door to a house, and she walked inside to a dark and empty room.

"After you," Ina held her hand out to Lily.

Entering inside the dank and damp house, Lily was almost startled to see how little there was. The floor was a dark wood, covered with hay to keep it warm, and a single, black table with a few chairs was all that was available for furnishings. A couple photographs hung on the wall, but otherwise, there was nothing. The depression Lily felt entering the house was crushing.

"Take a seat," the woman spoke over her shoulder as she pointed at the table before entering a backroom that was secured by a squeaky and flimsy wooden door.

With a gasp, Lily threw a hand to her chest in fright when she noticed a girl sitting in the corner of the room.

Lily thought the girl was maybe sixteen or seventeen years old, but it was difficult to tell due to her state. She simply sat on a stool in the corner, with her tongue hanging out of her mouth and drool caking her chin. Lily assumed she had some sort of disability, but found it sad that she was hidden away like this.

"I didn't see her at first," Ina whispered as she sat at the table.

"What is it you're looking for exactly?" Alina returned out of the backroom with a sack of flour.

"Anything you can spare for the war effort is appreciated." Ina nodded.

Alina didn't reply as she glanced between Lily and Ina coldly. Yet Lily didn't sense she was necessarily put off by them, but rather, anyone in a uniform. She seemed frail but strong, and, apart from the extreme differences in circumference, the woman reminded Lily of her own mother.

"I understand you've been under occupation for quite some time, but we're not the Germans," Lily spoke tenderly, yet she noticed that the moment she said 'Germans', the girl in the corner of the room seemed to moan.

"Why should I believe you're any different?" Alina asked impatiently as she patted the bag of flour. "This is all we have. I'm only giving it to you so you don't come back for more."

"Would it ease your burden if we made an exchange?" Ina asked as she gestured to the girl. "We could have our physicians attend to her?"

"No man is allowed near her." Alina shook her head.

"Man?" Lily frowned as she examined the girl. "Why would that matter?"

"She wasn't always like that." Alina paused as she grew upset. "This is what the Germans—"

The girl moaned louder.

"This is what those monsters did to her," Alina continued.

"They beat her?" Lily's heart bled for the girl.

"If only she was that lucky." Alina drew a deep breath, and Lily and Ina glanced at each other with a horrified expression as they understood the woman's meaning.

"She's your daughter?" Ina looked up at Alina.

"She was." Alina nodded. "Night after night, they took her from our home and then brought her back in the morning. She can't even talk. All she does is moan. She used to be so bright, so full of life. Now look at her. There's no life left in her."

"She needs a washing." Lily stood and walked closer to the girl and noticed that her eyes didn't even track Lily. She was staring off at something in the distance. Her spirit was utterly crushed.

"She won't let me near her." The mother drew a deep breath. "If you can convince her, I won't stand in your way."

"What's her name?" Ina asked as she also came to stand near the girl.

"Sasha," the woman replied.

"Hello, Sasha," Lily took the girl's hand, but she didn't react.

"Can you hear us?" Ina asked.

No response.

"Let's boil some water." Lily took command of the situation, and the two girls set about trying to right a wrong that should never have been committed.

"The house is yours while you take care of her," Alina spoke without much hope as she closed the door behind her.

Without needing further permission, Lily and Ina took over the house. They lit candles, set out a space with a large bucket of warm water, gathered some towels, and made sure the area stayed private for the girl.

While the tragedy of the day with Katya hadn't been forgotten, this somehow felt, to Lily, like a service to her. Lily didn't know how, but she felt as though she was reaching out to Katya. She imagined how her fallen comrade would feel in this situation, and she knew there was no earthly force that would contain the retribution she would deliver to the Nazis for this depravity.

"We're going to remove your dress. Is that alright?" Lily asked loudly, but the girl didn't respond.

"I'll see if I can stand her up." Ina pulled the girl to her feet and let her lean her head against her shoulder before huffing, "For such a skinny thing, you're not light."

"I'm going to undo your dress. We're going to give you a bath," Lily continued to talk loudly.

"She's not deaf," Ina grumbled. "And can you hurry? I don't want to drop her."

"I want to make sure she understands what's happening," Lily griped.

Soon, the girl had been stripped down to her undergarments, but both Lily and Ina agreed to keep those on her.

"How warm is the water?" Ina asked as they walked the girl over to the bucket.

"Not too bad. Just perfect, actually." Lily nodded as she tested it before bringing a chair closer to the bucket where they sat Sasha down.

"I'll start on her feet." Ina grabbed a towel and dipped it in the bucket of water before rubbing the girl's feet.

Lily did likewise as she wiped away the drool crusted on Sasha's chin and face, and she stared into the girl's eyes with heartbreak.

"Men are terrible creatures," Ina spoke softly but with hidden rage.

"Abominable." Lily agreed.

The two continued to wash the girl, pouring out their pity on her for her undeserving fate. Lily's heart was filled with rage for how anyone took pleasure in behaving this way. It was the absence of love or passion. This was pure lust, the hell of immorality, and Lily couldn't understand, couldn't fathom, how any man enjoyed this. Then again, she wondered if they were men at all or mere beasts.

"Times like these I'm glad I knew a man like Alexei," Lily spoke quietly and glanced at Ina before glancing away quickly.

"He was kind to you." Ina nodded as she looked up at Lily.

"About before." Lily swallowed as she looked sheepishly at Ina.

"You were scared." Ina nodded in her understanding.

"You deserve to be angry with me," Lily apologized as the tears welled. "I was cruel. We were all close."

Ina didn't reply as her lips trembled. Lily watched her struggling for the words, but none came until, at last, she burst into tears.

"Come here." Lily grabbed Ina's hand, and the two embraced as the tears flowed unrestricted.

"I'm sorry." Ina shook as she wept.

Lily didn't reply as she simply held her friend close. She needed Ina now more than ever, and she felt foolish for ever trying to push her away.

Suddenly, Lily felt a hand on her leg, and, looking down, Lily saw the girl looking up at her.

"Sasha?" Lily asked.

The girl didn't reply, but her eyes, at least, appeared conscious. She looked straight into Lily's eyes without emotion but with a measure of understanding.

"Do you know who we are?" Ina asked.

The girl glanced at Ina, but then glanced down at her feet, and Lily knew the shame, which was undeservedly poured out upon her, must be crippling.

"I'm sorry for what they did —"

The girl remained with her gaze low, and Lily and Ina glanced at each other hopelessly. Then, after a moment, the girl stretched forth her hand and clasped Ina's tightly.

"What have you done?!" Alina asked when she entered the house and saw the elevated state of her daughter.

Without waiting for an explanation, the woman ran over to Sophia and embraced her, and then wept over her with many kisses.

Ina and Lily stood back and watched the happy reunion with tearful eyes. It was an emotionally taxing day in many ways, and Lily didn't know quite what to make of it.

"This is the war, you know." Ina looked at Lily.

"What do you mean?" Lily asked.

"This is why we fight." Ina nodded at the mother and daughter. "Not so that we can kill, or become famous for our exploits, but so that we can redeem what was lost. I know all you want to do is distract yourself with fighting, but maybe we needed to remember why we volunteered in the first place."

"How right you are." Lily smiled at Ina.

"Take it!" The mother pointed to the bag of flour. "Take it all! Please! Take anything else you want! Thank you! Thank you! Thank you!"

"Will you be alright?" Lily asked Sasha.

Still, the girl didn't reply, but Lily understood that their small measure of devotion had awakened her from a terrible nightmare. The road ahead would be unbearable, but there still was a road, and Lily and Ina had helped Sasha find her footing.

With a nod of gratitude, Lily and Ina grabbed the bag of flour and returned to the truck.

"We won't have moldy bread for once." Ina chuckled.

"Alexei never minded anyway." Lily grinned, reminiscing.

"They're not gone, Lily." Ina reached out and took her friend's hand. "They're not gone."

Then, suddenly, Ina jumped out of the truck.

"What are you doing?!" Lily asked with worry as she looked around, wondering if the enemy was nearby.

"You're going to learn how to drive."

# Chapter Twenty-Five
# Ace

*"Success flourishes only in perseverance — ceaseless, restless perseverance."*

Manfred Von Richthofen

## August 1, 1943, near Khrustalnyi, Ukraine

"I'm trying to make my report," Lily grumbled as she gently pushed Antony out of the way.

She was lying on her cot and trying to complete her statement of recent events, which Antony saw as an invitation to play. Undeterred and convinced Lily's attitude was further encouragement for amusement, Antony sniffed her ear before biting down on her pencil and feigning a growl when Lily tried to take it out of his mouth.

"You goof!" Lily chuckled as she sat upright and took him in her arms. "This is probably one of the most important reports I've ever made, you know. I shot down an ace today. It was a great skirmish, but I'm the better pilot. Imagine how he'd react if he found out a girl shot him down?"

Antony barked.

"Exactly!" Lily raised her eyebrows. "He would likely sound something like that."

Lily grinned as she ran her hand through Antony's soft hair. She imagined herself many years from now with a dog of her own, and maybe two or three children eager to play with the pet.

Even though he was gone, Lily still found herself fantasizing about a life with Alexei. She pictured where they would live, if he would get along with her mother or brother, and if he would be a good father. She imagined he would, but worried that his arrogance would maybe impede him a little. Then again, Lily believed he was merely cocky to compensate for the terror of fighter combat, and once the war was over, his ego would cool.

Yet the more she contemplated life after the war, the more she became unnerved. This was all she knew. It felt almost dishonorable to simply return to a civilian life as if the friends she lost were mere blips in time.

333

"I should get back to it." Lily stood swiftly as Antony jumped safely from her lap.

There was a knock at the door.

Lily frowned, waiting to see if she had just imagined it. The knock came again.

Lily drew her pistol and held it down by her side as she walked slowly to the door and asked, "Who's there?"

"Colonel Martinuk," he replied. "I have some news for you."

*News?* Lily panicked. The people she cared about had dwindled lately, and she thought of Ina or Larisa or Nadia. Then her mind raced to some disaster that had befallen her mother or brother.

"Yes?!" Lily threw the door open in such a manner that almost surprised the colonel.

"That pilot you shot down today..." he removed his cap.

"What of him?" Lily grew eager to know what was wrong.

"He parachuted and was captured by our operatives."

"Oh?" Lily sighed in relief, and then wondered what was so distressing that the colonel had to come tell her personally.

"He's here." The colonel grew a dry smile of anticipation. "I found out he was captured and being held nearby. I asked if he'd like to meet the pilot who shot him, down and he agreed. He's a terribly arrogant fellow."

"That's intriguing." Lily threw her lips upside down. "He's here?"

"We have him in the command bunker." The colonel nodded in the direction.

"Alright." Lily drew a deep breath.

Throwing his hands behind his back, the colonel stepped aside for Lily to exit the bunker and the two began their trek to meet this pilot.

"You've been with us for quite some time now," the colonel began politely. "Over a year now, am I correct?"

"You're correct." Lily nodded.

"I wouldn't be surprised if they championed you as a Hero of the Soviet Union someday."

"I don't know about that, sir." Lily grew bashful.

"Also, did I see a dog back there?" the colonel asked with a knowing smirk.

"Ina has let herself go. I've found her to be rather hairy lately. She needs some maintenance."

"Just make sure Ina stays clear of the airfield when she is in need of maintenance, as you put it." The colonel winked as he opened the door to the command bunker for Lily.

Walking inside, Lily found the atmosphere to be tense. A German officer, still in a uniform that was decorated with more medals than Lily found reasonable, sat in the center of the dimly lit room. A few Soviet soldiers were surrounding him, and another officer, who was interrogating him, sat on a chair opposite.

"Ah, here the pilot is." The Soviet officer grinned at Lily.

"A colonel," the German officer replied in Russian as he stood and saluted Colonel Martinuk. "I was wondering how a Soviet could take me down, but now it makes sense. A decorated officer such as yourself is the only one who could best me."

"You're incorrect, sir." The colonel refused to salute the German back as he pointed at Lily and stated, "Behold, your demise."

The officer glanced at Lily, and then behind her, wondering who they were referring to. Finally, once it became apparent to him that they meant Lily, he scoffed and looked around the room, clearly believing this to be some sort of jest.

When no one shared in his amusement, he doubled down by throwing out his hands and asking, "Surely this is meant to embarrass me."

"I remember you." Lily nodded as she took the now vacated chair in front of the German officer.

"There is no way a little girl like you shot me down." The officer crossed his arms as he also sat.

"You were as overconfident in the air as you are now."

"Prove it." The officer laughed.

"With pleasure." Lily also laughed, matching his mocking energy as she continued. "You like to use the sun to hide."

"This isn't new." The officer shrugged. "That doesn't prove anything."

"It proves that your tactics are outdated." Lily leaned forward as she relished going in for the kill. Truthfully, she wouldn't have cared about his mocking or how arrogant he was, but Lily realized this wasn't merely about her.

"Outdated?" The officer glanced around the room, still believing he was the punchline of some silly joke. "My dear girl, I'm an ace pilot. You would have known that if you had been the one to shoot me down."

"There was another man, a Lieutenant Dobkin, a veteran of the Spanish Civil War, who liked to use the same tactic that you had employed. And, just as I did with him, I timed my barrel roll perfectly. At the last moment, when you thought I was at my most vulnerable, I was inverted, looking down at you through my cockpit."

"That was a man!" The officer stood quickly, and at once, a dozen weapons were trained on him.

Slowly raising his hands, the officer sat back down as he began to realize that Lily was, in fact, the pilot who had shot him down.

"The White Rose of Stalingrad is a man," he continued in disbelief.

"I'm sorry to disappoint you." Lily grinned.

"Propaganda." The officer shook his head. "I don't believe a word of it. It can't be you! You're just a little girl!"

"After my barrel roll, you broke right, or east if you need me to be specific." Lily used her hands to mimic planes as she positioned them how they would've been in the air.

Lily watched with immense pleasure as she continued to describe the dogfight, movement by intricate movement, and the officer's eye continued to widen and his jaw clenched tighter as his lips pursed.

Then, and with none of the respect that he had shown Colonel Martinuk, the officer nodded, relenting to the truth.

"That was satisfying," Colonel Martinuk spoke cheerfully to Lily as he escorted her out of the bunker.

"Almost as pleasant as killing him in the air." Lily agreed. "Almost."

"He'll never be able to tell a soul how he was shot down." The colonel laughed.

"Which, sadly, is more a reflection of my gender." Lily glanced at her watch as she realized she was due for another sortie. "What is going to happen to him now?"

"We'll trade him for some of our own prisoners of war."

"Bring our men back home." Lily nodded. "I like that."

"Well..." the colonel hesitated.

"Yes?" Lily frowned.

"Stalin has little care for men who surrendered. He considers them cowards and traitors. We merely don't want our men talking."

"I see." Lily contemplated the gravity of his statement.

"I'll walk you to your plane." The colonel held his hand out in the direction.

"Thank you, sir." Lily nodded.

"How is your new wing mate, by the way? Are they adjusting?" the colonel asked while, again, throwing his hands behind his back.

"Ivan is a good pilot and an exceptional fighter."

"But?" the colonel pressed.

"He's inexperienced." Lily threw her lips upside down as she continued, "And he's unlucky."

"Unlucky?" the colonel chuckled.

"You need luck to survive." Lily grew solemn. "Mine, fortunately, has yet to run out."

"Let's hope it never does." The colonel patted Lily on the back when they arrived at the hangar, and he went his own way.

Approaching her plane, Lily found Ina working diligently underneath.

With a gentle touch, Lily kicked Ina's boot, but she didn't react.

"Hello, Lily," Ina replied dryly.

"How did you know it was me?" Lily asked with disappointment.

"Because if it was anyone else, they'd be dead." Ina stood and wiped the oil off her hands.

"May Heaven spare the man that spurns you." Lily grinned.

"I heard they found the ace you shot down."

"He thought I was nothing more than propaganda." Lily laughed.

"He might not be far off." Ina rubbed her tired eyes.

"You alright?" Lily asked.

"Yes. Just exhausted. This war needs to end soon."

"Hopefully I can help that along." Lily climbed into her plane.

"I added another rose to your plane." Ina pointed.

"Thank you." Lily grinned.

"You're running out of room. Soon, your whole plane will just be a shade of white."

"Then let's hope this war does, in fact, end soon." Lily raised an eyebrow.

"Do you think, perhaps, that the white roses paint you as a target?"

"Perhaps." Lily clicked her tongue. "Or does it strike terror in the enemy's heart?"

"Roses aren't known for their ferocity."

"They do have thorns." Lily chuckled.

"So…you're prickly?" Ina squinted.

"It sounded better in my head." Lily waved to dismiss the subject before asking, "Where's Ivan?"

"He's in his plane." Ina pointed, and Lily looked to find her wing mate sitting in his cockpit.

"Excellent."

"Your birthday is coming up," Ina mentioned, and Lily spun toward her.

"How did you know that?" Lily frowned.

"Lily." Ina tilted her head. "Don't you remember?"

"Remember what?" Lily shrugged.

"When you first arrived, you argued with Colonel Baranov that 'flying was in your blood' because you were born on aviation day."

"Right." Lily grinned at the recollection. It felt like ages since she had become part of this regiment.

"Aviation day is coming up."

"Please promise you didn't plan anything too grandiose." Lily braced herself for Ina's response.

"I know how much you hate attention." Ina patted Lily's shoulder. "So I've notified everyone at the airfield to prepare something for your twenty-second birthday."

"You didn't." Lily searched Ina's eyes intently, hoping that she was lying.

"Your secret is safe with me." Ina winked. "I do enjoy torturing you, though."

"They should put you in charge of interrogations." Lily chuckled. "The way you can get into someone else's head is terrifying."

Ina laughed as Lily strapped into her parachute and entered the cockpit.

"Good hunting." Ina saluted before taking away the blocks on the wheels.

"Ivan?" Lily called into her headset.

"Ready to go when you are," Ivan replied quickly, and Lily felt he sounded a little too eager.

Applying power, Lily was soon taxied to the runway and then taken off to rejoin the ever-raging battle with Ivan as her wing mate.

Her destination was the city of Khrustalnyi in the Ukraine. The Soviet counter-offensive was gaining momentum, and although the air battles were still fierce, Lily was beginning to see a light at the end of the tunnel.

A tunnel which, Lily mused, had at one point seemed impossible to escape from. The Nazi war machine was brutal and accurate, but Hitler had failed to account for the Soviet fighting spirit.

Within a few minutes, the city came into view. The usual, horrid sights that had now become so familiar were on Lily's horizon. Black smoke, flashes of orange and yellow flames, explosions, destroyed buildings and homes, and the unfortunately common sight of bodies scattered around.

"Tanks at three o'clock," Ivan spoke into his headset.

"We should look for bombers," Lily replied.

"Yes, ma'am."

"You don't need to be so formal with me."

"Of course not, ma'am."

Lily chuckled.

"There." Lily nodded. "Ten o'clock."

"Copy." Ivan acknowledged, but Lily noticed that he didn't alter his course. It was times like this when she missed the synchronicity of Katya or the swift reactions of Alexei.

"When you're ready." Lily glanced over at him.

"Right." Ivan cleared his throat, and the two moved to attack.

"Cover me." Lily increased her speed as she decided to take the initiative.

Moving into position, Lily noticed that a swarm of fighters near the bombers was moving to protect their charge.

"Break left!" Lily shouted, but it was too late.

In her confusion, Lily put the number of fighters at about eight, and they were now chasing her. She noticed that they weren't concerned in the slightest with Ivan, and Lily assumed they were targeting her due to the white roses on the side of her plane. It was the only explanation for them to be targeting her in such a concentrated manner, and Lily wished that she had paid more attention to Ina's concern.

Fortune and providence, despite being Lily's close allies earlier in the day when she took down the German ace, were now absent.

A sudden and continuous burst of black smoke covered her entire windshield, and Lily assumed that the engine had been struck. Within mere seconds, she lost all power, and she felt her plane gliding toward the earth.

*Ivan can guide me down,* Lily thought and went to call him when she realized the radio was broken.

*I'm flying blind.* Lily tried to calm herself, but the instruments weren't reading correctly, and she couldn't see a thing. It was akin to flying at night, yet without instruments to guide her.

*I'll have to time it right.* Lily thought as she made sure her parachute was strapped on correctly.

With her heart pounding, her palms sweating, and her hands and face tingling, Lily pushed back the canopy to find that she was dangerously close to being outside of parachuting distance.

With a great leap, Lily jumped clear of the plane before immediately deploying her parachute. She watched with a clenched jaw as her beloved plane exploded upon impact with the ground.

It was then that Lily realized her grievous error. She was behind enemy lines.

"Shit!" Lily yelled as she glanced down to find that the magazine had fallen out of her pistol.

She searched her pockets for another magazine, but they were empty.

*I must've left it in the bunker,* Lily thought to herself.

There was no chance for escape, either, as Lily spotted a group of German soldiers who had her in their sights and were pointing wildly as to where they believed she would finally land.

She could hear their horrid shouting, and, from what she knew of German, none of it was polite.

If she had taken a moment to realize how close she was to enemy lines, Lily imagined she would've rather gone down with her plane. The image of the young girl who had been used night after night flashed through her mind, and Lily prayed that would not be her fate.

With a thud, she landed roughly on the ground, but the German soldiers offered her no chance to recover as they grabbed her abruptly by her arms and stood her to her feet.

They trained their weapons on her as one of the soldiers began inspecting her thoroughly, and a little too thoroughly, than Lily believed reasonable. His hands lingered in areas where he was searching for something other than weapons.

She bit her tongue from lashing out at him as she knew this would only invite violent retribution. Besides, she didn't believe his Nazi ears could handle the purity of her Russian tongue.

With a grunt, a soldier shoved her from behind, and Lily was led away, left to wonder what cruel and barbarous fate awaited her.

# Chapter Twenty-Six
# Interrogation

*"Monsters exist, but they are too few in number to be truly dangerous. More dangerous are the common men, the functionaries ready to believe and to act without asking questions."*

Primo Levi

Lily glanced at the man across from her in the transport truck who also appeared to be a prisoner of war. He was wearing a striped uniform with a red triangle on his chest, and had crude handcuffs on his hands and feet.

On either side of Lily were two German soldiers, and they casually smoked as they held their weapons across their laps.

The man across from her had a wound on his head that was not being treated, and Lily didn't imagine that either of the soldiers beside her would assist him. The blood ran down the side of his forehead and dried near his cheek. His hands were dirty, and his uniform was so tattered and worn out that Lily assumed he had been used for forced labor.

"Can I help him?" Lily asked in the best German that she could, but the soldier simply glared at her before looking out the back of the truck.

The man across from her raised his head as he looked at her, surprised at the concern from a stranger.

"Eyes down!" one of the soldiers shouted, and the man obeyed immediately.

The truck slowed and came to a stop, and Lily heard the driver talking with someone. They were speaking too fast for her to understand, but what she could discern were the words 'prisoner' and 'camp', and her heart began to pound in her chest in fear of the Germans discovering her Jewish heritage.

She recalled the horrific stories of how others were treated for their ethnicity, and she felt a tightening in her stomach that made her ill.

Another shout in German and the truck drove through a barbed wire gate that was heavily guarded with towers and soldiers carrying automatic rifles.

Immediately, as they entered the camp, Lily was struck by a horrid smell. It was so strong that she was forced to cover her nose to stop her from gagging.

Lily noticed that neither of the soldiers beside her nor the man across from her seemed disturbed in the slightest by the smell. The soldiers continued to smoke, and the man continued to stare at his feet, and she understood they were accustomed to this.

It didn't take long before Lily became aware of the source of the smell, and the shock of what she was seeing was so horrific that she almost forgot the stench.

Rotting bodies, lying face down in the dirt, were so decayed that they appeared as otherworldly animals. Some were still in their military uniforms while others were wearing the striped prisoner outfits.

As the truck continued into the camp, Lily found it difficult to distinguish between the living and the dead. Bodies that were mere skeletons lay with their mouths agape beside prisoners scarcely clinging to life.

Lily struggled to hold back the tears. If she was going to die and be reunited with Alexei, then it was supposed to be in glorious combat—not in this literal Hell.

The truck came to an abrupt halt, and within mere seconds other soldiers, with large dogs barking wildly, appeared at the back of the truck and began waving and shouting for Lily and the other man to exit.

With an unkind shove, Lily fell onto the ground, where the wind was knocked out of her. The dogs barked in her ear, and Lily, in fear and terror, curled into a ball to save herself from their ferocious bites.

A swift, sudden kick struck the back of Lily, and she heard the command for her to stand. She tried to roll to her side to get onto her knees, but another swift kick, followed by some mocking, kept her down.

Finally, the man who was with her on the truck helped her to her feet, and the guards escorted them toward what Lily assumed was a sort of office or command center.

Taking in her surroundings, Lily noticed that this camp was smaller than what she anticipated, and wondered if, maybe, there was still a chance for her.

But the sight of a half-starved prisoner walking rigidly past them caused Lily to doubt, and she immediately put away any inkling of optimism or hope.

"In!" a soldier behind Lily shouted as he forced her into the office building.

"Not you!" another shout came as they turned the man away and offered him a swift strike with the butt of their rifle.

Inside the office, Lily noticed there were a couple desks against a wall with some papers stacked up. A junior officer was writing something in a logbook and didn't bother to look up at Lily.

It was a dark office with rudimentary electricity, and Lily took particular notice of the lack of windows. The only light available was from dim lamps on the desks and the light coming in from the door behind her.

At the far end of the dark office was a room that was locked with a chain. Lily knew that she was bound for whatever was behind that locked door, and factoring in the element of her isolation, she didn't dare think about what she was certain the men were going to do with her.

With a shove, the men pushed her to the back of the room, where one of them unlocked the chain. It fell onto the floor with a heavy thud, and Lily nearly let a cry escape.

Her hands shook violently as she rubbed the back of her neck. She knew there was little sense in resisting and prayed, begged God or anyone who would listen, that her torture would be brief.

She wondered if they were planning some sort of revenge for the White Rose of Stalingrad, or if she had killed some of their comrades.

Regardless, the door was opened to a dark, windowless room, and Lily was forced inside.

Lily struggled to compose herself as she felt around in the dark, trying to become familiar with the room.

One of the guards flicked a light on, and Lily squinted as her eyes adjusted until she realized where she was.

This was an interrogation room.

A table was set in the middle of the room that was bolted to the floor. Handcuffs with chains were tied to the table, but Lily's attention was stolen by the blood on the floor, walls, chairs, and table.

One of the guards gave her an order as he threw a uniform onto the table, but he spoke too quickly, and Lily didn't understand what he had asked. She assumed that he wanted her to put the uniform on, but they remained in the room with her.

Not comprehending the request, Lily simply stood in place, taking in the room.

"Now!" one of the guards shouted and threw the uniform at her.

"Alone," Lily spoke in the best German that she knew, but both guards looked at each other before bursting into laughter.

She didn't know if she had said the wrong word or if they were laughing at her for the request. In either case, Lily refused to change in front of them.

Growing impatient, one of the guards stepped closer to Lily and, grabbing her collar, ripped the uniform in one swift motion. It was so sudden and violent that Lily simply froze in place.

Swiftly, and before Lily could even realize what had happened, her uniform was lying on the ground, and the guards were eyeing her with unforgivable gazes.

Turning away from them, Lily held up her hand when the guard approached her again, signifying that she would continue by herself.

Removing her trousers, Lily stood in the room in her undergarments as she quickly grabbed the prison uniform. She was about to put it on when she felt the end of a baton strike against her thigh.

Holding the uniform against her chest, Lily turned toward them with an angry scowl, wondering why that was necessary.

Then, gesturing to her undergarments with his baton, the guard indicated that she would need to remove the rest as well.

Red in the face with embarrassment that was mixed with rage, Lily stripped off her undergarments as the soldiers watched her with enjoyment before she quickly slipped on the prison uniform.

On the chest of the uniform, below the red triangle, was the number one six six seven zero, and Lily wondered what this signified.

"Sit." One of the soldiers pointed, but Lily refused. She knew it was stupid to become defiant when there was nothing she could do to overpower them. How she wished that she could face these guards in an airplane.

"Sit!" the other soldier grabbed her arm and forced her over to the chair, where he slammed her down.

Then, taking her trembling arms, they handcuffed her to the bloodied table before swiftly leaving and closing the door.

Lily's heart pounded in her chest, and she feared that she would vomit at any moment. She tried to keep her mind clear, but the blood on the table promised an unkind reception.

She tried to listen for any movement on the other side of the door, but it was quiet. All she could hear was the wind rustling against the side of the building, the distant shouting of orders, and the occasional creaking of the roof.

*Be with me,* Lily spoke inwardly to her father. She glanced down at the breast pocket of her torn uniform, remembering that his photo was in there. She wondered if she should have destroyed it before her capture. She didn't imagine that he was notorious enough to be known by the Nazis, but she wondered what would happen if they discovered that he was Jewish.

*I should've shot myself,* Lily thought.

She burst into tears.

A muffled voice could be heard on the other side of the door, and Lily heard what she thought were heavy boots walking toward her.

With a sniffle, and wiping her tears on her shoulders, Lily tried to hide her emotional state.

Swiftly, the door opened, and an officer with a pleasant smile and a charming appearance stood before her with his hand pressed against his chest as if he were greeting a dear acquaintance.

"How are you?" he asked in Russian, which surprised Lily.

Lily didn't reply as she watched him warily, trying to judge his character.

"You're right to be cautious." He closed the door, and Lily noticed that he was wearing a cape that was slung over one shoulder. His boots were a shiny black, and it was clear that they had just been polished, his uniform was pristine, without any blemish, and his short grey hair was cut to perfection.

Taking a seat across from her, the officer placed a folder on the table and opened it. Inside the folder were a few blank pieces of paper. Taking a pen from his breast pocket, the officer lined up the papers nicely on the table and then smiled brightly at her.

His ease and cheerfulness were unnerving to Lily, especially given the conditions that he was surrounded by. He was either willfully ignoring the enormity of the suffering, or he took pleasure in it. In either case, Lily knew to be distrustful of him.

"I know who you are." He clicked his pen, readying himself to write.

Lily didn't reply. She wasn't sure if this was a ploy to elicit information or if, in fact, he was aware of her.

"You killed a friend of mine, you know." He tilted his head, and Lily felt her heart falling into her stomach, fearing retribution.

Still, she remained silent and withdrawn as she stared at the table.

"Look," he began and leaned forward, but Lily backed away swiftly as the chains rattled on the table and the floor.

"No, no, no." He raised his hand as if he was taming a wild creature. "You mistake me. They died valiantly. It's an honor to meet the fabled White Rose of Stalingrad."

Lily remained quiet as her pulse raged in her neck, and she feared that at any moment, she would pass out.

She reminded herself to breathe, as she had been trained during combat, and she took a measured deep inhalation and exhalation.

"You must understand my excitement." The officer withdrew a silver case that he flipped open toward Lily to reveal cigarettes lined up neatly inside.

Lily shook her head as she refused the gesture.

"Me neither." The officer threw his lips upside down as he put the silver case back into his pocket. "Terrible habit."

With a deep sigh, the officer leaned forward and held his hands together gingerly as he stared at Lily with a polite smile.

"As I was saying," he cleared his throat. "I'm very excited to not only meet you, but I hope that we can come to an agreeable arrangement. There are very few pilots we've captured, but a female pilot, that's almost unheard of."

Lily swallowed as she pondered his statement. The camp here was hell, she admitted, and it would be tempting indeed to make an agreeable arrangement, as he had stated. Still, Lily didn't believe that she would be able to betray her fellow comrades. Alexei's sacrifice, Katya's sacrifice, Major Raskova's sacrifice, would all count for naught if she offered information on tactics or locations. She would be spitting on the graves of the most noble people she had ever known, and Lily resolved to keep silent.

"So," the officer clicked his pen as he set it to the paper and prepared to write, "What is your name and rank?"

Lily remained silently staring at the table.

The officer looked up at her with still a pleasant smile as he repeated, "Your full name and official rank?"

Lily refused a single syllable. He already knew her name, and she found his question curious.

"Am I not speaking the correct dialect?" the officer squinted. "I've been practicing my Russian for quite some time. I've spoken with many other prisoners, and they had no problem understanding me."

Silence.

"I see." The officer set his pen neatly beside his pad of paper before leaning back and interlocking his fingers across his chest.

Lily avoided eye contact, but she could still tell that he was staring at her. His gaze didn't seem menacing, and Lily didn't believe he would treat her in the horrible manner that so many other women had experienced, but it was evident that he was comfortable with silence, and that was the most unnerving trait to Lily.

The only sound in the room was his breathing and the rattling of the chains when Lily had to readjust in the chair. Still, she stared at the table, training her mind to think upon other things. She considered her mother and brother, and wished to tell them that she was still alive. The reports likely advised of her death with the plane being mostly destroyed, and Lily's heart broke for her family.

After what seemed to Lily like ten minutes, which was a long time for someone to simply stare at a person, the officer withdrew a cigarette, lit it, and took a generous puff.

"That usually works." The officer leaned forward, and Lily glanced into his eyes briefly to see that the pleasantness he previously displayed was retreating. "Often, if a prisoner doesn't want to speak, I remain silent. Naturally, they try to fill the void and ask me stupid questions like which camp they're in or if they'll live."

Lily glanced at her fingernails and noticed the dirt underneath them. Over the past few weeks, she had failed to maintain her usual standards of beauty. With the passing of Alexei, Lily's only thought was her plane and combat, and now she realized how much she had drowned out her own consciousness.

"I don't want to be unkind," the officer began with a more forceful tone, "but if you refuse to speak to me, I can make life very difficult for you. You see, I already know that you're Lily, or Lidya, Litvyak, and that you are a flight commander. I was merely being polite by asking you some simple questions. If you cooperate, you can live comfortably. If not, then there's nothing I can do to help you, and I really want to help you, Lily."

An itch began to develop on Lily's neck, and she tried to use her shoulder to reach it but was of little effect.

"You're itchy?" the officer asked as he stood, and Lily nearly shot back in fear as he approached her.

"Don't worry." He chuckled. "I'm not going to hurt you."

Her shoulders seized with terror as he dug his nails into her neck and lightly began to scratch.

"Did I get it?" he asked kindly as he tilted his head at her.

Lily nodded quickly. He had missed entirely, but Lily hated his proximity to her and would rather deal with the torture of an itch than his hand on her neck.

"Good." The officer rubbed her back gently.

Lily assumed that he was trying to calm her, and again, she didn't sense any sexual menace from him. Still, the act was too familiar for someone she was even close with, let alone an enemy officer.

"Alright." The officer returned to his seat as he grabbed the pen and prepared to write. "I will help you with the first question with respect to name and rank."

Scribbling quickly, yet with neat writing, the officer wrote down Lily's name. Somehow, seeing it written on the pad made Lily feel as though she would never leave. She felt that it was akin to writing on her tombstone.

*Here lies Lily,* she thought.

"Next question: Where were you stationed? Please provide exact coordinates." He looked up at her with a bright smile.

As expected, Lily kept quiet.

"How…" the officer squinted as he looked at the ceiling. "How were you such a good pilot? You, after all, are just a woman. What makes you better than men of pure blood?"

Lily recognized his game. He was trying to goad her into a response by attacking a vulnerability.

"I'm surprised the Soviets are so desperate that they're sending little girls up to fight." The officer began to write in the pad. "How many confirmed kills do you have?"

Silence.

"You had a fellow captain that you were in love with. An Alexei Solomatin." The officer clicked his tongue. "I read the papers. You two seemed to make a fine couple. You're both very attractive, smart, and capable pilots. Did it bother you when he died in such a pathetic way?"

Lily clenched her jaw to hide the trembling in her lips. She could stomach this despicable man slandering her, but to hear him insulting the man she loved was a trigger she found difficult to conceal.

"Are you Jewish?"

Lily's heart leaped into her throat, and she shook her head quickly.

"Now that is interesting." The officer grinned as he leaned back in his chair and tapped his chin. "You refuse to answer a single question, but asking if you're Jewish seemed to bother you. Why?"

Lily knew she had damned herself and wished that she had prepared for such a question. It was inevitable, after all, given her location, and she loathed that fear had overtaken her.

"I'll tell you what," the officer whispered. "I'll keep that a secret *if* you share some information with me. What do you say?"

Lily felt her throat becoming dry, and she could scarcely swallow.

"You loved him, didn't you?" the officer asked, and Lily sensed it was a genuine question.

Looking him in the eyes, Lily studied his sincerity before looking away.

"Hmm." He narrowed his gaze at her.

Then, after a moment, he reached into his pocket and retrieved something that was wrapped in white paper. Unwrapping the paper, the officer revealed a piece of bread that looked fresh, as if it had been made earlier that morning. It was absent of mold, smelled the way Lily remembered how bread was supposed to smell, and looked appetizing.

"Take it." He gestured.

Lily glanced at him as she judged his sincerity.

"There's no game." He raised his hand to profess his innocence. "I'm simply offering you a piece of bread."

Lily remained wary.

"Look, Lily, you saw how skinny those criminals are out there. This is the last piece of good food you'll ever touch. Eat it now, or you'll never eat anything wholesome again. You're going to die here. You know that, right? I mean, if you talk to me, I can make it comfortable here for you, but it's likely that you will starve to death or succumb to some disease that these animals seem to enjoy spreading to each other."

Lily couldn't believe the vernacular that he was using to describe the people she had seen coming into the camp. *Animals? Criminals?* Lily frowned as his words echoed in her mind.

"Have it your way," the officer sighed as he wrapped up the bread and stood. "I tried to help you, Lily. Remember that. I should mention that, in normal camps, there would be a female section. Since you're the only woman here, you'll have to stay with the men. I can't protect you from them, but if you want to talk, I could provide you with some alternative arrangements."

Unlocking the door, the officer left without offering her another look, and shut the door behind him.

Lily held in her emotions for as long as she could until, when she was certain that no one was within earshot, she broke down and began to weep.

She knew that the officer was right, that she would die here. How she wished, again, that she had been able to use the pistol on herself. A death by starvation was not how Lily imagined her final days.

A shout came from within the office, and Lily wiped her eyes on her sleeves as she tried to remove any trace of her momentary weakness.

The door swung open, startling Lily, and a couple soldiers rushed into the room as they grabbed her by the arm and yanked her to her feet. One of the soldiers uncuffed her and led her out of the office, back to the main camp, and toward a row of barracks.

Again, the stench struck Lily, and she spotted a body of a man leaning against a wall of a barrack, who was nothing more than skin and bones. He was so pale, and his eyes were so wide that Lily couldn't tell if he was living or dead.

The soldiers offered Lily a generous shove as they drove her toward a single barrack where she was forced inside.

The bunkhouse was crowded with men, and Lily noticed that they were in differing stages of deterioration. Some were either dead or close to dying, others were in the beginning stages of starvation while others, like Lily, had only just arrived.

The smell, Lily found, was much stronger and potent inside the barrack, and she found it difficult to not vomit. It was worse than anything she had ever smelled before, and she was forced to cover her nose with her hands.

Without a word or any instructions, the soldiers left Lily alone. Most of the men inside the barrack stared at her with curiosity while others, who had only recently arrived, looked at her in a way that no woman would appreciate.

"Do you know which camp we're in?" a man asked as he came to stand beside Lily, and she noticed it was the man who had been with her on the truck.

Lily shook her head as she remained wary of the stares from the men.

"What did they want to talk to you about?" the man asked aggressively.

"An officer asked me some questions," Lily replied, but she felt that her voice was hoarse, and she was desperate for some water.

"What kind of questions?" another man asked as he grew suspicious.

"He wanted information."

"What sort of information?" the man from the truck asked as he stood closer to her, and Lily backed away.

"Just about my…um…" Lily tried to think, but her mind was hampered by exhaustion, trauma, and fear.

"About your what?!" another man stood and came close to Lily.

"My unit." Lily swallowed, again feeling her dry throat.

"What did you tell them?" the man from the truck pressed.

"Nothing!" Lily replied fiercely, hoping a strong reply would dissuade his interrogation.

"She talked," another man scoffed. "Look at her. She's just a girl. She caved within minutes."

"I'm here, aren't I?" Lily defended. "He promised me an agreeable arrangement if I talked. Clearly, I didn't."

"Could be a double bluff," a man lying on a bunk called out.

"Could be, but—" the man from the truck began, but instantly drew silent as his eyes stared at the door.

Glancing in the direction, Lily noticed a man standing in the doorway. He held a baton down by his side and was wearing a brown uniform with a brown leather jacket that had an inverted green triangle sown into the chest.

He wasn't a Nazi, but Lily recognized that he wasn't a kind man either. She had heard of men, usually criminals charged with a violent offense, who were put in charge of the other prisoners. They were offered free reign to terrorize and keep the others in line in exchange for better food and housing. Lily knew, by his expression, that such rumors were true, and that she should be wary.

Slowly, the man walked into the bunker and came close to Lily. She kept her gaze at her feet as he stood near her.

Suddenly, he took hold of her hair and spun her around so that she was looking directly at him. His strength was astonishing, and Lily knew there was little, if anything, that she could do to overpower him.

"Relations are forbidden," the man spoke loudly so that everyone could hear, and the stench of tobacco on his breath was a welcome relief from what lingered in the bunker.

With a shove, the man pushed Lily onto the ground before he addressed the room again, "If I hear of anyone who touches her, I'll break every bone in his body."

With a huff, the man left the bunker, and the remaining men inside kept a cautious eye on her as they returned to their pitiful excuses for beds.

"If you don't know, he's not your friend," the man from the truck spoke cruelly to Lily. "If anything happens to you, he's a dead man. That's his only motivation. As soon as you cease being important, you're dead."

"We're on the same side!" Lily moaned. "Why are you treating me like this?!"

"If we're on the same side, then why did you talk?"

"I didn't talk!" Lily barked.

"Time will tell." The man from the truck pointed to a bunk near the corner of the room that had no straw or anything for padding. "That one is yours."

With a heavy heart, Lily grudgingly took her place on the bunk as, still, every man watched her closely. She was used to men's attention, but this was different. She knew how to deal with men who wanted her, but how to deal with men who didn't trust her and saw her as a threat was entirely foreign.

Rolling onto her side on the crudely made wooden bunk, with her back to the room, Lily allowed the tears to escape. She studied the etchings of the wood and noticed the names of the previous inhabitants etched into the frame. She refused to even consider adding her name, hating the thought of her life accounting to nothing more than an engraving in wood.

# Chapter Twenty-Seven
# A War Among Allies

*"I don't think of all the misery but of the beauty that remains."*

Anne Frank

A whistle blew, and Lily pried her eyes open to find that the sun had barely risen, but that the men in the bunkhouse were quickly filing outside. Even the men who were so weak that they could barely stand were moving as quickly as they could.

In a panic, Lily sat upright, but she winced at the strain on her body from having to sleep on what was essentially a wooden plank. Still, she didn't want to be late, and Lily knew that if these men were terrified, then she should follow suit.

Rushing out of the barrack, Lily noticed that all the barracks were emptying, and the men were filing into columns in the center of the camp. Swiftly, Lily found a place in line and stood tall. She was accustomed to such drills from her training, and she didn't dare fall out of order for fear of punishment.

The camp drew quiet as everyone was now in place, and Lily's stomach gurgled angrily at her. She realized that it had been almost twenty-four hours since she had last eaten, but looking around at the men who were mere skin and bones, she didn't dare complain.

The man with the green triangle who had 'protected' her yesterday in the bunk stood at the head of the column as he began reading off the list for the roll call in Russian. His knowledge of the language was almost perfect, and Lily wondered how someone could turn on their own people.

It was then that she noticed he wasn't alone. There were about four other men dressed like him, and they also had the green triangle on their uniforms. They were each in charge of their own columns, and Lily guessed there were about one hundred men in each column, which meant that this was a smaller P.O.W. camp. Still, she wondered how she could survive, and again felt her stomach rumbling.

Lily replied loudly when her number, one six six seven zero, was read, and she noticed a few heads turning when they realized that a woman was among them.

"Remain in your position," the man shouted loudly as he walked toward a small building opposite the barracks and was followed by the other men with green triangles.

Opening a small window in the building, the man took a bowl that was handed to him from a worker inside, and Lily understood that this was the kitchen. From a distance, Lily couldn't see what he was eating, but it looked better than anything she had eaten at the airfields.

It was then that Lily understood the cruelty of these men with the green triangles. Slowly and quietly, these men began eating while the columns of prisoners remained standing in place. It was a horrible form of torture, and Lily looked at the men who were near death from starvation, wondering how someone could be so unkind toward them.

She also found it odd, given their numbers, that they couldn't attack these men. They were outnumbered one hundred to one, but then Lily spotted the men in the guard towers with their automatic rifles. Lily suspected that if they revolted, many would die, but some would have a decent chance of not only surviving but maybe even returning to their previous designations.

Still, even when the men with green triangles had finished their meals, they sat on the ground and rested their legs for a moment, keeping those under their charge in terrible agony.

A groan came from near Lily, and she turned to watch a man collapse. He fell face-first into the dirt, but not a single prisoner near him dared to provide assistance, and Lily knew why.

At once, one of the green triangles came rushing over to the prisoner who had collapsed, baton at the ready, and stood over him with a menacing glare.

"Stand!" he shouted, but there was no response.

"Stand!" he shouted again, and when he didn't move, the man struck the prisoner on his back.

The man on the ground groaned in anguish, and he was so thin that Lily wondered if the strike had broken a rib. Another blow was delivered when the man still didn't stand, which was only met with another groan.

"Stand!" the green triangle began striking the man over and over again.

Lily winced at each blow as thud after thud was delivered until the groans ceased altogether.

Glancing out her peripherals, and not daring to bring any attention to herself, Lily noticed a pool of blood forming on the ground and that the man had been struck on the head.

She strained to hold back the tears at such merciless brutality. She didn't understand what the man's crime was that he deserved such a fate. He had been starving and collapsed after being forced to stand in place.

Without a shred of remorse, the green triangle ordered the men near the body to drag it over to what he called a crematorium.

Then, with shallow and angry breathing, the green triangle began pacing up and down the column, tapping his baton against his leg, and Lily thought that he was hoping that someone would give him another excuse to unleash his violent rage.

Calming a measure, the green triangle walked back toward the kitchen where he and his other comrades returned to sitting and leaning against the wall.

Curious as to what the protocol was, Lily looked slightly to her right to find that the man from the truck was beside her.

"Don't look at me!" he whispered through gritted teeth.

"What are we doing?" Lily asked quietly as she covered her mouth.

"Silence!" one of the green triangles stood and shouted, and at once, Lily obeyed.

The minutes stretched into what Lily believed were hours as the sun began to rise steadily in the sky. Her hunger gnawed at her, and Lily's legs began to ache. She was surprised that no other man, especially those who were nearly dead by starvation, collapsed in the swelling heat.

A bead of sweat rolled down her forehead, and Lily, in her desperation to quench her thirst, licked it into her mouth.

Finally, a whistle blew, almost startling Lily, and she turned to see that the kitchen window had opened, and a large pot of what she hoped was soup was set out on a table.

In surprising order, given the extreme hunger and physical constraints, the men, and Lily, lined up for the kitchen.

Lily was frustrated that she was near the end of the line and hoped that some soup would be left over. Still, she understood that complaining would be in ill taste and kept her mouth shut.

With a sluggish pace, the men grabbed a bowl and held it out for one of the kitchen staff, who filled it quickly and then angrily barked for them to keep moving.

Finally, Lily approached the kitchen, and she also noticed a large silver pot, which some of the men were dipping cups into, and she hoped it was coffee.

Grabbing a bowl, Lily held it out for the soup, which she was disappointed to find was essentially warm water with some cabbage leaves mixed in. The pot was nearly empty, and Lily counted herself lucky to receive at least something.

Taking some coffee as well, Lily realized that it was also little more than warm water, and there were a few black flakes from the coffee grounds. It smelled appetizing, but Lily knew there would be little substance in the taste.

"There's no more!" the kitchen staff shouted, and Lily watched as a handful of men behind her groaned in agony that they wouldn't be fed.

In angry desperation, one of the men pushed his way to an area beside the kitchen and began digging through some scraps of food and shoveled into his mouth some potato peels. Lily's heart shattered as she watched how he didn't care that he was also eating dirt.

The others, except one man, who also didn't get any soup, followed suit, and soon a squabble broke out over scraps. Lily watched with rage as the green triangles began laughing and mocking the men. She despised them with an unbearable hatred and believed they were worse than the Nazis.

Studying the man who had refused to engage in the squabble, then looking longingly back at her bowl of warm water, Lily walked over to him and offered him her food.

Without even a moment of hesitation, the man grabbed the bowl out of her hand so violently that Lily nearly let out a cry of surprise. Turning his back to her, the man ate quickly and without regard for decorum or propriety. The Nazis, and the Russians with green triangles, had reduced him, and many others, to nothing more than beasts where their only thought was food.

She did, however, keep the coffee, and she gulped it down quickly.

"That was kind," a voice spoke from behind her, and Lily noticed it was the man from the truck.

Lily didn't reply as she looked back at the man she had given her food to. A part of her wished that she had remained selfish.

"That wasn't a compliment," the man from the truck continued, and Lily looked at him warily.

"He was hungry," Lily replied.

"And now everyone else here knows that you have a weak will. They'll take advantage of you."

"We're stronger together," Lily replied unconvincingly as she felt herself growing weak with nothing but the horrible coffee to nourish her.

"I'm Nikolai." He extended his hand, and Lily looked down at it curiously, unsure if she could trust him.

"Lidya," she replied with her real name as she accepted the gesture of his handshake.

"I know who you are." He nodded and then added, "Sorry about yesterday. I shouldn't have doubted your loyalty."

"If anyone's loyalty is in question, it's the men with the green triangles," Lily spoke quietly.

"They're kapos," The man explained. "The Nazis use our own against us. It allows them to employ fewer staff at camps like this. Divide and conquer."

"Where did they capture you?" Lily asked as she crossed her arms but felt that she was about to faint from exhaustion and hunger.

"Kursk." He nodded in the direction. "I was taken a few weeks ago. They've been moving me from camp to camp as Soviets retake occupied land."

"Hopefully they take this camp soon and free all of us."

"You don't want that," the man scoffed.

"What do you mean?" Lily frowned.

A whistle blew, and Lily watched as the kapo assigned to her bunk stood on a little box as he addressed them, "You've spent too much time standing around, you'll need to complete your labor before the evening or there will be no rations."

A collective sigh with some restrained groans arose from the prisoners, and Lily wondered what labor he was referring to.

"Let's get to it." Nikolai nodded for Lily to follow him.

"Where are we going?" Lily asked as they walked toward a pile of rubble.

"We need to move all of this, every last stone, to the other side of the camp," Nikolai explained.

"What?" Lily was certain this was in jest, but when Nikolai remained serious and determined, she asked, "Whatever for?"

"To weaken us." Nikolai picked up a block.

"Weaken us?" Lily asked in confusion as she also picked up a block and began following him to the other side of the camp, past all the weary souls that were moving toward the pile of rubble.

"Destroy the mind and body with meaningless work." Nikolai huffed as he struggled to carry his block. "They use the same tactics in almost every camp I've been to. Tomorrow, they'll make us move the pile back."

"What did you mean before when you said that I don't want our men to find us?" Lily asked as she set her block down beside Nikolai's, and they began marching quickly back toward the pile.

"We need to pace ourselves." Nikolai wiped the sweat from his forehead as he ignored Lily. "Otherwise, we'll be exhausted before sundown."

"What did you mean earlier?" Lily pressed as she grabbed another block.

"We're prisoners of war." Nikolai shrugged as he also grabbed another block. "If we survive, the Soviets will believe that means we talked. We'll be questioned, tortured even, until we give them an answer they want to hear. No, Lidya, there is no escape. Our only hope is to flee somewhere west."

Lily recalled the story from Nadia of the night bomber who escaped the Nazis and made it back to Soviet lines only to be sentenced to death for treason.

Lily froze in place as she took his words to heart and understood that he was telling the truth. Even if she escaped or was liberated, she would likely be dealt with harshly by her own people. Her mother and brother would also be questioned, and she prayed that her officials, at least, believed she was dead. It would be a mercy to her family if she was counted as fallen in battle.

"Come on." Nikolai grabbed Lily's arm. "We have to keep moving. They'll beat you otherwise."

"What's the point?" Lily asked as she felt the tears forming.

Nikolai paused before answering, "There is no point. To anything. If you believe that, then carrying these rocks to an arbitrary place in the camp won't matter. The beatings they give won't matter. The lack of food won't matter. Do you understand? You must let go of everything. Only when nothing matters will you survive."

The tears streamed down Lily's cheek as she returned to carrying the blocks. It was arduous, back-breaking work, and even if the blocks were small and broken into pieces, the mere repetition was demanding.

Hour after hour, Lily and Nikolai, along with the other hundreds of prisoners, moved the large pile to the other side of the camp, but Lily noticed it was growing dark. She prayed that they would finish in time for them to be awarded evening rations.

Beatings of the other prisoners happened so frequently and severely that Lily began to grow numb to the occurrences. She hated how little it took for her to tune the world out, but hunger, even after a day of not eating, was playing against her. She knew that she needed to focus on the task, and hopefully, they would make good on their promise of providing nourishment.

"Prisoner one six six seven zero," came a shout from further in the camp and Lily noticed the officer who had interrogated her earlier was looking directly at her.

Setting her block down, Lily left the train of miserable and dejected creatures and walked over to the officer. Her hands were burning and sore, and she imagined they were bleeding, but she didn't dare look down at them for fear that she would reveal any weakness. She needed to remain strong and resolute.

Coming to a halt in front of the officer, Lily stood at attention with her gaze straight ahead. Still, her gaze was stolen by an apple held down by his side, and she could scarcely keep her mouth from salivating.

"We should continue our discussion from yesterday," the officer spoke politely as he took a generous bite out of the apple and Lily struggled to think of anything other than food.

"I should continue my work." Lily shook her head.

"She speaks?" the officer grinned cruelly. "I was almost concerned that you were mute."

"May I continue?" Lily asked as she stared straight ahead.

"We need to talk." The officer shook his head as he took another bite.

"I refuse." Lily swallowed before adding, "Respectfully."

"That's not how it works here," the officer replied quickly as his previous cheer began to fade in his annoyance with her.

"If we don't complete the task, we don't eat," Lily pressed.

"I don't care." The officer shrugged.

Lily didn't know what course of action to take. She knew that if she went willingly with the officer, the men in the camp would understandably be suspicious. However, if she refused, Lily knew that violence would be used against her to force compliance.

"Bring her." The officer nodded to one of his Nazi guards, and they quickly approached Lily.

"Don't touch me!" Lily demanded, but the guard cared little for her opinion as he took her roughly by the arm and led her back to the office where she had been tied to the table the previous day.

"In here," the officer spoke calmly as he removed his jacket and sat at the table as Lily was again chained.

Resuming her demeanor from yesterday, Lily refused to even look at him or offer a single syllable as the door was closed and she was shut into this battle of wills.

"Let's try this again, shall we?" the officer asked, but Lily detected the bitter tone in his voice.

Opening the folder, which had the pad of paper that contained nothing more than her name and rank, the officer seemed to understand that Lily was unwilling to budge.

"Yesterday, I offered you a reward." The officer paused as he stared at the table. "Today, I offer you the promise of punishment."

Lily clenched her jaw as she waited for whatever harrowing retribution he had planned.

"Where was your airfield located?" the officer asked without even grabbing his pen, perceiving Lily's silence.

"Did any man touch you?" the officer asked, which surprised Lily, and she glanced at him quickly before shaking her head and looking back at the table.

"Who was your commanding officer? How are the airfields defended? What are the precise tactics employed by your regiment?"

As usual, Lily remained silent.

"I expected as much," the officer sighed before stating, "This gives me no pleasure. I hope you know that."

Lily felt her pulse raging in her neck.

Standing quickly, the officer walked over to Lily as he stood over her. She didn't dare look up at him, but his body heat radiated against her arm, and Lily feared that he would act barbarically toward her.

Taking a key from his pocket, the officer unlocked her handcuffs before walking back to his side of the table, where he picked up his folder and pen.

"How does two weeks sound?" the officer asked as he opened the door.

"Two weeks?" Lily asked. She had wanted to remain silent, but curiosity gnawed at her.

"In here." He looked around the windowless room.

"Sir?" Lily asked.

"I'll come back in two weeks." He shut off the light and closed the door behind him, leaving her in total darkness.

Lily stood quickly, and her chair flew backward as she stared in the direction of the door, praying it would open again. Her punishment had been delivered so swiftly that she barely had a moment to process what it meant.

As her eyes adjusted, Lily was able to detect a sliver of light under the door from the office. Still, she stumbled as she walked around the room, not entirely sure what she intended, but found the punishment intolerable.

Lily was a flier, someone who not only enjoyed but needed wide open space. Being confined to a small room where many had been beaten or possibly even killed was enough to drive her mad. It was a genius move by the officer, and Lily slunk down to her knees as she began to weep.

# Chapter Twenty-Eight
# Raven

*"For the dead and the living, we must bear witness."*

Elie Wiesel

Some shuffling could be heard on the other side of the door. Lily knew it was time to eat. That was the only reason anyone came to the door. She didn't know how many days had passed since she had been locked in this room. She tried to count backward from the number of feeding times, but she was certain they had skipped a few meals.

The door opened, and Lily shielded her eyes from the dim light that blinded her. A bowl was nearly tossed inside, spilling some of its contents.

Lily crawled swiftly over to the bowl, lifted it to her lips, and drank the warm water that contained a few cabbage leaves, desperate for any nourishment.

Wiping her face, Lily let the bowl fall onto the floor as she leaned against the wall. The smell in the room was becoming unbearable, even though it originated from her.

There was nowhere for her to relieve herself, and Lily hated how the Nazis, in every extent possible, made her feel less than human. They stripped every morsel of dignity from her, and she almost laughed and cried at the same time as she imagined someone like Larisa being forced into a situation like this. She recalled the days of the two of them sitting in a café in Moscow, taking tea like ladies, but now she was a disgusting creature, no better than an animal in a cage.

Yet, as Lily stared into the darkness, the shape of a man began to form in the opposite corner of the room. She couldn't see his face or tell who he was, but the man was in uniform, and his hands were down by his sides.

Lily imagined that, in normal circumstances, this would scare her half to death, but there was something comforting about the apparition. The man seemed to be watching her from a protective point of view, as if he was caring for her.

At first, Lily thought the man was Alexei, but the longer she stared into the corner, his shape seemed to take on that of her father.

A tear rolled down her cheek as she wondered if this meant that death was approaching her, and his visitation was to take her to that uncharted realm.

Then, as if reading her thoughts, the spirit shook his head slowly, and Lily seemed to understand him as if he were communicating to her without words. An impression dropped into her heart, and Lily knew that this was not her end.

A door slammed from further in the office, and the ghost departed.

"Thank you," Lily whispered. She wasn't sure who had come to visit her, but in either case, she appreciated the comforting sign.

Keys rattled on the other side of the door that was swiftly opened and two guards burst inside. Taking her by the arms, the guards rushed her out of the office. The brightness of the sun was blinding to Lily, and she squeezed her eyes shut as the guards led her to some unknown destination.

A large hiss of steam, followed by some barking, startled Lily, and she pried one eye open to realize that she was being led toward a train. A couple guards were standing near the train with large dogs that were eager to devour anyone their masters permitted them. She noticed that Nikolai, and a handful of other men, were also being led to the train.

Yet the closer they came to the train, the more confused Lily became. She realized that the train didn't have any passenger cars, only cattle cars. She assumed this meant the train wasn't for her after all, but she didn't understand why she, and the other men, were being led towards it.

It was only when the ramp was placed against the cattle car that Lily understood they were, in fact, going to be transported like animals.

A whistle blew, and the guards forced Lily, and the others, up the ramp as the dogs barked at their heels, snapping their jaws near Lily's thigh, eager to take a bite out of her flesh.

After she was securely on the train, Lily looked back into the camp to find that the officer who had interrogated her was standing with his hands behind his back and smiling pleasantly at her. She found his character so jarring, so wicked that she was thankful to be leaving this camp. Then, again, she doubted her destination would be any improvement.

After she and the other men were packed into the car, the door was slid shut and Lily listened as a heavy lock was placed on the door.

With her head spinning, Lily shuffled closer to Nikolai and asked, "What now?"

Nikolai shook his head and placed his finger to his lips for her to be quiet.

With a nod of understanding, Lily searched for an area in the car to sit and picked a corner by the door. Nikolai joined her a few moments later as he sat a few feet away from her.

The car remained quiet as each man, and Lily, waited for the train to begin its hellish journey. She didn't know how long they would be traveling, but she understood this would be a brutal ride, especially considering there was no food, nowhere to relieve oneself, and the heat in the car was already sweltering.

After what Lily guessed was a couple hours of them sitting and staring at the walls of the car, the train finally jolted to a start, and the excursion to what Lily assumed would be their new barbaric home was underway.

"Now we can talk," Nikolai began as the sound of the train engine drowned them out.

"Do you know where we're going?" Lily asked.

Nikolai shook his head.

"They didn't give me any explanation." Lily stared at her hands, which, in the light, she realized were filthy.

"We're animals to them. Why should they waste their breath?" Nikolai shrugged.

"Do you think we're going West?" Lily stared out the small slit in the wood on the car to see if she could gauge their direction. How she wished that she could simply peek at the instruments in her plane.

"I imagine so." Nikolai nodded. "The guards were nervous the last couple of days. From my experience in other camps, this means our men are advancing."

"Too bad they didn't capture the camp before we were sent away." Lily played nervously with her fingers.

"Too bad?" Nikolai scoffed. "Don't you remember what I said a couple weeks ago? If our Soviet comrades liberate us, we're going straight to the Gulags."

"A couple weeks?" Lily frowned.

"You lost track of time." Nikolai nodded in his understanding. "That's common. You were in solitary for two weeks."

Lily chuckled slightly in her mesmerization before she broke down and burst into tears.

"Enough of that!" Nikolai spoke through gritted teeth. "You can't let anyone else see you crying."

"I know." Lily rubbed her eyes. "This is Hell."

"You haven't seen anything yet." Nikolai shook his head. "You were at a small camp. Hopefully we won't be sent to a larger one. You think food was scarce here? You'd better have something you can trade if you want to eat in a larger camp. Fortunately, you're a woman. You have something every man wants. Sadly, the guards are not permitted to fraternize with the opposite sex, so there goes your advantage."

"What should I trade then?" Lily asked as she drew a deep breath.

"Cigarettes are the currency in most camps." Nikolai threw his lips upside down. "That's about it, really. Oh, trading jobs can help, too."

"Thank you." Lily nodded at Nikolai. "I'm not sure I deserve your assistance."

Nikolai examined her kindly for a moment before stating, "I heard your name being cursed in the other camps. You made our country proud."

Lily's eyes welled as she took to heart his accounting and only hoped that her mother was just as proud of her. Still, she knew that, even if she survived this ordeal, she would never be able to speak to her mother again. For Anna and Yuri's safety, she would have to disappear.

After a good stretch of time, at least a few hours, as far as Lily could tell, the train began to slow down until it finally came to a halt and Lily heard the familiar barking of dogs.

Some shouting in German came from the other side of the door as it was unlocked and then slid open.

To Lily's horror, she saw a score of people, possibly one hundred, forced to wait in line for the train. They were in terrible condition, much like the previous camp where she had been interned, and Lily noticed that many of them were sick. Their eyes were red, their gazes were glassy, and their skin was pale.

With a whistle and some more shouting in German, the guards forced the prisoners inside the cattle car until the bodies were so packed that Lily was forced to stand. There was no room to sit or lie down.

Since she was shorter than most people, Lily was forced to stand on her tiptoes just to catch a breath. She didn't understand why the guards forced so many into a single car, and wondered why they wouldn't utilize the other cars on the train as well.

Eventually, the door was shut, and the stench of the starving, dying, and sick around Lily was sorrowfully becoming normal. Still, Lily was forced to breathe out her mouth so that she didn't gag.

The train began again, and Lily noticed that not a word or even a whisper was spoken by anyone. The people, whether they were prisoners of war or sent to the camps because of the Nazis' degenerate policies of hatred, were entirely demoralized.

Lily noticed that only a handful of prisoners wore red triangles, and most had a yellow star. Many of these prisoners were here simply because of the coincidence of birth. There were many other triangles and colors, and while Lily didn't understand what they signified, she gathered that they likely indicated something the Nazis considered degenerate.

Hours upon hours passed as Lily was packed in tightly with other prisoners. She slipped in and out of consciousness during the journey, but she recalled moments, where the train would stop, and the other cattle cars were then filled with people.

"He's dead," a man from near Lily spoke plainly, and Lily looked over to see the deathly stare of a deceased prisoner.

There was nothing they could do. There was nowhere to place him or give him some dignity in death. Lily understood that they would be left, the living and the dead, standing in place until they arrived at their destination, whenever or wherever that may be.

Lily wasn't religious, having grown up in a society that suppressed anything spiritual, but she recalled, to an extent, her grandmother's Jewish prayers for the dead. Silently, and in her heart, Lily offered up a prayer for the man's soul. She didn't believe that anyone was listening, but still, she prayed.

The world around Lily began to dim as the journey continued, and she realized that the sun was setting. She had been on the train since the sun was barely rising until its setting. Her legs were aching, her stomach was growling, and her head pounded. She was certain that, being in such close proximity to so many sick and dying, coupled with her malnutrition, that she would likely contract something.

The image of the ghost in her solitary cell passed through her mind as a reminder, and Lily knew that she would be all right. She didn't know how, as it seemed impossible, but something in her spirit reminded her to keep the course.

"I miss you," Lily whispered to Alexei, not caring that others should hear her.

Finally, the train came to a halt, and Lily noticed bright lights through the slits in the car wall. Whistles, dogs barking, and shouting sprung up suddenly as the door slid open, and the guards, showing no clemency, forced those who had been cramped into this car for hours on end down the ramp at a hurried pace.

Lily's heart fell into her stomach. Shielding her eyes from the blinding lights on the guard towers, she realized this was a large camp. The rows upon rows of barracks and people were almost too much for Lily to bear. She felt her legs growing weak and numb as she couldn't stand the inhumanity.

With dogs at their heels and guards swatting their batons at anyone who came close enough, the sick, dying, and starving were herded past rows of housing that was too nice for the prisoners, and Lily assumed this is where the SS lived.

Eventually, they came to a square in front of the barracks, and Lily noticed that most of the prisoners in the camp were women. In fact, all the prisoners that she could see inside the camp were women.

"Attention!" an officer at the head of the square stood on a small block so that he could stand above them.

The square drew quiet, and Lily assumed they were just as worried as she was about what would happen to them. She had heard of prisoners being selected for execution, and Lily reminded herself to appear as strong and healthy as she could summon.

The officer continued to speak in German, and Lily found it difficult to make out most of what he was saying. She did, however, understand that she was in a camp called Ravensbrück.

She also understood that he mentioned the woman's portion of the camp was behind them, and the men's was close by. She could clearly detect the sentiment that any fraternization with the opposite sex was forbidden under pain of death.

The rest of what he shouted angrily, Lily couldn't decipher. She felt that he was shouting instructions, and she prayed that someone here could translate well enough.

Suddenly, a doctor wearing a white lab coat began inspecting the group. An assistant was standing near him with a clipboard in hand and marking something that Lily hoped was to help those who were sick. Somehow, she didn't believe that would be the case.

The doctor, who seemed entirely disinterested in the prisoners and inspected them as if they were cattle, began to order those who were frail and sick over to a separate section of the square. Again, Lily hoped it was for their benefit, but she doubted that the doctor had selected them for respite.

After a handful of those who were in the worst condition had been separated, the other guards began shouting, and Lily realized it was time to go into the camp. She found the inequality between the SS portion and the prisoner portion of the camp revolting. The SS had houses that she wouldn't necessarily consider luxurious, but in comparison to the prisoner barracks, they were palaces.

Following along in the throng of people that were being forced inside the camp, Lily, and the other women that had been collected by the train, were set aside in the women's portion of the camp, which, Lily realized, was quite a bit larger than the men's portion.

Lily noticed that some other women who were wearing green triangles were waiting for them, and by the fierce look they were offering, Lily knew they were likely going to be brutal.

The kapos organized the women, using their batons and flashlights, into columns and rows, and Lily tried to gauge the people she was imprisoned with. Many seemed like humble mothers or others caught in terrible circumstances. None of them, besides the kapos, appeared like criminals to Lily.

The kapos began speaking, but Lily couldn't decipher the language. It was Eastern European, and she assumed it was maybe Polish, but wasn't certain.

Then, without explanation, the kapos began shouting and pointing toward the barracks, and Lily followed along with the women as they were hurried to a bunkhouse that was closer to the gate.

Lily wasn't certain how many women she was with, but she assumed it had to be at least thirty or forty, and when they came to the barrack, Lily's spirit suffered another crushing defeat when she realized that it was already close to full. There was no way that all the new women would be able to live in this barrack in even slight comfort with the number of women who were already inhabiting it.

The women inside the barrack were stuffed into the bunks at three a person, and Lily assumed she would likely be sleeping on the floor.

The kapos shouted inside the barracks as they shined their lights right into the eyes of the other women, and Lily didn't understand why it was necessary to be so cruel.

Regardless, Lily resolved to keep to herself, and she found a spot in the corner of the room by the door where she could sit and rest her legs for a moment.

Despite the fact it was summer, Lily found it cold in the barracks that were not insulated by any meaning of the word. She imagined that winter, if she survived that long, would be brutal indeed.

Still, she clung to that image of the ghost in the solitary cell, and to the hope that life would go on after this. Pulling her legs up to her chest, Lily turned her gaze as she wept, hoping that no one would be able to see her tears.

# Chapter Twenty-Nine
# Liberation

*"The entire time I was in the camp it was as if I had a double personality. My real self seemed to be observing what was happening to my physical self."*

Sarah Helm

## April 28, 1945

Nearly two years had passed since Lily's plane was shot down and she was captured, but that time in her life felt like such a distant memory that she almost didn't believe it had ever happened. Not to mention how foreign it had been to the life, if she could call it that, that she was now accustomed to.

Hunger, Lily was certain, was the best keeper of time. Every day seemed to stretch, every hour felt tenfold, because she was perpetually hungry. All she could contemplate was food, all she cared about was the next meal, and Lily found it surprising how she had survived on starvation rations for so long.

Many thousands had died since arriving at the camp, and Lily had watched as body after body would be taken away. At first, the bodies, Lily assumed, were taken to some sort of mass grave, but at some point in the winter, Lily noticed a crematorium was being constructed. Since then, the bodies were burned, and the smell was horrendous.

For almost two years, Lily's routine had been the same. She had been fortunate enough to be assigned to the laundry. While the work was tiresome, usually spanning eleven to twelve hours a day while only breaking briefly for lunch, it meant that she worked indoors. Otherwise, Lily didn't believe she would've been able to survive the winter. She had seen how quickly the other prisoners had succumbed to frostbite in the pathetic excuse for winter clothes that had been given them. With such little care for the prisoners, treatable injuries such as frostbite were often fatal.

Lily's day began at five in the morning for the roll call, then she would partake in the bland breakfast, which was either brown water for coffee or an herbal tea that, again, was merely water. Lily, however, had noticed that most of the prisoners who survived would keep the black bread, which was distributed in the evening, and consume it in the morning, which gave them a bit more energy, and she adopted this practice.

At lunch, she was given soup—a mix of some ingredients that were so poorly cooked, the only thing she could identify was the potatoes. Still, after nearly two years, Lily could not discern what other elements made up the soup. In the end, it didn't matter, and, as usual, she forced it down while trying not to gag. The soup was so dreadful that even while she was near starvation, Lily found it difficult to consume.

In the evening, she was given a small slice of sausage, some black bread, some margarine, and some cheese. Lily assumed that if she was the cook in charge, she would've put some effort into feeding the tens of thousands that depended on her survival, but unfortunately, this was not the case. The sausage was either too dry or undercooked, the bread was often moldy, which reminded her of Alexei, the margarine was a discolored yellow that Lily couldn't stomach, and the cheese was also usually moldy.

Another aspect of survival that Lily observed in the other women was camaraderie. She would often find groups of women singing in the evening in their bunks or sharing stories from home. They made the best effort to try and ease their sorrows, but Lily, having picked up on some of the language, heard them often speaking of their families, wondering where they were or what had happened to them.

With regard to languages, Lily could hear a handful being spoken at any given time. She was thankful when she met someone who spoke Russian, but that was seldom. She did, however, learn that many spoke French and that most of these women had been part of the resistance in France. Others spoke Polish, and they were usually in the camp because they were Jewish. There were also many others from a variety of Soviet Union countries, but many of them spoke Ukrainian or other languages that had some similarities to Russian but still quite foreign to her.

But with respect to camaraderie, Lily found none. She, rather, found that survival for her lay in sticking to herself. She kept her head down and paid no attention to anyone or anything apart from her work. It felt cruel, like she was dead inside, but it was the only way for her to exist. She witnessed beatings on a daily occurrence, waking up to dead bodies in the bunk had become the norm, and rampant disease that went left untreated was the custom. Those who did become too sick to work were temporarily transferred to the 'hospital', which was a wicked joke. The beds were overrun, the nurses didn't try to help their patients by any stretch of the imagination, and the sick were often taken to be murdered since they offered no more use to the SS.

Day after endless day, she carried out the same harrowing, pitiful, and thankless routine. Her only comfort lay in the fact that she had successfully hidden her Jewish identity.

Today, after roll call, Lily took her coffee and her black bread, consumed them quickly, and then left for the SS workshops to complete her never ceasing laundry duty. Her hands had become so dry from the constant immersion in water that they seemed to Lily like the hands of an elderly woman and not those of a twenty-three-year-old.

Arriving at the shop for the laundry, Lily entered to find a group of women huddled together in the center of the room and whispering to each other. They stopped suddenly when Lily entered, but then resumed when they realized it was only her, and Lily assumed they were worried she was one of the guards, or worse yet, a kapo.

Curious as to what was so captivating, Lily came closer to the group as she tried to listen in. They were speaking in French, but Lily was able to understand a couple words here and there such as 'march' and 'death'. Still, nothing that she could piece together to form a coherent sentence.

A shout came from behind Lily, and she turned to see a guard yelling at them. From what she understood of German, he was telling them to get back to work. Yet Lily found his demeanor odd.

He seemed nervous. A slight tremor rippled up his arm as he held the weapon down by his side. At first, Lily assumed this meant he maybe had an injury, but then she noticed that he was sweating. His eyes darted back out into the camp, and Lily wondered what he was so afraid of.

Then, Lily recalled Nikolai, from the first camp she had been sent to, mentioning that the guards were nervous whenever the Soviets were approaching. She wondered if that could be the case now. It had been so long since she had come to this camp and without any news of the outside world that Lily almost assumed the Germans had won the war.

While trying to remain inconspicuous, Lily kept an eye on the guard as she began her duties for the day. She submerged the SS uniforms and blankets in the terrible chemical that burned her skin.

Lily listened to the other French girls as they began their work as well, and she recalled when she first entered training with Nadia and Larisa. How she missed those friendships, and she hoped both girls were still alive.

Apart from hunger, and being surrounded by a living hell, the worst part of her time in the camps was the solitude. She was surrounded by tens of thousands of women, yet Lily didn't count any of them as her friend.

Not from any hostility from the other women, but rather, Lily shut herself off from everyone.

It was too painful to become a friend with someone who, in the span of a couple weeks, would succumb to disease or be sent for execution, or be transferred to another camp. It was agonizing, and Lily believed the only way for her to mentally and emotionally survive would be to isolate herself as much as humanly possible. She ate alone, she worked alone, she spoke only when necessary, and the lively, witty Lily that she had known slowly withered away.

Lilly missed what the girls like Larisa and Nadia brought out in her. She missed flying with comrades and offering clever remarks in response to Larisa or Nadia's antics. She missed divulging the secrets of her romance to Ina or Katya. She missed the trivial arguments with Yuri that, given her experience in this camp, seemed so needless it was almost offensive. She missed, really, herself.

Lily had, apart from her physical self, died. There was nothing about her that had any trace of her former days. Her curls had flattened due to malnutrition, her bouncy personality was absent, her longing for companionship with the girls around her nonexistent, and her rebellion against the standards men had arbitrarily attributed to her sex was quashed. She was merely a husk, a body, a uniform with a number.

A couple shots rang out in the camp, and Lily, along with the other girls in the laundry, was startled. While it wasn't unusual for shots to be heard, with the current circumstances of the guard's nervousness and the girls' anxious whispers, Lily knew that something foul was afoot.

Walking toward the door to peek into the camp. Lily held a hand over her mouth in shock at what she was witnessing.

The entirety of the camp, every single prisoner, man and woman, was being driven toward the camp exit. Lily noticed that every single guard, and some that were only in half their uniform, were pointing their weapons at the prisoners and shouting orders at them.

The other girls soon arrived at the door with Lily, and they also seemed to understand the implications. Lily wondered if it would be best for them to hide in the laundry.

*Maybe the guards have forgotten about us?* Lily wondered.

But it was too late. Lily and the girls' curiosity had caused them to be noticed by a guard, and he approached them quickly while aiming his gun at them and shouting rabidly.

Raising her hands above her head, Lily complied as she was forced into the great throng of people exiting the camp.

The guards seemed to Lily to surpass mere nervousness as she noticed more than half of them seemed to have jumped into action. Many were dressed in nothing more than trousers and an undershirt, while others had their uniform jackets over their undershirts. It was utter chaos as they moved toward the train station, and Lily imagined this was not planned.

An explosion erupted from further in the camp, and many of the prisoners ducked down quickly, thinking they were under attack. It was soon evident to everyone, though, that this was caused by the Nazis. They were eradicating evidence.

Further confusing Lily as they approached the train station was the absence of a train. She didn't imagine that they would be able to pack this many people into the cars as it was, but for it not to even be there was odd.

Yet when they marched past the train station, Lily's heart fell into her stomach. The words the French girls had mentioned before swung back into her mind, and Lily knew this was a death march. There would be no food, no resting, and Lily's only consolation was that this meant her people were winning and her family was likely safe.

*We're heading north.* Lily frowned. *Why aren't we going west? That can only mean that the Western Allies are advancing into Germany. Maybe France was able to fight back? Or did the English invade? I hate not knowing.*

A shot rang out, and Lily was shaken when she looked further up the road to find that a guard had murdered a prisoner in cold blood. She watched as the frail body of the woman collapsed onto the ground. She was likely too weak to march, and the Nazi had gunned her down without remorse.

A cry escaped from a woman near Lily, who was also weak from malnutrition as she stumbled. A guard shouted at her to stand up as he pointed his gun at her head.

At once, Lily rushed to her side and threw her arms around her shoulder as she helped the woman to her feet. Without paying further attention to the guard, Lily, while shaking and struggling even with the fragile weight of the woman, helped her walk.

"Merci," the woman could barely utter the word, and Lily didn't have the strength to reply.

"You survived?" a man asked with surprise as he took the other woman's arm and slung it around his shoulder as well, which Lily greatly appreciated.

"Do I know you?" Lily asked with a dry voice, happy for someone to speak Russian to.

"Nikolai," he replied quickly, and Lily was shocked at his appearance.

His beard was thick, and his cheeks were sunken in. He looked so different from the man she had been on the truck with to the prisoner of war camp, that if he had not told her his name, she would've never been able to identify him.

"I see you're still showing your weakness by helping others," Nikolai offered the best attempt at a grin that he could afford. "I almost didn't recognize you."

*Me?* Lily frowned. *I know I probably look different, but my appearance hasn't altered that much, has it?*

"You don't know, do you?" Nikolai asked as he discerned the meaning behind her frown.

"Know what?" Lily asked as she tried to look at him, but carrying the woman required all the strength she could muster.

"Here," Nikolai grunted as he passed her a pocket mirror.

"How did you get this?" Lily asked as she took it from him. She couldn't remember the last time she had seen something of any value worthy of note, and she imagined the Nazis would've likely confiscated it.

"Don't advertise it!" Nikolai griped as he glanced over his shoulder.

"Sorry," Lily cleared her throat as she held it down by her side.

Then, after a few more steps, as Lily needed to gather her strength to make the attempt, she opened the mirror and inspected herself.

At first, Lily thought she was looking at a reflection of the woman she was assisting, and when she realized it was her own image, she fell into shock. Her cheeks were so thin and sunken into her face that all Lily could see were her own cheekbones. Without any fat around her eyes, they appeared wide as if she was in a constant state of terror. Her hair was so long, straight, and brown, that Lily almost thought it was a wig.

The reflection of herself was so alarming that Lily didn't know what to think. She knew her appearance had altered, but to actually see the difference was staggering.

"That's not me," Lily whispered.

"Count it as a blessing," Nikolai grunted.

"How?"

"If we're discovered, hopefully, by our own men, they won't recognize you. Surviving two years in an enemy camp? They'll be certain that you talked. They'll brand you as a traitor."

Lily didn't reply as she took his harrowing statement to heart.

"Do you know where we're going?" Lily asked after a few minutes.

"No idea." He shook his head.

"What's your plan if the Soviets do intercept us?" Lily asked.

"We have more hope of trying to escape." Nikolai looked around, and Lily understood that he was counting the guards. "They're nervous. They're going to make mistakes."

"Escape where?"

"Switzerland," he whispered.

"Switzerland?" Lily frowned, hoping he would elaborate.

"They take in many neutrals, especially Jews."

Lily turned her gaze away quickly. She had taken great pains to hide her identity, and Lily didn't want to reveal anything in these final moments where escape or liberation were actual possibilities.

"Listen, my friend," Nikolai began as he struggled with the woman's weight. "We are going to be marching for days. We can't carry her the whole time."

"We can't leave her." Lily shook her head and was glad the woman didn't speak Russian, otherwise his suggestion would've been disheartening at best.

"We leave her, or all three of us die."

"You don't need to stay." Lily shook her head. "I'll take her on my own."

Nikolai stared at her for a moment, and Lily found his gaze peculiar. It was as if he didn't understand her, and he couldn't seem to make sense of her sacrifice.

"It's foolish for all of us to die." Nikolai frowned.

"That's why us women of war were so effective," Lily replied as she recalled the girls she fought beside. "We knew that we were stronger together. When one of us faltered, the others were there to help them. We survive as one, not as individuals."

Nikolai didn't reply as he stared at the ground as they walked, and Lily spotted a hill that they were about to climb. It was steep, and she knew it was about to be treacherous. Still, she was resolved to help out this woman, otherwise she knew there was little difference between her and her captors. She needed to prove to herself that, even at her lowest and most degraded form, she was better than them.

Hour after thankless and painful hour, Lily, Nikolai, and this French woman walked. Lily's legs ached, and each step she was almost certain would be her last. There were many bodies of others who collapsed along the side of the road. She wished that she could offer to help them as well, but many had already died from exhaustion.

Their Nazi guards showed little clemency or concern for their prisoners as they marched them without cessation. Adding to the cruelty, the guards would drink liberally from their canteens and sometimes intentionally spilling water in front of those dying of thirst.

"My friend," Nikolai panted.

Lily glanced over at him, unable to even offer a vague response.

"She's dead."

Glancing at the woman, Lily was surprised that she hadn't noticed. She had been so surrounded by dead and the dying, that when a woman died with her arms around her it wasn't immediately evident.

Nodding in the direction, Lily indicated that they should place her by the side of the road.

Lying her down, out of the way of those who were walking, Lily was about to close the woman's eyes when a guard began shouting at them.

"One moment, please!" Nikolai held his hands together gently.

A shot rang out, and Lily screamed as Nikolai fell to the ground with blood oozing out of his chest.

With wide eyes, Nikolai looked at Lily with fear and angst before his gaze turned to Heaven.

"Up!" the guard shouted at Lily, and she had no choice but to comply.

If she had enough hydration for tears, she would've cried for Nikolai, but she wept inwardly for him at the cruelty as she rejoined the march.

Dragging foot after each foot, Lily drove herself onward. She tried to distract herself with pleasant thoughts, but nothing could suppress the burning in her muscles and the aching in her bones or the sorrow she felt for Nikolai. He had been so close to escaping, and the guard didn't give him even a moment to comply.

Then, a sound arose. A sound that Lily had not heard for nearly two years. A sound that brought a smile to Lily's face unlike any other sound could.

Glancing up at the sky, Lily spotted a plane, which she guessed was at about one thousand feet, and it had the unmistakable outline of a Yak. It was a Soviet plane.

After a few minutes, as the Nazis debated among themselves if the plane was friend or foe, they finally realized it was not German and began opening fire. It was useless, and Lily almost laughed at their pathetic and terrified attempt.

Unphased, the Soviet plane turned back toward the east, and Lily prayed that it had spotted them and was about to report the sighting.

# Chapter Thirty
# The Trampled Rose

*"For thy sweet love remember'd such wealth brings
That I scorn to change my state with kings."*

William Shakespeare

<u>April 30, 1945</u>

Dawn began to break, but Lily could scarcely look in the direction of the striking sunrise. The beauty of the oranges and pinks streaking across the sky was lost on her, and she would rather entertain a thousand grim mornings in exchange for even a drop of water.

They had marched for two days, and Lily lost track of the people who had died along the journey. Bodies by the side of the road were more common than trees, which, Lily perceived, they were now surrounded by.

They were walking down a gravel road that was flanked on either side by forest. Lily wondered if the Soviets would be able to find them now that they had entered the thicket.

While Lily found it peculiar that the guards were not growing weary, she spotted, on more than a handful of occasions, where they would take a pill. This pill seemed to give them a sort of craze, and Lily noticed that their empathy evaporated entirely.

She had heard of the use of drugs by the Nazis, particularly in their astounding lightning conquest of France. They marched over great distances without sleep or rest. She had even heard of many of her Soviet comrades taking drugs to keep them awake during the night or to give a boost to concentration during the day. Still, she didn't recall seeing any of them lose empathy or become crazed like these Nazi guards.

It had been two days since the Soviet plane had spotted this death throng, and Lily wondered what had become of the surveillance. She prayed that their liberation would be quick.

*Maybe the plane didn't see us?* Lily wondered as she glanced down at her feet. The pebbles of the gravel road were unbearable to walk on with the poor excuse for shoes that had been distributed to them back at the camp, and she could feel her blisters growing with each and every step. Still, she kept walking.

She began to contemplate her time in the camp, and she wondered if her father had similar experiences in the Gulags. While she would never have asked for this to happen to her, a part of her was somehow appreciative that she could suffer what her father endured. She felt closer to him, understanding what he might've gone through. She only prayed that he hadn't lasted for years as she had, and that his death had been quick. She recalled the ghost that appeared in her cell nearly two years ago, and she wondered if, indeed, that was him.

She remembered that his photograph was in the breast pocket of her pilot's uniform, and she wished that she had taken the opportunity to hide it on her. She wondered where it was, and prayed that the Nazis had not discovered it.

*Maybe the —*

A guard near Lily collapsed, and she watched him clasping his neck as blood oozed out and stained his hands a deathly red.

Surprised, but partially wondering if she was merely hallucinating, Lily kept walking. Her legs seemed to be automated, and Lily walked by the guard as he choked on his own blood in agony.

Then, another guard fell, and another and another as Lily grew aware of bullets flying past her. An explosion from a grenade startled a group of guards and prisoners alike, but Lily remained unphased.

Lily watched as a few guards stripped out of their uniforms and fled while others shot widely back at their hidden enemy in the trees surrounding them.

Unable to react, Lily merely watched what was happening around her. She was delirious from near starvation, thirst, and exhaustion, but she had enough whereabouts to believe that the Soviets had discovered them.

After a few moments, Lily realized she was on the ground. She didn't remember falling or losing consciousness, and she had no recollection of the last few minutes.

Whatever had happened, Lily realized that the fight was already over. She was surrounded by Soviet soldiers who were capturing the Nazi guards or else chasing those who had fled. Many of the Soviet soldiers were offering water to other prisoners or else food from their rations.

"Here," a kind voice spoke to Lily as a soldier knelt in front of her and offered his canteen to her.

Without a moment of hesitation, Lily grabbed the canteen and drank liberally. Her stomach began to ache as she drank and drank, but Lily didn't care. The quenching of her thirst was so relieving that she burst into sobs.

"Easy, easy." The soldier tried to take the canteen back, but Lily twisted away. She had become like the man she offered her food to in the prisoner-of-war camp. She had been reduced to nothing more than a beast with one primal instinct: survive.

"Can you understand me?" the soldier asked, but Lily wasn't sure if she should feign ignorance. Remembering Nikolai's warning, if they found out who she was, it could be disastrous, and not only for her, but for her mother and brother too.

Without a word of acknowledgement, Lily handed the canteen back to the soldier and nodded her thanks.

"Keep it." He patted her shoulder before reaching into his pocket and retrieving a piece of chocolate.

The tears welled in Lily's eyes as she looked at the sweet. She never imagined that she would behold such a beautiful thing again in her lifetime, and she took it quickly from him after he offered it to her.

Lily closed her eyes as she shoved the entire bar into her mouth, not caring how she appeared or that some shavings from the chocolate should fall onto the ground. The gratification alone was enough for Lily to never want for anything again, and she never knew that it could taste this good.

"I don't know if you can understand me, but the Swedish Red Cross is helping us. They've assisted with other camps we've come across." He pointed behind Lily, and she turned to see some nurses and doctors inspecting and triaging prisoners.

"Where are you from?" the soldier asked Lily, but again, she remained quiet. She didn't know who to trust, and so she pretended that she didn't understand him.

"If you can provide verification of your identification, it will be much easier to return you to your home. If not, you'll be sent to a displaced persons camp."

Lily felt her stomach churning as she sat on the ground and was confident she was about to vomit. Turning away, Lily dry heaved, but nothing came up.

"Help!" the soldier shouted, and within seconds Lily was surrounded by what she hoped were medical staff.

Lily felt herself losing consciousness, and a darkness began to envelop her as she drifted into oblivion.

Shooting her eyes open, Lily awoke with a start. Taking in her surroundings, Lily realized she was in a medical tent, and she was hooked up to an IV. Much like when she had been shot down and broken her leg, Lily found the scene in the tent to be rather chaotic.

Nurses were running back and forth between patients who were in agony. Lily noticed many people had their feet in bandages or with ointment being applied, others were being fed slowly, and others, despite all assistance, appeared to be drawing closer to death.

"How are you?" a woman asked in French, and Lily watched as she sat at the foot of her cot.

The woman was wearing a military uniform with the Red Cross band around her arm, but still, Lily remained wary.

"Do you speak French?" the woman continued, and Lily gestured with her hand to indicate she knew a little.

"What is your native tongue?" the woman asked, but Lily didn't answer.

"I'll speak slowly then, how does that sound?"

Lily nodded.

"Name?"

Lily paused before replying, "Katya. Katya Solomatin."

"Not a very French name." the woman grinned, but Lily didn't share in her amusement. She was too exhausted to even force a smile.

"Family?"

Lily shook her head.

"Deceased?"

Lily nodded.

"All of them?"

Lily nodded.

"I'm sorry." The woman reached out to squeeze her hand, but Lily withdrew sharply. She didn't mean for such a harsh reaction, but for the last two years, the only contact she received from others was in the form of a beating.

"Do you have anyone that you can reach out to?"

"Husband," Lily lied while pointing to her chest and speaking in the best French she knew how. "Switzerland."

"Where in Switzerland?"

"Geneva," Lily replied. It was the only city she could think of in the country.

"Where in Geneva?"

Lily shrugged.

"You're wearing a red triangle." The woman pointed to Lily's uniform. "Were you a prisoner of war?"

Lily shook her head as she struggled to think of the word before replying, "Resistance."

"You fought in France?"

Lily nodded.

"Do you have—"

Lily held up her hand to interrupt her and then gestured that she would like a pen and paper.

"Sure. I'll be right back." The woman stood and walked out of the tent quickly.

Lily stared at the tent ceiling as she tried to commit to memory the fabrication she just told the Red Cross woman. She knew that any deviation would cause suspicion, and Lily had to stick to her new truth.

"Here." The woman held out the pen and paper to Lily.

With a thankful nod, Lily took the items, but offered a quick look to the woman to indicate she would prefer some privacy.

"I'll give you a moment." The woman smiled gently.

Staring at the blank piece of paper, Lily didn't know how to properly begin her letter. It felt strange even thinking of communicating with her mother again, and Lily knew she would have to be deceptive to hide any traces of who she really was. It was dangerous, but Lily couldn't leave her mother with the belief that she was dead.

*Dear Anna,*

Lily began in the letter as her lips trembled.

*I had the extraordinary privilege of fighting alongside your daughter, Lily. She spoke often of you, and Yuri.*

Lily paused. She didn't know what else to add. How she wished to tell her mother that she was alright, but could she? If Anna was aware, then she could be in the precarious position of having to lie to the authorities which could be extremely dangerous.

The tears rolled down her cheeks as Lily scrunched up the letter and tossed it onto the floor. For the love she bore her mother and brother, Lily would permit the falsehood that she was dead. It was the only way to protect them, and that, after all, was the sole reason she had joined the Soviet Air Force. For the sake of her mother and brother, for the sake of love, she would leave everything behind.

In either case, Lily wasn't convinced she could even return to conventional society in Moscow. The only way for her survival, she believed, was forward. In the end, she knew her mother would understand.

◆◆◆

June 6, 1945

The train arrived in Geneva, Switzerland, and Lily looked out the window with a faint smile at her new home.

This is the furthest she had ever traveled west, and Lily found the architecture to be a wonderful change from the concrete forest of Moscow. That's not to say that her home city was without beauty, and in many places it was unrivaled, but the living quarters were bleak and dismal. By contrast, here, in Geneva, Lily found the apartments and flats to be charming.

After just over a month in the displaced persons camp, Lily was able to mostly heal from her physical trauma. The blisters on her feet were gone, her hair, while still straighter than usual, was at least regaining some body, and her face was not nearly as lean.

Lily was eternally grateful to those who helped her regain health and even provided her with some clothes, some money for the traveling, and even organized a job for her. Otherwise, Lily had nothing.

While the dress, which was a dark burgundy, was not one that Lily would've picked out for herself, she wondered when she could wear proper fitting clothes again. She had been proud of her appearance, which she knew was vain, and Lily hoped to salvage what the Nazis had tried to destroy.

Looking at the address on the little slip of paper in her hand, Lily drew a deep breath.

Hailing a taxi, Lily handed the driver the address, but he looked back at her with a curious glance.

"It's correct," Lily confirmed, and the driver shrugged before they began their journey.

Lily stared out the window with a grin as she took in the beautiful sights of the city. They drove by majestic fountains and grand palaces, squares bustling with people being entertained with food or artists, and green, lush parks with couples holding hands or little children running about.

Eventually, they drove out of the city and into the country, where, after a few minutes, the driver stopped near a flying club.

Paying the fare, Lily exited the cab and watched with delight as a plane flew overhead before performing an amateurish, yet noble, barrel roll.

"You're our new instructor?" a voice asked, and Lily turned to see a tall man approaching her.

"Yes," Lily replied. She had taken the time in the dispersed persons camp to obtain a better handle on the French language, and wished that she had made greater strides previously.

"Excellent." The man smiled at her charmingly, and Lily was relieved, for once, that he didn't make a comment about her gender. "How was your journey?"

"Pleasant." Lily nodded.

"I'm so happy that you're here. This way, please." The man held his hand out for Lily to walk beside him. "We're in need of some more female instructors. I have a daughter myself, you see, and, well, after her mother and I divorced, she hasn't really been around. She used to come to the club with her mother, but I think the number of men here intimidate her. If she sees another woman like yourself flying, then maybe she will be persuaded."

"I—" Lily began.

"Sorry, I said way more than I should've." The man twisted his face in agony. "A terrible habit when I'm nervous."

"Divorced?" Lily asked as she took a moment to inspect him secretly, and if she was honest, was quite pleased with the detail of his marital status.

"Yes," he cleared his throat. "I hope that my impropriety hasn't discouraged you?"

"On the contrary."

"Maybe I should be worried then?" he offered a nervous laugh.

"I'm going to marry you," Lily spoke in Russian, and the man frowned in confusion.

"I'm sorry?" the man tilted his head.

"I asked when I could get into a plane?"

"Oh, I see." The man chuckled as he held a hand to his chest. "I know a bit of Russian, and for a moment, I thought you said something about marriage."

"Don't be silly," Lily lied with a grin.

"Plane, right, well, um, I suppose you can take one now." He shrugged. "Do you require anything?"

"No." Lily shook her head.

"You're making things too easy for me." He giggled, and Lily found his antics more than amusing. "Follow me, please."

The two walked across the field in silence, which, Lily noticed, greatly bothered him. She understood that he was a man who abhorred a vacuum and needed to fill the space with talking.

"You're, um, flight log is impressive." He nodded. "But there is quite a gap since you last flew. The war put an end to that for you, I'm guessing?"

"In a sense, yes." Lily threw her lips upside down as they arrived at the hangar and she stood before a single propeller plane that was of sleeker design than the Po-2, but she assumed wouldn't be nearly as fast as a Yak-1 or 9.

"Beautiful, no?" the man asked as she ran his hand along the wing, which was painted red.

"Very." Lily nodded before adding, "Do you want to come up with me?"

"Me?" the man threw a hand to his chest as he asked in surprise before continuing, "No one has ever asked me before. Probably due to my nervous nature. Or, maybe, I—"

"Yes or no will do," Lily spoke strongly as he reminded her of Nadia.

"Yes, please." The man smiled brightly at her.

"Good." Lily nodded as she climbed into the plane, not caring that she was still in a dress.

With the engine started and the blocks moved away from the wheel by an assistant, Lily taxied to the runway. Tears streamed down her cheeks as she gripped the controls tightly.

Pressing the throttle forward, Lily applied speed to the vehicle, and she was, once again, finally, airborne. She climbed rapidly to a height of six thousand feet, and Lily couldn't keep away the tears.

She thought of Alexei, Katya, Nadia, Ina, Larisa, Major Raskova, Colonel Baranov, her mother and brother, and all the others that she had known or lost over the years. How she wished to ascend to Heaven in her plane and be rejoined to Alexei.

"I love you," Lily spoke quietly to Alexei.

"Thank you for being with me," she spoke to her father.

"I'll always sing your songs," Lily smiled as she spoke to Katya.

Lily took a moment to take in the majestic sights of the Swiss countryside, with its bright green pastures complimented by dark blue lakes and rivers that were guarded by imposing snow-capped mountains.

"I'm sorry, but I have to close off my past." Lily sniffled. "I need to move on. I need to make room for healing, and keeping you near to my heart will take up too much space for others. I love you all, and I always will, but that Lily you knew is dead. She was killed in the camp, and she can't reemerge. I will be reborn anew, and I'll make you proud by living a good life. I promise."

"Are you talking to me?" the man shouted, and Lily smiled.

"Do you have your parachute?" Lily called over her shoulder.

"My what? Where? I don't remember you asking me to wear one!" he panicked.

"Are you strapped in?" Lily asked with a grin of anticipation.

"Yes! Why?!"

"No reason." Lily laughed liberally as she spun into a barrel roll and the man screamed in terror.

# Author's Notes

There are some distinctions that need to be understood for my reasoning with respect to a number of historical controversies.

Firstly, and simply, Lily's name. While not necessarily a controversy, you will find a few variations of her name, ranging from Lydia, Lilya, and Lily. I chose the variation of the name Lily as I seemed to connect to this one the strongest.

Secondly, there is some controversy as to who the first woman was to shoot down an enemy aircraft. If you throw the question into Google, you will get Lily as a result. This, however, is not a suitable form of research, and further investigation is required to review. The dates, which I have seen, highly suggest that it was Valeria, as I wrote in the book, and not Lily. There is no consensus among historians, that I have found, and it very well could've been Lily, but I've chosen to go with Valeria as the dates, to me, seems most plausible. I hope this displays my impartiality to the subject.

Lastly, there is controversy of Lily's death. It was initially believed that she died when she was shot down on August 1, 1943. Ina Pasportnikova, however, believed otherwise, and, for thirty-six years, searched for Lily's crash site.

After reviewing, along with a team of researchers, ninety crash sites, and many lost pilots killed in action, it was determined that a female pilot had been buried in a village called Dmitrievka. Initially, it was assumed that this could be Lily.

The body was reportedly exhumed, and it was concluded to be Lily. This fact, unfortunately, remains clouded, and there are claims that the body was never exhumed, but rather, the body was compared against reports.

Other researchers are convinced that Lily was taken captive and held in a prisoner-of-war camp. I find their evidence the most compelling.

Finally, a Swiss broadcast in the year 2000 reportedly featured a former female Soviet fighter pilot. A former night bomber was watching this broadcast and was convinced this was Lily. The woman in the broadcast was married and had three children, and my heart wants to believe that this was, in fact, Lily.

On May 6, 1990, President Gorbachev posthumously awarded Lily with the Hero of the Soviet Union.

At the end of her career, Lily was credited with twelve autonomous victories, including one observation balloon, and three aircraft shot down jointly with her comrades.

Printed in the USA
CPSIA information can be obtained
at www.ICGtesting.com
LVHW012232030624
782196LV00035B/1010